THE ROGUE RIDER

SPARKS SERIES BOOK IV

KERRY LAW

Copyright © 2024 Kerry Law

All rights reserved

ISBN-13: 979-8-3239-5692-0

For Colin
Love you as big as the sky

TO MARLIDESH
NALLEIN
FIR DU MERG
SORAMERG
TAUMERG
NEPZUG
VORTHENS
LAKE CEIL
HELVETHI LANDS
ARDNANLICH FOREST
BROKEN BAY
LORSOKE
GRIYDAK SEA
KIERELL AND BEYOND
CITY OF KIERELL

CHAPTER 1

FAMILY

Elka picked up a silver cake fork and twirled it around her fingers. The balance was all wrong compared to her throwing knives, but she reckoned she could get it to stick in the far wall. She'd get shouted at if she started throwing cutlery around the dining room, but it would at least mean someone would pay attention to her. Sighing, she returned the fork to its place.

Her eldest brother, Torsgen Haggaur, sat at the top of the table, as was his right as head of the family. Frannack, the middle child, sat to Torsgen's right. The chair to his left was filled with the skinny bottom of Ottomak Klein, Head of the Landowners Guild and member of the Gierungsrat, the city states' ruling council. Elka sat elbow to elbow with Frannack, though he mostly ignored her. Pudding was served by servants whose feet made no sound on the plush teal carpet. Elka stabbed a fork into her bilplum tart and left it there. She didn't have much of a sweet tooth and would have preferred another round of spiced roast potatoes to the cake.

'You've redecorated, I see,' Ottomak was saying around a mouthful of tart.

Elka saw the smile on Torsgen's face—proud with a side order of smug. She didn't fault him for it. He'd worked hard for every luxury they had.

'I love this table.' Ottomak ran a hand over the pale wood. It had been varnished and polished till it reflected the glow of the gas lanterns mounted around the walls. 'It's a Vornelia, yes?'

'Of course,' Torsgen replied, sipping his neat gin from a crystal glass.

Elka had turned seventeen last month and now demanded gin with her dinner too. Torsgen and Frannack were twelve and ten years older than her, and she hoped that soon they'd stop treating her like their baby sister. She didn't actually like gin, though. She only forced it down because it was what Torsgen drank.

'You can tell by the legs. She has such a unique style.' Ottomak was still going on about the table.

The legs of the table were black metal decorated with cogs, stylised versions of the gears that powered their family's textile mills. It had been a bespoke commission from Vornelia, and Elka thought it looked pretty good, but she wished Ottomak would shut up about their furniture and talk business. She knew he wouldn't. He and her brothers would have already discussed whatever he was here to discuss, before dinner, without her.

Torsgen and Frannack kept her at arm's length from

the family business. Apparently she hadn't earned her place in their inner circle yet. She was only here tonight at dinner to look pretty. A task she enjoyed failing by scowling at the world from under her long fringe and occasionally fiddling with the silver ring through her nose. It was a piercing Torsgen hated, saying it was unladylike—a comment that had almost made Elka get her lip pierced too, just to rile him.

Elka's eyes drifted over the luxury in the room, barely seeing it. She knew that when she was a baby, and her brothers were teenagers, they'd lived in the single room of a basement in one of the worst areas of Taumerg. But she couldn't remember that.

She picked the bilplums from her tart and ate the pastry while staring out of the tall, diamond-paned windows at the room's far end. In daylight they gave a view across the Rorg Canal. Most of the canals in Taumerg were used for transporting goods but the Rorg was one of a few used only for leisure. Yesterday, Elka and her friends had hired one of the colourfully painted barges for the day; they'd driven the boat as far up as the Last Lock, drinking themselves silly on cheap wine all the way. She'd even let Daan finally kiss her, after a whole summer of flirting. The memory made her lips tingle.

'I appreciate your ambition, but where will you source a workforce to power such a mill?'

Ottomak's words pulled Elka's attention away from Daan's lips and back into the room. This sounded like business talk. She'd grown skilled at listening in to conversations and piecing together her family's business, even if her brothers wouldn't let her get involved. She knew that it was thanks to Torsgen's drive and Frannack's mechanical knowledge that they'd become the owners of three very successful textile mills. That, and the fact that they had no problem stepping around the law when required. Elka had learned early on what greasing the right palms with enough galders could achieve. Especially when those palms belonged to the Zachen Guard who policed the city.

And now her brothers had ambitious plans to build a mill twice as large as any other in the city.

'There are plenty of folk always looking for work,' Frannack said, waving towards the city of Taumerg that lay beyond their windows.

Ottomak gave an awkward little cough. 'The Hagguar family does not have the best reputation for…ah…treating workers as well as they may expect.'

'Sourcing a workforce is my problem,' Torsgen fixed his cold stare on the Head of the Landowners Guild. 'Your only job is to secure me the land.'

Elka had watched Torsgen give that same look to everyone from employees to officials of the Gierungsrat and it worked every time. No one could meet the frosty intensity in his pale blue eyes.

The dining room door opened and a shadow slipped into the room. A moment later, Claujar was at Torsgen's side. The older man had been with the family since Elka was a toddler. As a little girl she'd called him Uncle Claujar. Then, when she was twelve, she'd eavesdropped on him one night talking with her brothers and learned that he wasn't related to her at all. He looked like a gentleman in his fancy suits, but his connections, which were why her brothers employed him, were with Taumerg's criminal underworld. She'd been fourteen before she understood that the missing little finger on his left hand meant he'd done a stretch in gaol.

Frannack began asking Ottomak if he'd see the latest play showing at the Clockwork Theatre and Elka wished he'd shut up so she could hear what Claujar was whispering to Torsgen. But of course, secrecy was why Frannack was loudly extolling the virtues of the play's leads. She watched Torsgen nod and slip Claujar a leather wallet. Then Claujar left without ever looking at Elka.

The appearance of Claujar meant Torsgen would disappear in the middle of the night and return in the morning with blood on his boots. Elka didn't know what Claujar did for her brothers, or where Torsgen went when he slipped off with the older man at his side. But she longed to find out. Often she imagined following them. In these daydreams, Torsgen would get into some sort of trouble and she'd spring from the shadows, throwing knives in her hands, and save him. Then he'd see that she deserved her place in the family and that she could be more than a decoration at the dinner table.

After dinner Elka followed her brothers out into the hallway as they bade goodnight to Ottomak. Her boots clicked on the red and black tiled floor. She was supposed to wear dainty silk slippers to dinner but that didn't fit with the person she was trying to be. Someone in her brothers' inner circle, a person with the power of the Hagguar family name behind them—that person wore boots.

Elka watched the handshakes between her brothers and their guest, longing to stand beside them and shake hands too. The front door opened with a mechanised hiss of steam—one of Frannack's inventions—and Ottomak left. Torsgen slipped off his dinner jacket. It was cut in the most fashionable of styles and made using fabric from their own mills patterned with blue and purple flowers. He passed it to the servant who'd brought Ottomak's coat, without even looking at her, checked his gold pocket watch, then disappeared upstairs. He took them two at a time.

'You did well tonight,' Frannack said, resting a patronising hand on her shoulder.

Elka shrugged out from under him and glared. 'I didn't *do* anything.'

He smiled and shook his head, the same way he'd done when she was seven and demanding to be allowed to go and play in Vonspaark by herself. Elka loved her brothers, but she hated the way they still treated her like she was a little girl. Out of the two, though, she reckoned she had more chance of convincing Frannack to let her be useful. There were only two years between Torsgen and Frannack, but to Elka, Frannack had always seemed a lot younger. Where Torsgen was calm to the point of being cold, Frannack seemed to have a hundred new ideas every minute and he was often talking through theories on mechanics with anyone who'd listen.

'What did you talk about with Ottomak before dinner?' Elka demanded to know.

'Just the site of our new mill,' Frannack replied, distracted as he tugged his notebook from his inside jacket pocket.

'And that took four hours?' Elka knew how long they'd been in Torsgen's study because she'd sat on the stairs and watched the closed door the entire time.

'It's complicated.'

'Complicated how?'

Frannack held his notebook against his chest and looked across at her. She'd apparently inherited her mother's height and was tall enough to look her brothers in the eye. Somehow, that only added insult to injury when they kept her in the dark.

'We were destitute, Elka, and—'

'I know,' she interrupted him, but Frannack ploughed on as if he hadn't heard.

'After our parents died we had nothing, and this,' his wave took in their expensive townhouse, 'everything that we have now, we didn't get because some benefactor gave it to us. Torsgen and I worked for this, every single day.'

Elka opened her mouth to interrupt again but Frannack stepped close, resting his hand on her shoulder as if holding her in place so his words could land on her.

'Now we are successful, we are powerful. Everyone in Taumerg knows the name Hagguar. Torsgen and I have earned that. Our brother runs this business, and yes he uses Claujar's contacts, but it's Torsgen who's there in every one of those…meetings.'

Elka didn't miss the pause before Frannack chose the word meetings. She knew there was more to what Torsgen did for them. And she longed to be part of it.

'Everyone who is anyone in Taumerg wears clothes made from the fabrics we produce. Our mills are the most successful in the city, and that's thanks to the machines I've designed.' Frannack tapped her on the head with his notebook.

'But you don't build them, Mila does,' Elka pointed out, keen to prove she knew something of how their family empire functioned.

'True, because Mila is the best puffer in Taumerg.'

It had taken Elka years of listening to her brothers to realise that puffers was a slang term for the engineers who manufactured the steam-powered machines that Taumerg's factories relied upon.

'You only say that because you fancy her,' she said with a smirk.

'Don't be childish, Elka.'

'But Mila isn't even a Hagguar!'

'No, but she has skills and knowledge we can use. She brings something to the table. As do I, as does Torsgen. What can you bring, Elka?'

She glared at him, but this time she had no reply. What did she bring? She wasn't powerful and driven like

Torsgen. She didn't have a mechanical mind like Frannack. She didn't have a network of contacts in the underworld like Claujar. She was good at memorising things but what use was that to anyone?

'If our mother had still been alive she'd have been lady of this household.' Sadness washed through Frannack's eyes. He remembered their mother, but she'd died from complications two weeks after Elka was born. 'That's what you should be bringing, Elka. You should be running this household, welcoming our guests, and acting with poise and dignity.'

Frannack looked pointedly at her pierced nose, heeled boots, and the garter of throwing knives strapped to her thigh—something else she wasn't meant to wear to dinner. Then Frannack was walking away, chewing his pencil and flicking through the mechanical drawings in his notebook.

'Frannack! I can be useful. Please!' Elka yelled after him.

Frannack had reached the door at the end of the hallway, the one that led to his basement workshop, and he didn't bother replying. Even a flimsy lie would have been better than being ignored. He turned, one hand on the doorknob and gave her an indulgent smile. 'Above all else what matters most?'

Elka sighed as she gave the well-learned answer. 'Family does.'

Alone Elka trudged up the stairs, heading for her bedroom on the fifth floor. Running the household was a role she desperately didn't want to be pushed into—

dealing with the servants, planning fancy dinners, smiling sweetly as the men around her did the real business.

Now she was seventeen, Elka could have taken one of the suites of rooms on a lower floor like her brothers had. But she liked her childhood room nestled at the top of the house, mainly because she had the whole top floor to herself. And that felt a little bit like being in charge, even if it was only over a couple of rooms.

Their house, like all others in Taumerg, had a network of pipes and cogs running up the outside. These controlled their hot water and gas. In Elka's house the pipes burrowed through the walls of the fifth floor and emerged just beyond her bedroom. It lent her floor an industrial look, rather than the polished luxury of downstairs. Elka liked it because it made her bedroom the warmest room in the house.

Her bedroom had originally been two rooms but when she was thirteen she'd insisted Frannack find a way to knock through and create one big room. There had been a lot of boring discussions about roof beams but finally Elka got her way. Stepping into her bedroom now she felt the annoyance in her chest ease a little.

The ceiling sloped steeply on either side, almost meeting the floor, but three big windows on the far wall stopped the room from feeling cramped. The diamond-paned glass made patterns of moonlight across Elka's wooden floor and it danced up her legs as she crossed to her bed. The big metal frame took up almost half of what had been her original bedroom and was piled high with pillows. A fluffy shape uncurled and a little pink nose poked out from between a yellow blanket and a cushion covered in striped blue fabric. Elka smiled and sank her fingers into the cat's thick ginger fur.

'Hello, you. Good nap?' Then she gave a wry laugh. 'Of course it was, when do you ever not have a good nap.'

Ember purred at the attention. He was a stray she'd befriended when she was eight years old. She'd snuck him into the house and managed to keep him secret for three whole weeks before one of the servants told Torsgen. Her brothers had insisted she get rid of the 'mangy creature' but she'd fought for the right to keep him and eventually they'd relented. Now Ember was an old cat, his mouse-hunting days behind him, and he spent most of his time curled up on her bed.

Elka rummaged under the pillows and pulled out a slim book with an emerald-green cover. Taking it with her, she sat in one of the armchairs she'd positioned in front of the big windows. With a soft pad of footsteps Ember jumped up onto the armchair opposite, gave her a croaky meow and began grooming his tail. Far below barges glided along the Rorg Canal, lanterns on their prows, and on the paved streets the very best of Taumerg's high society strutted along. Rooftops marched away in every direction, tall townhouses giving way to workshops and factories the closer the city got to the River Ireden. From up here Elka could see all three of the Hagguar textile mills—the empire her brothers had built.

Crossing her long legs, Elka propped the book on her knee and ran her fingers over the embossed title on the cover. *The Saviour of Kierell by Callant Barrell.* It had cost her nearly fifty galders because it had been printed in Kierell and only a few copies had made it as far as Taumerg. Then she'd had to teach herself Kierellian to be able to read it.

Everyone had heard stories about the battle with the Empty Warriors that had almost destroyed Kierell three years ago, but Elka had never known the actual details until she stumbled across this book in a tiny shop on Polkstraab. The book told the story of Aimee Wood, the young Sky Rider who'd saved the city and defeated Pagrin, the evil Master of Sparks.

Elka flipped open the book to the line drawing printed on the page after the title. It showed a young woman with short curls and a scimitar in each hand. Behind her a dragon stretched open its wings, filling the page.

'Did you really do everything this book says you did?' Elka asked the drawing.

She wasn't sure how much of the tale she believed—some of it seemed too epic to be true, even though Callant claimed to be a friend of Aimee—but she'd read the book cover to cover four times now. And every time she wished she could be as brave, determined and powerful as Aimee. Elka felt trapped in her life, unable to prove to her brothers that she deserved a place in their inner circle, that she could be more than just the pretty face of the Hagguar family.

She flicked through the book, the gentle shush of rustling pages reminding her of hundreds of evenings spent in this armchair, a cup of Marlidesh coffee by her elbow and the lights of Taumerg twinkling beyond her windows.

'What can you bring?' she repeated Frannack's words.

Normally *The Saviour of Kierell* was a comfort read but tonight she slammed it closed, annoyed with Aimee and the life she lived that allowed her to be a hero.

CHAPTER 2

A WAY IN

THE STREETS OF Taumerg bustled around Elka as she made her slow way home. The city was a horseshoe-shaped curve against the River Ireden with canals running through it like the spokes of a wheel. Elka followed the Njmega Canal, its waters busy with barges. The whirr and clunk of their steam-powered engines mingled with the other sounds of the city—the clop of horses' hooves on the cobbles, the shouts of a lad hawking newspapers, the tinkle of bells above shop doors. Taumerg had always been an industrial city but as the curve of it expanded, more residential areas were created, home to streets with small shops and cafes. It was here that Elka liked to walk.

She used to make a point of visiting each of the three Hagguar mills every week. She'd make the foreman give her a tour and talk her through that week's production—figures she'd then memorise. She didn't know what she was really looking out for on these tours amongst the gears and wheels, the machines puffing steam as workers turned a complex maze of valves. But she assimilated every scrap of information she could, trying to find a role for herself. Until one day six months ago when Torsgen had caught her at it. He'd dragged her from the mill by her elbow. His accusations still lurked in the back of her mind.

Was she trying to make the family look foolish?

Hadn't he taught her how important reputation was?

Did she think their rivals employed silly girls to inspect their factories?

As she crossed a cobbled footbridge Elka looked to the city's industrial north. It was a calm, late summer's day and the smoke from the factories hung in the sky like a cloud.

'Miss Hagguar?'

A voice behind startled her and she spun to see Nail looking at her, one eyebrow reaching towards the neatly combed hair on the top of his head. The sides were shaved bare. Without meaning to she'd stopped in the middle of the bridge, her gaze caught by the factories, and she wasn't sure how long she'd stood there. Long enough for Nail to think she was being odd.

'This is your least favourite job, isn't it? Babysitting me when I go shopping,' Elka asked him as she started walking again.

His footsteps followed, always a respectful distance behind. When he didn't reply she glanced over her shoulder at him. He was only a few years older than her. He wore a smart three-piece suit, the fabric a deep purple with a subtle floral pattern—from the Hagguar mills, of course. He dressed like a gentleman but his bulk suggested that he ate metal cogs for breakfast with a side order of iron bars.

'What else do you do for my brothers?' Elka tried.

Nail only gave her a nod and kept walking. She held up the paper bag she carried, the one full of pastries from Makje's Bakery on Tinstraab. 'I'll give you one if you tell me.'

'It's not my place to say, Miss Hagguar.'

Elka's sigh felt like it came all the way up from her boots. Nail was always polite, respectful and frustratingly tightlipped. But Elka had seen the holster underneath his fashionable gentleman's jacket and she knew he carried one of the new clockwork pistols. They cost over a thousand galders each and Elka had begged Torsgen for one, and of course, been refused. It irked her that her brother had given one to Nail, a nobody. And it annoyed her that her brothers thought she needed a minder when she was out. Even without a pistol she could take care of herself. She'd been practising with her throwing knives since she was thirteen. And it made her spark boil that Torsgen thought she was important enough to protect but not valuable enough to be given a proper job.

'What do you know of the new mill my brothers are planning to build?' Elka threw the question over her shoulder, even though she knew Nail wouldn't answer. Did he know the answer? Was he only hired muscle? It was so frustrating that she didn't even know which of the family's employees were in her brothers' confidences.

Each business in Taumerg had a *Ragel*—a ruling committee who were in charge and made all the decisions. Elka didn't even know who sat on the Hagguar Ragel. Though she knew who definitely *didn't* have a place on it. Her.

She'd overheard smatterings about the new super mill and pieced together that there were two problems. The first was building machines big enough to handle the amount of fabric they wanted to weave. Frannack and Mila were working on this but one of their earlier prototypes had exploded. Elka didn't have a mechanical brain so she couldn't help solve that problem. The second was the issue Ottomak had touched on the other night at dinner. Where could they find a workforce able to keep up? People needed to sleep, they needed breaks to eat, they got injured by the machinery and had to be paid compensation.

Could Elka solve that problem? The issue was, she had no idea where to start.

She turned at the corner where the Njmega Canal met the Rorg Canal and onto her street. Noticing an odd quiet she looked up and spotted one of the Vorjagen—the Hunters. Elka had heard countless stories about them. Everyone had, because they loved stirring up controversy. They hunted prowlers on the tundra, selling the pelts and heads in Soramerg and the bones to travelling shaman from Marlidesh.

The Vorjagen walking down her street had shaved

his head—like they all did—and his skull was covered in tattoos of claws and snarling beasts. His coat flapped open as he walked and Elka spotted at least one small crossbow on his belt, along with two long daggers, and he had a knock-pistol strapped to his thigh. People quietened as he passed, as if he was pulling a cloak of silence behind him.

Determined not to be intimidated Elka strode on past him. Though she did notice that the Vorjagen and Nail exchanged nods, and she wondered at that. Her brothers wouldn't have any dealings with a cult of brutish hunters, would they?

Nail left her at her front door, wishing her a goodbye that was muffled by the mechanised hiss of steam as the door opened. Inside she tried to emulate the way Torsgen arrived home, looking around with a cool distain and holding out her coat for one of the servants to take. Except that when Ida appeared her facade cracked instantly.

'You did it!' Elka exclaimed, waving her hands at the servant's head. Yesterday her pale hair had been bound in braids that almost reached her waist. Today it bobbed around her chin as Ida swished her head side to side to let Elka admire it.

'What do you think?' Ida smiled shyly.

'It suits you. And now we won't have to have the "will I or won't I get it cut" conversation every morning when you bring my breakfast tray.'

Ida's laugh was a soft tinkle as she took Elka's coat and retreated into the warren of servant's tunnels behind the staircase.

Elka gripped her bag of pastries and looked ahead into an afternoon of doing nothing. She thought of the dozens of sketch books she had stacked on a shelf in her room. Each was filled with designs and patterns for new fabrics. She'd always loved designing outfits, especially ones for girls that were beautiful but also practical. She'd drawn dresses that looked like they had full skirts but were actually wide-legged trousers, silken shirts with sleeves wide enough to conceal a dagger strapped to the wearer's wrist, and trousers for herself with a clever holder for her throwing knives sewn into the thigh and disguised by the pattern of the fabric. She'd once presented her sketches to Torsgen and Frannack, thinking that perhaps being a genius fabric designer could be her role in the family business. But Frannack had laughed at her drawings and Torsgen had barely even looked at them.

She hadn't designed any new fabrics for months. She used to love it but now it felt pointless, and every time she looked at her sketchbooks she just became annoyed.

A door banged open and Frannack appeared from his workshop. He had goggles with optic attachments shoved up onto his forehead making his hair stick up. He and Torsgen wore their hair the same as Nail, and the same as every other broad-shouldered, well-suited man they employed—long on top and shaved at the sides. Frannack looked up from the open notebook in his hand and seemed surprised to see her.

'Have you seen Torsgen? We were supposed to meet an hour ago?'

Elka shook her head. 'What are you meeting about?' she tried asking.

Frannack waved a hand stained with engine oil. 'Stuff.'

Just then the front door hissed and Torsgen strode in. As he swept off his coat Elka noticed that he too was wearing a clockwork pistol in a hostler under his arm.

'Nice. Can I get one?' she asked, pointing to the pistol. Torsgen ignored her, just as she'd known he would.

Today he wore a sky-blue waistcoat patterned with white flowers, and a pair of striped navy trousers. Fashionable as always.

'Shall we?'

He looked to Frannack and gestured to the stairs. Torsgen didn't apologise for keeping their brother waiting. Torsgen never apologised and always expected the world to run on his timetable. Elka wanted desperately for the invitation to have been extended to her as well but there was no way Torsgen would let her sit in on the meeting. She had a bright spark, she knew she did, and sometimes she wished Torsgen could see it. Maybe then he'd value her more. Just as she had that thought her brother turned to her as he passed.

'Tell the kitchen to bring a fresh pot of coffee to my study.'

Elka kept her glare in check because she had her own way of joining their meeting. So she plastered a smile on her face and waggled the paper bag she still held. 'I have pastries from Makje's too,' she said, playing the part of the good hostess, all she was worth apparently.

Her brothers headed up the stairs and she waited till she heard the study door close behind them. Then she ran to the kitchen, flung in the order for coffee, tossed the bag of pastries at Ida, and sprinted up the stairs. The advantage of being mostly ignored as a child was that Elka had explored their house extensively. She knew all the best eavesdropping spots.

She slipped into an empty guest bedroom on the third floor, clicked open a small door concealed in the room's wood panelling and crawled inside. All the bedrooms had these hidden spaces which gave access to the network of pipes and valves running up the outside of the townhouse. There was a hatch the size of two dinner plates that opened to the outside wall but Elka ignored it. She liked this particular cubby hole because the dusty floorboards were gappy, and by sacrificing the point of one of her throwing knives, she'd been able to cut a tiny spy hole in the ceiling of her brother's study.

Lifting up two floorboards, she pressed her eye to the hole and smiled. She could hear Torsgen and Frannack perfectly. Torsgen sat with his customary stillness, hands resting on a tabletop created from one giant metal cog covered with a single circular pane of glass. Frannack had his notebook balanced on his knee and his work goggles still on his head.

'I just can't figure it out,' Frannack was saying. 'I

thought we had it with the last prototype but we can't get the tension right. More than half the threads keep snapping. Mila thinks it's because the frame's so much larger and the weight's being distributed incorrectly. I keep running the numbers,' he tapped his notebook with a pencil, 'but I still can't get the tension correct.'

'You'll figure it out,' Torsgen said with confidence.

'What if I can't?' As he looked up Elka saw the worry creasing her brother's forehead.

'I didn't steal all those books on mechanics when we were teenagers just for you to fail me now.' There was a rim of frost on Torsgen's words that made Elka shiver. His cold tone never seemed to bother Frannack. Though, when he was lost in a mechanical problem, Frannack often didn't seem to notice the world around him.

A knock at the door of Torsgen's study halted the conversation. Both men sat in silent thought as Ida carried in a tray. The rich smell of freshly brewed coffee drifted up to Elka's hiding place and brought with it a resurgence in her annoyance. She should be down there, drinking that coffee and sharing her thoughts on their project. As Ida left, closing the door behind her, Frannack continued.

'It's only that we've invested so many galders in this project.' Frannack shook his head accidentally dislodging his goggles which fell off the back. He left them on the floor as he continued. 'Between the metal for the prototypes and how much Ottomak is asking for the land, I'm worried, Torsgen. If this goes wrong, it'll wipe us out.'

'That won't happen.'

Torsgen's reply was confident but Frannack's words had Elka worried too. She hadn't known her brothers had invested so much into their plans for a super mill. She'd always longed to see her family's accounts but Torsgen employed a young woman, Dellaga, to handle them. Their lifestyle told her that they had hundreds of thousands of galders. How much of that had Torsgen risked on his plans? If the family ran out of money she'd never get a chance to be someone important, to play a role, or have a purpose.

'Alright, let's say that Mila and I get the loom working,' Frannack flicked to another page in his notebook, 'that still doesn't solve the problem of actually working it. It's no use spending thousands of galders on building such a huge mill if it only every produces as much fabric as one of our other mills.'

'Frannack, I know that.'

'And even if we employ more people it won't be enough,' Frannack continued as if he hadn't heard Torsgen. 'What we're building is too big and too powerful to be operated by people. We'd need a workforce that can work our mill every hour of the day and night without stops. And we have accidents in our normal mills. Well, with machines as large as we're proposing those will increase tenfold. Workers that are injured cannot do their jobs. We'll run out of people.'

Frannack closed his notebook with a snap and stared across the table at Torsgen.

'We need a super-human workforce with sparks brighter than the sun.'

'Or no sparks at all,' Elka found herself whispering.

'I can't conjure a workforce like that. Can you, Torsgen? It's not something I can build.'

'But what if you could.' Elka's voice was soft as cobwebs.

She lifted her eye from the spy hole, her mind whirring like a cog. She leaned back against the bare walls of the cubby hole, something she never normally did because she hated getting dust on her clothes. She wasn't paying attention to her surroundings though, because in her mind she was skimming through the final chapters of the *Saviour of Kierell*. She pretty much had it memorised.

What if she could find a way for Frannack to make a workforce? One that wasn't human. It would give them an edge none of their rivals could compete with. And, more importantly, it would force Torsgen to give her a place in the family's Ragel.

She wasn't sure she liked the callous way her brothers were talking about workers getting injured. No one should have to worry about their limbs being caught and chewed up by a mechanised loom. But Elka knew all about making men who weren't human, who would follow orders and who didn't have sparks. In Callant's book they'd been Empty Warriors, but what if Elka could find a way to make a different sort. Endless Workers perhaps. But to do that she'd need one of the Quorelle's bracelets.

Her mind reached the last chapter of *The Saviour of Kierell* where Aimee had flown miles out into the Griydak Sea and dropped Kyelli's bracelet beneath the cold waves. It was lost forever. Her mind skimmed back a few chapters, searching for the clue she knew was there. She'd spotted it before but never had a reason to linger on it.

And there it was. Elka smiled as excitement bubbled in her chest.

There was no mention in the book of what had happened to Pagrin's bracelet. Aimee had killed him and Jess had torn off his head, but where did his bracelet go? So, if someone had kept it… The gears in Elka's mind whirred faster as if someone had just added another burst of steam to the machine of her brain.

Access to Pagrin's bracelet could be the missing piece her brothers needed. If Torsgen wore the bracelet he'd be able to create hundreds of Endless Workers. But he wouldn't be able to do that without her. Elka highly doubted Torsgen had read *The Saviour of Kierell* so for once she knew more than her brother.

'Endless Workers.' She smiled as she said the invented name. She liked it and would make sure that was what they'd be called.

Torsgen and Frannack continued talking below but Elka had stopped listening. There was a flaw in her plan. According to Callant's story a bracelet wearer needed sparks to create Empty Warriors, or Endless Workers, and Torsgen only had his own spark. Where would he get more?

Elka dismissed this problem. Frannack would think of a solution. The bracelet was a machine, albeit one from hundreds of years ago, but if anyone could reverse-engineer it, it would be Frannack with his huge brain. Elka was sure he'd find a way to alter it so Torsgen could use it without needing extra sparks.

So, that only left figuring out what had happened to Pagrin's bracelet. And surely there was only one answer to that. The bracelet was important, it could be dangerous, and its value was unmeasurable. It would need protecting. And Kierell had guardians whose job it was to protect the city.

Elka would need to steal the bracelet from the Sky Riders.

CHAPTER 3

ALL THAT MATTERS

ELKA PACED HER bedroom from the windows to the door and back. Ember watched from his nest on her bed, his green eyes fixed on her as if she'd hypnotised him. It had been five days since she'd eavesdropped on her brothers, and for every moment of each one of those days her brain had been whirring. This was it. This was her way to prove to Torsgen and Frannack that she deserved to be an equal partner in their family business and have a place in their Ragel.

After eavesdropping, Elka had sat in her armchair by her bedroom window all night. She hadn't slept, just watched darkness douse the city, her mind alive with thoughts. As the night deepened and the lights winked out, still she sat there. Ember had given up on her, uncurled from her lap and gone to bed himself.

She'd turned over everything she'd learned from *The Saviour of Kierell*, like Frannack inspecting a new machine for flaws. The more she thought about it the more her excitement fizzed like the bubbles in sparkling wine. And as the pink ribbon of dawn seeped into the sky, she'd worked out her plan.

She would travel to Kierell, make the climb and become a Sky Rider. Then steal Pagrin's bracelet.

Now it was time to put her plan into action. Fate had dropped this in her lap, the opportunity she'd been searching for, the way to prove herself.

'So why am I nervous?' she asked Ember, spinning on her heel at the windows and heading back towards the door, socks sliding on the floorboards.

Ember gave a croaky old-man meow and snuggled into his blanket, resting his chin on his paws.

'You're right,' she told him, coming to a halt by the bed. 'I'm scared of leaving all this behind.'

She flopped down on the bed beside Ember and sank her fingers into his thick fur. She thought of the everyday luxuries she'd be giving up by leaving Taumerg, like piped hot water, servants to bring her breakfast in bed when she didn't feel like getting up, and money to spend in the city's cafes. She knew from Callant's book that in the Ring Mountains there would be only bare caves and cold winds.

The travelling bag she'd packed for the journey sat at her bed's foot and was far too small for her liking. Having only a few possessions fitted with the story she'd concocted of being a nobody from the cities. But it pained her to leave all her stuff behind, especially her clothes. A huge wardrobe sat against the wall to the left of her door and was so full of outfits that she'd forgotten half of what was in there.

Elka looked down at her current attire. Red trousers with a bold floral pattern, a cream silk shirt embroidered with gold thread at the cuffs, and over the top, a fitted pink waistcoat in a floral design that clashed perfectly with her trousers. All made with the most expensive fabrics her family's mills produced. Bold and bright was fashionable and she was not looking forward to swapping it for the dull black of the Riders.

Still, at least it would only be for a year.

'Just one year out of my life, Ember, and when I come back it'll be the three of us running the business. I'll get to sit at the top of the table beside Torsgen and Frannack. Maybe they'll even put me in charge of the new mill.'

Elka pictured herself on a high walkway above a factory floor, the rhythmic sound of hundreds of looms swish-clicking below her. Her mill, her workers, building a new future for Taumerg with her family at the head. She adjusted the image, adding a belt and two clockwork pistols, their wooden grips inlaid with gold. Because her plan would make her enemies, but she wouldn't let that stop her. Not if it meant winning a place at her brothers' side.

Ember nudged her palm, wanting his head stroked. 'You'd better still be alive when I get back,' she told him. He purred softly.

Standing up she lifted her travel bag onto the bed and checked its contents one last time. She knew Torsgen would quiz her on every element of her plan, including the cover story she'd concocted, and fully expected him to search her bag before she left. That was why she'd hidden the contraband at the bottom of a drawstring pouch and packed lace underwear on top. Torsgen and Frannack would never rifle through her pants.

She'd allowed herself two small items of contraband. The first, a block of red henna. Torsgen would deem it completely unnecessary, but that was only because he'd been born with dark hair that shimmered like midnight, instead of the mousy brown Elka had. She'd been dying it red since she was twelve. And the second was a small purse of galders. Her cover was that she was a nobody from the cities but the thought of being completely broke for a year gave Elka shivers. She wasn't sure if galders would be accepted as currency in Kierell but gold was gold, surely.

She would be taking her throwing knives but she'd also stolen another weapon to take. Her brothers weren't careless enough to leave a clockwork pistol lying around but Elka had taken a knock-pistol from a drawer in Frannack's study. The weapon wasn't lethal. It shot capsules of redbane root which would burst in a cloud of smoke and knock someone unconscious. She'd packed it into a small pouch along with the mask she'd need to wear to protect herself if she ever fired it.

So she was ready, yet she hesitated.

She'd heard her brothers earlier, heading into the third floor sitting room. They'd be discussing business without her. All she had to do was march downstairs and announce her plan.

Instead she walked back to her tall windows. She'd spent the last five days formulating her plan. It had taken until this morning to find the perfect caravan she could travel with to Kierell. And during that time she'd ignored three hand-delivered notes from Daan. The memory of the kiss they'd shared was still sweet on her lips and if she closed her eyes she could smell the black pepper and oak moss scent he wore. Her skin remembered the way he'd brushed her long fringe away from her eyes and her fingers felt the ghost of his, entwined with her own. She imagined how bright her spark must have shone that day they spent together on the barge.

But if she'd answered his notes and gone to see him, she'd have fallen through the door that his kiss had opened between them. And then she'd stay in Taumerg. And she'd be a nobody, overlooked by her brothers, and never earning a metal shaving of the respect they commanded. Torsgen wouldn't let a silly thing like love stop him from reaching his goals, so she wouldn't either. Even if, when she thought of Daan's dark eyelashes and his mischievous smile, she forgot all about mills, and Endless Workers, and dragons.

'I'll only be gone a year. Please don't forget me, Daan.'

She was so close to the windows as she whispered the plea that her breath misted the glass. Then she marched back across her bedroom, pulled on her heeled boots and headed downstairs. The door to the sitting room was firmly closed and Elka pushed it open without knocking. Picturing the way Torsgen entered a room she straightened her shoulders, kept her eyes up and her lips in a resolute line.

'Sparks, Elka, you aren't needed here.' Torsgen's words were sharp at the edges and cold in the middle.

She ignored him and headed for the drinks cabinet. It was circular and stood on four spindly legs of iron rods. The door was pale wood edged with rivets and Elka turned the metal valve which acted as a handle. Inside coloured bottles with stylised labels were lined up in neat rows. She chose the purple bottle of Old Wheel Explorer Gin, Torsgen's favourite, and poured herself a generous measure into a cut crystal tumbler.

'Elka?' Torsgen was annoyed now, she could tell from the way he elongated her name.

She turned to face the room, gin in hand. Her brothers were seated around a large table, its surface inlaid with cogs painted black and gold. Both of them were watching her and Elka had to stop herself from grinning at the attention. Her palm was sweaty against the glass and her heart was hammering like a piston but she kept her nerves hidden.

'I know of the problems we're going to have getting workers for our super mill,' Elka began tipping her glass towards her brothers, 'and I know that we've invested enough galders in this project that if it doesn't work out then we'll be broke.'

'Blazing sparks, Elka! How do you know that?' Frannack interrupted her.

He'd had his notebook balanced on his knee but it fell to the floor as he made to push himself to his feet.

Until Torsgen's hand on his arm stopped him.

'But it's alright,' Elka continued, glossing over the interruption, 'because I have the solution.'

She let that statement settle in the room for a moment. Frannack looked at her like she was a puzzle he couldn't solve, but Torsgen's eyes had narrowed. She took a sip of her gin, and suppressed the shudder in her throat as she swallowed the horrible stuff.

'Alright, little sister,' Torsgen finally said, leaning back in his chair and mirroring her by sipping his own gin. 'Explain to me what you're thinking.'

Hope blossomed in Elka's chest but she kept her face calm like Torsgen's. Amazingly her brothers listened, without interrupting her, as she explained about the Quorelle's bracelets and what they could do. She laid out her reasoning that the Sky Riders had kept Pagrin's bracelet. Frannack looked sceptical but if Torsgen was a dial then the needle of his interest had swung from cold blue to hot red.

'You need someone to infiltrate the Sky Riders,' she told them. 'And since only girls are allow to become Sky Riders, and I am the only Hagguar of the requisite gender, I'll be the one travelling to Kierell.'

'How?' Frannack spluttered.

'With the ManFiney caravan,' Elka countered. 'I deliberately chose one that's small, with only three wagons, and it's owned by a Kierellian family so no one should recognise me.' She looked directly at Torsgen. 'I would not risk our reputation by letting any of our rivals get a hint of what we're planning.'

Was that a flicker of respect she saw in Torsgen's eyes?

'The ManFiney caravan will travel first to Nepzug, which is half a day from Vorthens and right on the edge of the Helvethi-controlled land. Caravans from Taumerg can travel there safely enough, it's only when you head out south of Nepzug that you need protection,' Elka said, laying out all the careful steps of her plan.

'Elka, you can't go traipsing off—' Frannack started again but Elka talked over him.

'Protection which I'll have because at Nepzug my caravan will meet with Sky Riders who are accompanying the Jimenai caravan back from Kierell. The Jimenai caravan will be safe to continue from Nepzug back here and so the Riders will then escort my caravan safely to their city.'

'My caravan?' Frannack had collected his notebook from the floor and waved it at her. 'You're speaking as if you're already going.'

Elka took a deep breath. 'I am. I paid for passage with the ManFiney caravan this afternoon. I leave tomorrow morning.'

Frannack turned to Torsgen but their older brother had his steely blue eyes fixed on Elka. She wanted to cross all her fingers and her toes, like she'd done when she'd laid out her case for keeping Ember. It had worked then. But she was trying not to act like a little girl, so instead she took another sip of her revolting gin and waited.

Torsgen placed down his own glass and ran his fingers through his dark hair.

'And when you arrive in Kierell?' he finally broke the silence.

'I'll make the climb and become a Sky Rider,' Elka replied. 'And once I've infiltrated the Riders, and become one of them, then I can steal the bracelet.'

'This is ridiculous,' Frannack scoffed, still looking at Torsgen and not Elka.

She'd had enough of him dismissing her. She marched to the table and slammed her glass down in front of Frannack.

'No it isn't!' she yelled then took a breath to get herself back under control. It was Torsgen she needed to convince anyway, and he never lost his temper. 'It's the perfect plan. There's no better way to get the bracelet back to Taumerg than on a dragon. You're not the only one who can study, Frannack, I've done my research.

'In the three years since the Battle for Kierell, and the peace the Kierellians have made with the Helevthi, the routes across the tundra have opened up. But they still need Riders to protect caravans from prowlers and the two Helvethi tribes who are resisting the changing times.' Elka leaned on the table and turned her attention to her elder brother. 'Sky Riders also act as diplomats. We might never see them here in Taumerg but they visit the Gierungsrat in Soramerg. And as diplomats Sky Riders are not subject to searches or customs checks, and no one in Kierell questions the comings and goings of a Rider.'

Frannack opened his mouth to speak but Torsgen held up a hand to silence him. Elka had always struggled to meet her brother's intense gaze but she forced herself not to look away. If she backed down now, showed even the slightest wavering of her commitment, Torsgen would dismiss her and her carefully wrought plan. She could see the gears turning behind his eyes.

'You'd need to be able to speak Kierellian?' Torsgen pointed out.

'As if that hadn't occurred to me,' Elka retorted, in Kierellian.

She caught the slight frown on Torsgen's forehead and had to tuck in her smile. He didn't speak Kierellian. Another reason why she was the only Hagguar qualified for this task.

'You'll need to be able to explain yourself to the Riders,' Torsgen continued. 'I've never heard of anyone from the cities travelling to Kierell to become a Rider. They'll want to know why you've made the climb. And why you want to become one of them.'

Elka felt a smug smile twitching at her lips. She'd thought of this and had it all worked out.

'I'll tell them that I've heard stories of Kierell and I'm excited that it's a city with a future still to be shaped. Taumerg is so built and fixed, everything is established, and I want to be someone who makes a difference. And I feel I can do that in Kierell.'

'You'll need to put more emotion into it when you deliver that line in Kierell. At the moment it sounds like you're in a job interview,' Torsgen commented.

Elka thought that was rich, coming from a man who kept his emotions as locked as a rusted cog. But she realised that it sounded like Torsgen was approving her plan. A firework of excitement exploded in her chest.

'So?' she asked, making the word sound decisive and not pleading. Torsgen had picked his gin off the table and leaned back in his chair, a small smile on his face.

'Seems the Hagguar spirit doesn't just reside in the men of this family,' he said.

Another firework went off in her chest, one of the fizzing, spinning ones.

'Torsgen, you can't be serious.' Frannack slammed his notebook down on the table. 'This is too important. We can't let the future of our business rest on the shoulders of a silly girl. If we screw this up we'll have wasted thousands of galders. All the contracts we've agreed, the bribes, everything that's in place…' he ran out of words as his exasperation got the better of him.

'You have a better plan?' Torsgen countered.

Frannack had no reply to that, so Torsgen turned back to Elka.

'Right, so Frannack and Mila will continue until they have a working prototype of a new loom, I will secure us the land to build on and Elka will steal us the bracelet we need to create an unstoppable workforce.'

This time Elka couldn't stop her smile. She was in.

'But,' Torsgen caught her smile and fixed her with his steely eyes. 'This is not some adventure in a book. I'm not giving you leave to disappear down to Kierell and take in the sights. How long does it take to become a Sky Rider?'

'Girls who survive the climb train for a year before being allowed their dragons,' Elka replied.

'Alright, you will make the climb, become a Rider, steal the bracelet and be back here by the mid-winter feast next year. Understood?'

She nodded.

'And if you're successful, you'll be given a seat on the Hagguar Ragel.'

Elka turned to leave, afraid that if she lingered her brother might change his mind and retract the offer. As she pulled open the door Torsgen called to her.

'And, Elka?'

She looked back, one hand on the doorknob, heart hammering with nerves.

'Once you make the climb you'll have to live with the Sky Riders, pretend to be their friend. Until you get a dragon and become a Rider you'll have to live a lie. Are you prepared for that?'

'I am,' she replied, firmly. 'I won't forget that I'm a Hagguar.'

'You won't be seduced by a life amongst the dragons?'

'No, that's not where I belong. I'll stick to my task and when the times comes, I will betray the Riders.'

'Because above all else, what matters?' Torsgen tested her with the question.

'Family matters,' Elka replied without hesitation.

CHAPTER 4

HOPE AND DISAPPOINTMENT

One year after leaving Taumerg

ELKA CROUCHED BEHIND a jagged pillar of rock and peered across the nesting site. The persistent drizzle was a hazy curtain across the rocky hollow but through it Elka could make out five coloured smudges. Five hatchlings to choose from. When they'd woken to find the Ring Mountains enveloped in rain this morning, Aimee had told them that they could wait for a dry day. Tariga, the other recruit who'd been training with Elka, had liked that idea but Elka had insisted that they go today.

She'd surprised herself by enjoying the year of training, despite how hard it was. She liked looking at the muscles in her arms, the ridges on her abdomen, and feeling the strength in her calves when she ran. The grips of scimitars felt at home in her hands now and she loved the power they gave her. But she could feel her self-appointed mission chafing more and more each day, like wet socks she was unable to change. Her brothers were waiting for her. The future of their family was on hold until she got back with the bracelet.

'Have I told you how much I hate the rain?' Tariga called over in a loud whisper. She was tucked behind another pillar of rock, shield propped against her knees as she squeezed water from her blonde braid.

'Only every day last winter and so far every day this autumn,' Elka replied, eyes back on the hatchlings.

'I'm a child of summer. In my mind I'm sprawled on the warm grass of a meadow, iced cloudberry juice in my hand.'

Tariga had made the climb only a week after Elka did and she'd then proceeded to spend the next three months coaxing Elka into a friendship. At first Elka had rebuffed her—she wasn't here to make friends—but Tariga's relentless cheerfulness had finally worn her down. And anyway, being friendly with the Riders was a good extra layer to her cover.

'I can see five hatchlings,' Elka said, getting back to business.

'One each and three to defend ourselves against. Easy.'

Tariga threw her a wink and Elka's mouth twitched into a grin. She double-checked the straps fixing her shield to her arm and wiped rain droplets off the thin sheet of orallion. The shiny metal covering the whole front of her shield would act as a mirror, casting the hatchlings' reflections back at them and confusing them. Or at least it would if it wasn't blurry with rainwater. One of the reasons Aimee had suggested they wait.

'How are we supposed to choose? I can barely even see them.' Tariga was peering through the drizzle, water dripping off her button nose. Everything about Tariga was soft, round and cute, but Elka knew from painful experience that she was a daemon with a blade. She'd even once beaten Aimee in a bout.

'Dull sparks,' Tariga cursed. 'I can't see any green ones.'

'There has to be,' Elka insisted, 'and I'm claiming him.'

'No way! If there's a green one, she's mine.'

For the last few weeks both girls had talked endlessly about what colour their dragon would be and what they'd name him or her. And both had decided they wanted a green dragon like Jess.

Elka had quickly discovered that Tariga hero-worshiped Aimee and she'd found herself admitting that she'd read *The Saviour of Kierell* and thought Aimee was pretty awesome too. They'd both tried to hide their awe at being trained by the young woman who'd stopped an army and saved an entire city. A girl-crush on her instructor was the last thing Elka needed and she'd hoped that being drilled by Aimee day after day would make her hate Kierell's hero. She sort of did when, after only a few weeks of training, Elka was convinced she'd torn every muscle, ligament and tendon in her body. But it was only thanks to Aimee's firm but gentle encouragement, and her complete belief in them, that Elka had survived her first few months. So she and Tariga continued to whisper about how one day they'd be as amazing as Aimee.

'I thought you wanted a male dragon,' Tariga continued, 'and I'll bet any green ones are female. You can't call a male dragon Jess.'

'You can't call yours Jess either, that name's taken.'

'Jessie?' Tariga's smile said she'd won the argument.

'Jester?' Elka countered.

Both girls laughed, then fell silent as they heard the hatchlings roar.

'They know we're here,' Tariga whispered. 'Okay, being serious now, which one are you going for? I think we should decide before we go in there.'

Elka peered through the drizzle at the coloured blurs. There definitely wasn't a green one. She heard the click-clack of their talons as they came closer. They'd be able to smell the girls, even through the rain. She and Tariga would need to go soon—attack before they were attacked.

Tariga's dream had been to get a double of Jess, but Elka wanted a male dragon. She saw how large Faradair and Malgerus were, how strong Black was, and she knew that's what she'd need from a dragon. She was aiming for a clean getaway once she'd stolen the bracelet but a childhood of listening to Frannack's fastidiousness had taught her to always have a back-up plan. So, if she was chased, she didn't want to get caught half way across the tundra because her dragon was small and slow.

'Elka, we need to get moving,' Tariga urged. 'And not just because every layer I'm wearing is now soaked. Even my underwear.'

The hatchlings were emerging out of the drizzle, close enough for Elka to see them properly for the first time. She'd spent the last year living amongst the dragons in Anteill but they were bonded creatures. These ones were wild and she was prey. Fear tingled in her fingertips and squeezed the breath in her throat. If she was eaten by a hatchling her brothers would never find out what had happened to her.

One hatchling was ahead of the others, its scales the deep indigo of a fresh bruise, shimmering in the rain. Elka assessed its long neck and legs, and the spiralled horns that looked too big for its head. It roared, the sound echoing around the stoney hollow. The other hatchlings kept back, deferring to this one.

'I want him,' Elka announced, eyes fixed on the indigo hatchling.

'Really? He looks pretty vicious.' Tariga sounded nervous, but she had her shield up ready to go. 'Alright, I'm having the golden one. She'll match my hair.'

Elka rolled her eyes at Tariga's inability to be serious for even a single moment. Despite her skills with a blade, if she'd been a Hagguar family employee, Torsgen would have kicked her out after five minutes.

'Shame she can't breathe fire yet,' Tariga was still talking, staring at the golden hatchling at the back. 'I could do with some heat to warm my toes. I swear I can't feel a single one of them.'

'Are you good to go?' Elka asked, pushing down her fear and steadying her breath like Aimee had taught them.

'Let's do this!' Tariga yelled and leapt from behind her pillar.

'*Mi sparken!*' Elka swore in Glavic, the other girl's speed taking her by surprise.

She sprang from behind the pillar and careened down the scree slope. An avalanche of small stones cascaded down into the hatchlings and all but Elka's one roared and jumped back.

'You're mine!' Elka yelled at him, still speaking Glavic.

As her boots sank into the scree she jumped, propelling herself off the slope and down into the hollow of the nesting site. She landed in a crouch, shield held before her. Her hatchling was two feet away and he glared at her, yellow eyes narrowed to slits. Elka grinned. He was ideal.

He stalked towards her, cautious but unafraid, his long talons clacking on the rock. He gave a hiss and smoke leaked from between his wicked-looking teeth. Elka's grin only widened. She opened her mind as Aimee had taught them to and felt the hatchling brush against her consciousness. Elka reached out with her mind, pressing against him. He met her, pushing back, and Elka thrilled to feel the connection she'd read about in Callant's book.

She risked a glance away from her hatchling. Tariga had circled round behind the others, drawing the attention of the golden one and another with ocean-blue scales. The other two, a pearly white and smokey grey, were still crouched behind Elka's hatchling as if waiting for orders.

Shifting her shield Elka watched her hatchling's eyes follow his own reflection.

'Come on, you're smarter than that,' Elka coaxed, in the same way Frannack had done when he was teaching her mechanics.

At the sound of her voice the hatchling's eyes snapped back to hers. And he attacked. Launching off those long back legs he sprang at her just as Elka had been hoping he would. She raised her shield and flattened her body to the wet rock. The screech of the hatchling's talons on the orallion stabbed Elka's eardrums like needles. She lay on her back, shield above her, hatchling on top. Under his weight her shield arm buckled, elbow jabbing painfully into her breasts. The smell of woodsmoke filled her nose and sharp teeth snapped an inch from her eyelashes.

The hatchling's tail whipped around and Elka felt the bite of its barbs. She screamed as it tore through her boot and cut a line of hot pain up her shin. Feeling like her shoulders might pop she heaved upwards with the shield, flipping the hatchling off. It landed on the rock beside her in a scramble of limbs and talons. But before it could right itself Elka pounced.

She flung her shield away and threw herself on top of the hatchling. It writhed and roared beneath her. Elka tore the lilybel tablet from her shirt pocket and flung it down the hatchling's gullet. Grabbing its jaw with both hands she clamped it closed. She felt claws tear her arm and warm blood ran down her skin. The hatchling was trying to open its mouth to bite, and the strength of its jaw made Elka's finger bones feel like they might pop through her skin and ping away.

'Come on,' she willed the lilybel to take effect.

A blur of shimmering white filled her vision and Elka was thrown backwards off her hatchling. The pearlescent one had pounced on her. Instinct took over and Elka rolled with the hatchling, springing to her feet. Sharp pain lanced down her shin. The hatchling leapt at her again and she spun to the side, kicking it in the ribs as it went past. She heard a crunch and the hatchling roared. It whipped around, angry now, ruff of feathers around its neck flared, wings spread wide.

Elka crouched, keeping her eyes on the hatchling, and felt around on the rock with her cold, wet fingers.

'Come on,' she whispered, this time aimed at herself.

Her fingers found a shard of slate. It wasn't a throwing knife but it would do. With a practiced flick of her wrist she sent it straight at the hatchling. The sharp point burst the hatchling's eyeball and it roared in pain, clawing at its ruined eye. Elka looked back to her own hatchling and was relieved to see he was unconscious. She pulled the silver horn free from her belt.

'Tariga?' she yelled. The rain was falling heavier now and the other recruit was a blur. Elka felt a niggle of worry. 'You alright?'

'Blow the horn!'

She did. The note rang out, echoing around the hollow of the nesting site, and a moment later Elka heard the tumbling hiss of scree. She dropped to her knees, wrapping a protective arm around her hatchling so the Riders would know not to kill him. She was sure the Riders knew their job, but Torsgen always liked to check those he hired were doing as instructed.

Lyrria and Nathine were black blurs, their scimitars silvery streaks in the rain. In a matter of moments the three unbonded hatchlings were dead and the coppery stench of blood caught in Elka's throat. She let out a breath she hadn't realised she'd been holding and looked down at her hatchling.

She'd done it, she had a dragon. Yes, she still had to survive her first flight, and find Pagrin's bracelet, but the pieces of her plan were clicking into place like the well-oiled cogs in one of Frannack's machines.

'Welcome to the Hagguar family,' she whispered to her dragon in Glavic.

She saw black boots, and her eyes travelled up over a curved blade slick with viscous dragon blood to see Nathine smiling down at her. The Rider's high ponytail was coming loose and she had a smear of blood on her cheek.

'Nice dragon. Have you already got a name picked out for her?'

For a moment Elka thought she'd misheard. Then she doubted her grasp of Kierellian even though she knew it was perfect.

'Her?' Elka looked from Nathine down to the unconscious hatchling.

'Yeah, your dragon's female.'

Now the adrenaline from the fight was ebbing away Elka properly looked at her hatchling. Her limbs were long, gangly, but her head was narrow and graceful. She *was* female. Elka tasted porridge in the back of her throat and thought she was going to be sick. She'd been an idiot and chosen the wrong dragon. Her panicked eyes swept the nesting site but the others were definitely dead, rain washing the blood from fatal wounds in their necks and torsos. She thought of Torsgen's stern, calculating face. He wouldn't have made a mistake like this.

'Alright let's get your hatchlings home,' Nathine continued, unaware of the despair seeping through Elka like blood through a bandage. 'Cake's on me. Well, I don't mean I'll actually bake it but I'll swipe some from the kitchen for you.' She turned away. 'Lyrria, chuck me a harness.'

* * *

ELKA TRUDGED THROUGH the dark tunnel, every footstep sending a fresh burst of pain up her injured leg. The cut was deep and had needed stitches. Elka's mouth twisted as she thought of the scar it would leave. She stumbled, catching her toe on a ridge of rock and almost dropping her dragon's breath orb.

'*Mi sparken!*' she swore.

This far from Anteill, if her orb smashed she'd be blind and lost in the dark. Dragon's breath orbs were pretty but why couldn't Riders use gas lanterns like normal people? She was too tired to do this properly, she knew that, but her mistake at the nesting site today had gnawed at her all evening. She'd made excuses about being sore from her wounds and left dinner early. But she'd only pretended to go back to her room. Instead she'd headed for the deep tunnels, same as she did every night she got the chance.

The warren of caves inside the Ring Mountains was far larger than the part where the Riders lived—there were miles of tunnels and Elka had been secretly exploring them. In her first few months after surviving the climb she'd searched everywhere in Anteill, even sneaking into Rider's bedrooms when they were away on missions. Frannack had taught her to pick a lock when she was seven years old. And then to encourage her to practice he often locked her out of the house on wintery nights. The first time it had taken her nearly an hour to get back in. She could do it now in under thirty seconds, even when Frannack changed the locks without telling her.

But there had been no sign of the bracelet. Since then she'd widened her search but after almost a year she'd still not found her way through all of the tunnels. With every failed excursion down a cold, dark, musty tunnel she'd grown more and more frustrated. Added to her failure to get a strong male dragon, it felt as if her plan was drifting away like smoke.

But going home empty-handed wasn't an option. Torsgen would retract his offer to grant her a seat on the Ragel and she'd be nothing but their useless little sister.

So even though her whole body ached she'd forced herself back into the tunnels, searching for a hidden room, a secret trapdoor, anywhere the Riders might have stashed Pagrin's bracelet.

This time when her boot scuffed the edge of a crystal stalagmite she couldn't stop her fall. Pain shot through her kneecaps and she yelped as the dragon's breath orb tumbled from her fingers. The tunnel floor knocked the breath from her lungs and she lay sprawled in the shadows. Her orb bounced along the rock and came to rest against a vein of sparkling rose-coloured quartz. She stared at it, waiting for the moment it would crack and release the captured flames, leaving her in the pitch dark. That would just be typical. But thankfully it stayed in one piece.

Elka rolled over onto her back. The little orb was too small to light up the tunnel's ceiling and she stared up into velvet shadows. Her leg and arm hurt, her knees throbbed and a ridge of rock was digging right into the back of her skull. She hadn't bathed today, and the clean clothes she put on before dinner were now dusty with spiderwebs and she dreaded to think what else. She sniffed her armpit and winced.

Right then she'd have traded her dragon, and all the clothes in her wardrobe back home, just to be curled up in her armchair with a good book and Ember in her lap. Only the thought of Torsgen's face made her get up. She didn't picture him angry, Torsgen didn't get angry—she pictured him disappointed. She saw him looking at her like a worker who hadn't fulfilled their quota and was deemed to be of no more use to them. You couldn't fire someone from your family, but you could disown them. And she'd no doubt Torsgen would do that if she failed.

So Elka pushed up to her feet, retrieved the troublesome orb and continued through the dark. It would be another few months before her first flight but that gave her a deadline to work to. If she could find the bracelet before then, she'd hide it in her room, then as soon as she was flying she could take off back to Taumerg with it. Mission accomplished.

She just had to find the damn thing first.

CHAPTER 5

HOLDING BACK

THE TUNNEL LED Elka out onto a small ledge overlooking the tundra. She'd been here before. It wasn't far from the boundaries of Anteill, in one of the first tunnels she'd explored. The mouth of the tunnel was encrusted with crystals—milky white and rose pink—and they sparkled as the first rays of the new day reached out across the endless grass towards Elka. She didn't notice the beauty. Her eyes were fixed on the far north.

Taumerg was up there. Her home, her proper one. These caves weren't where she belonged, despite the way the Riders had easily enfolded her into their community, barely a question asked about her life before the climb. Her family was up there too. It wasn't here with these women. Her place in the world was in Taumerg, waiting for her to claim it. She came out to this ledge at least once a week to stare towards the north and remind herself of these facts.

Sometimes she let herself remember the boy that she

hoped was waiting for her there. But she didn't do that too often. Every time she thought about the way Daan had cupped her face when he'd kissed her, or his terrible jokes that somehow always made her laugh, she would regret leaving him.

She'd searched the tunnels all night and found nothing but dust and spiders. Mad plans had been flitting through her mind. Kidnap Jara and force her to tell where the bracelet was hidden. Smash all the orbs, setting Anteill alight, and follow whichever Rider was sent to save the bracelet from the blaze. Steal Jess and threaten to kill her unless Aimee handed over the bracelet. She'd dismissed every one of them and then worried what that said about her commitment to the mission.

Her brothers wouldn't have flinched from doing any of those things.

Elka squeezed the dragon's breath orb in her hand, knuckles white against the textured glass. The sun rose higher, the rays hitting her face, blinding her to the view northwards. A memory popped into her head unbidden. Not of home, but of one of her first days of training. Aimee had been working them hard—stretches, drills, runs, climbs—and they hadn't even touched a training blade yet. Every muscle in Elka's body felt like it was being shredded. Then Aimee had sent her and Tariga for a long run, all the way round the Ring Mountains.

Elka had nearly plummeted to her death three times, but Tariga had been there. She'd pulled Elka back up and kept her going with her endless chatter, even if most of that chatter was complaints about the weather. The winter's first snow arrived while they were scrambling around Norwen Peak, slushy stuff that make the rock slippy as a frozen canal. Elka had hated every moment of it.

But finally they were back, and Aimee had been waiting for them at the entrance to Anteill, two big blankets over her shoulders. She'd wrapped her recruits in them and led them down into the warmth of the dining cavern where Pelathina waited with steaming mugs of hot choc. And as Elka huddled on a bench, her toes tingling as they came back to life, hot choc with a hint of spice warming her tongue, she'd felt something. Not belonging, because obviously she didn't belong here, but satisfied maybe. Other Riders passed by, giving them a knowing smile, or stopping for a moment to share the stories of the first time they'd run the circuit of the mountains. Elka wasn't the same as those women but in that moment she'd felt it, the kinship.

She pushed aside the memory. It wasn't useful or relevant. She needed to get back. Her dragon would be waking in a few hours and she was expected to be there. Her failure to bond a male dragon weighed on her shoulders like an iron girder.

Elka trudged from the tunnels back into the well-lit corridors of Anteill. She was wondering if she could squeeze in an hour of sleep before her dragon awoke when she rounded a corner and bumped right into Aimee and Tariga.

'Elka!' Aimee gasped then laughed as she narrowly

avoided smacking her head off Elka's chin. 'Congratulations for yesterday. Your dragon's beautiful.'

She was beautiful, with her shimmering indigo scales, but she was a she. Even if she'd been rainbow coloured and could magically conjure Elka a proper cup of Marlidesh coffee, she wasn't the dragon she wanted. But she couldn't tell Aimee that, so instead she changed the subject.

'Going down to the bathing caves?' she asked, noting the towels Aimee and Tariga were carrying.

'Wanna come?' Tariga asked.

The word yes was on her tongue. The thought of a long soak in the naturally hot water of the bathing pools was like a balm in her mind. She could let her frustration seep away into clear water that sparkled with crystals. She could let the tightness of her wounds release.

'Come on,' Aimee nudged her. 'Pelathina's already down there.' When she said her girlfriend's name, Aimee's face lit up as if her spark was glowing through her skin.

Every now and then a moment like this caught her unawares and Elka felt completely star-struck. The hero of Kierell was chatting to her like a friend. She wasn't just a line drawing in a book, she was a real person standing right here. Elka felt herself turning, facing towards the bathing caves, smiling back at Aimee. Then she stopped herself. She'd been getting too close to these women recently and she'd sworn to her brothers that she wouldn't be seduced by their friendship.

'I'm going to get some breakfast,' she lied.

'Pff,' Tariga waved away her excuse. 'We can do that afterwards.'

'You have fun,' she said and quickly walked away.

She didn't look back and she didn't look up until she stopped outside her own bedroom door. She'd done the right thing, she knew she had. It was what Torsgen would have done. He didn't share baths and laughter with the people he made use of to keep their business growing. So why was the look of hurt she'd glimpsed on Aimee's face prickling in her memory like a shard of metal wedged in her mind?

From the doorway Elka surveyed her room—a little cave with a single bed, patchwork blanket on top, two tiny cupboards for clothes and nothing on the walls but weird-looking lumps of jagged crystal. She longed for her own spacious room, her view of the city, her full-length mirror, armchairs and books.

She threw the dragon's breath orb on her bed, slammed the door and headed off down the corridor the other way. It was still early and Anteill was quiet. She met no one on her way to the Heart. As she stepped into the huge cavern, the woodsmoke smell of dragons filling her nose, she felt the now familiar surge of awe. But she took a deep breath and squashed it. It was just a big cave with some lizards in it. What was so special about that?

In the middle of the Heart, lying on the floor, chest rising and falling gently, was her dragon. Elka didn't move from the entrance. Years of eavesdropping on Torsgen had taught her that everyone had a price and everyone was a tool to be used. Dragons were the same. Her dragon was supposed to be the tool to get her back to Taumerg without anyone catching her. But she'd picked a tack hammer when she was meant to have chosen a mallet. She imagined Frannack frowning at her.

A whole year of training, of longing for a dragon, and now she had one and she didn't want her.

Tariga's golden-scaled dragon was sleeping beside hers. It was smaller than the one Elka had chosen, another female, so she couldn't even swap with her.

Elka sighed and thought of Frannack. In his last letter to her he'd explained in excruciating detail about Mila's latest loom prototype. It was the fifth configuration they'd tried and it was finally working. Frannack and Mila hadn't given up and they'd worked with the materials they had to make something useful.

'I'll just need to do the same,' Elka said.

Crossing the Heart she knelt beside her unconscious dragon. She was lying with her head and shoulders in a shaft of sunlight which softened the colour of her scales from indigo to a blue-violet. The ruff of feathers around her neck twitched as she stirred in her sleep. Elka laid a tentative hand on her ribs. She expected to be able to feel the fire inside but her dragon's scales were cool. Her neck and limbs were long, gangly even, and Elka could see how she'd mistaken her for a male. Not that she forgave herself.

'Alright, you're not what I wanted,' Elka spoke to her dragon in Glavic, 'but I'm stuck with you, so you're going to have to prove to me that you can be faster than even a male dragon.'

Her dragon stirred, talons scraping on the cavern floor, but her eyes stayed closed. Elka felt a pressure in her mind. It was like someone had tied a very thin thread around her brain and now they were giving it a gentle tug. It was her dragon, trying to strengthen the tentative bond between them.

Elka held herself back, not giving in to the tugging.

'Oh no, you don't get to just saunter into this family,' Elka told her. 'You'll have to earn your place. Just like I am.'

She sat for the next hour, one hand on her dragon, waiting for her to wake. The whole time she could feel her dragon exploring the bond in their minds, confused as to why it wasn't as open as it had been yesterday.

Footsteps echoed in the Heart and Elka looked up to see Tariga running towards her, huge grin on her round face. Her fellow recruit plopped down beside her and elbowed Elka in the ribs.

'It's almost time.' She practically sang the words. 'Have you got a name picked out? I'm still unsure about mine.'

Elka rolled her eyes. As well as the jokey argument about each naming their dragons after Jess, she'd been listening to Tariga fall in love with and then dismiss hundreds of names for the last few months.

'You'll end up not deciding and just calling her "dragon",' Elka teased.

'Well, at least that would be original, wouldn't it?

I'll bet no one else has ever named their dragon "dragon".' Tariga was stroking her dragon's feathers. They were the colour of summer sunlight and Elka grudgingly agreed that Tariga's dragon did match her hair. Even though that was a stupid reason to have chosen her.

'What about you? Sometimes you're so quiet and mysterious that I think you're conjuring up a really dramatic name.' Tariga elbowed her again. 'Go on, you can tell me. I promise not to laugh and I'll be honest and tell you if it's a rubbish one.'

'More rubbish than "dragon"?'

Her eyes drifted down to the scales rising and falling underneath her hand and she felt again the disappointment of not bonding a dragon like Black or Faradair. Unexpected tears welled in her eyes and Tariga spotted them before she could dash them away.

'Hey, I get it. It's almost unbelievable that we're finally here. I never in a million years dreamed this is where I'd be when I was seventeen. I was sure I'd be working with my sister, sculpting pots all day long. Ugh, sticky clay fingers.' She waggled her hands at Elka. 'Even after the war, when *everyone* was talking about Aimee and how she'd saved the whole city, I never thought I could be someone as amazing as that.'

Elka felt an unwanted surge of affection for her fellow recruit. She'd misinterpreted Elka's tears, which was totally fine, and now she was trying to comfort her.

As if on cue Aimee walked into the Heart. She had Nathine and Ryka with her, those two with coats and scimitars on, flying goggles dangling from their fingertips. Elka watched as Nathine and Ryka called down their dragons. Malgerus swept round the cavern three times, showing off, his orange scales flashing in the shafts of light, before he landed. Smaja, the pale green of new leaves, landed lightly beside him. Elka still hated that the Riders' outfits were black and boring, even if they did make their dragons' colourful scales look more vibrant in contrast.

'They look spark-shiningly awesome, don't they?' Tariga said in a loud whisper, her eyes also on the Riders. 'And that'll be us in a few months, after we've made our first flight.'

The other girl practically squealed with excitement. Elka approved of the fact that there were steps to becoming a Rider. Girls had to prove themselves by first surviving the climb, then by not quitting during the arduous training, not getting eaten by a hatchling when they stole their dragons and finally by making a successful first flight. But sometimes she wondered how Tariga had survived to make it so far. She was just so…soft.

Tariga had gone back to wittering on about dragon names but Elka tuned her out. Instead she was listening to Aimee and Nathine. Ryka had mounted up but the other two were chatting as Nathine fixed Malgerus's saddle. Since arriving in Anteill, Elka had put her eavesdropping skills to good use. She listened in to every conversation she could, hoping to glean a clue about where the bracelet was hidden.

'Are you going to see Lukas before you head out to Ardnanlich?' Aimee asked.

'Yeah, I promised him I would,' Nathine replied with a sigh in her voice but Elka knew it was put on. She'd heard Nathine talk about her little brother often enough to know that her complaints were masking her love.

'How's his training going?' Aimee asked with a smile.

'Ugh, you know he's still got three years before he can even apply to join the guards but the little fool is learning swordwork already.'

'I heard Halfen's teaching him.'

Elka saw it, the twinkle in Aimee's smile as she wound Nathine up about her boyfriend.

'Silly boys playing at heroes.' Nathine sounded scathing but her mouth twitched in a smile at the mention of Halfen.

As Nathine swung up into her saddle Aimee kept talking but beneath Elka's hand her dragon sucked in a deep breath. Elka froze. Was she waking up? Her dragon's eyelids fluttered, not quite opening yet. She felt the swirl of nerves in her belly.

'Ah, sparks! It's happening.' Tariga's dragon was waking too and she was crouched over her, face pressed up close to her dragon's snout.

Elka kept a hand on her dragon's ribs but didn't shuffle any closer. The disappointment at not bonding the dragon she wanted was still raw. The tugging in her mind grew more insistent as her dragon's mind slipped free of the lilybel. She had no doubt that beside her Tariga was throwing herself fully into her connection, excited and gushing. Elka opened her mind, enough to let her dragon know she was there but not enough to fully give herself to her. Her dragon was going to have to earn that.

She heard the whoosh of wings as Nathine and Ryka took off, away on some mission. Elka had tried to learn only what she needed to about the Riders' work in order to keep her cover in place. She wasn't planning to be here long enough to be given a mission herself.

A shadow passed over Elka as Aimee came and crouched beside her. The Rider watched both dragons with a proud smile. Elka knew that pride was for her, for the two recruits that Aimee had steered, encouraged and supported through all their training. But Elka turned her eyes away, back to her dragon. She'd save basking in someone's pride for when she returned triumphant to her brothers.

Then her dragon was awake.

The surge along their connection almost mentally bowled Elka over. It was so intense, so full of love and longing.

'Whoah, steady on,' she said in Glavic, pulling her hand back from her dragon's scales.

'You alright?' Aimee asked, concern flickering over her face.

'Yeah,' Elka brushed her off, placing a tentative hand back on her dragon.

'Come on Ray, that's it girl,' Tariga was coaxing her

dragon up to standing.

'Ray?' Elka called over.

'Yeah, because she's the colour of a ray of sunlight.'

Right then Elka wished Nathine was back. Surely the one person who would appreciate the barfing gesture she wished to make.

Elka's dragon was staring at her, reptilian eyes giving away nothing. But Elka could feel her in her mind, pushing, questioning. Elka leaned forward and touched her nose to her dragon's snout, the scales cool against her skin. She thought of the way her hatchling had been the first to attack them at the nesting site. She'd appeared as a leader, a dragon the others deferred to. Elka expected her to push back, but instead she tucked in her neck, retreating from Elka's contact.

'*Mi sparken*,' Elka swore. 'Where's the fierce dragon who fooled me?' she asked, speaking in Glavic so Aimee wouldn't understand.

'What are you going to call her?' Aimee asked, still crouched beside Elka.

'Everyone is so obsessed with names,' Elka complained to her dragon, then switched to Kierellian. 'I don't know yet. I've got a few ideas but can't settle on one,' she lied.

In fact, she hadn't even bothered to think of a single name. She wasn't sure yet if her dragon had earned one.

CHAPTER 6

ACCEPTED

'Storm?'

'No.'

'Hjema?'

'No.'

Tariga turned to her with a wicked smile. 'Grape?'

'No!' Elka yelled, exasperation bursting from her. 'Why Grape?'

'Because she's purple,' Tariga explained, pointing at Elka's dragon.

'She's indigo, and you can't name a dragon after a piece of fruit.'

Tariga shrugged, still grinning. She'd been doing this for the last three weeks, randomly suggesting names because Elka still hadn't given her dragon one. She kept telling people it was because she couldn't decide, but really she still didn't feel her dragon deserved a name. Instead of getting better—stronger and faster like all hatchlings as they grew—Elka's dragon was becoming slower and more timid. It was frustrating the spark out of her.

They were in the Heart playing games that were supposedly designed to teach them how to give their dragons orders. But Elka's dragon never listened, always seeming to do the exact opposite of what she asked. Or even worse was when Elka got angry and her dragon cowered to the floor, wings tucked in, head lowered. She was pathetic and each day Elka grew more and more frustrated that she was stuck with her.

Every morning when she woke after a brief sleep she would sense her dragon, there in her mind, waiting for her. It was like having a needy younger sibling who followed her around. Except she couldn't shut her dragon in another room and ignore her because she was inside her mind. If her dragon had been strong and full of life Elka would have embraced the bond.

She tried to keep herself stoic, but she could sense a lot more from her dragon than she wanted to. She felt her puzzlement, tinged with fear, at being taken from the nesting site. Most of all she felt her hatchling's need to belong, to be part of a clutch. And she was looking to Elka to fill that hole. A dragon's clutch was its family but this wasn't how families worked—you didn't just ask to be loved and instantly get given a place. As her brothers had told her so often, you had to prove that you belonged, that you could bring useful skills. So far Elka had deemed her dragon to be failing on all accounts.

She stood beside her nameless dragon, fiddling with the ring in her nose, as she watched Tariga and Ray.

Aimee and Pelathina were standing at opposite ends of the Heart, beyond the ring of shepherd crook poles. They took it in turns to throw coloured balls towards Tariga. It was impressive the way she was managing to get Ray to ignore the blue ones, so that Tariga could bat them away with a training sword, but catch the green ones in her mouth.

'Pelathina, both at once. Go!' Aimee yelled.

She and her girlfriend both lobbed balls at the same time into the centre of the Heart.

'Argh!' Tariga shouted. Instead of trying to catch any of them, Ray hunched down, raising her wings so they protected her Rider. Balls flew over their heads or smacked off Ray's wings.

'That wasn't fair!' Tariga complained.

'No,' Aimee agreed as she walked into the centre of the Heart, 'but you got a fright, yes?'

'Of course I did.' Tariga pointed at the balls still rolling on the floor beside Ray.

'But you kept your shock to yourself, you didn't share it with Ray, and she protected you, instead of freaking out. You're learning control, and your bond is strengthening.'

Tariga beamed at the praise and Elka scowled. She and her dragon had been failing at this game to the point where she'd refused to play any more. Her dragon always seemed confused even when Elka gave her clear orders and she was tired of yelling at her. She rubbed her eyes. They felt gritty and sore. It wasn't helping that she was spending every night deep in the mountain's tunnels, searching and failing to find the bracelet. She knew it would be easier to convince her dragon to do what she was told if she wasn't so tired, but she refused to let herself sleep away the nights when Torsgen's deadline was looming. The mid-winter feast, the date she'd promised to return by, bearing the bracelet, was only two months away.

She heard footsteps from behind and her dragon turned, snapping at Pelathina. The Rider held up both hands, and took a step back.

'Are you alright?' Pelathina asked gently.

'Yeah, fine,' Elka shot back, knowing full well that her dragon's behaviour was betraying her.

'I know that sometimes you like to keep to yourself,' Pelathina continued, lowering her arms slowly, 'and no one is judging you for that.'

Elka blinked in surprise and brushed her long fringe from her eyes, giving herself a moment to think. She didn't know Pelathina well. One of Aimee's main jobs with the Riders was to train the recruits but her girlfriend was often away on missions. Elka didn't think she'd spent enough time around Pelathina for the Rider to notice anything about her. It worried her that maybe her cover wasn't as good as she'd thought. Was Pelathina suspicious of her?

'Holding back was fine while you were a recruit. We all do whatever it takes to get through the training.' Pelathina smiled, dimples appearing in her cheeks. 'I used to sneak into the kitchens in the middle of the night and drink cream straight from the jug.'

'Why cream?'

Pelathina laughed. 'I thought it would make me stronger.'

Maybe she wasn't suspicious, maybe she was just being friendly. Sometimes, in the middle of the night, Elka would place a dragon's breath orb on her pillow and stare into the swirling flames. She'd imagine being able to let go of all the lies and the constant worries that the Riders somehow knew what she was planning. She wondered what it would be like to let the fake Elka be burned away by those flames. But they were just tired-brain thoughts, that wasn't how she really felt.

'But now that you have your dragon you can't keep yourself walled off,' Pelathina continued. 'If you do, your dragon will reject you.'

A sliver of worry crept up Elka's spine. 'What would happen then?'

'If you can't bond your dragon she'll revert to wild. And we can't let a wild dragon live, it isn't safe. Your dragon would be killed and you'd have to wait for the spring batch of hatchlings and try again then. And that's the best-case scenario.'

Elka gripped her dragon's saddle. She couldn't start again in the spring. Her deadline was two months away.

'And the worst-case scenario?' she asked.

Pelathina's eyes slipped over to her girlfriend. 'Ask Aimee to tell you about what happened to Hayetta on her first flight.'

As if sensing her gaze Aimee glanced over and caught Pelathina's eye. The look of love they shared sent a pang through Elka's heart. For a moment she thought of Daan and wondered if he remembered her.

'You're from Marlidesh, aren't you?' Elka asked, Pelathina's deep bronze skin reminding her of Daan's colouring.

There were lots of people from the sunny north in Taumerg, with complexions ranging from warm beige to dark brown, but she hadn't expected to find any down here. In fact, Pelathina was the only one she'd seen. Daan had been born in Taumerg but his parents were from Marlidesh and Elka remembered that every winter when the canals froze they'd complained twice as much as everyone else of the cold.

'Aren't you freezing?' Elka's question followed her train of thought.

Pelathina laughed. 'Not always,' she replied, her dark eyes slipping across the room to her girlfriend.

'Why did you come all the way down here?'

'Tell you what,' Pelathina turned back to her, still smiling. 'If you and your still-to-be-named dragon can complete three challenges for me, I'll tell you what made me abandon the sunshine for days and days of rain.'

'And snow,' Elka added.

'*Raarish*,' Pelathina shivered, 'don't get me started on snow.'

Pelathina's smile was infectious and Elka felt her own mouth twisting upwards. This was the most she'd ever spoken with Aimee's girlfriend, but she felt drawn to her because she too wasn't from here.

'Alright, stupid, let's see if you can do even one of

these challenges,' Elka spoke to her dragon in Glavic.

'You probably shouldn't name her Stupid, the other Riders will laugh,' Pelathina said, also in Glavic.

Elka spun to the Rider, panic fluttering in her chest. 'You speak Glavic?'

'And Helvetherin, and Irankish obviously. But you're just procrastinating now.' She made a shooing motion.

Elka stared at her for a moment longer, mind rushing faster than a dragon's flight, trying to remember if she'd ever said anything in front of Pelathina that would give herself away. But the Rider was still smiling at her, and surely she'd have told Aimee if she had heard one of their recruits talking to herself about stealing from them.

Still, Elka cursed her carelessness. She'd been among the Riders too long—she was letting her guard down.

'Concentrate,' she whispered to herself.

Her thoughts felt like the ends of old ropes, all tangled and fraying. She could feel her dragon pressing against her mind, longing for Elka's acceptance, wanting the comfort of a Rider. But Elka didn't need a life companion, she simply needed a fast ride back to Taumerg. She slammed shut the door in her mind, tired of her dragon's persistent neediness.

She did that at the same time as she grabbed her saddle. And that was her mistake.

Her dragon jerked away from her, both mentally and physically. Elka felt a tear in her mind and a lurch under her hands. She was swinging a leg over her saddle as her dragon skittered away from her. Elka lost her grip and fell. She yelped as she tumbled sideways, instinctively putting out an arm to brace herself. Then she screamed as her palm slapped the cavern floor and her bodyweight followed.

Razor-edged pain shot through Elka's wrist.

She rolled onto her side, curling into a ball around her arm. Her breath snorted in her nose. Pain washed up her arm in waves. It felt like her wrist had snapped in two. She had to know if it was broken but she didn't want to look. Biting her lip, she steeled herself and looked down, expecting to see a bone jutting from her arm. But her skin was smooth. Somewhere above her people were shouting but their words were gibberish. The pain was all she could think about and her brain was too panicked to translate their Kierellian.

She tried to wiggle her fingers and couldn't. Couldn't feel them at all. She retched, tasting vomit in the back of her throat. The voices grew more insistent and Elka felt a gentle hand on her shoulder. She didn't want it, didn't want anyone. So she screamed and the hand retreated. She squeezed her eyes shut and felt tears leak down her face. The voices kept on, buzzing around her like angry bees.

'Go away!' she yelled, in Glavic or Kierellian, she wasn't sure which.

A broken wrist would take two months to heal. Time when she couldn't practice with her dragon. Time when Riders would fuss over her and it would be hard to sneak away and search for the bracelet. Her first flight would be delayed. And that was only if the Riders didn't decide she'd be better waiting until spring and trying again with a new hatchling.

She was failing. And her chance at earning a place on the Ragel was drifting away like steam from a chimney.

She choked on snot and tried to spit it out. But she was still curled on her side and it dribbled down her chin. She was pathetic. Crying just like the useless little girl her brothers thought she was.

Then she realised the voices had faded and the sounds of the cavern had softened. She opened her eyes and found herself in an indigo-tinged bubble. The scent of woodsmoke made its way through the snot blocking her nose. Feathers fluttered gently against her face. Her dragon had lain down beside her, her body a crescent around Elka's, her wings over them both like a canopy, sealing them away from the world.

A small voice at the back of her mind reminded her that it was her dragon's fault she'd fallen. But the beat of pain in her wrist drowned out that voice. She'd been strong for a year—leaving her home and her friends, surviving the climb, sticking with the training, searching every day for the bracelet, keeping her secrets, holding herself back from this community which kept trying to pull her in with laughter, and cake, and support. And now she was tired and hurting and just wanted someone to lean on for a little while.

And she had listened to Aimee during the months of training, so she knew that really it was her fault that her dragon had baulked. It was her own fault that she'd fallen.

Her dragon snorted a small puff of smoke that wreathed Elka's face with warmth.

She looked into her dragon's yellow eye. 'Thank you,' she whispered.

Closing her eyes she let herself relax for the first time since she'd joined the ManFiney caravan heading for Kierell. As her mind softened she felt her dragon's strength, like one of the pillars of rock out on the mountainside. Something she could lean against.

'Alright, we'll try it,' she whispered and for the first time, opened her mind fully to her dragon. She gasped, sending a fresh jolt of pain through her wrist.

That persistent neediness she'd loathed so much was gone. The moment she accepted her dragon, agreed to be part of her clutch, her dragon felt settled. And now that she knew her place, knew where she belonged, her dragon was happy to be herself. Elka sensed the strength, bravery and independence which had made her dragon leader of the hatchlings.

'Perhaps this can work.'

Her dragon responded by licking her face, rough tongue scrapping up Elka's cheek and into her hair.

'Ugh, okay don't do that ever again, you horrible creature,' she ordered, but there was the soft edge of laughter in her voice.

'Elka?'

It was Aimee's voice, coming from outside her cocoon.

'I just want to know if you're alright?'

Elka gave her dragon a nudge and was astonished when she obeyed and opened up her wings. Pushing herself up to sitting with her good arm Elka found three anxious faces staring down at her. She wasn't sure how to take their concern. There was a cog in her mind spinning her towards them, urging her to accept the friendship they so willingly offered. And sparks, right now she wanted some friends. But there was a piston beside the cog pounding away every day, urging her to complete her mission and leave. That piston reminded her that she was going to betray these women.

'May I see?' Aimee asked softly, pointing to Elka's arm.

Bracing herself for the pain she held out her hand. Surprisingly it didn't hurt as much as she'd expected. Aimee gently pulled back Elka's sleeve and she could see her wrist was red and swollen but no bones were poking out. Aimee's fingers were cool on her hot skin as she gently prodded Elka's wrist.

'I'm not a proper healer, we'll need to get Emilla to examine it, but I've seen a lot of training-related injuries.'

There was a small frown on Aimee's forehead, right at the point where the colourless half of her face met the tanned half. It smoothed out and she gave a small smile.

'I don't think it's broken, just sprained. You're going to have some epic bruising though.'

Elka let out her relief in a whoosh of breath. Not broken meant it would heal quicker. She leaned back, resting herself against her dragon and tried sending some of her relief to her. She responded with a rumbling growl and a strong urge to be in the open sky.

'Soon,' Elka told her and found herself excited by the prospect, and not just because flying would mean she had a way back home.

'Here, I can help you up,' Tariga offered, crouching beside Elka and holding out an arm.

Elka pushed her away, gently, and looked to Aimee. 'Can I stay here, just for a moment?' She stroked her dragon's ruff of feathers. 'With her.'

Aimee smiled such a smile of understanding that Elka wondered if anyone had ever looked at her like that before. Like they understood what she needed.

'Of course,' Aimee said, rising and pulling Pelathina and Tariga away with her.

Elka leaned her head back against her dragon and closed her eyes. The jagged edge had faded from the pain in her wrist, leaving a dull, throbbing ache. She'd need to go to the infirmary soon, get it strapped up, but for now she just wanted to sit. It felt like she hadn't stopped moving since she left Taumerg.

'You did it,' she told her dragon, speaking quietly even though Pelathina was now flying around the cavern on Skydance, demonstrating techniques to Tariga. 'When I shut you out, you could have flown off and left me. But you stuck around. I reckon that proves your commitment to me.'

There was a soft rasp of scales as her dragon wrapped her long neck around Elka's shoulders. Back in Taumerg, a lifetime ago, Elka's friends had hugged her.

She'd let Daan hug her, and more. But no one in her family had ever hugged her. She rested her cheek against her dragon's feathers, marvelling at their softness compared to her scales. Dragon hugs were good.

'Welcome to the Hagguar family,' she said, smiling, still with her eyes closed.

And then it came to her, the perfect name for her dragon.

'I'm going to call you Inelle.'

Her dragon snorted a puff of smoke that went right up Elka's nose. She snorted, coughed and laughed all at the same time. Then winced as she jostled her wrist.

'Ha, I'll take that as your agreement.' She opened her eyes, meeting her dragon's intense stare. 'Inelle,' she said again, smiling.

It was the Glavic word for family.

CHAPTER 7

STORIES AND LIES

Two years after leaving Taumerg

LIGHT DRIZZLE PATTERED on Inelle's wings as Elka waited to take off. She could feel how eager her dragon was to get back into the sky, the need tugging at the connection in her mind. Elka shared her dragon's desire to get going because she absolutely loved flying. She loved the way people looked up at her with awe in their faces as she and Inelle swept overhead. It was a great feeling to be noticed and no one could miss you when you had a dragon.

Over the past few months a little voice had taken up residence in the back of Elka's mind, and now it reminded her that she'd been in Kierell for almost two years. A whole year longer than planned. It also pointed out that she'd still not found Pagrin's bracelet. Every day she'd tell herself that she'd go looking for it tomorrow, but then tomorrow would arrive and there would be more exciting things to do.

When her mid-winter deadline had come and gone

she'd written to her brothers, and feared their reply. When the letter finally arrived Torsgen had barely written three lines but his disappointment oozed from every word. She'd let them down. She couldn't be trusted. No Hagguar would abandon their family as she had.

She'd crumpled up the letter, torn it into a hundred pieces, then got Inelle to incinerate them. When the next one arrived she'd burned it without even reading it.

Inelle growled and fluttered her wings, impatient.

'I told you, we're waiting for Aimee,' she said to her dragon in Glavic. Originally she'd started speaking to Inelle in Glavic as a way of reminding herself who she was and where she was from, but then it had simply become habit. Beneath her, Inelle stretched out her wings and shook herself, rain droplets flying from her indigo scales. Inelle had grown large for a female, not bulky like Malgerus or Black, but long-limbed.

Elka heard a short roar behind her and turned to see Aimee and Jess swooping over the brick wall surrounding Lorsoke.

'Come on, come on,' she urged the other Rider, palms itching with the longing to get back into the sky.

When Elka had first passed through Lorsoke on her way to Kierell two years ago it had been bustling with workers as they turned it from a trading post into a proper town. Now it had brick buildings, and inns and cafes catering to every taste. On her first trips out here as a Rider, Elka had always gone to the same little cafe because it was run by a man from Taumerg, and he baked proper pastries. But on their last trip here Aimee had taken her to a Helvethi inn where they flavoured all their stews, regardless of the type of meat, with juniper berries. It tasted amazing.

'Good to go?' Aimee called as Jess followed the line of the paved road that ran from Lorsoke all the way to Kierell.

'I've been ready all morning,' Elka shouted back in Glavic.

She watched the frown appear on Aimee's small face as she worked at the translation in her mind. Elka had been teaching her Glavic. Apparently Pelathina had tried to teach her once but love and learning hadn't mixed well and they'd mostly just fallen out. Though Elka suspected they did it so they could enjoy making up again.

'You have not!' Aimee yelled back, her Glavic heavily accented. 'You are shopping for socks half the morning!'

Elka laughed because that was true. Lorsoke had a mix of traders in a way that Kierell didn't yet and Elka liked how it reminded her of city life back in Taumerg. She liked the little shop on the corner of Krue Lane that sold colourful clothing. It wasn't high fashion like she'd worn in her old life, but she'd still managed to find a pair of socks with pink, yellow and blue stripes. She figured she could wear them under her Rider boots and no one would know.

Elka pulled down her flying goggles and pushed Inelle's horns. Her dragon took off. The whoosh of wings, the lightness in her stomach, the rush of air, none of it had grown old. She and Inelle had been bonded for just over a year now and Elka still felt the thrill of having her own dragon. After their rocky start she and Inelle had bonded quickly and now she'd forgotten what it was like to not have a dragon.

The little voice at the back of her mind reminded her that she'd once vowed not to be seduced by the life of a Rider. But then the rush of flying blew through her brain and washed that voice away.

Jess and Inelle flew above the newly constructed road, passing a stream of caravans underneath. The three-day route from Kierell to Lorsoke was safe now, thanks to the *Nokhori*. It was the Helvetherin word for friendship and what they'd called the alliance between the centaurs and the people of Kierell.

During her year of training Elka had not left Anteill—she couldn't without a dragon. But now she was a Rider she saw the excitement in Kierell at the progress they'd made in the five years since they defeated the Empty Warriors. It was hard not to get swept up in it. Previously, when that happened, she would take a mental step back and imagine looking at Kierell through Torsgen's eyes. He would see a cultureless backwater. But recently she kept forgetting to do that.

'You want to take it today?' Aimee called over, waving a leather tube sealed with wax. She'd switched back to Kierellian.

It contained letters from the Sulchinn tribe for the Uneven Council. The two sets of leaders had been negotiating for months as the councillors in Kierell tried to bring the Sulchinn into the *Nokhori*. This was the third set of letters Aimee and Elka had carried this month.

'You can keep it out of a bog this time,' Aimee continued, pointing the tube at Elka.

Elka felt a laugh tickle her throat. Last week, while stopping to let their dragons hunt for hares, Aimee had dropped the tube of letters. She'd then tripped over it and sent it spinning towards a slimy green bog. On instinct Elka had dived for it, slipped, skidded along the wet grass, rescued the tube but ended up in the bog herself. Aimee had tried to pull her out, but in doing so had also fallen in. They'd had to each scramble out and Elka had lost a boot to the sucking depths. Afterwards they'd both laughed until they couldn't breathe.

'You keep it, I trust you,' she told the other Rider with a smile.

'I'm not sure I do,' Aimee replied but she tucked the leather tube safely in her saddlebags. 'Last time after we got home Pelathina found bog slime and soggy stalks of grass in my underwear.'

'Argh! I don't want to hear about what you and Pelathina get up to!' Unable to put her hands over her ears because they were gripping Inelle's horns, she hunched up her shoulders.

Aimee threw her a wink and a laugh but then she seemed to read something in Elka's face and her smile dropped.

'I've never asked you, did you leave someone behind

when you came to Kierell? I know you don't have any parents, so I mean someone else you loved. A boy? Girl?'

Elka could still picture Daan's smile, but when she tried to remember some of the terrible jokes he was always telling her mind drew a blank. Her memories of him were old and thin now like worn out cloth. It made her sad.

'We should be having this conversation in Glavic,' Elka said, deflecting Aimee's question and switching languages. 'What's the Glavic for flying, again? You forgot yesterday.'

Elka tensed, expecting Aimee to push back, but she didn't. Instead she let the topic of who Elka loved drop and smiled sweetly.

'*Vliagen*,' she said, then continued in Glavic. 'Which is greatly a more useful word than some of the others you are teaching me.'

Elka couldn't help laughing. She'd spent a while on the flight out to Lorsoke teaching Aimee several very rude words which Aimee had mastered before Elka told her their meanings. Aimee's blush had been the brightest one Elka had ever seen. Even the colourless half of her face went red.

'Okay, you are telling me about Taumerg,' Aimee continued. 'I want to learn more of your city.'

The rain pitter-pattered on the dragon's wings as they flew but there was no wind today which meant they could fly and talk instead of shouting at each other. As part of their Glavic lessons Aimee had been asking Elka more about Taumerg. On the one hand it was pretty amazing to have someone like Aimee wanting to know about her home, but the more they talked the harder Elka had to lie. And it felt like most of her lies were stretched too thin already. She worried some of them would break soon.

And would that be so bad? Sometimes she fantasied about letting them all drift away, putting aside her cover story and just being herself. But that would mean being a Rider, and Elka wasn't a Rider. She was a Hagguar. Though it was getting harder and harder to remember that because being a Rider was incredible.

'Elka?' Aimee's voice cut into her thoughts. 'Your head's lost in a cloud,' she said in Kierellian.

'In Glavic,' Elka prompted, and Aimee repeated the sentence.

'So, you were lived in the area near the river,' Aimee continued in Glavic. 'And here is where the factories are constructed.'

Elka nodded though for a moment she longed to tell Aimee the truth and describe the bedroom she still missed. She knew Aimee would love the view of the city from her window.

'Where's your favourite place?' Aimee asked.

'In Taumerg?'

Aimee nodded and Elka thought about the question. Not because she had to consider it, but because she had to check if an answer she gave would expose her in any way. She sighed, tired of all the lies. Inelle snorted a puff of smoke that quickly dissipated in the rain.

'The streets around the western branch of the

Njmega Canal,' she finally replied, deciding that since Aimee had never been to Taumerg she'd have no clue that a nobody born in the factory district would be very unwelcome in that upmarket area. 'I liked all the little shops and cafes there.'

Aimee smiled, her cheeks bunching up against her flying goggles. 'Maybe one day we are going there together?' she suggested.

The simple statement, which was nothing really between friends, felt like it was grinding against Elka's heart. She would love to sit at a cafe on Blummestraab with the young woman who'd saved a whole city and who commanded respect in every room she entered. She would have loved to knit together the two pieces of her life.

Guilt at failing in her self-appointed mission niggled at her, mostly at night when she lay down in her cosy little cave to sleep and knew she should be getting back up to go searching for Pagrin's bracelet. She would do it, of course she would, she just needed a little more time.

They reached the Ring Mountains in early evening along with another band of drizzly rain. This was Elka's second autumn in Kierell and she'd become like Tariga—complaining about the days and days of rain. As Inelle dived through the vents and into the Heart Elka was planning her evening: dry clothes, a quick dinner grabbed from the kitchen and then she really would resume her search of the tunnels.

'Tonight,' she promised herself as she removed Inelle's saddle, 'I'll find the bracelet and then I'll take it back to Torsgen, just like I vowed to.'

Inelle nudged her and blew hot smokey breath over her.

'Don't worry, you'll be coming with me.'

She told herself that was because she needed Inelle to get back to Taumerg quickly once she had the bracelet, and not because she was so attached to her dragon now that the thought of leaving her hurt like a piston pounding her heart to bloody pulp.

'Elka, wanna grab some food?' Aimee asked as Jess swept through the streams of rain from the vents and settled on a high ledge. 'Tariga and Pelathina should be back from the harbour. They're probably already eating.'

Elka opened her mouth to say yes. She loved sitting with the other Riders in the glow of dragon's breath orbs, sharing food and stories of their missions. But the little voice in her head was being especially loud today and it reminded her that being a part of this world was not why she was here.

'I'd love to,' she said, telling herself the words only sounded true because she was so good at lying, 'but I'm pretty tired. I think I'll skip dinner.'

'I could bring something to your room?' Aimee offered.

'No, honestly it's fine,' she said quickly, hoisting her saddlebags over one shoulder. 'I just need some dry clothes and sleep.'

She tried to ignore the flicker of disappointment on Aimee's face.

'Aimee! Elka! Please tell me it went well,' a new voice called out across the Heart.

Its owner strode between the shepherd crook poles and their dragon's breath orbs, blond ponytail swishing and green eyes sparkling. Jara. There was a confidence to the Riders' leader that always reminded Elka of her brother, Torsgen. When Elka tried to mimic Torsgen's conviction it felt sometimes like she was only trying it on for size, whereas Jara wore hers comfortably like an old pair of boots, moulded to the shape of her feet.

Aimee tugged the tube of letters from her saddlebag and handed it over. 'Well, the Sulchinn tribe have replied to the council so the next step will be setting up a proper meeting.'

'And they've agreed to that?' Jara asked, taking the tube.

Aimee nodded and Jara's smile widened. 'And did you bring me…'

Her words trailed off as Aimee produced a small, wrapped package from her coat pocket. Jara tucked the tube under her arm, rustled the package open and took a bite of one of the biscuits inside. Her eyes fluttered closed in bliss.

'You're the absolute best, Aimee.'

The biscuits, which the Helvethi called *emegs*, were Jara's favourite. Elka had tried them on her first trip as a Rider out on the tundra. They were nutty and sweet and salty in a combination she'd never had before. They were alright. Certainly not as good as a proper Taumerg smoked onion pastry. Some days she missed Makje's

Bakery so much that her stomach growled just thinking about it.

'Don't let Nathine see you have them. She'll steal the lot,' Aimee warned.

Jara laughed and made a show of hiding the package inside her coat. Elka wished they'd both leave because the longer they lingered the more she wanted to stay with them and sack off going back to searching the tunnels.

She knew ducking out of the conversation would be rude, but she had to get out of there before her resolve cracked. 'I'm going to—' she began but Jara cut her off.

'Here.' Jara flipped the tube of letters out from under her arm and held it towards Elka. 'Can you take this to the council.'

It wasn't a question, it was an order. And Elka was delighted. She loved dealing with the Uneven Council. As a Rider they not only noticed her but they respected her and valued her opinion.

'Sure.' Elka snatched the letters from Jara.

'You're keen,' her leader commented, before nibbling another biscuit.

'Yeah, what happened to needing sleep and dry clothes?' Aimee asked.

Elka faltered, her mind skipping over lies, searching for one that fit just right. How could she explain that being someone important was what she'd longed for her whole life and talking to the council made her feel like that? As far as Jara was concerned she was simply a no one, just a girl from the north looking for adventure and a place in the world.

None of her lies seemed to fit so she risked a truth. 'I really like the council chamber.'

'Says the girl from a city twice the size of Kierell.' Jara shook her head but either believed Elka or didn't really care because she sauntered away again, package of biscuits still in her hand.

'You sure you don't want me to save you some pudding?' Aimee asked.

Elka shook her head. 'Let Nathine eat all the pudding. But maybe save me some toast.'

'I promise.'

Elka whistled for her dragon as Aimee left the Heart. She could probably have easily gotten out of taking the letters to the council—Aimee would have gone in her place if Elka had thought of an excuse. And she should have. She should be heading for the tunnels.

'I'll go later,' she told Inelle as her dragon landed beside her. 'We'll only be gone an hour at most.' She stroked her dragon's feathers. 'Do you think we can beat our record for flying down the mountains?'

Inelle snorted a puff of smoke and Elka gave her dragon a wicked grin. She'd been practicing flying as fast as she could now Inelle was fully grown, setting herself challenges and then trying to beat her time. From the floor of the Heart until the moment Inelle broke from her dive down the side of the mountains was one of their challenges. They'd yet to do it in less than three hundred heartbeats.

'Tonight we will,' Elka told her dragon as she boosted herself up into her saddle.

Flying really fast had begun as a way of preparing. Once she had the bracelet she'd need to get back to Taumerg as quickly as she could. But also, flying really fast was amazingly good fun.

CHAPTER 8

STILL FINDING NOTHING

…two hundred and eighty-four…two hundred and eighty-five…two hundred and eighty-six…

Sharp grey rock flashed past them. Elka's hair streamed behind her. The wind pressed on her face like a slap, making her cheeks sting.

…two hundred and eighty-seven…

Her dragon was a dart of muscles and indigo scales. Elka gripped her horns so tightly she knew she'd have spiralled imprints on her palms. The peaked roofs and cobbled streets of Kierell rushed towards them.

…two hundred and eighty-eight…

Inelle's wings snapped open, rising from her dive at the last moment.

'Yes!' Elka yelled into the evening sky. 'A new record, Inelle!'

Elka felt the surge of shared triumph flowing through their connection. She pulled Inelle's left horn, squeezing with her knees and steering her dragon over the warehouses of Barter and towards Quorelle Square.

There were no other Riders around but still Inelle was showing off, enjoying the victory. She flapped her long wings, fast but still graceful, and she was snorting small puffs of smoke then biting them. She would catch them in her mouth and then let the tendrils float out from between her teeth. As Inelle rode the sky above Kierell, Elka could feel every shift in her powerful muscles. Elka was sure Inelle could outrun even the male dragons now.

They landed in the centre of Quorelle Square beside the statue of a Rider and her dragon, the dragon's wings open wide as if in flight. In Elka's book, *The Saviour of Kierell*, that statue had been one of Kyelli and Marhorn but it had been damaged during the Battle for Kierell. Elka had learned that instead of repairing it the council had voted unanimously to replace it with one of a Rider. It was supposed to be a generic Rider representing all the women who'd fought to protect the city. But the Rider was small and curly hair poked out from under her hat.

Leaving Inelle, Elka ran up the steps of the council chamber two at a time. The guards on the door nodded to her as she slipped inside. Elka was used to tall, skinny buildings lining canals, so the cavernous space of the council chamber always amazed her. Even though it was evening the place still bustled. Elka skidded to a halt on the polished marble floor and grabbed the arm of a passing clerk.

'Where's Councillor Myconn?'

The clerk almost brushed her off till he clocked her

Rider's outfit. Elka smiled at that. 'High gallery,' he told her.

Elka let him scuttle off and headed for the stairs. She had to weave between ladders and workers all the way up. They were busy replacing the old sconces with proper gas lighting—the first building in the city to have it installed. Elka had rolled her eyes at all the excitement. She'd grown up with gas lights. But still, she liked that Kierell was installing them, it made the city feel more like home.

She reached the high gallery and rapped her knuckles on the wooden door.

'Enter,' a voice called.

Kierell might be old fashioned, and sometimes Elka found it too quaint, but she did love the view from the high gallery. The curved wall with its full-length windows perfectly mirrored the curve of the Ring Mountains beyond. And right now the sunset was bleeding across the sky, painting the peaks of the mountains pink and orange.

There were two councillors sitting at the big table, papers laid out in neat piles before them. There had been an election the year Elka arrived in Kierell and she'd taken it upon herself to learn the names and previous occupations of all eleven members of the council. It was what Torsgen would have done. Tonight she was facing Myconn SaSturn, Jara's twin brother and councillor for a third term, as denoted by the three bands tattooed around his left wrist. The other was Bylettie Cups, with two bands around her wrist, and only daughter of a couple who owned five inns across the city. Bylettie also had the natural red hair that Elka had always tried to emulate with henna and for that she envied the woman.

Elka smiled as she noticed Myconn was wearing a short coat more in keeping with Taumerg's fashions than Kierell's. The fabric was a drab dark grey, however, and Elka wanted to design him something brighter. With his pale hair he'd suit perhaps a teal jacket and a nice orange waistcoat to clash with it.

'I hope you've come to tell us that it went well?' Myconn asked, echoing what his sister had said earlier.

Elka laid the tube of letters on the table and rolled it across to the councillors. 'The Helvethi have replied and agreed to a meeting.'

She saw the relief on both the councillors' faces as they shared a smile. Bylettie opened the tube, tugging the rolled-up papers free. Elka lingered as they scanned the letters, hoping they might ask her opinion on something. She didn't really expect them to and jumped a little when Myconn spoke.

'What do you think?' he asked.

'About what?' The question had taken her by surprise but in a pleasant way. Her brothers had never asked for her thoughts.

'Well, you've met with the Sulchinn several times now. Spoken to them, eaten with them. In your opinion are they genuinely committed to joining the *Nokhori*?'

Bylettie looked up from the letters, watching her too. A smile tugged at the corners of Elka's lips but she reigned it in, keeping her face professional. But sparks, it felt good to have these two important decision makers treating her like an equal.

'Yes, I think they'll join,' she told them.

'You're from Taumerg, yes?' Myconn asked and continued when she nodded. 'And what do they think of the *Nokhori* there? I don't expect you to know what the Gierungsrat in Soramerg are discussing, or even the Guild heads in your own city, but perhaps you know the feeling of the ordinary people. Are they pleased the tundra is opening up and becoming safer?'

'Myconn, if you're going to quiz the girl at least let her have a seat.' Bylettie shook her head and gestured for Elka to sit.

She eagerly pulled out a chair but sat down so quickly that she smacked her scimitars off the back. Wincing, she hoped the councillors hadn't noticed.

'Tea?' Bylettie asked, lifting a teapot.

Elka nodded and took the cup she poured. 'I love your dress,' Elka said, and meant it. The cream of Bylettie's outfit wasn't what she'd personally have chosen but it set off the councillor's red hair beautifully.

'And I like your piercing,' Bylettie pointed to her own nose.

Elka smiled as she remembered how much Torsgen hated it, saying it made her look like a common worker and not a respectable lady. She almost told Bylettie this and stopped herself just in time by biting the inside of her cheek.

'So, Taumerg?' Myconn prompting, taking the seat

opposite her. The sunset was behind him and it made his blond hair glow.

Elka wheeled out one of her practised answers and as she said it, she realised that this time she actually meant it. 'Without the *Nokhori* I wouldn't have been able to travel safely to Kierell. I wouldn't have become a Rider. So for me, it's a very good thing.'

'Why did you come all the way from Taumerg to become a Rider?' Bylettie asked as she unrolled another of the letters.

Elka was always prepared for this question, and she'd answered it enough times now to be good at it. She smiled. 'Because this is where the future is. Taumerg is old, and everything is fixed. It feels like there's nothing new there. Growing up I always wanted to be someone who could play a part in changing things for the better.'

The little voice in her mind had become a whisper as it tried to remind her that it was her family's business she wanted to play a part in, not Kierell's future. And that it was the amount of galders in the Hagguar coffers that she wanted to help improve, not this city at the bottom of the world.

'And are your family proud?' Myconn asked.

'I don't have any, it's just me.' That practiced lie slipped out easily but tonight it tasted sour. These important people were respecting her as a young woman with thoughts, opinions and power, and all she was doing was lying to them. Suddenly she wanted to get out of there before they delved any deeper into who she was.

'You're busy and I should leave you to read the Sulchinn's letters,' Elka said, standing.

But as she turned to the door her thoughts went to the task ahead. More hours of searching through dark tunnels, wondering why she was doing this and if it was still worth it. She'd begun to suspect that maybe she had it wrong and the Riders didn't have the bracelet. And if that was the case, she should just give up, shouldn't she?

Elka felt all twisted inside and for the first time in her life she didn't know who she was. She still felt the desire to be someone, to prove herself. Sometimes it felt like she'd done that by becoming a Rider. But that wouldn't get her a seat on the Hagguar Ragel. That wouldn't earn the respect of her brothers.

Feeling like she was a ball of yarn unravelling Elka clung to the thing that had brought her here in the first place—finding Pagrin's bracelet. If the Riders didn't have it, then maybe the Uneven Council did. And stealing from them wouldn't make her feel as guilty as stealing from the Riders. But she couldn't just ask them outright.

With one hand still on the door she turned back. 'I've always wondered about after the war,' she began and the councillors both looked up. 'Were you ever tempted to keep it and use it?'

She watched for any tell in Myconn's face, any twitch or flicker of his eyes that told her he was about to lie. But instead he looked genuinely confused. 'Use what?'

Perhaps she'd been too subtle. She took a deep breath. 'The Quorelle's bracelet. You could have made Empty Warriors of your own and used them to... I dunno,' she waved vaguely pretending she'd never really thought this through, 'maybe clear the tundra of centaurs, or... perhaps make workers to build factories like we have back in Taumerg.'

Myconn's eyes changed the exact same way she'd seen Jara's do, going from soft moss to hard emerald. The colour drained from Bylettie's face and her knuckles whitened as she gripped one of the letters, crumpling it. Myconn rose, slowly, hands flat on the tabletop.

'I shall forgive you that comment because you're from Taumerg. You weren't here, you couldn't possibly understand the horror those monsters brought to Kierell.'

'I would have thought Jara would have explained our history to you,' Bylettie added, her voice tight with anger.

Myconn threw her a look, clearly not liking a criticism of his twin. Was his anger a front though, to hide a secret the council were guarding? He'd been a councillor for ten years. Even if not all the councillors knew they'd kept Pagrin's bracelet, surely Myconn would.

'No, I wasn't here,' Elka pressed on, committed now to testing him. 'But the stories made it to my city and from what I understand the Empty Warriors were only monsters because their master was twisted and evil. If someone peaceable used the bracelet you could make warriors tied to a more noble purpose, yes? Someone…maybe a councillor, like you.'

The anger exploded across Myconn's face like a firework. 'We lost three councillors! Murdered by Pagrin. Two of them were close friends of mine. One of them… she…' his voice croaked and his words trailed off before he took a deep breath and rallied himself. 'The entire harbour district was destroyed. Hundreds of guards were killed, thousands of people. Sparks! Many of them burned alive in their own homes!'

'And all by an enemy with no mercy and no humanity. One that couldn't be spoken too, reasoned or negotiated with,' Bylettie added, throwing the crumpled letter onto the table.

'If it hadn't been for Aimee, and Jara's Riders, every single person in Kierell would be dead.' Myconn was a shadow now, backlit by the sunset behind him. 'If Aimee hadn't dropped Kyelli's bracelet into the sea I would have smashed it to pieces myself. Then dropped it into the sea.'

'It's power that no one should ever have,' Bylettie said quietly. As a tear slipped down her cheek Elka wondered who she'd lost in the war. 'One person cannot be trusted with the bracelet, no matter their intentions.'

The anger and sorrow from the two councillors was palpable, pressing against Elka, almost shoving her out of the door. She knew fake, she'd seen it in her own mirror for two years, and these emotions were real.

'I'm sorry, I didn't understand,' she mumbled and hurried away down the corridor.

As she wove between the ladders balanced on the stairs she felt chastised and angry. At herself? At Myconn? She wasn't sure. She was convinced that the council didn't have Pargin's bracelet, and likely didn't even know about it. Myconn had only mentioned Kyelli's. So that led her right back to her theory that Riders had kept it and not told the council.

'So where is the blasted thing?' Elka spat the words through gritted teeth.

'Excuse me?'

One of the guards at the doors had heard her though she'd spoken in Glavic.

'Sorry, nothing,' Elka switched to Kierellian and threw him one of her practiced smiles. She dropped it a second later, hurried down the steps and across the square. She was watching Inelle glide down from the library roof and didn't spot Halfen at first.

'Elka!' he called, running over, patchwork guards' cloak flapping behind him.

Elka smiled because she needed a distraction from her own thoughts and Halfen was a nice one. He and Nathine made a sweet couple though she really didn't know how he put up with her sometimes. Perhaps he was the calm to her storm.

Elka had gotten to know Halfen, both through her duties as a Rider, but also because he joined them whenever he was off duty. Aimee had made such an effort to include Elka in her group of friends, mistaking her stoicism for shyness. At first Elka had swerved whenever she could, but sometimes she was caught without an excuse and had been forced to join trips down into Kierell. Now she loved an afternoon off spent with any combination of Aimee, Pelathina, Tariga, Nathine and Halfen.

Inelle landed in the square with a clack of talons on flagstones and snorted a greeting at Halfen. Elka wanted to stay and chat but she'd promised herself that she'd get back into the tunnels tonight and if she delayed any longer she knew she'd never go.

'Hi, Halfen. I'm sorry I can't stay, I'm in the middle of something for Jara.'

Not strictly a lie.

'Oh sure, no worries.' Halfen had tilted his good ear towards her, like he always did when someone was speaking. He couldn't hear a thing out the other one. 'I'll bet your job's more exciting than mine.'

He was complaining but still wore a smile on his round face.

'Is Captain Tenth still giving you all the rubbish assignments?' Elka asked as she boosted herself up into her saddle.

'Yeah, but don't tell Nathine. She's already threatened to get Malgerus to bite off Tenth's head three times this year.'

Elka laughed though she could picture Nathine doing exactly that.

'Well, good luck with your boring job.'

Halfen winked at her and pulled a book from his pocket. 'I'll get through it.'

Elka pushed Inelle's horns and her dragon took off.

Halfen gave her a cheerful wave which she returned. The sunset had bled down behind the mountains leaving a darkening sky the same indigo as Inelle's scales. Stars began to twinkle and Elka hung back her head to admire them.

There were days when she longed for the buzz of a proper city, for the comfort of her townhouse, and the mix of cafes that sold food from everywhere. But the sky above Kierell was so much better than at home. In Taumerg smoke from the city's factories clouded the sky and at night, the orange glow of lights cast a haze over the rooftops. Stars were something people wrote about in books—fanciful, romantic imaginings. But here, the sky went on forever and with the easy flap of her wings, Inelle could lift her above the lights of Kierell. Hundreds of thousands of stars shone like tiny flakes of silver and looking at them made Elka feel both small and immensely free at the same time.

Soon they were up in the mountains, Inelle heading straight for the vents leading into the Heart. Elka took the knowledge that the council didn't have the bracelet and fed it into her, admittedly waning, motivation for searching the tunnels underneath Anteill.

'Tonight I'll find it,' she promised Inelle as her dragon swept through shadows coating the training ground. 'Then we'll go home.'

The problem was, she wasn't sure anymore if she was already home.

CHAPTER 9

GETTING DESPERATE

THE BLADE CUT the air above her head as Elka ducked. Another followed a split second later. Watery morning sunlight glinted on the scimitars as they carved up the space where she'd been. She tucked and rolled, squeezing the leather grips of her own blades. Springing to her feet she whipped up her scimitars in time to block the next strike. Ringing metal sounded in the mountaintops. Her breath misted on the air above their crossed blades.

'Enough?' Aimee asked her.

The other Rider twisted her wrist, sliding her blade free of Elka's. The sudden loss of pressure against her scimitars made Elka stumble and in that moment she felt Aimee press her blade against her ribs.

'Dead,' Aimee announced with a smile.

Elka lowered her blades and rolled her shoulders. After flying for hours yesterday they were aching now, but it was an ache she'd come to relish. It meant she'd done something.

'Again,' Elka said, moving into first stance, left foot back, right forward, both blades up and ready.

'Are you sure?' Aimee brushed her strand of white curls off her sweaty cheek with the back of her hand. 'That's two points to me now and one to Tariga.'

The other Rider, standing to Aimee's right, gave Elka a cheery wave with her scimitar still gripped in her hand. Her round cheeks were flushed and her sweaty black shirt clung to her soft curves. But her breathing was steady despite the fact that they'd been sparring for almost an hour. The ground was frosty, the air biting cold as the Riders sucked it deep into their lungs, but all three had stripped off their coats as they sweated in the chilly morning.

Elka blew her long fringe out of her eyes. 'Again,' she repeated.

She watched as Aimee scrutinised her for a moment.

'What? You scared I'll show you up in front of Tariga?' Elka said in Glavic, a cheeky smile on her face. Aimee matched it with a grin of her own that told Elka she'd understood. 'Let's see if your swordwork is as good as your Glavic.'

Aimee laughed, then attacked.

'Hey, I heard my name. What did she say?' Tariga called over the ring of meeting blades.

Elka ignored the other girl, needing all her concentration to focus on trying to beat Aimee. The small Rider was so damn fast.

'I'm supposed to be the teacher,' Aimee said. She slashed high, low, high in a deadly combination that

Elka only just blocked.

'Yeah, but in all the stories the pupil eventually surpasses their old teacher.'

'Old? I'm twenty-three!'

Their blades matched their banter, clashing in the air between them. Elka thrilled at the strength and power in her body as she danced and wove around Aimee, searching for an opening. But sparks, she was nimble and darted like a hummingbird, never attacking from where Elka expected.

The current crop of recruits Aimee was training were away on their run around the Ring Mountains so Elka had suggested they have a sparring session. Then she'd gone and dragged Tariga from her bed too. The other girl had huffed at being out in the cold, insisting she was actually allergic to frost, but she was smiling now. And this morning Elka needed the distraction of burning muscles and clashing blades, of thinking about nothing more than avoiding the next strike, of looking for nothing more than an opening. Because she'd dreamed of Taumerg last night and woke feeling guilty and conflicted.

'Come on, Tariga!' Aimee called over.

Tariga was standing with both her blades balanced casually on her shoulders, tips crossed behind her head, watching the others fight. She smiled, opening her mouth as if she was about to speak but it was a feint. Instead she lunged at Elka, whipping her blades down so fast they were a blur. Aimee sprang back to let her in, as if they'd planned it.

'Traitors! Cheats!' Elka yelled.

'Can't handle two at once?' Tariga grinned behind the flash of her blades.

Elka met Tariga's attack and pressed into it. Within a minute she was breathing hard trying to catch every one of Tariga's strikes. The girl was fast as the wind. Elka lost herself in the deadly dance, letting everything beyond the reach of their blades disappear. Tariga came at her hard, twirling her blades and slashing them low. Elka caught them on the edge of hers and stabbed forward with both points. Tariga laughed and ducked under her attack, rolling and springing up behind her. Elka spun on her toes but she slid on the frosty ground and found herself back on the defensive as Tariga slashed at her neck, belly and hips.

'You're still tucking in your right elbow,' Aimee called. 'Keep it out and open or it'll limit your strikes.'

Their old teacher was circling round them, her blades down by her sides but she walked on her toes, ready.

'I'm not one of your recruits any more,' Elka shouted back as her blade whistled by Tariga's cheek. The other girl skipped aside and stuck out her tongue.

'Every girl I train will always be one of my recruits,' Aimee told her.

Elka had her back to Aimee now but she could hear the smile in her voice. Then she felt a cheeky tap on her right elbow as Aimee sprang back into the fight. Elka pulled one blade from her attack on Tariga and whipped it around to clash with Aimee's. Then she twisted both wrists at once, freeing her blades, and danced back. They might both be faster than her but she was a lot taller and had the reach. Tariga was short and Aimee seemed to have reached age twelve and decided not to grow anymore. Elka's long limbs gave her an advantage and she was going to use it. This time the win would be hers. Because right then, she needed a win.

She went on the attack, using every combination of moves that Aimee had taught her. Her feet danced, her blades sang, and her heart soared as she felt the strength and power in her own body. Aimee and Tariga had to work together, taking turns to attack her lest they tangle their blades. But Elka was free to attack where she could.

Slashing high she caught Aimee's blade on her own and shoved the shorter woman back, then immediately spun to knock aside Tariga's scimitar as it stabbed towards her thigh. The blade screeched the length of hers, bringing Tariga close enough for Elka to launch a kick at her. Her boot collided with Tariga's stomach and the girl stumbled back with an 'oof'.

But in taking out Tariga Elka had exposed her side. Aimee attacked but Elka's long arms let her twist aside and strike through Aimee's guard. Her left scimitar pricked Aimee's shoulder.

'Point to me!' Elka yelled, triumphant.

'It only counts if she's dead. That's just a flesh wound.'

Tariga followed her words with another attack, forcing Elka back. She was being pushed towards the edge of the training ground and she felt shale crunch under her boots. Sweat stuck her fringe to her forehead and she knew her cheeks must be as red as Tariga's. For a brief second, she wondered what the Elka from two years ago would think if she saw herself now.

Despite feeling like her shoulders had been wrung through a mangle, Elka caught every one of Tariga's strikes, the metal of their blades kissing together then springing apart. Elka's eyes flickered, watching Tariga's moves, hoping for an opening. Over Tariga's shoulder she could see Aimee circling, waiting for her chance to strike.

Tariga got through her guard, left scimitar tapping her knee then right pressing against her upper arm. But neither were kill strikes. Elka whooped as she pressed forward, both blades high, deadly tips pointing down, aiming right for Tariga's collarbones. She had her. The win was hers.

And then it wasn't. A cry of frustration tore up Elka's throat as Tariga dropped to her knees and swept both blades high above her head, moving fast as a darting firefly. Tariga's blades cut hers aside and Elka's arms were pushed wide, leaving her exposed. It was the moment Aimee had obviously been waiting for and her blade came slashing towards Elka's chest, edge catching the sunlight.

'*Mi Sparken!*' Elka swore, only just managing to block her.

But the move threw her off balance and forced her back. Her calves banged up against rock and she felt the lip of it against the back of her knees. They'd pressed her to the edge of the training ground.

'Done?' Aimee asked.

'Never!'

For a moment Elka imagined herself as the hero in a book with her picture drawn at the front, her and Inelle. Caught up in the fantasy she attacked. But she wasn't in a good position and the move was clumsy. Aimee caught her right scimitar on both of hers and twisted her blades sharply. Elka's scimitar pinged from her grip and skittered away across the rock. Showing off, Tariga spun her grips, blades slicing, then brought them both down on Elka's left scimitar. It clattered to the ground.

She was disarmed but she was a hero and wouldn't surrender. In the moment where Aimee and Tariga thought they had her beat she spun, hooked a heel on the rocky ledge behind her and boosted herself up. Crouching above the two other Riders she whipped three throwing knives from the garter around her thigh. Holding them between the fingers of her right hand, metal icy cold against her skin, she grinned at the other two.

'Oh, and who's cheating now?' Tariga looked pointedly at her knives.

'I've got ten presses says you can't make a kill shot with all three.' Aimee gestured to the training dummies standing like statues at the edge of the plateau.

Elka closed her eyes and took a deep breath, steadying her thumping heart. The tips of the knives pricked gently against her palm. Opening her eyes she sighted on the middle dummy and threw her knives in quick succession. Each one spun once in the air then hit its mark with a satisfying thunk, sinking into the straw on the dummy's forehead, neck and right between his legs.

'Really? Groin not heart? Is there something you want to talk about?' Tariga looked her at, pale eyebrows raised high, then she clanged her scimitars together. 'That's it, that's the real reason why you left Taumerg. Some boy broke your heart, didn't he? Well, he'd regret it if he could see you now.'

Daan's face floated behind her eyes—dusky skin, soft hair, lips she still ached to taste. Other memories of Taumerg had become blurry with time, but not Daan. She'd never told any of the Riders about him and now it was too late because she'd have to admit she'd been lying for years. So, shoving Daan aside she forced herself to laugh and wink at Tariga. Aimee offered her a hand and helped her jump back down off the rocky ledge. As Elka was gathering up her fallen blades she heard footsteps crunching on the frost.

'What are you lot doing out here apart from letting the cold suck out your sparks?' Nathine called as she walked towards them. She'd pulled her hat down low and her scarf up high.

'Apparently we're hardcore,' Tariga replied, but she was gathering up their coats and Elka gratefully slipped hers on. The wind was pressing her sweaty shirt to her back, making her shiver. She slid her scimitars into their sheaths and held them under one arm as she went to retrieve her knives.

'We,' Nathine made a circle with her finger, taking them all in, 'have no duties until this afternoon so we're going for breakfast down in Kierell. I need waffles.'

'Sounds great,' Tariga smiled.

'Is Pelathina—' Aimee began but Nathine cut her off.

'Yes, don't fall off your dragon, she's coming too. I swear sometimes you two are sharing a spark now. Watching you gaze lovingly at each other would be enough to put me off my waffles if I wasn't so hungry.'

'Oh, and you and Halfen?' Aimee retorted.

'Pff, that's different.'

Elka slid her knives back into their garter and her stomach rumbled. Breakfast did sound like a good idea. She joined the others just as Nathine tugged a letter from her coat pocket.

'Here, you've got post.' Nathine held out the letter to her.

Elka immediately recognised Torsgen's handwriting and her stomach tightened. The letter sat there, balanced on Nathine's hand, like a coiled spring. She remembered the way the last letter from her brother had burned, changing from paper and ink to ashes in a second as Inelle blew dragon's breath over it.

'Aren't you going to take it?' Nathine asked. 'It's not heavy but my hand's getting cold.'

Still she hesitated, dreading to think what words Torsgen had for her in this one.

'Elka?' Aimee's voice was soft as snowflakes.

She grabbed the letter, feeling the stiff paper crinkle

in her hand. 'Sorry, I was away in a dream.'

Tariga clapped, a delighted smile on her face. 'Aha! It's from the boy, isn't it? I told you he'd regret leaving you. I'll bet that's him begging you to fly back and sweep him off his feet.'

Elka swallowed her dread and forced a smile on her face. Nathine, of course, jumped on Tariga's assumption.

'A secret lover, eh? Interesting.' She folded her arms and gave Elka a knowing look. 'So when you told us you hadn't left anyone behind in Taumerg, no family, no friends, no boys pining for you, that wasn't true?'

Elka knew the girls were teasing her but still her skin prickled with the truth of being named a liar and her heart juddered against her ribs like a malfunctioning piston.

'Leave her alone, Nathine. Let Elka have her secrets,' Aimee said, chastising her friend and gifting Elka with a wink.

Somehow Aimee defending her made her feel worse than Nathine's accusation had.

'Didn't someone mention waffles?' Tariga gave a *come on* wave and started back towards Anteill.

Aimee and Nathine followed, but Elka hung back. She'd worried that after burning Torsgen's last letter and not replying he might have given up on her. She kinda hoped he had, but it seemed he hadn't.

'I'll catch you up,' Elka called, waving the letter at the others.

Nathine threw her a smirk, but Aimee's brow rumpled with concern. 'Since that letter appeared you've looked like worries are gnawing at your spark. If you need someone, I'll sit and listen over a cup of tea if you want to talk.'

'Me too,' Tariga called over her shoulder.

Right then Elka felt like she was two people facing two different futures. One was a Rider, attached forever to these amazing young women who called her friend. And the other was a Hagguar being pulled back towards her brothers and the life she'd once longed for.

'I won't be long,' she called to them.

'Don't be. If you're not in the Heart in ten minutes we'll go without you. I'll still order you breakfast, but I'll eat it,' Nathine promised.

'She will,' Aimee warned.

Then they disappeared into the mouth of Anteill, the darkness at the edge of the tunnel swallowing them. Elka was left alone with the words her brother had deemed worthy of sending hundreds of miles. And Torsgen would never have paid galders to send her praise or the latest gossip from their city. She flipped the envelope over and stared at her name. She could see Torsgen's anger in the sharp angles of his handwriting, the deep press of his pen. But worse than that was what he'd written.

Elka, Sky Rider

He'd left off her surname. She hadn't used her full name for almost two years but still, the deliberate omission stung. She tore open the envelope and gingerly slid the letter free as if it might scald her fingers. As with the few others he'd sent it was in Glavic and used a cypher only she and her brothers knew. Taking her own notebook and pencil from her coat pocket she knelt on the rock. Her knees melted the frost but she barely felt the cold. Scribbling on one of the back pages she deciphered Torsgen's letter.

Elka

I'll grant you the benefit of doubt and assume that my previous letter was lost in transit and that's why you have neither replied nor arrived home.

But you've worn out my patience, girl. Our family Ragel works like a well-oiled machine. You've become a bent cog and any part of a machine that doesn't work is removed. And replaced with a new one that fits.

You will return home within a week of receiving this letter, I've seen to that. Perhaps I'm wrong and you've already obtained the bracelet but something yet holds you in Kierell. If that's the case I will remind you that we're changing the world, Elka. I thought you were going to prove to me that you deserve a place beside us, but clearly you're not as committed to this family as you claim to be. If you've failed in your task then I've taken steps to ensure that the bracelet is obtained by other means.

Either way you will return home.

Torsgen

Elka crumpled up his letter, and tore the translation from her notebook, scrunching it in her fist too. She realised her hands were shaking, her heart beating against her ribs. Torsgen's letter was like being doused by a bucket of freezing water when she'd been sleeping in the sun.

A few days, that's all she had before she had to leave, with or without the bracelet. Or Torsgen would make her return. What did that mean? What had he set in motion? Her mind whirred but Torsgen's plans had always been unknowable to her. And now that the moment was here, she realised that she didn't want to leave the Riders.

CHAPTER 10

FRIENDS AND THREATS

Elka followed the others down Marhorn Street, the busiest in Kierell. Shops with colourful striped awnings lined both sides and a row of wooden stalls ran down the middle like a spine. Elka had always liked it because the buzz reminded her of Taumerg. But today the resemblance seemed flimsy. Torsgen's letter played through her mind over and over. She had a handful of days, then she had to leave. Or he'd make her leave? How? And without the bracelet she'd be going back to a world where she was nothing but a pretty face at a dining table, smiling and powerless. All she'd accomplished as a Rider would mean nothing.

Nathine led the way, striding through the crowd. Tariga chatted away by her shoulder. Aimee and Pelathina followed, hand in hand. Elka brought up the rear but her steps seemed to be slowing of their own accord, the others pulling steadily ahead. They'd left their dragons perched on the library roof and Elka could feel Inelle's unease, which was actually her own unease reflected back at her. She knew her dragon would be shifting around, unable to settle. She tried to take a firmer hold of her emotions, to be calmer.

They passed a stall with a red and gold striped awning and the smell of fresh pastries caught in Elka's nose. Turning she saw the woman behind the stall was from Taumerg—her bright, patterned clothes gave her away. She wore a skirt of soft green, a white shirt and over the top she'd buttoned a yellow waistcoat dotted with stars. Elka glanced down at her own outfit. She'd forgotten what it was like to wear anything other than black. Neat trays of pastries lined the woman's stall but Elka turned away, not letting herself remember the taste.

The others had pulled ahead and as her eyes spotted their dark coats in the crowd Elka felt a presence behind her, and a firm hand gripped her elbow.

'One moment of your time, miss.'

It was a voice she recognised and the shock of hearing it here made her compliant. The hand on her elbow pushed her forwards, steering her between the stalls and into a narrow alley. Behind her the man's footsteps were loud on the cobbles. Half way down the alley, where the shadows thickened, he pulled her to a stop. Spinning her around he slammed her against the wall. His big hands gripped her shoulders, pressing her into the red bricks.

'Sorry if I hurt you, miss, but there will be worse to come if you don't listen to me.'

'Nail! What the blazing sparks are you doing here?'

She stared into a face that she hadn't seen in two

years. His dark eyes were soft, gentle almost, but the set of his jaw was hard. It seemed hairstyles hadn't changed in the time she'd been away as he still wore his long on top, shaved at the sides. For a fleeting moment she wondered if her brothers still looked the same and realised that she could hardly picture their faces anymore.

'Your brother sent me,' Nail said, taking a step closer till she could smell the bitter coffee on his breath. 'It seemed his letters were not getting through so he sent me with a message.'

'I did get his letter!' Elka protested.

Nail's hands were like weights on her shoulders pressing her down. The moment he'd grabbed her everything she'd learned during her training fled from her head. Aimee had taught her how to take down an enemy stronger than she was but the shock of seeing Nail here made her limbs feel weak as stalks of grass. Nail could trample all over her and she'd forgotten that she could stop him. They'd all left their scimitars back in Anteill but she still had her throwing knives strapped to her thigh. But her fingers didn't reach for them.

'I haven't forgotten them, or my duty.' Elka's words burst out fast and panicked. 'I haven't...'

Failed. She trailed off, because she had failed. And this was what Torsgen meant by taking steps. He'd sent one of his thugs to drag her home like a wayward child.

'Your brother gave me two choices to present to you,' Nail continued as if she hadn't even spoken. 'You can fly back to Taumerg within the week, taking with you the item you yourself claim you are here to find. If you do that Torsgen will forgive you your tardiness and the seat on the Ragel will be yours.'

'Nail, listen I...'

The weight vanished from her left shoulder as he lifted his hand and backhanded her across the face. For a moment there was only shock then the pain hit. She tasted blood and realised she'd bitten her tongue.

'I am sorry for my rough treatment, miss, but your brother thought you may need reminding of where your loyalties lie.'

With the same hand that had slapped her he gently straightened her head and then replaced his grip on her shoulder. Elka did nothing to stop him. Because he was right. She had forgotten it, been seduced by this world and the women who rode dragons. She'd forgotten that above all else, family was what mattered.

'I shouldn't...' she began but a single raised finger from Nail was enough to silence her.

'If you don't fly back to Taumerg within the week, bearing the item, then you will be travelling back with the Koch caravan. With me. And without your dragon.'

Suddenly Nail had a clockwork pistol in his hand, the barrel pressed under her chin. It took a second for the full meaning of his words to sink in. And when they did it felt like a bullet had already torn through her chest. If she failed, Nail was instructed to kill her dragon.

'No, please, Inelle is part of me now. I need her,' Elka begged.

'Then you will complete your task and I'll see you flying over those mountains a few days from now.'

The metal of the pistol had warmed on her skin as it pressed her head back. She stared into those gentle eyes, out of place in the mean-looking face. She knew without a doubt that Nail would do it. He'd apologise to her afterwards but he'd put a bullet in Inelle and not even hesitate.

Elka felt a tear slip down her cheek and cursed herself for showing weakness. Nail would tell Torsgen how she'd acted. With his message delivered Nail released her and stepped back. The clockwork pistol disappeared back into his tailored coat.

'I apologise for the discomfort, miss, but I will be watching you.'

He patted the concealed pistol and gave her a small nod. Then he was gone, back out of the alley and sucked into the crowd on Marhorn street. Elka bent over, hands on knees, breath whooshing out of her. Her cheek stung from his slap and her heart was hammering her ribs like a piston in overdrive.

'*Yur jak!*' she swore, straightening and yelling the curse in Glavic. 'I hope your spark winks out and you die right now!'

She threw her words down the alley, defiant now Nail's pistol was no longer at her throat. She felt the warmth of Inelle in her mind, sending her comfort though she didn't know what had upset her Rider. She'd grown so used to having Inelle in her mind that losing her would be like losing a part of herself.

Which meant she had to find the bracelet in the next few days or she'd lose Inelle, along with any chance to ever again prove her worth to her brothers.

'Sparks,' she swore softly, in Kierellian this time.

She didn't know where to start. She could go back to the tunnels but she'd abandoned that search months ago and could never cover all the ground before Nail killed Inelle and dragged her home. The pressure felt like it was squeezing her chest, building up like steam that hadn't been released. It folded her in half, bent over with one hand pressed against the alley wall opposite. She stared down at her boots. Black boots. Rider's boots. Scuffed from this morning's sparring. A muddy imprint on one where Nail had stepped on her toes. Her mind felt stuck, unable to think about anything beyond her boots. Unable to even panic about what she should do.

'Here she is!'

The bright call bounced down the alley, jolting Elka's thoughts. She straightened up to see Tariga hurrying towards her, coat tails flapping around her legs.

'Are you alright?' Tariga asked, grabbing her shoulders just as Nail had done, but her hands were small, gentle, and her face was creased with concern.

The entrance to the alley darkened as Aimee, Nathine and Pelathina crowded in too. The first thing Elka felt was joy at seeing the girls who'd become her friends. They'd come to find her. Their drawn-together eyebrows said they were worried about her. Then she felt relief that they hadn't found her a few minutes earlier when Nail was here. How would she have explained that? Then she felt anger. At herself for failing. At Nail for threatening Inelle. At these girls because they cared about her.

'Uh oh, you look like you're going to be sick. Are you?' Tariga stepped aside and wrapped an arm around her shoulders. 'There, coast is clear now, you go right ahead and vomit.'

Elka swallowed her emotions. 'I'm all good.' She forced herself to look into Tariga's face. 'I felt faint for a moment. Probably just because I haven't eaten this morning.'

The lie slipped easily from her tongue but it tasted bitter.

'Well, the waffles aren't going to eat themselves,' Nathine called.

'Elka prefers savoury,' Tariga called.

'Then she can have fried potato pancakes instead.'

'Mmm, salty fluffiness,' Tariga said with an encouraging smile as she guided Elka back down the alley, just as Nail had guided her in. It felt like when she was a child and Torsgen had steered her life, telling her which school she'd go to, what subjects she'd study, which influential families she'd mix with. But right then Elka felt too empty to resist.

As they stepped back out into the bustle of Marhorn Street Aimee gave her a look, one that said she hadn't believed Elka's insistence that she was alright. Elka felt numb as she was led to the cafe. Her mind was paralysed. Stuck on the fear of losing Inelle and held there by the desperation of not knowing what to do. She was sure both Aimee and Pelathina asked her again if she was alright but she couldn't remember what answer she'd given. What lie she'd told.

The shock of seeing Nail here, someone from her previous life, made everything around her feel unreal. They must have arrived at the cafe, and someone must have ordered her breakfast but none of it seemed to be registering, everything was just flowing around her.

'What am *I* going to do about it?'

The question broke into her thoughts and she realised it was what she'd been thinking, over and over, while she chewed her pancakes without tasting them. Had she asked the question? Panicked she looked around but no one's attention was on her.

'Yeah, it's your turn,' Aimee was insisting.

'Ha, I think you'll find you're wrong there, love,' Pelathina replied.

Elka relaxed, the conversation was not about her. She wasn't part of it. She hadn't been found out. Aware now, she looked around, and was almost surprised to see they were tucked in the corner of a small courtyard, sitting outside for probably the last time this year. The autumn sun was squeezing out the last of its warmth and had melted that morning's frost. Hemmed in by red brick buildings on three sides and a neat row of silver birch trees on the fourth, the courtyard was a pretty spot for a cafe. Wooden chairs scraped on cobbles as other patrons came and went. Elka wasn't sure how long they'd been sitting there but her plate was empty and there were only dregs in her coffee mug.

'You're not reading that again, Aimee, are you?' Nathine waved a fork at the book Aimee had pulled from her pocket and sat on the table.

'No, I'm lending it to Halfen.'

She stuck out her tongue and slid the book over to Nathine's boyfriend. He smiled his thanks and flicked it open to scan the first page. Elka wasn't even sure that she'd noticed Halfen had joined them.

'Oh, so you're going to rot his brain as well as your own. Thanks very much.' Nathine rolled her eyes.

'Hey!' Aimee and Halfen both objected at the same time, then laughed.

'They're good books,' Aimee insisted, Halfen nodding in agreement as the words on the first page sucked him in.

'Uh-huh,' Nathine folded her arms. 'A master thief with a secret identity who always pulls off impossible heists and never gets caught.' She snorted. 'Nonsense.'

'Sounds like you've read them,' Pelathina joined in.

'As if I would!' Nathine objected.

'You should give them a try. I've got volume one, I can lend you it,' Halfen offered, giving Nathine a playful nudge.

'Oh, yes please.' Nathine fluttered her eyelashes at him. 'Then I'll have something I can use to beat some sense into you.'

Halfen wrapped an arm around Nathine but looked to Aimee. 'Next time you're up in the sky, can you push her off her dragon for me?'

Nathine snorted. 'She can try.'

Then she tried to elbow Halfen in the ribs but he caught her arm and pulled her in for a kiss. Elka blushed but couldn't tear her eyes away as they shared a kiss that was way too intimate for a public place. The feel of the one kiss she'd shared with Daan was long gone like snow melted in the spring.

When they finally pulled apart Nathine gave the table a smug grin. Then she finished her tea and waved the cup at the book in Halfen's hands. 'I like Callant and all, but he has more imagination than talent.'

Halfen just rolled his eyes and slipped the book into a pocket in his colourful patchwork cloak. As he did, Elka caught sight of the title, *The Daring Adventures of Jakob Blade, Volume 6 by Callant Barrell*. She thought of another book by Callant, one she had hidden at home. *The Saviour of Kierell* had allowed her the insight into the Riders that had given her the edge over her brothers in terms of knowledge. It had allowed her to convince Torsgen to let her come.

She glanced across the table at Aimee—the 'Saviour of Kierell'. The colourless half of her face looked even paler because her summer tan was lingering on the other half and her pure white eyelashes made the brown of her eye look even darker. She was jabbing a fork at Nathine as they laughed and argued over books. And everyone laughed harder when the piece of waffle on Aimee's fork pinged off and landed in Halfen's tea.

Everyone apart from Elka.

Earlier this morning she would have joined in, her

laughter mixing with theirs, but Nail's unexpected appearance had reminded her that she was here to betray these women. They weren't meant to be her friends.

'I've never read any of Callant's books,' Tariga was saying.

'I wouldn't bother,' Nathine said, pouring herself more tea.

'I'd recommend starting with his *Knife Edge* series,' Aimee said, ignoring Nathine. 'He wrote those while he was still a councillor and they were the first books in Kierell to be printed on the Barrell Press.'

'And then he and his husband set up Kierell's first publishers and what did he call it?' Nathine asked with a smirk.

Aimee blushed. 'Jess's Books.'

Pelathina wrapped an arm around her girlfriend and kissed the top of her head. The laughter and teasing continued, filling the little courtyard with the sound of friendship. The comfort of it felt like a chain pulled around Elka's chest and tightened till her ribs would crack and pierce her heart. She'd spent so long fighting the accepting community of the Riders, like it was a whirlpool sucking her in. The rock she'd clung to was the memory of her brothers, her home and her desire to earn a place there. She saw now that at some point she'd let go of that rock and been happy to do so.

Aimee caught her eye, and before she could look away she saw the same look of concern on her face that she'd worn earlier. Elka silently begged Aimee to ignore her, to for once not be kind. But of course, that wasn't

Aimee's way.

'In volume six Jakob travels to Taumerg. Maybe Elka could read it and tell us how accurate it is,' Aimee suggested. 'I mean, could Jakob really have avoided being caught by the Zachen Guards when he stole a barge?'

Aimee could tell she was upset about something and she was trying to pull her into the conversation, to give her a way of forgetting whatever was bothering her. All Elka had to do was step into it but instead she shook her head, long fringe brushing her eyes.

'I doubt my Kierellian is good enough to read books,' she lied.

She saw the shadow of hurt as it flitted across Aimee's face. Turning away, Elka stared down at the crumbs on her plate. The pancakes felt like a stone sitting in her stomach and she wished she hadn't eaten them. Sometimes, when she stopped to think about it, it amazed her that the brave young woman she'd read about, the hero who'd saved a whole city, was sitting right there at the other end of the table. And had become her friend.

What was she going to do?

She felt a tear drip from her lashes and quickly wiped it away before anyone saw. She'd been an idiot to abandon her search for the bracelet. She'd done what she promised not to—been seduced by the world of the Riders and now she'd made herself vulnerable. She had to get up from this chair and go to find Pagrin's bracelet. Friendship be damned. Cover story be damned. She'd always known she'd have to betray these women.

If she didn't, Inelle would only have days to live.

CHAPTER 11

BREAKTHROUGH

Elka put her hands on the table, about to push herself up and leave when Halfen's insistent tone drew her attention back to the conversation.

'It's not that bad.' Nathine was frowning at him and he took her hand, clearly trying to placate her. 'It's not worth you swooping into the barracks in a blaze of glory and incinerating Captain Tenth.'

Nathine huffed in disagreement.

'So what is your un-exciting, but not worth getting worked up about, new assignment?' Pelathina asked.

'Are you going to finish that?' Nathine butted in before Halfen could answer, pointing at Pelathina's half-eaten waffles. Elka caught Halfen rolling his eyes at his girlfriend but luckily for him Nathine was fixed on the food.

'Yes,' Pelathina replied, licking cream off her fork.

'Well you're taking long enough with it. If you give up, let me know,' Nathine said, her eyes still on the waffles.

'You already finished off mine!' Tariga looked both impressed and slightly queasy at Nathine's capacity for making food disappear.

'So, Halfen, your new assignment,' Aimee tried to get their conversation back on track.

Elka's legs quivered with the desire to get up and run away. But she didn't have a reason to leave and her brain was busy scrambling through her stock of lies, trying to pick one that would fit. She didn't want anyone to follow her. Especially not Aimee.

'Look, it's just guarding some old precious stuff at the university. Struan had the job before me but he retired last week.' Halfen gave Nathine a stern look. 'And it's fine. The scholars give me loads of cups of tea and I get to be inside. It's way better than patrolling the streets in the rain hoping to spot a pickpocket.'

Elka's attention snagged on the phrase 'precious stuff'. Her heart skipped a beat in her chest then sped up as if to make up for it. Something old that required a guard. Could it be the bracelet?

It felt like misaligned gears were slotting into place in Elka's mind. She'd memorised then picked over every story Aimee and the others had told her about the Battle for Kierell. She knew the scholars at the university had taken an Empty Warrior's breastplate to study. After the fighting had they also taken Pagrin's bracelet? It was the sort of priceless artefact scholars dreamed of studying.

The cogs in Elka's mind whirred as if a burst of fresh steam had been fired through them.

Had she just stumbled over the answer, here, now?

The conversation continued around her, everyone oblivious to the fireworks that had just exploded inside Elka's brain.

'So a job that an old guard with a gammy leg previously did has now been lumped on you,' Nathine grumbled, then reached over and stole a corner off Pelathina's waffle. Pelathina tried to stab her with her fork but Nathine was too fast.

'Yeah, but imagine Jakob Blade tried to steal the stuff and Halfen had to fight him off,' Tariga added, eyes wide with how exciting that would be.

Nathine threw up her hands in disgust. 'He isn't real!'

Aimee laughed as she stole the other corner off Pelathina's waffle.

'Hey, do you all mind!' Pelathina wrapped her arms protectively around her plate.

'You need to learn to eat faster, my love,' Aimee said around a mouth full of waffle.

The silliness was getting to Elka. She wanted to scream at them all to shut up about fictional thieves and waffles and demand Halfen explain what he meant by 'precious stuff'. She felt the pressure of Inelle in her mind and could almost hear the scraping of talons as she pictured her dragon on the library roof, shuffling as she shared her Rider's impatience. Her wings would be partly unfurled, jostling Skydance beside her.

Elka's mind skittered over excuses she could use to get away. Then could she blag her way into the university? Claim she was working on some important task for Jara?

'I dunno,' Halfen was saying, 'but knowing the scholars it'll probably be some pieces of ancient pottery from the early days of Kierell that they dug up over there.' He waved vaguely towards the north-east curve of the mountains.

'In Cog Town?' Aimee asked.

It was the sobriquet for the area north of the harbour district where Kierell had started building factories, using knowledge learned from the city states. Elka had flown over it a few times. It was still in construction, and at first it had given her a nostalgic pang for home, but now she smiled to see a piece of her old world clicking into place in her new one. In the last year she'd even spotted puffers down here in Kierell. They stood out because they dressed unlike anyone in Kierell, wearing rust-red waistcoats with dozens of pockets and their legs wrapped with belts and holders for all their tools. The only thing that made the puffers look a little like they belonged here were their circular goggles—almost identical to the ones Riders wore for flying.

But what mattered to Elka right then was that Cog Town was next to the meadow where the Riders had fought their final battle against the Empty Warriors. It was where Aimee had killed Pagrin. Elka had been to that meadow. Every summer on the anniversary of the day after battle the Riders and their dragons gathered there at sunrise. This summer had been the first time Elka was there, standing with the others, a dragon's breath orb held in her cupped hands, Inelle standing at her shoulder. They'd waited while the darkness sank away into the west, the other Riders remembering those they'd lost to the Empty Warriors, and watched the light flow back into the world.

'Yeah, I overheard some of the scholars talking about how the workers in Cog Town keep finding stuff and they think that spot is where our ancestors camped when they first arrived,' Halfen explained.

'What sort of stuff?' Elka asked, her voice too loud as she struggled to sound only mildly interested.

Halfen shrugged. 'Bits of bottle, an old dagger. Apparently someone found a dragon's tooth.'

'Where do they…you know… keep it all?'

Halfen waved in the direction of the university. 'It's all at the top of Vunskap Tower, though I've only been up once. Mostly I just stand guard at the bottom of the staircase. Which is fine by me,' he added hurriedly as Nathine glared again.

Elka reached under the table and pressed her hands on her knees to stop her legs from bouncing. She wanted to jump up and fly to the university right now. Shards of pottery and broken bottles didn't need guarding, no matter how old they were. That must be a cover. It must be.

The scholars had taken and kept Pagrin's bracelet. Elka stared through the birch trees at the courtyard's edge, her mind picking out the route to the university. She wouldn't even need Inelle—she could run there in five minutes.

She heard the flapping of wings and looked up. She

half expected to see Inelle, flying to her Rider because she'd sensed her need to move. But the dragon landing in the courtyard was a brighter purple.

'Hey, Lyrria,' Tariga called over.

Lyrria swung from her saddle and sauntered over to their table. Elka twisted around and gripped the back of her chair. Could she use the distraction of Lyrria's arrival to disappear? She almost did it, but a sensible voice in her head, one that sounded very like Frannack, told her not to be rash. If she barged into the university and stole the bracelet now, everyone would know she'd taken it. She and Inelle would barely get over Norwen Peak before they were chased.

She fiddled with the ring in her nose and forced herself to think. She'd be better waiting till tonight and sneaking into the university then. Would that give her enough of a head start? She pictured Malgerus. His wings were a quarter again bigger than Inelle's, and Black and Faradair were even larger. If both she and a guarded relic disappeared at the same time, the Riders would have no choice but to hunt her.

She couldn't arrive back in Taumerg with half the Riders on her tail. Even if she got the bracelet to Torsgen, his men couldn't fight off dragons. It would be the same as failing. And in response for bringing Riders to their door, she had no doubt Torsgen would order Nail to use that pistol.

Lyrria stole a chair from another table and joined them, sitting at the opposite end from Aimee. Elka had noticed an awkwardness between the two women before but right then she couldn't care less.

'We weren't supposed to be meeting till later, were we?' Tariga asked, a look of mild panic on her face that she'd missed something.

Lyrria smiled, showing her crooked front teeth. 'Don't worry, nothing has changed for us. You still have the joy of joining Intilde for harbour protection duty for the next three days.'

Elka shivered at the thought of harbour duty. It was her least favourite assignment because even in the height of summer it was never warm out above the grey swell of the Griydak Sea. The building work to extend the harbour and make it suitable for larger ships had ramped up in the last month as they tried to get as much done as they could before winter set in. But the building works drew salt drakes from the deeper southern sea and they were growing bolder. Last week one had leapt from the waves and snatched a man right off the harbour wall. It had happened so fast that the dragons hadn't had a chance to react. Jara had doubled the Riders at the harbour since then.

Elka wondered when her next shift out above the cold sea would be. Then caught herself. What was she thinking? She wouldn't be here tomorrow. On hearing Lyrria talk about duties her mind had slipped back into that of a Rider.

'It's these lovely others who have a change to their week ahead,' Lyrria continued, smiling round the table at them.

That sharpened Elka's attention. If she was about to

be sent off somewhere that would ruin her plans to steal the bracelet tonight. She began circulating possible excuses in her mind.

'You know that Councillor SaSellen's caravan left for Lorsoke yesterday? Well, he's made a specific request that our renowned hero, Aimee Wood, be the Rider to lead it from there to Nepzug.'

'I thought Ryka was already assigned to lead that one?' Nathine said.

'She was and she's briefed and ready to go,' Pelathina answered.

'I know all that but SaSellen's a very important councillor and this is a very important caravan.' Lyrria wiggled a finger at them like they were her pupils. 'I have sat through so many council meetings where he's told us in great detail how the progress in Cog Town depends on his trade for iron ore.'

'Darell SaSellen is head of the Metalworkers Guild,' Aimee explained for Elka's benefit. Elka didn't care if he was head of the Turnip Guild; she was too busy wondering if somehow she could use Aimee's absence to her advantage. Because if anyone was going to feel her betrayal and come chasing straight after her, it would be Kierell's hero. Elka suspected she'd chase down a wayward recruit to the ends of the world.

'Yes, and all those shiny cog machines require more metal than Kierell can produce, hence SaSellen's trade with the mines in Fir du Merg. And you should thank me all for giving you the short version of that.' Lyrria grinned at them. 'You'll need to leave tomorrow morning in order to meet them at Lorsoke.'

'That still doesn't mean he needs me,' Aimee said. 'I've got three recruits to train at the moment.'

'Oh I know, but the future of Cog Town relies on this caravan so who better to protect it than our very own hero,' Lyrria repeated. A flush crept up Aimee's neck and cheeks. Pelathina smiled and gave her hand a squeeze. 'Seriously though,' Lyrria's tone changed, 'this is important and Jara's agreed.'

'What about my recruits?' Aimee asked.

'I'll take over their training till you get back.' Lyrria leaned back in her chair, arms behind her head. 'I think I still remember what to do. I did train this girl once who went on to totally defeat a whole army.'

'Can I choose who comes with me?' Aimee asked, her face still flushed.

'Yeah, Jara said you could and I figured you'd take this lot,' Lyrria swept open her arms to encompass the Riders around the table, 'hence why I'm here.'

Elka pressed a hand over her mouth to hide her smile. This was perfect. Travelling tomorrow with Aimee gave her a legitimate reason for leaving Kierell. All she had to do was sneak away from the caravan before it reached Nepzug. That, and steal Pagrin's bracelet tonight.

'You figured right,' Aimee said with a smile. 'Nathine? Pelathina?' Both women nodded their assent then Elka felt Aimee's eyes on her. 'A caravan travelling that far should really have four Riders with it, but I know you've not been feeling well, Elka. I can ask someone else.'

'No, I'll come,' Elka practically shouted and Aimee looked taken aback.

'You're just back from Lorsoke so maybe what you need is a day or two of resting. That could explain why you were dizzy earlier.'

'I'm totally fine now,' Elka insisted, desperate not to let this chance slip away. 'And even if I fall asleep Inelle will keep on flying,' she added, trying to make light of her insistence on coming.

It was the wrong thing to say. Concern crowded Aimee's face and she looked thoughtful as she tucked curly strands of pure white hair behind her ear.

'Elka, I'm sorry but I need Riders who'll be fully alert. The Helvethi are still a threat and at this time of year prowlers will be looking to fatten up for the winter.'

'And a caravan will look very tasty to them,' Lyrria added, not helping.

Aimee was shaking her head and Elka felt her chance slipping through her fingers like engine oil.

'No, I didn't mean what I said. It was a joke but I'm clearly not good at humour in Kierellian.'

She didn't want to beg. Nail's threats had awoken the Haggaur in her, and Torsgen would never beg. She could feel herself slipping back into the person she'd been, like putting on a winter coat that she'd shoved to the back of her wardrobe all summer.

Aimee looked at her for a long moment and Elka couldn't read her eyes. Finally she nodded.

'Alright.'

Relief flushed through Elka. Aimee was still giving her a look she couldn't decipher and Elka vowed to avoid her as much as she could on the trip.

All she had to do now was hope that her hunch about the scholars was right and steal Pagrin's bracelet tonight.

CHAPTER 12

NOT THE PLAN

THE NIGHT BREEZE was soft on Inelle's wings as they glided above the city. It was just after midnight and the streets below were filled with deep shadows. Peaked roofs jutted up, their edges painted with moonlight. Elka spotted a guard patrol as she flew above Marhorn Street. A few looked up but Riders in the city were a common sight and they would assume she was working. Inelle flew over a couple on Spine Street, the doors of the Falling Stars Inn closing behind them as he held her arm and she twirled. Their drunken laughter bounced off the walls as Inelle turned her wings and headed north.

The brick walls of the university rose to a collection of peaked roofs, each one steeper than the last. They made the whole roof look like a miniature mountain range. Squeezing her thighs and pushing gently on Inelle's horns, Elka guided her dragon along tree-lined Hylwen Street to a brick archway marking the entrance to the scholar's world. With a powerful thrust of her wings Inelle took them up and over the arch and into the university grounds. Vunskap Tower stood proudly in the north-west corner.

Elka could feel Inelle's joy as she navigated the mountain range of roofs, swooping under eaves, around chimney stacks, and diving down the steep peaks, her tail flicking out to avoid the gutters. Like all dragons Inelle enjoyed the open sky but she especially loved flying when she could twist and turn, dodging obstacles. She liked to show off and Elka knew she did it for her. Ever since she'd named her dragon, Inelle had shared Elka's drive to succeed. In Inelle this had manifested as a desire to keep proving to her Rider that she was the best, at flying, at fighting, at soaring, at diving. So tonight she flew on silent wings.

Elka kept her eyes on the maze of lanes and courtyards below them, body tense as she prepared to swoop away if she was spotted. She saw lanterns glowing in a few windows but no one was about.

'Quietly now,' Elka whispered to her dragon as they neared Vunskap Tower.

Elka felt Inelle's understanding as a pulse in her mind. Her dragon slowed, circling the peaked roof of the square tower. There were four large windows, one on each side, and they were all dark. Satisfied that the tower was empty Elka ordered Inelle to land. Her dragon gracefully folded her wings, her talons making the barest scraping sound as she landed on the slate tiles. No one below would have heard them. Elka sent a thank you through their connection and felt Inelle's warm glow at her praise.

'Don't think, just do,' Elka told herself. 'And then tomorrow Inelle will be safe.'

She slipped from her saddle and slid carefully down the slates of the roof, bracing her feet in the gutter to stop herself from tumbling off the edge. Inelle watched her intently, yellow eyes bright in the moonlight, as Elka lowered herself off the roof until she was hanging under the eaves. A quick glance down told her the window's wide sill was directly below her but a six-feet drop away. She didn't let herself think about what would happen if she missed.

She opened her hands and dropped. Her stomach flew up into her throat but her feet landed square on the window sill. Quickly she gripped the frame and pressed herself against the glass. Two years ago she'd have been way too scared to try that. Still gripping the frame, she lowered herself hand over hand until she was crouched on the sill.

'Quick but steady, come on, come on,' she encouraged herself.

Jabbing the window with her elbow she smashed a hole in the glass. Pulling her lock picks from inside her boot she braced her back against the window jamb. Then she carefully reached through the broken glass, feeling for the latch on the other side. Even though she couldn't see what she was doing, Elka made short work of the window's lock.

Easing the sash up slowly in case it creaked, Elka slipped a leg through then ducked her body under and in. Sitting on the sill she let her eyes adjust to the darkness inside. Moonlight made silver squares on the floor but the walls were cloaked in shadow. Slowly, shapes emerged from the gloom. Three long trestle tables sat in the middle of the room piled with boxes and lumpy things concealed by sheets. Elka decided to start there.

Copying her brothers she had learned to walk into a room like she owned it but Aimee had taught her to move soft and quiet as a cloud. The combination gave Elka a stride that was purposeful but stealthy. She whipped the sheet off the first table and felt a twang of despair. Memories of pointless hours spent wandering the tunnels flashed through her mind.

'It would've been too easy if it was just sitting there with a sign saying "Pagrin's bracelet",' Elka whispered to herself as she ran her fingers over pieces of broken pottery.

Other relics were laid out on the table—a tarnished silver necklace, the hilt of a sword with its blade snapped off, a shoe with rotten laces and its sole peeling away. Elka wrinkled her nose at these so-called treasures. Moving to the next table she opened every box on it. More of the same, but these objects were all wrapped and labelled. She didn't bother putting them back, just left them piled on the table.

'Okay, if I was a scholar where would I hide something so valuable I hadn't even admitted to the council or Riders that I had it?'

Elka spun slowly on her heel, taking in the rest of

the room. One wall was covered by a hanging showing a map of Kierell. Striding over she flung it aside and ran her fingers across the wall behind it. Nothing, no concealed catches or hidden hinges. She banged the heel of her hand over the wood panelling, listening. None of the sections sounded hollow.

'Alright, yes, that would have been too obvious as well.'

She knew she was talking to herself to keep the mounting despair at bay. Dropping to her hands and knees she crawled to the rug covering the floor underneath a bookcase. She noticed it was from Taumerg, the bold floral design looking out of place in this stuffy, traditional setting. With an expectant tug she flipped up the rug.

'*Mi sparken!*' she swore.

No trapdoor. She tapped all the floorboards, growing more and more annoyed at each solid knock. Trying to be like Torsgen, to keep her anger in check, to be methodical, she tapped her way round the entire room, knocking on every wall panel, each floorboard.

Nothing.

Striding over to the bookcase she began yanking books from the shelves. They tumbled to the floor, pages fluttering, spines cracking. She banged the back of the bookcase, willing a secret compartment to spring open. It had to be here. She was out of time. She *had* to find the bracelet tonight.

Books lay scattered around her feet as she reached the middle shelf. With a growl she swept these ones off in one go. They tumbled to the floor and amongst the thuds Elka heard a metallic clink.

Just at the same time as the door swung open.

Elka froze, feet buried by books, and winced at the light from a lantern held high.

'Elka?'

Her heart started to pound and her muscles twitched as they flooded with adrenaline.

'What…?'

Halfen's voice trailed off as he lowered the lantern and looked around the mess of the room. As his light swept across the floor it caught on a curved shimmer of gold. Elka's eyes snapped to it. A book lay spilled open, its inside cut away to make a deep hole in the pages. To make a hiding place. And on the floorboards beside it was a wide gold cuff.

Pagrin's bracelet.

'Oh shit,' Halfen swore.

He was looking at the bracelet too and clearly he recognised it for what it was. His face had gone ashen, his eyes wide. His shock told Elka he hadn't known it was here. More curses tumbled from Halfen's lips as he bent to retrieve the bracelet. But Elka beat him to it. Slapping aside his hand she snatched it up, clutching it to her chest. She'd done it. She'd got it. All she had to do was get it home and Inelle would be safe.

'Elka, you don't know what that is,' Halfen said, a quiver in his voice. He held out his hand. 'Pass it to me, please.'

She shook her head and gripped the bracelet tighter.

She heard a scraping of talons on the roof and sent Inelle the command to stay.

'Please, just put it down. It's dangerous,' Halfen continued as if he was trying to protect her.

His naivety tore at her. He hadn't yet questioned why she was here, he was too busy worrying she'd hurt herself.

Halfen stared at her, confusion scrunching up his round face. The same face that had beamed at Nathine earlier, so full of love. He ran a hand over his cropped hair. The same hand that had caressed the small of Nathine's back.

'You could turn around, go back down those stairs and pretend you never saw me,' Elka said, even though she knew he'd never do that.

She watched as the realisation dawned on him, eyes widening, mouth hanging open.

'That bracelet shouldn't exist, it should have been destroyed.' He reached out a hand towards her, nice and gentle. 'Elka, you don't know what that can do. It's…' his words trailed off.

She saw memories flicker behind his eyes, pain creasing at the edges.

'No, *you* don't understand. I have to take this. My family needs it.' She slipped the bracelet into her coat pocket.

'Sparks! Elka, no one needs that bracelet! The power it gives a person is wrong and immoral.' He rasped a hand over his hair again. 'You weren't here, you didn't see the Battle for Kierell.'

'I know!' Elka shot back. 'You've all told me a hundred times that I wasn't here, that I couldn't understand. But you can't understand either why I need this. I made a promise and I have to keep it. If I don't...' her words trailed off as she remembered feeling Nail's pistol under her chin.

'A promise to who, Elka?' Halfen was shaking his head.

Seeing the fear on his face was eating away at her resolve. She touched her connection with Inelle and felt her dragon's reassurance. She tried to imagine what it would be like to lose Inelle and found she couldn't. Her dragon was too much a part of her now.

She felt tears heavy on her eyelashes and blinked them away. 'We won't use the bracelet to make Empty Warriors, I promise. That's not why I need to take it.'

'Who's we? Elka, what's going on.'

'I can't tell you. Halfen, go back down the stairs and let me leave. Please.'

'But you're a Rider!' Halfen exclaimed, as if that would make her suddenly change her mind and hand over the bracelet. 'I can't let you take it,' he said firmly.

'But I have to!' Elka shouted.

She saw the determination on his face. He really wasn't going to let her leave with it. She touched her connection with Inelle, then slid free both her scimitars.

Halfen shook his head then swung the lantern at her. It crashed into her shoulder sending her flying across one of the tables. Shards of broken pottery crunched under her as Elka slid along its length. She smacked her head on one of the wooden boxes and tumbled from the table. The world went black for a moment and panic clawed at her throat. But no blade pierced her body. Shaking her vision clear she sprang to her feet, blades held low and ready. Above, she heard Inelle growl.

'Stay!' she yelled at her dragon.

Halfen still held the lantern and had drawn his sword too. But he hadn't advanced.

'Elka, when you became a Rider you swore an oath to dedicate your life to protecting others. That bracelet, the power it gives a person, goes against all that the Riders stand for.'

'But I'm not a real Rider.'

It was true, it had always been true, but still it hurt to say it. More tears beaded on her eyelashes and she shook her head to get rid of them.

'What? Yes you are. You're one of them.'

'I'm not! I have a family and I swore an oath to them first!' Elka yelled. And attacked.

Four quick steps took her around the table and her blades clashed with Halfen's. She cut high and low, using her height and all the skills Aimee had drilled into her. But Halfen planted his feet and blocked her, blade in one hand, lantern in the other.

Jumping back, she swung both scimitars wide then dashed forward, crossing her blades with quick slices. Halfen caught her swords on his, metal screeching together, tangling their blades. Elka pressed forwards and he stumbled back, dropping the lantern. Glass smashed and with a whoosh the flames caught the corner of the hanging map.

'Marhorn's sparks!'

'*Mi sparken!*'

They both swore at the same time and stared at each other for a moment.

'Elka—'

'No!'

She couldn't stand to listen to any more words about her duty as a Rider. She knew she was betraying them—that had always been her plan—but it hurt like someone was ripping the spark right out of her chest. She couldn't think about it, or she might stop.

So she sliced for Halfen's hip with her right scimitar but he caught the strike with a two-handed blow of his own. She slashed high with her left blade but he spun away and her scimitar sliced through nothing but his guard's cloak. She tried herding him towards the flames which were now roaring up the map but he stepped around each of her blows, always blocking her.

Their blades clashed together, again and again, metal singing. They were close, dancing this deadly dance. She could smell the sandalwood scent he wore. She saw the freckles on his nose and the look in his eyes. They'd gone steely. He wasn't trying to protect her now. He was trying to stop a thief.

Elka felt sweat run down her face as the flames heated the room. From the corner of her eye she saw them jump from the map to the jumble of books on the floor. Smoke was roiling above their heads and gathering in

Elka's lungs. Halfen knocked aside one of her blades and thrust for her stomach. She jerked back as if pulled by a rope around her lower back. One heel crunched on a piece of pottery and the other tripped on the broken sword hilt.

She skidded, fell, winced as she waited for the bite of Halfen's blade and rolled aside. She kicked her way under one of the tables and came up with it between her and Halfen. He looked at her, eyes furious, head as always tilted slightly to the side, favouring the ear that could still hear.

'They all trust you,' he coughed around his words as smoke filled the room. 'Nathine trusts you. She's your friend!'

A stream of images flickered through Elka's mind of all the times she'd drank tea with Nathine, flown through the clouds with her, been beaten by her during training, shared cake with her in a dining cavern glowing with dragon's breath. Elka heard Inelle growl as she shoved aside the memories of friendship.

'It wasn't real!' she yelled, not sure if she was telling Halfen or herself.

She crouched to spring up onto the table but Halfen shoved it towards her at the same moment. The edge smashed into her chest and Elka screamed as she felt a rib crack. Halfen followed his shove, leaping over the table, one hand on it, legs kicking out at her face. Elka dropped to the floor and he sailed over her head. As he landed she sprang at him, all finesse with her blades abandoned. Sharp pain flared like lightning in her side as she smacked into him. Her knees cracked against his and her head smashed into his chin.

Halfen's blade went skittering across the floor as he fell backwards. Even above the roar of the flames Elka heard the crack as his head hit the windowsill. He slumped boneless to the floor, his colourful cloak draping his body. Elka stood over him, breathing hard through the pain in her ribs. She still had both her scimitars and she squeezed the grips so tight it felt like her fingers would never let go.

'Don't get up,' she whispered, not brave enough to bend down and check if he was alive.

Inside she felt torn in two. Part of her was screaming at what she'd done. That was the Rider part. That half of her baulked at having hurt a city guard and shuddered to imagine the disappointment on Aimee's face, after all the months she'd spent training and encouraging her. That part hoped Halfen was still breathing.

But the Hagguar half of her wanted him to be dead so she could get away free. That part longed for success in her mission and yearned to protect Inelle.

A gust of wind blew Elka's long fringe from her face and sent the crackling flames up the table legs. She looked through the open window to see Inelle circling, waiting for her Rider. Elka had to go. Someone would see the flames. And they'd see Inelle. No one could know a Rider had been here. Checking Pagrin's bracelet was safe inside her pocket, Elka put a hand on the windowsill.

Then Halfen groaned.

Elka felt sick as she looked down and saw him pushing himself to his knees. A thick river of red ran down the back of his head and neck, soaking the collar of his cloak. While Elka hesitated, Halfen didn't. He shook his head once, spraying droplets of red, then barrelled into her. Lightning bolts of pain shot up her ribs as she grappled with him. They were both injured and he was groggy. Elka felt the heat of flames licking at her back as Halfen shoved her. She twisted her arm, cracking her elbow into his nose, then pushed to get him off her. Halfen staggered back, blood spilling down his face, and caught the back of his knees on the window ledge.

Then he tumbled backwards out of the open window and was gone.

'No!' Elka yelled.

CHAPTER 13

BLOOD AND GUILT

Elka heard the sickening thud as Halfen's body hit the cobbles four storeys below. She gripped the window ledge and felt her hands slide on the wood. Looking down, she saw they were red with blood from Halfen's head wound. It was under her nails, in the creases on her joints, and as she turned her hands over it coated her palms. Her breath became panicky gasps. She wanted the blood gone. She pressed her hands down her thighs but they came away smeared, still red. Beyond the window Inelle called to her.

She had to go, right now.

Elka braced herself on the window jamb and was about to climb through when the horror of what she'd done came rushing up her throat in a wave of bile. She puked out the window, her vomit splattering the side of the tower. The heat of the flames pressed against her back and her cracked rib jabbed her insides like a thousand pins. Inelle tugged at her mind and without her, Elka might have let go and followed Halfen down to the cobbles.

The room behind her was gone, eaten by the flames. Elka climbed out of the window, grinding her teeth against the pain, and crouched on the sill she signalled for Inelle. As her dragon swooped in close, Elka readied to jump across into her saddle.

Then she fell.

Her right foot slipped off the window ledge into nothingness. Elka scrambled at the wall but her fingernails broke on the bricks. Fear and disbelief punched through her mind.

For three seconds she plummeted, unable to think, too shocked to scream. Until Inelle snatched her from the air. The long talons on her back feet wrapped around Elka's body and her wings beat a steady rhythm as she lifted her Rider up into the sky.

Elka caught sight of Halfen's broken body and she retched. Then the rooftops shrank below her as Inelle carried her up and away. The flames were a beacon, waving at the city from the tower's open window. Elka was too high in the sky to hear but the alarm must have been raised by now. Inelle kept rising until Elka felt moisture on her skin and realised they were hidden by the clouds.

'Clever dragon,' she croaked, her throat raw from smoke.

She tried to wall off the pulsing pain from her cracked rib and keep it from Inelle but she could feel her dragon's concern. It was comforting. The Riders didn't know what she'd done yet but they would, and then they'd hate her. But at least she'd still have Inelle.

Peering through the clouds she couldn't tell where they were but trusted Inelle to take her somewhere safe. She was feeling dizzy from being carried rather than flying, so was grateful when the mountains emerged from the clouds and Inelle gently laid her down on a rocky plateau. She closed her eyes and felt her dragon curl around her, wrapping her in smooth scales and the smell of woodsmoke.

'We can't stay here,' she told Inelle and her dragon snorted in agreement.

Halfen's shocked face as he fell out of the window flashed behind Elka's eyes and she rolled onto her side and was sick again, bringing up nothing but stringy drool. Then she gasped at the cut-glass pain in her side.

She'd never killed a person before. Out on the tundra Inelle had killed two prowlers and once, protecting a caravan from an attack by the Tsyent tribe, she'd wounded a Helvethi. But now she had blood on her hands, literally.

'I didn't mean to,' she whispered.

She stared through the clouds, the lights of Kierell a fuzzy blur far below. By now the Riders on watch tonight would have seen the fire and flown to investigate. Would the scholars lie about why their tower had been ransacked and burnt? Elka pictured Jara's sharp stare and knew that under that they'd crack. They'd tell her what they'd kept and what was now missing. And then there was the dead guard lying broken on the cobblestones.

Elka knew she should stick to her plan. Act normal and leave with the caravan in a few hours. But the thought of flying back into Anteill and facing the Riders made her want to be sick again. As a thief she could have managed to lie to them for another couple of days, but as a murderer, she couldn't face them.

She had to leave, right now.

She thought for a moment of the possessions she'd accumulated over her two years here. She didn't have much in her little room but there had been a few things she'd planned to take back to Taumerg—mementos of her time as a Rider. She'd have to leave them all behind. At least she had her scimitars, and her throwing knives. She also had the knock-pistol she'd brought all the way from Taumerg. She'd stuck it in her inside coat pocket in case she'd needed it tonight, and then in the fight with Halfen she'd forgotten all about it.

The guilt twisted in her guts and tears spilled down her cheeks. She wiped them away on the cuff of her coat.

'Come on, get up,' Elka said to herself and Inelle. Her dragon uncurled from around her and Elka grabbed her saddle. Inelle rose as Elka swung a leg over, sucking in a sharp breath against the pain in her ribs. 'Time to fly faster than a cog can spin.'

Inelle snorted a puff of smoke then took off. Her long wings flapped slow and steady until she'd carried them above the clouds. Up here Kierell was hidden. The highest peaks of the Ring Mountains poked up through the carpet of clouds and above them the sky sparkled with stars. It was breathtakingly beautiful and it broke Elka's heart to be leaving.

But there was no going back.

'Go!' she shouted, and Inelle roared in reply.

Her wingbeats increased, her long tail stretched out straight behind her, and she shot across the sky. All those months of practising flying fast were about to pay off.

Once the Riders realised she was missing, it wouldn't take them long to put the pieces together and chase her. She could only hope that the distraction of the fire at the university and Halfen's death would give her enough of a head start. And if Aimee or the others caught her? Elka looked down at her blood-smeared hands gripping Inelle's horns and shuddered. No, it wouldn't come to that.

They passed the tip of Norwen Peak and Elka tried not to think about how this was the last time she'd ever see it. When she'd first arrived in Kierell the Ring Mountains had looked forbidding and inhospitable. But they'd become her home and she'd grown to appreciate the wild, untameable beauty of them.

'Stop it!' she chided herself, her words lost in the wind as Inelle sped through the night.

She shouldn't have been dwelling on what she was leaving behind; instead she should have been excited that she was finally getting to go home. She should have been pleased that she'd completed her mission and earned her place in the Hagguar Ragel.

It was early autumn but the weather was unusually

kind to them on the tundra. The endless wind still blew but the skies stayed clear of rain. On and on Inelle flew, her powerful wings eating up the distance. As dawn glided soft and pink across the sky, Elka spotted Lorsoke on the horizon. She debated for a moment about swinging wide to avoid flying over the town but decided to stick with her straight route.

The sun rose and onwards they flew. Every few minutes Elka would turn in her saddle, dreading to see wings in the sky behind. It remained clear. Halfen's blood had long ago dried on her hands, cracking and flaking away. But some of it was still there, in the lines on her palms and in blood-red crescents under her nails. Every time she looked at her hands the guilt would grind at her insides like rusted gears. More than once she found herself crying, the tears cold on her cheeks.

She flew through the whole day. Rain showers passed over them, soaking her clothes and beading on Inelle's scales. Her bum and thighs screamed with cramps, then went completely numb. Her stomach rumbled and growled with hunger. The needle-sharp pain in her cracked rib hurt only when she moved, then only when she breathed in, and then it hurt all the time and she couldn't remember what it felt like not to be in pain.

Finally as the sky around her put on its sunset dress, Elka admitted to herself that they needed to stop. The sky had been empty behind her all day so she decided she could risk an hour of rest. Inelle's wingbeats had slowed through the afternoon and Elka could feel her exhaustion, like a weight tugging on her mind.

She pushed on Inelle's spiralled horns, guiding her dragon down. They landed on a patch of long grass bordered on one side by heather and a small stream on the other. For a moment Elka felt too sore to move and wondered how she'd get out of her saddle. Then Inelle crouched down, belly to the grass.

'Thank you,' Elka gave her a smile as she stepped from her saddle, body protesting.

The dusk was deepening and Inelle cocked her head, listening.

'Alright, go hunt,' Elka told her, but tightened her grip on their bond so she wouldn't go too far.

As Inelle flew into the sinking shadows Elka crouched by the stream. Bracing herself for the cold she plunged both her hands into the flowing water. She rubbed them together then pulled them out. Still bloody. Grabbing a handful of moss, she shoved them back under. Using the moss she scrubbed at her palms and dug under her nails, desperate to get rid of every speck of Halfen's blood. Only when her fingers went numb with the cold did she pull them out.

She wished she could also wash away the memory of Halfen's face as he fell.

Elka heard the clash of teeth as Inelle hunted. She had no food for herself but there was something she needed more—pain relief. Looking around she spotted a bush of snathforg and picked a dozen of its leaves. They would dull her pain. Then she sat on a grassy tussock and pulled her scarf from her coat pocket. It wasn't a proper bandage but it would have to do. Striping off her coat and shirt she shivered as the night air raised goosebumps on her skin.

'Ah! *Dul sparken*,' she swore as she wound her scarf around her ribs. It was awkward to hold it in place and tie it tight at the same time.

An unwanted memory of being in the infirmary back at Anteill pushed to the front of her mind. One day when they were still recruits, Tariga had gotten through her guard and smacked her shoulder with a training blade. Aimee had taken her straight to the infirmary, full of concern; Tariga had been overly apologetic; Emilla had been sweet and kind, telling her nothing was broken, but that she'd have epic bruises. Elka had been hurting—Tariga had smacked her really hard—but she'd been wrapped in the friendship of the Riders.

Now she was alone, crying with the pain as she struggled to get her shirt back on. She'd placed the snathforg leaves in her coat pocket and the little spiked leaves pointed up at her like a quiver of arrow tips. It was better to brew them into a tea but Elka didn't have the luxury of time. She popped three of the dried leaves in her mouth and crunched them. They softened and turned to a bitter paste on her tongue. Clamping her jaw closed with a hand she forced herself to swallow.

Inelle came back, spots of blood on her snout, and curled up around her Rider. Elka sat cross-legged in the grass and stroked her scales. The moon was rising and its silver light danced over the gold ring on her index finger.

Her Rider's jewellery.

She hadn't planned on being a Rider long enough to ever be given it and had always felt torn whenever she looked at it. Part of her was proud to have earned her jewellery, to be strong, brave and dedicated enough in the eyes of the Riders that they saw her as one of them. But the other part of her felt that wearing it was a betrayal of her family.

She twisted the gold band on her finger. It was wide and flat, and engraved with a tiny ship, its sails filled in with mother of pearl. It was beautiful. And Aimee had given her it.

Elka still remembered the moment she'd slipped it on her finger. It was a week after her first mission protecting the ships and workers extending the harbour beyond the Ring Mountains. The work drew salt drakes from the cold, deep southern waters and it was the Riders' task to patrol the harbour's boundary keeping watch for the monsters. The first day Elka had been out there in the cold and spitting rain, two female salt drakes had come hunting.

Lyrria had spotted them first. They looked frosted, with white-blue scales and jagged spines down their backs like shards of ice. And when one broke the surface Elka saw more teeth than any creature should ever have. Fear had sunk claws into her belly but to her own surprise she hadn't let it control her. Her year of training had kicked in and she'd followed Lyrria and Dyrenna in a swooping falcon attack. Inelle had followed Midnight and Black, adding her own blast of flames as they skimmed the grey waves with the salt drakes just below them. But at the nadir of their dive, just as Inelle began flapping to take them back into the sky, one of the salt drakes twisted and leapt clear of the sea. Its body was as long as a dragon's and its clawed flippers were bigger than Elka.

The salt drake's teeth snapped closed on Inelle's tail and she roared in pain. But so did the salt drake as the barbs on Inelle's tail punctured its mouth. Elka felt Inelle's pain and with it came a flush of protective anger. How dare something hurt *her* dragon.

Without stopping to think she took a hand from Inelle's horns, grabbed two of the throwing knives from the garter on her thigh, holding them between her fingers, and twisted round in her saddle. Breathing in she marked her target, and breathing out she threw. Both knives sank to their hilt in the salt drake's eye. Thick purplish blood spurted from its burst eyeball. The monster roared and released Inelle. Elka and her dragon climbed into the sky as the monster sank beneath the waves.

Inelle still had the scars on her tail from the salt drake's teeth—thin lines of pink cutting through her indigo scales. And in the dining cavern one week later Aimee had appeared with Elka's jewellery. The Riders around her had cheered, all crowding in to admire her ring. Lyrria had told the story again of how Elka single-handedly took out a massive salt drake, exaggerating the details even more than on the previous ten times she'd told the tale.

And for that evening Elka had let down her guard and allowed herself to be pulled into the Riders' world. She'd laughed, beamed at the compliments given to her ring, listened to the stories of how other Riders earned their jewellery, and even reenacted the encounter with the salt drake on top of a table with Lyrria pretending to be the monster while Elka threw a wooden spoon at her.

'But it was all pretend,' she told herself now and tugged the ring off her finger.

Slipping it over the end of a branch on the nearest heather bush she decided she'd leave it there. Once she was back home she wouldn't be a Rider anymore. She'd never actually been one in the first place.

As she settled back against Inelle her aching leg muscles twitched. And as if in a chain reaction, those twinges of pain set off the ache in her cracked rib. She ran her tongue round her teeth, searching for any dregs of snathforg leaves she could swallow.

'Just an hour of rest,' she told Inelle, 'then we'll fly again.'

Her dragon snorted a puff of smoke that wreathed her face in warmth.

'You can sleep because you need your strength to fly. I'll keep watch.'

Elka pulled a pouch from deep inside her coat pockets. Unwrapping it she took out her knock-pistol. Checking the capsules of redbane root were still loaded she aimed it at the sky, sighting on the moon. The smooth wooden grip felt comforting in her hand. She liked her scimitars and was proud that she'd learned to fight with them, but pistols were the weapons she'd grown up longing to wield.

She lowered the knock-pistol, resting it across her palms, and ran a finger over the intricate gears that would power it, sending a puff of redbane root into the face of her targets. She hoped she wouldn't have to use it.

As she sat, resting against her dragon, looking up at the stars, it all caught up with her. The desperate fear of losing Inelle, the twisting guilt at causing Halfen's death, and the pang of loss at no longer being a Rider. It all crashed down on her and she doubled up, gasping for breath. Tears blurred her eyes and sobs tore through her chest.

She felt teeth on her wrist. Opening her eyes she saw Inelle holding her left wrist in her mouth. It was the wrist she'd hurt the day she'd named Inelle, the day they'd properly bonded. A sad smile tugged at Elka's lips.

'You're right,' she told her dragon, 'we're family. We don't need the Riders. We'll be fine with each other.'

She closed her eyes, resting against Inelle, just for a moment.

It was cramp in her leg that woke her hours later. Elka jolted up, yelling as pins and needles stabbed her foot. Then panic gripped her chest. The moon was sinking, it would be dawn soon, and she'd slept almost the whole night.

'Why didn't you wake me?' she cried at Inelle but

her dragon only cocked her head at her.

Then she heard a sound that sent a spike of fear right through her heart—the rustle of wings on the wind.

'There!'

The shout came from the sky. The Riders. They'd found her.

CHAPTER 14

BETRAYAL

'*MI SPARKEN!*' ELKA swore.

Inelle rose from her crouch with a whoosh of wings. Elka grabbed her saddle, ready to boost herself up and flee. Displaced air swept over her and Inelle growled, giving Elka a warning. She ducked and claws tore the air where her head had been. In the moonlight she caught a glimpse of orange scales and panic surged through her veins. Of all the Riders, why did it have to be Nathine who'd caught her?

'Traitor!'

Elka winced as the word hit home. She grabbed Inelle's saddle again but something dropped from the sky and barrelled into her. Elka hissed in pain as she was slammed to the ground. There was a weight on top of her and agony danced up and down her ribs. The cold edge of a blade pressed against her neck.

'I'm going to kill you for Halfen.'

Nathine was so close that her breath washed over Elka's chin. The fury in her eyes hit harder than a punch to the face.

Panic flooded into her mind from Inelle. Turning her head, Elka saw Malgerus pinning her dragon to the ground. Inelle snapped at him. Malgerus roared then clamped his jaw around Inelle's neck. Her wings and ruff of feathers fluttered frantically.

'No!' Elka yelled in Glavic. 'Inelle, be still.'

She felt her dragon's rising panic like steam in a boiler but Inelle held off from fighting Malgerus. If she did, he'd kill her.

'Nathine!' someone yelled and Elka recognised Aimee's voice. Being caught by the women she'd most closely betrayed felt like swallowing shards of metal. From the corner of her eye she watched two more dragons land, moonlight caressing scales of emerald green and sapphire blue.

Then hands were grabbing Nathine and yanking her off Elka. Nathine yelled and kicked but Aimee and Pelathina pulled her away. Elka struggled to her feet.

'Traitor!' Nathine yelled again, then spat at her. The globule splatted on Elka's cheek. She wiped it away with her coat sleeve.

'Nathine!' Aimee shouted. 'We don't know what's going on here, so can you please take a deep breath and calm down.'

Scrubbing angry tears from her face, Nathine told Aimee where she could shove her calm.

'She killed Halfen!' Nathine yelled, stabbing a scimitar at Elka. 'I'm going to let Malgerus rip open her belly and eat her insides while she watches and screams.'

Tears mingled with snot on Nathine's face and the whole lot dripped from her chin. Her high ponytail had gotten twisted to the side and long strands of hair caught on her sticky face. The fierce look in her eyes told Elka that she meant every word of what she said.

Aimee and Pelathina stood on either side of their friend, and all three had blades drawn. Elka didn't dare reach back and unsheathe one of her own, not while Malgerus had Inelle pinned. She heard the rustle of wings and the slither of scales. Turning her head she saw Jess and Skydance take up positions to her left and right. She was surrounded.

Every nerve in Elka's body screamed at her to run. But without Inelle she couldn't get away. Inelle shared her dread and growled, low and threatening.

'Don't,' Elka whispered in Glavic, terrified that she'd saved Inelle from Nail's bullets only to lose her here to another dragon.

'Call off Mal,' Aimee ordered Nathine.

'No!' Nathine spat the word.

'I did say that we maybe shouldn't have brought her,' Pelathina threw a look at Nathine, then Aimee.

'As if you could have stopped me,' Nathine scoffed.

Elka wished they had. She wished Jara had sent any other Riders after her apart from these three. She watched as Aimee pulled Nathine's face round until she was facing her.

'Nathine, we don't know for sure that Elka killed Halfen or that she was the one who stole Pagrin's bracelet.'

Aimee's trust, and willingness to give her the benefit of the doubt, cut Elka deeper than Nathine's insults had. She wished she could be the girl that the Saviour of Kierell thought she was. But she reminded herself that she'd never been that girl. It had all been an act.

'If she's innocent then why did she run?' Nathine snapped.

'Because I didn't have a choice,' Elka insisted quietly in Glavic.

But she saw now that yesterday she did have a choice. She'd been so shaken by Nail's appearance and his threats that it hadn't occurred to her to resist. She could have told the Riders everything, and yes they'd have been upset that she'd lied to them, but they'd also have protected her. They'd have helped her save Inelle. But that was before Halfen fell. Now the door to that future had firmly closed. And maybe she'd been a fool to open it in the first place.

'Family is everything,' she whispered to herself in Glavic.

'You mean Inelle? She's why you're out here?' Pelathina asked in Kierellian.

Elka shook her head, using the movement as a way to look around, searching for an opening, something she could use to escape.

'Let's get back to Anteill where we can properly listen to Elka and sort out this misunderstanding,' Aimee said, her voice surprisingly calm.

'Misunderstanding?' Nathine yelled. 'Which part of Halfen being dead is unclear?'

Malgerus growled, still towering over Inelle, pinning her to the grass.

Aimee looked at Elka then, the colourless half of her face made even paler by the moonlight. Elka saw in her eyes that Aimee didn't want to believe that she'd betrayed them.

'Nathine's wrong, isn't she?' Elka could hear the desperation in Aimee's voice. 'You didn't steal Pagrin's bracelet or kill Halfen, did you?'

'Oh, love.' Pelathina's voice was half a whisper and it was all it took to make Aimee see the truth. Elka watched as her face crumpled.

The lump of Pagrin's bracelet dug into her hip. She imagined for the briefest moment taking it out and handing it back to Aimee. But a thief could be forgiven. A murderer could not. She remembered the girl she'd been two years ago when she first arrived in Kierell, full of confidence and ambition. That girl hadn't cared about lying, or worried about betraying these women.

Elka tried to be that girl again. Because that's who she really was, wasn't it? It was like slipping into an old outfit that didn't quite fit anymore—the boots pinched her toes and the sleeves of the shirt were too short.

'I used to have nightmares about it.' Aimee's voice was as soft as the wind in the grass. 'I'd dream that the bracelet was stuck on my wrist again and that Pagrin was there beside me. And he'd make me touch people. He'd force me to steal their sparks and kill them. I'd wake up kicking and screaming. Once I kicked Pelathina in the shin so hard that she had a bruise.'

'Well instead of you stealing sparks, this time it'll be her!' Nathine jutted her chin at Elka. 'Let me kill the backstabbing, boyfriend-murdering bitch!'

Elka's eyes flicked from dragon to Rider to dragon, desperately trying to think of a way to get free. Inelle was tugging at her mind, scared and confused.

'Do you have it with you? Or did you hide it somewhere?' Aimee asked. Elka tried to think of a lie but inspiration wouldn't come so she just shook her head.

'Why?'

It was Pelathina who'd asked. Elka turned to face her.

'You wouldn't understand,' Elka told her. 'But I really didn't have a choice.'

'Tell us, we'll listen,' Pelathina said softly but Elka shook her head again.

She wanted to open up, to explain everything to these girls who'd become her friends but the little voice in her head was back. And it was telling her to ditch them and get out of there.

When Aimee spoke, though, her words almost silenced the little voice. 'I always tried to make you feel welcome because feeling like an outsider sucks. Believe me, I know.' She looked across at Elka, pleading. 'I don't understand. Please, just come back with us and explain.'

'Aimee! Don't you dare take her side!' Nathine shouted.

'I'm not!' Aimee finally snapped and yelled back. Then she stepped over to Jess and Elka flinched as

Aimee pulled manacles from her saddlebag.

Elka felt like one of Frannack's prototype looms—tension stretched to breaking point, dangerously close to exploding.

'But I won't let you kill her,' Aimee said as she passed Nathine. 'We're taking her back to Anteill as planned and she'll face judgement there.'

Aimee came to stand in front of Elka. The small Rider looked up at her.

'I can't go back to Kierell,' Elka said. 'But please believe that I really didn't mean to hurt Halfen.'

'Liar!' Nathine said but this time the word came out in a croak, not a shout. Her grief was winning over her anger. 'I'll bet he was trying to be a hero. Stupid boy with his stupid face.'

Elka heard the love underneath Nathine's insult, a love she'd shattered along with Halfen's bones. The look Aimee gave her best friend was so full of sympathy and understanding that Elka had to turn away. An image flashed into her mind of Nathine and Halfen sharing their way-too-intimate kiss at the cafe yesterday. She felt again her hands sticky and wet with Halfen's blood. Her stomach spasmed and bile rose in her throat. She leaned over, hands on knees, clamping her lips closed to stop herself from throwing up again.

As she stared at the soggy grass between her boots she shifted the cogs in her mind, coming up with a new plan now that she had been caught and her original had been torn to tatters. Frannack had always taught her that when one solution didn't work as intended you found a way around to a different solution. Elka reached into her coat, and her fingers tightened around a bundle hidden deep within an inside pocket. As she straightened she deftly tucked the bundle up her sleeve. Sensing something, Inelle growled, long and low. Elka sent her a wave of calm, telling her to stay where she was and not to fight Malgerus.

'Elka?'

Aimee had stepped close, manacles jangling in her hand. Elka could still see hurt and sympathy in the softness of her eyes and the crease on her forehead. But she knew from reading Callant's book, and from suffering months of training under Aimee's tutelage, that the small Rider had steel in her. Elka remembered the way her brothers had bribed guild heads and city guards back in Taumerg. That would never work on Aimee. She'd always do what was right.

And the right thing was to take Elka back to Kierell to face punishment for what she'd done. Elka tried not to admire Aimee for her conviction. Instead she lined up the lies behind her teeth.

'Okay, I'll come back to Kierell with you,' she said.

Aimee nodded and stepped closer.

'I'm going to put these on you and then I'm going to search you for the bracelet,' Aimee told her.

'And if you twitch in any way that I think looks suspicious, I'm going to stab you,' Nathine added.

Elka nodded her understanding. 'I'm cold. Can I put my hat on for the flight?' she asked, this lie slipping out easier than she'd thought.

Aimee looked to the scimitar hilts behind Elka's head and the throwing knives on her thigh, thinking she was checking all Elka's weapons. 'Alright.'

Elka pulled a wad of fabric from her pocket and slipped it over her head. Then down so it covered her nose and mouth. It wasn't a hat. It was the mask that accompanied her knock-pistol.

She let the pistol drop from her sleeve and into her palm. Wrapping her fingers around the grip she raised it, the muzzle aimed directly at Nathine's face. Then she pulled the trigger. The redbane capsule was pierced and expelled in a puff of red smoke. Nathine's eyes widened in surprise as she breathed it in. Elka didn't wait to see her fall, she was already leaping towards Pelathina. Spinning the cogs on the frame she loaded another capsule into the pistol's firing chamber.

She caught movement from the corner of her eye and ducked as Skydance's tail whistled through the air. Pelathina was yelling. Aimee was too. All four dragons were roaring. Elka sprang to her feet and fired. Red smoke shot from the pistol but Pelathina had dived behind Skydance.

'*Mi sparken!*'

The redbane drifted across Elka's face but her mask protected her. It made her eyes sting, though. Blinking away tears she almost missed Pelathina rolling underneath Skydance then lunging for her. Elka tried to get away but Pelathina grabbed her ankles and pulled. Elka fell, gripping the pistol tight to her chest. Pelathina climbed on top of her, grabbing her arm and trying to roll her over. Elka threw an elbow up and felt it collide with Pelathina's jaw. The Rider gasped and her grip slackened.

Elka took her chance, yanking her arm free of Pelathina, spinning the pistol's cogs and firing. This time the redbane smoke engulfed Pelathina's head. Her eyes glazed over and she collapsed, landing on the grass beside Skydance.

'Pellie!' Aimee yelled.

Elka scrambled to her feet and backed away from Skydance, but without his Rider to command him the dragon was confused. Elka watched as he nudged Pelathina's unconscious body with his snout. Elka left them, sliding on the wet grass as she turned to face the last Rider standing.

'What did you do to them?' Aimee's voice was high and panicky.

She was crouched over Nathine, holding her friend's limp hand in her own. Jess was a dark shadow behind her, wings outstretched, blocking off the moon. Elka scanned the heather for Malgerus. Relief washed through her when she spotted him crouched on the edge of the stream, head cocked to the side as he stared at his unconscious Rider, not understanding why she wasn't giving him commands.

With a snap of leathery wings Inelle soared across the long grass and landed beside Elka. Having her dragon by her side again felt like putting on the final item of clothing that brought a whole outfit together.

Aimee let go of Nathine's hand and stood. She had

one scimitar in her grip and her dragon standing right behind her. She looked like the line drawing at the front of Callant's book.

'I am sorry,' Elka said in Glavic, her voice muffled by the mask she wore.

'Then don't do this,' Aimee replied in Kierellian. 'You weren't in Kierell when the Empty Warriors attacked, so you can't imagine what it's like to see an army driven by anger and hate, one that isn't human and that will not stop until they've extinguished the sparks of everyone that you love.'

'I promise the bracelet won't be used to make Empty Warriors,' Elka told her.

Aimee took a step towards her. 'The bracelet is a power that no one should have. It might seem like the solution to whatever problem you're trying to fix, but I promise it isn't. The power of the bracelet will corrupt the wearer, whatever their original intentions.'

There was no way she could make Aimee understand. The thought saddened her but also hardened her resolve. She clicked the cogs on the knock-pistol, loading another capsule.

Aimee sprang at her, fast and nimble as always. Elka had never been able to beat her in a sparring bout. But Aimee fought with bladed weapons. She'd never faced an opponent with a pistol. Before Aimee was even close enough to swing, Elka fired. Red smoke wreathed Aimee's face and a second later she breathed it in. She collapsed instantly. Aimee was small and the capsules in the pistol were large enough to knock out a man. Jess's growl was a loud rumble as she sank to her belly on the grass beside her Rider.

Elka looked around. Three unconscious Riders, all watched over by their confused dragons. She held her breath for a moment, fearful that the dragons might attack her. But they didn't. None of them understood what she'd done and as far as they were concerned, she and Inelle were part of their clutch. Elka let out her breath in a whoosh and pulled down her mask. She sucked cold night air into her lungs.

Inelle nudged her with her snout then gently bit her left wrist.

'I know,' Elka said softly, running a hand over her quivering feathers. 'Family.'

Elka tucked away her pistol and knelt beside Aimee's unconscious body. The redbane was potent and all three Riders would be unconscious for hours, maybe even half a day. But then they'd chase her again. No lies now could hide the fact that she was guilty.

Elka rolled her shoulders, trying to get the outfit of the old Elka to settle more comfortably on her again. That Elka was so close to completing her mission and returning triumphant. This was what she'd dreamed of. A place on the Hagguar Ragel was waiting for her.

Pulling one of her throwing knives from the garter on her thigh she pressed the knife to the skin of Aimee's throat. A warm trickle of blood ran over her fingers.

But then she stopped.

She had to do this, she knew that. Torsgen wouldn't hesitate. He'd have slit Aimee's throat the moment she fell unconscious.

But this was Aimee! The girl she'd read about, who'd saved a whole city. The person who'd trained her and made her stronger than she ever thought she could be. The Rider who gave out nothing but kindness and support. Her spark shone so brightly. How could Elka be the one to snuff it out?

She squeezed her eyes and felt tears in her lashes. Indecision tore at her insides like dragon's claws.

CHAPTER 15

DUST AND CELEBRATIONS

She couldn't do it. Aimee's blood on her fingers felt just like Halfen's—slick and wrong. She tucked her knife away and stood. She could put the manacles on Aimee but, one of the others would free her, and it would waste valuable time. If she was to reach Taumerg before the Riders she'd need every second.

So she tucked away her knock-pistol and checked Pagrin's bracelet was still secure in her pocket. A minute later she was in her saddle and Inelle took her up into the sky. The other three dragons watched her go but thankfully none of them followed.

'Show me that you can beat the wind,' Elka said to her dragon and felt the burst of power in Inelle's muscles as she increased her speed.

They shredded the clouds and the starlight couldn't catch them as Inelle flew across the tundra. The speed was intoxicating and Elka felt that if they went fast enough the wind would strip away her guilt and carry off her bloody memories. Even with her gloves on Elka's fingers grew numb with the cold as she gripped Inelle's spiralled horns, but they didn't stop. A rain shower caught them at dawn, soaking Elka to the skin and beading on Inelle's scales. Still, they kept flying. As soft grey light bled into the sky Elka risked a glance behind—she hadn't dared look around all night.

The sky was empty of dragons.

Yet she didn't slow. She wouldn't let herself believe she'd gotten away until they made it back to Taumerg. Inelle had been flying at full speed for hours and Elka could feel the edges of her dragon's exhaustion. Still she pushed her horns, urging her to keep going. The sunrise kissed the grass and the rolling hills but Elka saw none of its beauty. On and on they flew.

At midday she spotted Vorthens, the town clinging to the side of its hill, cupped by vineyards. Elka kept feeding her desperation to Inelle and her dragon pushed on through the weariness that clung to them both, eager to please her Rider. She was exhausted, though, Elka could feel it. More than once she'd felt her own eyes closing. Every muscle from her hips to her toes kept alternating between numbness and stabbing cramps. She'd chewed the last of her snathforg leaves hours ago and they'd worn off. With every breath pain flicked across her ribs.

They flew over Nepzug, Elka noticing with surprise how big the town had grown in the two years she'd been away. Then, as sunset painted the sky pink, she spotted the chimneys of Taumerg.

Home.

And the sky was still clear behind her. She'd done it, she'd gotten away.

Elka's brain felt pickled in tiredness and she didn't know what to think as she guided Inelle over the outskirts of her city. She flew straight along the Rorg Canal, following it until she spotted her own tall townhouse. Unlike Kierell, Taumerg wasn't built with dragons in mind. There were no flat roofs to perch on and the buildings were all too high for Elka to climb down from. She'd just have to land in the street and make an entrance.

People jumped aside, yelping in surprise as Inelle landed right by the steps to Elka's front door. She practically fell out of her saddle she was so tired, but when she heard the awed comments she stood tall. When she left Taumerg she'd been just a girl, dismissed as the Hagguar brothers' baby sister. Now she stood on her own street as a Rider, with a dragon at her back.

With a hiss of steam the mechanised front door of her house opened. Torsgen appeared, come to see what the fuss was on his doorstep. He hadn't changed. Same hairstyle, shaved at the sides and long on top, at odds with his fashionably tailored suit. Same stoic face and cold, calculating eyes. Elka watched him for a brief moment as he failed to recognise her. She threw him a tired smile and saw the surprise on his face, there and gone in a second. He didn't return her smile.

'Up onto the roof,' Elka ordered her dragon. It would be awkward for her to perch up there and Elka would need to find somewhere better for her to rest but it would do for now.

Torsgen's eyes followed Inelle and Elka couldn't read his thoughts behind them.

'Welcome home. You must be tired. I'll have a bath drawn and food brought.' Torsgen swept an arm towards the hallway behind him. Elka could tell he wanted to get her inside and away from the prying eyes of the gawping crowd. News that a Rider had landed at the Hagguar family door would be all over the city by morning.

There were seven steps to the front door. Elka's legs were quivering from riding Inelle for so long that it felt like there were seven hundred. The pain from her cracked rib had become an insistent pulse all down her side. The door hissed closed behind her. She was home. The house looked the same, smelled the same, but somehow it all looked different too, as if she was looking at it through a pair of glasses not made for her eyes.

Hands grabbed her arms and shoved her against the wall, knocking the breath from her lungs.

'Two years, Elka.'

Torsgen's face was inches from hers, his cold eyes like shards of ice. He didn't yell, and that made it worse.

'I put my trust in you, and you disappeared for two years. I should have known you weren't old enough to take your responsibilities seriously.' He pulled her away from the wall only to slam her back against it. He still hadn't raised his voice. 'This family has no use for people who shirk their duties.'

'No, no, wait Torsgen, I got it.'

Elka shoved away his hands and reached into her coat, pulling out the bracelet. Torsgen snatched it from her, turning the gold cuff over in his hands. Finally, he smiled.

'Pagrin's bracelet. Power once held only by immortals but now ours. With this we can change the future.' He looked at her and there was something new in his eyes. Respect? 'Well done, Elka.'

His praise went right into her chest, stoking her spark, warming her. She'd never had a well done from Torsgen, ever.

Still smiling he slipped the bracelet into his trouser pocket and headed for the stairs. Three steps up he turned and looked back at her.

'Get a bath, and some more appropriate clothes, and I'll ask the staff to prepare us a late supper. We'll celebrate that you're back.'

As he continued up the stairs Frannack burst from an upper room and came barrelling down the stairs. He too was just as Elka had remembered, hair ruffled on top, glasses askew on his nose and smudges of ink on his fingers.

'Torsgen?'

'She bloody did it.' Torsgen continued up the stairs, pointing at Elka still at the bottom and clapping Frannack on the shoulder as he passed.

Frannack spotted Elka then and his eyes went wide behind his glasses. He ran down the rest of the stairs then stopped awkwardly in front of her.

'You're back,' he said.

Elka laughed and squeezed him in a hug, forgetting her cracked rib and wincing in pain. Frannack didn't seem to notice. He pulled back and looked her up and down.

'You look... dirty.'

Elka laughed again, and as she did realised that she'd missed Frannack. 'What's new with you?'

'Torsgen told you about the new loom?' Elka nodded quickly before Frannack began a detailed explanation of it. 'It works and we've already built three and have plans for another five. And Torsgen has secured us land to build the mill on. Or almost has. There are some details to sort.'

Frannack looked like he was going to keep talking so Elka interrupted him. 'You can tell me about it over supper.'

The lure of a bath was too strong and Elka left Frannack in the hall, dragging her aching body up the five flights of stairs to her rooms at the top of the house.

It felt weird being there. Almost like the last two years hadn't happened. She was in her own bathroom, stripping off her clothes and running a bath before it even dawned on her that she used to wait for the servants to do this for her.

As she stepped into the tub she saw the scar on her shin, the one she'd gotten at the nesting site when she'd stolen Inelle. Amongst the Riders that scar had been a mark of honour. Here, it wouldn't mean anything to anyone. She shoved that thought aside.

Sinking into the hot water was delightful. She lay

back and stared up at the rafters and pipes above her head. She was back in a proper house. She imagined the last two years sluicing off her and into the bath water, and sank down under the surface, watching bubbles rise from her nose.

Aimee's face popped into her mind, unconscious with blood on her neck. Elka burst up from the water with a gasp.

'No, it'll be fine,' she told herself.

The sky had been clear the whole way back, no dragons following her. Aimee wouldn't give up but really what could she do? Elka was back with her family. She was safe. Here it was Aimee who was a nobody.

She nodded, having reassured herself, but the pleasure of the bath was ruined so she got out and padded with wet feet across the hall to her bedroom. During her first few months in Anteill all she'd dreamed about was being back here in her own room. Stepping inside, Elka waited to feel joy. It didn't come.

She looked around and saw everything was dusty and spider webs decorated her windows. Clearly the servants had been told not to bother cleaning this room. She felt Inelle in her mind, restless and worried, and heard a scratching of talons on tiles right above her head. She sent her a wave of comfort and a promise that she'd find her somewhere better to sleep tomorrow.

'After a good dusting you'll feel like mine again,' she told the room.

Dropping her towel, she stood naked before the big wardrobe she'd missed so much. She swung the doors open and trousers, dresses, shirts, waistcoats and scarves all slithered out, landing in a heap at her feet. Even without them the wardrobe was still full. Elka had forgotten that she had quite so many clothes. But now she could choose to wear any of them, whenever she wanted, and mix and match any colours she liked. No more black.

First she had to re-bandage her ribs, and she didn't want Torsgen to know she was injured because he'd ask questions. So that meant no servants. Instead Elka tore up one of her older shirts and wrapped the strips tight around herself. Then she needed clothes. But presented with a hundred choices she couldn't decide what she wanted to wear. She picked a green shirt with a bold leaf pattern from the top of the bundle at her feet and pair of dark grey trousers patterned with flowers in the same colour. For her feet she chose yellow silk slippers. Looking at herself in the mirror, she shrugged. She couldn't quite remember how she'd managed the clashing colours and patterns she'd worn before.

'I'm just out of practice,' she told herself.

As she walked downstairs to the dining room she trailed her hand along the banister, trying to slot herself back into the Elka she'd been before she left. In the dining room the table was set for three, soft light from the gas lanterns twinkling on cut crystal glasses. Torsgen appeared a moment later, Frannack at his heels. Her eldest brother took his seat at the head of the table, Frannack sitting at his right hand. With his foot Torsgen pushed out the chair at his left hand.

'Go on,' he said to Elka.

She took the seat she'd always dreamed of filling. The servants had laid out a simple supper of cold pheasant—Torsgen's favourite—fresh bread, savoury tarts and a chutney of kweap berries. All food Elka had loved, and missed. Filling her plate, she listened as Torsgen filled her in on the running of the Hagguar family business for the last two years. He told her to make time to sit down with Dellaga sometime soon. She was the young woman who did their accounts and whom Elka had barely been permitted to speak to before.

Frannack went on to give her all the complicated details of the machines he and Mila had been building. Elka didn't follow half of it but she smiled because she knew how much Frannack loved what he did.

Neither of her brothers asked about her time in Kierell or her journey to becoming a Rider. But that was okay because Elka didn't want to talk about it.

'I take it all this,' Elka waved to take in the room and the three of them, 'means that I have my seat on the Ragel now?'

Torsgen sipped his gin and nodded. 'You've earned it.'

She'd done it. She'd earned her place and now she'd be given all the respect a Haggaur was due. She waited to feel something. A kaleidoscope of butterflies in her stomach maybe. But if they were there, they remained still. She was probably just too tired to take it all in right now.

'Where's the bracelet?' she asked around a mouthful of tart.

'Safe,' Torsgen replied.

'How will we use it to create Endless Workers?' Elka asked. 'We need a way to make the bracelet work without needing hundreds of sparks.'

'Endless Workers?' Torsgen raised an eyebrow.

Elka nodded. 'That's what they should be called.'

'Alright.' Torsgen tipped his glass towards her then drank. 'And don't worry about using the bracelet. Frannack's already been working on a solution to that.'

Frannack threw their older brother a look and Torsgen narrowed his eyes. If Elka hadn't been so tired she might have read more into that than she did.

Torsgen lifted the gin bottle to pour her some but Elka quickly placed her hand over her glass. She hadn't drunk any alcohol since she left Taumerg, and after the one glass of wine that she'd already had she could feel her control over Inelle slackening. It made her feel less close to her dragon and she didn't like that.

'I thought we were celebrating,' Torsgen tipped the bottle towards her.

'I'm tired. Any more and I'll fall asleep,' Elka lied. She didn't want to explain to Torsgen about her bond with Inelle.

Torsgen leaned back in his chair, gin cupped in his hand. The curtains were open behind him and the orange glow of the city made a halo around him. 'I'm pleased that you remembered the debt you owe us.'

'It's a debt that we both owe you for lifting us out of

poverty,' Frannack said, indicating himself and Elka and nodding towards Torsgen.

'And you had already fulfilled yours by becoming one of the best engineering minds in Taumerg. Now Elka has fulfilled hers by bringing us the means to create an unlimited and completely controllable workforce.'

Frannack smiled his lopsided smile at her. Elka tried to stir up some pride in her chest but she was too tired.

'Because above all else, what matters?' Torsgen asked.

'Family matters,' Frannack and Elka replied together.

'So,' Torsgen said, leaning forward, elbows on the table, 'you had no trouble getting away from Kierell unsuspected?'

A series of images flashed past her eyes—Halfen as he fell, Pelathina collapsing unconscious, Aimee's blood on her fingers.

'A clean getaway,' she lied smoothly.

Elka had thought that now she was home she could stop lying. Hopefully once she settled back into her life she wouldn't need to anymore. It was only for tonight that she needed to keep up the lies. She pretended that her original plan had worked and told her brothers that she'd left Kierell legitimately with the SaSellen caravan.

'So the other Riders who were with the caravan? They won't come looking for you?' Torsgen's gaze was fixed on her and Elka found it hard to look away.

'No, I killed them.'

The lie was out of her mouth before she'd realised

she was going to tell it. Torsgen raised his eyebrows and looked mildly impressed. It was an expression he'd never directed at her before. She looked to Frannack, wondering what his reaction would be but he'd taken out his notebook and was scribbling in it.

Suddenly the room felt oppressive and Elka wanted to leave. Standing she excused herself, saying once again that she was tired. Her hand was on the door handle—steel and brass and stylishly fashioned to look like a section of pipe—when Torsgen spoke again.

'The dragon will need to be disposed of.'

'What?' Elka spun back to face the room.

'Well you don't need it anymore.' The look on Torsgen's face was calculating. 'Being a Rider was only ever your cover story and it's not as if they'd ever let you back into their ranks now. Not if you've murdered three of them.'

Elka's mouth was as dry as if she'd flown with it wide open. She should have expected this. Of course Torsgen wouldn't want her to have a bond with something outside of the family. It felt like one final test of her loyalty.

'You're right. I'll get rid of her,' Elka said, hoping that this one really was the last lie she'd have to tell.

Torsgen nodded. 'Remember, you're a Hagguar, not a Rider.'

'I know,' Elka threw him a quick smile and left.

Walking up the stairs to the bedroom that didn't feel like hers, Elka repeated his words.

'I'm a Hagguar. I have a seat on the Ragel. *This* is

my family.'

She was home, Inelle was safe, she'd succeeded in her mission and she was on the cusp of becoming someone important and powerful.

She reached her floor. 'I never really was a Rider so I can't miss being one.'

Today she was victorious.

So why did she feel so hollow?

CHAPTER 16

BROKEN THREADS

It wasn't until Elka woke the following morning that she noticed something was missing. She used to be awakened by a little pink nose pressing against her face and a croaky meow as Ember demanded his breakfast. Jumping out of bed, she realised her cat wasn't here and hadn't been last night either. On the roof she heard Inelle growl and tried to scrape together some calm to send her dragon.

She searched her room, calling Ember's name. He wasn't in any of his usual spots. Could he have gone out hunting? Elka shook her head. He was too old for that, more interested in a warm blanket than mice. Maybe he'd sensed Inelle on the roof and that had frightened him. Perhaps he was hiding somewhere else in the house.

Still in her nightshirt Elka headed downstairs to look for him. On the fourth floor landing she met Ida carrying a breakfast tray heaped with toast and savoury pastries. The sight made Elka's stomach growl like a dragon.

Ida greeted her with a huge smile. She'd kept her hair short and it bounced around her chin as she shook her head in disbelief.

'Cook said you were back but I suspected it might be a prank. I thought that she was making me carry this,' she nodded to her tray, 'all the way up here just so they could laugh at how gullible I am.'

Elka smiled too, then felt guilty. Ida had been her friend as well as her servant but Elka had hardly spared her a thought while she'd been in Kierell.

'That looks amazing,' Elka pointed to the tray of food, 'but I'm trying to find Ember.'

A look of sympathy softened Ida's face. 'He died last winter while you were away.'

Ida's words punched her in the heart and she sat down, bum thumping onto the bottom stair. Torsgen hadn't told her: in not one of his letters had he let her know Ember was gone. Ida was speaking but Elka couldn't hear her over the ringing in her ears. She turned and ran back up the stairs. Standing outside her bedroom door she stared up at the pipes on the ceiling, as if she could look through and see Inelle.

Her dragon knew she was upset and she sent Elka such a huge wave of love that she collapsed to her knees. She longed to reach out and touch Inelle, to breathe in her smokey smell and feel her leathery wings wrap themselves around her, keeping her safe. But she couldn't get onto the roof and Inelle wouldn't fit inside the house.

'This is stupid!' she yelled. If she'd been at home in the Heart she could have easily hugged her dragon.

'Elka?'

A soft voice in her ear and a gentle hand on her shoulder told her Ida had followed her upstairs. She'd placed the breakfast tray on the floor and crouched beside Elka.

'I'm sorry about Ember. Nothing dreadful happened to him, he was just old. We buried him out in the garden.'

Kneeling on the floor, Elka noticed it had been cleaned. Had the servants done that while she slept? The door to her bathroom was open and the wooden floor gleamed in there too. But what happened to…

Eka jumped up and ran into her bathroom. They were gone.

'Ida, where are my clothes?' Her words came out clipped.

'The ones you left in here? I was going to wash them this morning but Master Torsgen ordered them to be thrown out.' Ida obviously saw the anguish on her face. 'They *were* filthy.'

This second punch to the heart was too much and Elka yelled. On the roof Inelle roared. Ida's face paled as she heard the dragon right above them. It hurt Elka to imagine her Rider's coat thrown out with the kitchen scraps. She'd worked so hard to earn those clothes. And her flying goggles had been in her coat pocket. It wasn't Ida's fault though, Elka had to remind herself of that before she yelled at the servant who'd once been her friend.

She also reminded herself that she'd never really liked wearing black anyway. No, she was only this upset because of the news about Ember.

'I'm sorry for shouting.' She put a hand on Ida's shoulder. 'I'm tired. It was a long journey back from Kierell, and I haven't had any proper Marlidesh coffee for two years so it's no wonder I'm being a grumpy stuck-up princess.'

Ida smiled but her eyes kept darting up to the roof. 'How about I bring you a freshly brewed pot of proper coffee to go with those pastries.'

She disappeared back down the stairs without waiting for an answer. Elka walked back into her bedroom and heard the clack of talons above as Inelle followed her. She looked to her scimitars, propped up on one of her armchairs and was grateful she hadn't left those in the bathroom. Would Torsgen have ordered them thrown out too?

Standing in front of her wardrobe, and the heap of clothes she'd left on the floor last night, she wondered what to put on. She realised she'd pictured herself flying across Taumerg today on Inelle and wearing her black Rider's outfit.

'I'm just getting settled back in, then we'll be fine,' she told her dragon but even to her own ears her words sounded hesitant and she pictured Inelle snorting smoke to show her disbelief.

She also didn't yet know how she was going to get around the lie she'd told Torsgen. He'd asked her to get rid of Inelle to test her loyalty, but there was no way she was giving up her dragon.

* * *

THREE DAYS LATER she was still trying to pick up the threads of her old life, which was now her entire future. Inelle was struggling to settle in the city. Elka thought she would enjoy swooping around the tall houses and the factory chimneys, skimming along the canals and exploring all the new smells. But her dragon seemed withdrawn and kept pulling against Elka, trying to tug her up into the open sky.

Elka had discovered that flying in a non-Rider outfit made her feel all wrong. None of her coats were flexible enough for mounting and dismounting a dragon so she'd had to cut long slits in one of them to make it practical.

Her second night home she'd snuck into the kitchen at night and brewed a really strong batch of snathforg tea. It dulled the pain in her ribs to a manageable ache but she was still uncomfortable and that wasn't helping her dragon settle either.

She and Inelle followed the Amms Canal to the west of the city. She smiled when workers on the barges pointed up at her, enjoying being noticed and gawked at. But still Inelle's feathers quivered with unease. Then she spotted the open space of Rokspaark and steered Inelle down. Taumerg was so built up that there were few places they could land, which was why she'd suggested to Daan that they meet in the park.

Daan.

His note had arrived yesterday. News travelled fast across the city and he knew she was back. Elka was surprised, delighted, nervous and worried when he asked to meet her for coffee. It seemed he hadn't forgotten her, but that didn't mean he felt the same as he had two years ago.

She'd sat in the armchair by her window last night, watching the lights come on across the city, and assessed how she felt. While she'd been in Kierell she'd tried not to think about Daan too much, because the memories were bittersweet. It had been difficult sometimes when she'd seen Aimee and Pelathina together. Those two were wrapped together in their own little bubble of love and it was hard not to be envious of what they shared.

Since Daan's note had arrived, though, she hadn't been able to stop thinking about him. She'd missed his smile, and his bad jokes, missed feeling his fingers brush against hers and the way sometimes, when he looked at her just so, she felt tingles in her belly.

She'd been trying not to dwell on all that she'd left behind in Anteill. She was back where she was supposed to be, forging the life she'd always wanted. She'd ruined all the friendships she'd made with the Riders, but instead she could build something with Daan.

And the more she thought about him, the more she wanted him. Like the embers of a fire stirred back to life.

Inelle landed on soft grass surrounded by hoolegode

trees, their heart-shaped leaves turned golden by autumn. Elka dismounted, still feeling wrong in her outfit of red patterned trousers and waistcoat, shirt of pale yellow, and with no gloves or Rider's goggles. At least she still had her scimitars in their holster and crossed on her back.

The cafe was at the edge of the park and Daan was already there. Elka took a moment to familiarise herself with the place because she was too nervous to look right at Daan. It was one of the many cafes Daan's family owned. It was a sunny day and the doors had all been opened so Elka could see right in. The tabletops balanced on black metal frames and the low stools had red leather seats. The front of the bar was a length of silvery metal, riveted together but also engraved with an overlapping pattern of cogs. It was industrial but stylish.

Elka couldn't help thinking it would look great in the evening with some dragon's breath orbs hanging above it.

When she'd looked everywhere else she finally let her eyes rest on Daan. The butterflies in her stomach went crazy. He was even more beautiful than she'd remembered. Dusky skin and high cheekbones she longed to run her fingers over. And his smile seemed to fill his face. He waved and held up a brass coffee pot.

'You'll need to bring it to me, I can't leave her,' Elka shouted over to him, while she stroked Inelle's feathers.

She could feel Inelle's uncertainty, and worried about leaving her alone in a park full of strangers. Daan approached cautiously, coffee pot in one hand, two cups in the other. Under Elka's instruction Inelle lowered her belly to the grass and curled her tail around herself. Elka sat down too and patted the grass beside her. Daan hesitated.

'Who are you and what have you done with Elka?' he asked.

Elka had imagined many greetings but that question hadn't been among them.

'Excuse me?' She stared up at him.

'The Elka I knew would never have sat down in a park in case she got grass stains on her trousers.' Daan was shaking his head but smiling.

Elka realised that what he'd said was true and for a moment she looked at herself through his eyes. And what she saw was a girl of two halves—one part Rider and one part Hagguar.

'Wait till I tell you about the time I fell in a bog out on the tundra,' Elka said, breaking the silence that had started to feel awkward.

Both of Daan's eyebrows shot skyward. Finally he sat too, crossing his long legs and placing the coffee in the triangle space they made.

'He's flippin' huge,' Daan said, his eyes roving all over Inelle.

'She,' Elka corrected. 'Inelle's a female. The males are larger.'

'Sparks!' Daan whistled through his teeth. Then he seemed to run out of words and smiled at her awkwardly.

Elka wondered if he was feeling the same uncomfortable mix of emotions as she was—excitement at seeing him, worry about how and if they should pick up where they left off and anxious about maybe facing a rejection. The silence grew and grew. Daan's knee jiggled. Elka fiddled with the ring in her nose. Desperately she tried to think of something to say. Then her eyes fell on the coffee pot.

'Are you going to pour that coffee?' she asked.

Daan smiled, looking relieved that she'd broken the silence. 'This? No, this one's my pot. You can go and fetch your own,' he teased making Elka smile too.

'Ha ha, come on.' She waved at the pot.

Daan poured and passed her a cup. Elka closed her eyes for a moment, savouring the rich, bitter chocolate aroma.

'So, one day you vanished and then two years later you reappear. Wanna tell me about that?' Daan was keeping his voice casual but Elka heard the hurt behind his words.

'I would have thought that where I went was obvious.' She patted Inelle who gave a rumbly growl. Her dragon had closed her eyes and was soaking up the autumn sunshine. It was warmer here than it had been down in Kierell and even if Inelle wasn't enjoying Taumerg, she was enjoying the sun.

'Yeah, alright, the dragon is a bit of a clue, but why are you a Sky Rider?'

Elka didn't want to lie to Daan. Now that he was beside her, her feelings from last night were even stronger—she really wanted to pick up where they'd left off, but she didn't want to start something with him by lying.

'I had a job to do for Torsgen,' she said. It wasn't strictly a lie.

'Because dragons are really good at weaving? I'd have thought the threads would keep getting caught on their talons,' Daan joked.

His eyes kept darting from her to Inelle as if he couldn't decide who to look at. But every time his eyes were on her dragon it gave Elka a chance to admire his face without him noticing. She'd thought she'd remembered what he looked like but the picture in her mind was a pale comparison to the real Daan. The taste of his lips had faded too, but everything—the months of flirting, the tentative touches, that wonderful kiss—it all came flooding back now. Inelle fluttered her ruff of feathers and made a noise that was almost like a purr. Elka was thankful that Daan couldn't read dragon's reactions. She still wasn't sure where they stood and didn't want to embarrass herself.

'Have you seen much of Jennta?' she asked to distract Daan from the why around Inelle's presence. If Elka's childhood friendships had been a tripod, Jennta was the other leg supporting her and Daan.

'You didn't hear?' Daan had been lifting his cup to his lips but stopped half way.

'Not much news made its way to me in Kierell,' Elka replied, swallowing the lump in her throat as she remembered Ember.

'Jennta went missing.'

'Missing?'

'Well, not missing like you did but...' Daan took a slow sip of his coffee and Elka had to forcibly drag her eyes from his lips. 'It was just weird the way it happened.'

'The way what happened?'

'You remember that her family owned a button factory, over in Unsk district?' Elka nodded and waved him on impatiently. 'Well, about six months ago your brothers bought their factory and after that Jennta and her parents disappeared.' Daan made a ta-da gesture with his free hand, as if at the end of a magic trick.

'Disappeared?'

'It's odd that there's an echo here since we're outside.' Elka punched him on the arm and Daan laughed. Then his face turned serious. 'All the rumours said they'd taken the profits from the sale and moved to Soramerg but Jennta never said goodbye. And her manners always were better than yours.'

Something niggled at Elka, and it wasn't Daan's bad jokes. It wasn't unusual for Torsgen to buy other businesses and Elka had eavesdropped on enough conversations over the years to know that Torsgen often used the threat of violence to force sales. But that wouldn't explain why Jennta had disappeared.

'I think you're reading too much into this,' Elka said and finished the rest of her coffee. 'I'm sure she's in Soramerg living the high life.'

'You're different,' Daan said, his dark eyes firmly fixed on her now.

I am, I'm a murderer. The thought popped into her head unbidden.

'I'm not,' she insisted.

'You never used to hide things before or keep secrets.'

'Remember that time we hid that expensive bottle of cloudberry liqueur from your parents?' she tried, hoping to knock the cogs in his brain into a different alignment with a fun memory. He only stared at her. 'I'm not hiding anything,' she insisted, spreading her arms wide as if to prove her point.

'Alright, then tell me why you were really in Kierell.'

She didn't want to do this, she didn't want to lie to Daan. She wanted him to smile at her and tease her like he used to.

She pushed herself to her feet. Inelle responded instantly, rising beside her. 'I need to go. I'm meeting Torsgen and Frannack at the mill.'

Daan sprang to his feet as well. He knocked over his coffee cup, dark liquid spilling across the grass. Elka waited for some joke about coffee stains adding to grass stains but it didn't come.

'Elka.'

She looked down to see Daan's long fingers on her arm. She had to fight the urge to stroke them.

'What did he make you do?' Daan asked.

Elka was confused. 'Who?'

'Torsgen.'

'Nothing.' She pulled her arm from his grip, insulted that he thought she just ran around doing what

Torsgen ordered. 'It was my idea.'

'What was?'

'Going to Kierell.'

'Okay, but why?'

They'd circled back to this and Elka felt frustration bubbling inside her. This wasn't how she'd thought seeing Daan again would go. She'd let her imagination run free last night, picturing dozens of scenarios that were way more romantic than standing arguing while spilled coffee pooled around their feet.

'I earned my place on the Hagguar Ragel,' Elka told him. The more she said that out loud the more she felt the pride that hadn't been there the night she returned to Taumerg.

A shadow moved behind Daan's eyes. 'Elka, that's great. I know you've always struggled to get your brothers to value you, but...' His words trailed off and he pressed his lips together.

'But what, Daan?' Elka demanded, some of her frustration boiling over.

'Just don't lose yourself, okay?'

He didn't know it, but it was exactly the wrong thing to say. For three days now Elka had been struggling to remember who she was and the fight between the two halves of herself was wearing her out. Inelle growled, a deep rumbling threat and Daan took several steps back. His fingers twitched as if he wanted to reach for her again but didn't dare.

Elka felt like an idiot. She shouldn't have come here. As Inelle rose, Elka jumped up into her saddle. Daan began to say something but his words were swallowed by the thump-thumping of Inelle's wings as Elka flew away and left him.

CHAPTER 17

NOT SAFE

Anger roiled in Elka, making her grip Inelle's horns too tightly as she guided her dragon across the city. Her Rider's gloves had been amongst the clothes thrown out and all the others she owned felt too flimsy for flying in. So her hands were bare and she knew she'd have spiralled imprints on her palms. She was angry that her reunion with Daan had felt all spiky, and angry at herself for flying away.

As they followed the Amms Canal towards the river, Inelle began pulling beneath her. It started with her snapping at the air, then she began twisting her head around to the right, towards south Taumerg and the rolling hills beyond. Inelle's unease felt like dark smoke blowing through Elka's mind.

'We're not going back,' Elka told her. 'We can't.'

Inelle tugged again, twisting her head almost all the way around so she could look behind. Dragons lived as part of a clutch, and she'd taken Inelle away from hers. Elka felt a loneliness rise in her mind and wasn't sure if it originated from her or Inelle.

Taking a deep breath she pictured a giant piston, pushing all the anger, loneliness and confusion out of her brain. Then she sent a wave of calm to Inelle. She felt her dragon relax beneath her and her wingbeats grew more steady.

'We'll make our own clutch here,' Elka told her.

It would have taken Elka well over an hour to walk from Rokspaark to her family's largest mill, but with Inelle she could fly across the whole city in a quarter of that time. The River Ireden shimmered to their left as they flew over the factory district. Inelle swooped between plumes of smoke from the chimneys, swirling them with the tips of her wings.

They landed in the wide street in front of the mill's large double doors. Elka dismounted and told Inelle to wait for her up on the roof. In Kierell she'd grown used to seeing dragons perched on rooftops but here Inelle looked out of place on the peaked roof, like a strange gargoyle in a row of chimneys. She was beautiful, though, her indigo scales shimmering in the sun.

As Elka turned to go into the warehouse a poster on the opposite wall caught her eye. Dozens had been stuck over the brickwork in a haphazard jumble—adverts, political messages, job offers—but the three newest ones, not yet peeling at the edges, drew her attention. All three were for missing teenagers, two boys and a girl. It made her think of Jennta, and Daan's insistence that she'd disappeared.

She stepped over to the wall and looked more closely. In the printed line drawings of the missing teenagers, all three were wearing the boiler suits of factory workers. The address at the bottom of the posters—the home they'd disappeared from—was the same on all three. Elka recognised the street as one of the rows of tenements near the docks. Many families sent their teenagers to work in the factories and often they'd move from their family homes into boarding houses.

At first Elka couldn't work out what about the posters was holding her attention. She didn't know these kids. It wasn't until Inelle gave a short, sharp roar that it occurred to her that she was thinking like a Rider. She was looking for people to protect.

Shoving aside thoughts of missing teenagers, Elka turned to the factory doors. They were twice her height, painted bright red and with her family name stencilled across them in gold and black. Turning the big cog in the middle of the left-hand door made a series of smaller cogs turn and with a hiss of steam the doors swung open. Elka stepped inside and pulled the metal chain which would close them again.

The noise hit her immediately. The clack and whoosh of looms, the hiss of steam, the clanking of gears, men yelling orders—it all tumbled together and seemed to grow louder the longer Elka stood there. For a brief moment she wished she was wrapped in the silence of the Ring Mountains. She looked up to the roof high above, held up by a network of metal girders, and the row of skylights along the south side. Through them she could see Inelle, a dark shadow against the sky.

'Elka!'

Torsgen called to her from the metal walkway that circled the inside of the factory. It was raised high above the floor where hundreds of people worked. He jerked his chin, telling her to join him. She knew her boots were noisy on the metal staircase but she couldn't hear them above the din from below. At the top of the staircase were three rooms—an office each for Torsgen and Frannack and an outer office where Dellaga worked. Following Torsgen into the outer office Elka was relieved when he closed the door, shutting out most of the mill's noise. Dellaga wasn't at her desk and for the moment she and Torsgen were alone.

'What happened to Jennta?' Elka's mouth blurted out the question before her brain had even realised she was going to ask it. Apparently the Rider part of her was still hung up on the posters and missing teenagers.

'Who?' Torsgen frowned at her.

'Her parents owned the button factory over in Unsk district. You bought it.'

'So?'

'Apparently afterwards Jennta and her family disappeared.'

Torsgen shrugged and turned away, picking up a leather-bound notebook from Dellaga's desk. 'I don't give a single dull spark what people do with themselves after our business is done.'

Torsgen moved to the window that looked out over the factory floor. Copper pipes ran along the wall under the window and disappeared through the floor. Elka tensed as Torsgen's gaze swept from the factory floor up to the skylights. She knew what was coming. He'd ordered her Rider's clothing to be thrown out and he'd told her that she couldn't keep Inelle. He was doing it to test her. Arriving home with Pagrin's bracelet hadn't been enough to make up for taking a year longer than she'd promised. Torsgen wanted her to prove to him that her loyalties lay with their family and not with the Riders.

Elka needed to find a way to show him that she could be a loyal, dedicated Hagguar, but also still have a dragon. Until then she'd have to buy herself, and Inelle, some time.

'Elka, why is there a dragon on our roof?' His voice was cold and hard.

'It's temporary.'

'I distinctly remember a conversation where you promised you'd get rid of it.'

'Her,' Elka whispered.

'What?' Torsgen turned to face her.

'I will,' Elka began, annoyed at herself for lying but not seeing any other options at the moment. 'But I can't exactly leave a dragon's body to rot in our back garden, can I? And I'm not digging a grave that deep.'

'Well, fly out to the forests around Fir du Merg, deal with it there and get a barge back.' Torsgen strode back to Dellaga's desk. 'I'll not have this conversation again, Elka.'

'I'll do it,' she continued to lie, 'but that'll take days and right now we're busy with plans for our new factory.' Elka waved towards the offices where she presumed Frannack and Mila were waiting.

Torsgen slammed his hand down on Dellaga's desk, making Elka jump. He very rarely succumbed to anger and seeing it made an unwelcome fear prickle in Elka's fingertips. Torsgen dragged a sheet of paper from the desk and thrust it at Elka. She took it, realising it was a poster encouraging membership of the Vorjagen—the Hunters. She remembered them. The group, that bordered on being a cult, who hunted prowlers on the tundra. They sold the pelts and heads in Soramerg and the bones to travelling shaman from Marlidesh. The poster in Elka's hand advertised membership to their bloodthirsty ranks, stating that the entrance qualification was to have killed a prowler solo.

'Why do you have this?' Elka waved the paper at Torsgen.

'Because we have a useful arrangement with the Vorjagen.'

A cold shiver ran down Elka's spine. 'What? Why?'

Elka thought of the few Vorjagen she'd seen strutting through Taumerg, wearing knives, pistols and crossbows like they were the finest of jewels, heads shaved and tattooed with snarling beasts and skulls. Torsgen shrugged, as if doing business with a group who prided themselves on killing was no big deal. 'They pay a fee to transport their goods on Hagguar barges. And in return, they will lend us men if required.'

'You mean thugs?'

Torsgen shrugged again. 'Men who work hard and

are skilled at what they do.'

'But you already have half the Zachen Guards in your pocket, why do you need the Vorjagen too?'

Torsgen snatched the poster from Elka and shoved it in her face. 'The Vorjagen have made no secret of the fact that they'd hunt dragons if they got the chance. In exchange for giving them that chance I could probably double what we charge them for transport.'

Elka's stomach dropped down into her boots. She imagined those thugs whooping and cheering as they fought to become the first to take down a dragon. Her dragon. She grabbed the connection in her mind, squeezing tight. Feeling her, but not knowing what was wrong, Inelle sent a wave of love that almost made Elka cry.

'If you don't deal with that dragon, I'll tell the Vorjagen to hunt it down.'

Threat delivered, Torsgen stepped back, crumpled the poster and tossed it to the floor. 'You have two days, then the dragon becomes prey.' Torsgen straightened his waistcoat. 'Right, we're late for our meeting.'

Torsgen stepped into his office, leaving the door open for Elka and expecting her to follow. Hands shaking, and mind whirring, Elka joined him and tried to keep her attention on the meeting, but she barely heard a word of what Frannack and Mila were saying.

She'd thought that by stealing Pagrin's bracelet and flying back to Taumerg, that she'd saved Inelle. Nail's threat to shoot her was null and void now. But her dragon was still in danger. The gears in Elka's mind spun faster and faster as she tried to think of a way to save Inelle and also keep her place on the Ragel.

'Elka!'

She startled from her thoughts and noticed that everyone was staring at her. Torsgen narrowed his eyes.

'Were you listening?'

'Of course,' Elka replied quickly.

'I didn't grant you a place on the Ragel so you could sit and daydream.' Torsgen's voice was icy.

'Obviously.' Elka tried throwing him a smile. 'I just need more coffee.'

She reached across the piles of papers, showing lists of figures and sketches of machines, for the pot in the middle of the table. Frannack had already turned his attention back to his notebook and was chewing the end of his pencil. Mila was watching her, though. The puffer wore a pair of goggles on her forehead, keeping a mass of curly hair out of her eyes. Elka didn't really know Mila, but since she'd destroyed the friendships she had with the Riders, said all the wrong things to Daan, and apparently Jennta was missing, she felt the need to try and make new friends. So she gave Mila a smile. The puffer only frowned back.

'We could try copper,' Frannack suddenly said, his eyes still on his notebook. 'It's a better conductor.'

Mila put a hand on Frannack's arm. 'Not now.' Her eyes flicked to Elka.

'Try copper for what?' Elka asked.

Frannack looked up, his brow furrowed in confusion at her question. He didn't seem to have noticed

Mila's hand. 'For the tank. It could work better with the—'

'That's a problem best saved for another discussion,' Torsgen interrupted him.

Elka's eyes swivelled to her older brother but he ignored her gaze, instead picking up a leather folder from the table.

'What tank? What are you working on?' Elka turned back to Frannack but he was looking at Torsgen and Torsgen shook his head.

'It's a different project,' Frannack mumbled, pencil end back in his mouth.

'What project?' Elka demanded. 'I'm on the Ragel now so I need to know what's going on. If there are new plans we're working on then you should be sharing them with me.'

Frannack and Mila both deferred to Torsgen. He took a long sip of his coffee, watching Elka over the rim of his cup.

'Yes, you have a place on the Ragel now, but we all have our own jobs, our own special skills.' He placed his cup back down. 'So, leave the mechanical problems to Frannack and Mila. I need you to get Ottomak Klein to sign this.'

He slid the leather folder across the table and Elka caught it with one hand. 'What is it?'

'It's the contract for the sale of the land where we're going to build our mill.'

'I thought that was already sorted?' Elka picked up the folder and flicked through it.

'There were a few issues to straighten out but it's sorted now.'

It was the first task Torsgen had given her as a proper member of the Ragel. It rankled her that it was such a simple job—take Ottomak some papers to sign—but Elka reminded herself that two years ago she'd never have even known that there were papers which needed signing.

'Alright.' She pushed back her chair to leave but Torsgen shook his head.

'I want Claujar to accompany you but he won't be available until this evening.'

'Why do I need to take Claujar?'

'Because I'm telling you to.'

For a moment arguments buzzed on Elka's tongue, making her feel again like the rebellious teenager who'd got her nose pierced to annoy her big brother. Then it occurred to her that this job might be another test and that Torsgen wanted Claujar to watch how she performed. Well, if that was the case then she was going to ace it. Doing so might buy her a little more time to think of a way to keep Inelle safe.

'Tell Claujar I'll meet him outside our house at eight o'clock this evening then,' Elka said, sitting back down. 'And tell him not to be late.'

This time she met Torsgen's hard stare with one of her own. He held it for a moment then, apparently satisfied, he nodded. Elka allowed herself a small smile. Okay, being on the Ragel wasn't as easy as her younger self had hoped but life was teaching her that nothing ever was. She'd survived the climb and the trip to the nesting site to steal Inelle, so she should be able to pass Torsgen's little loyalty tests.

Then she chastised herself for thinking like a Rider again and turned her attention back to the meeting, vowing to listen to everything from now on. She even pulled out a journal and began taking notes.

CHAPTER 18

OUR JOB

Elka stood waiting on the steps to their townhouse as shadows filled the streets and lantern light shimmered on the canals. She heard boots on the cobbles and turned to see Claujar striding down the street, his gait smooth and efficient. As he passed under a gas lantern Elka saw his immaculate suit, buttons shining, and thought he looked like nothing more than a gentleman heading out for an evening drink. But to her, his hair gave him away: he wore it the same style as her brothers, the same as the criminals did—shaved at the sides and long on top.

Elka turned up the collar of the deep red coat that she'd altered to make like her Rider's one, and stepped down onto the cobbles.

'I'll meet you there,' she said before Claujar could speak.

Confusion creased his face until Elka whistled and Inelle landed, perching on the edge of the Rorg Canal. He raised an eyebrow at the dragon but said nothing.

Elka pressed her lips together to stop herself from smiling. She'd been a little scared of Claujar when she was younger but here she was now, off on a job with him and her calling the shots.

'Know where you're going?' Claujar asked, eyes still on her dragon.

'Of course.'

Elka mounted up and she'd barely settled in her saddle before Inelle took off. Her dragon sensed her enjoyment at giving Claujar orders and responded by showing off, swooping low over rooftops and flicking her tail through smoke from the chimneys. It was such a pleasure to have someone to share her emotions with. As a child Elka had kept everything hidden from her brothers, knowing they only saw sadness as weakness and joy as childish. Being able to express those emotions now, and feel them reflected back at her from Inelle, was freeing.

It would take Claujar longer to walk to Ottomak Klein's house than it would take her and Inelle to fly there, so she had some time. She used it to think, steering Inelle the long way around. She wondered if she could convince Torsgen that Inelle, and her speed, could be an asset to them.

They flew towards the south of the city, Inelle still swooping low, following the contours of Taumerg's skyline. The house they wanted was a four-storey townhouse in the middle of a narrow street. It was too tight for Inelle to land there so Elka guided her down onto the metal railings of a wide bridge across the

Njmega Canal. They startled a couple who'd been kissing under the soft glow of a gas lantern and Elka smirked. She gave the two young men a cheery wave as she dismounted. They stared wide-eyed at Inelle before hurrying away.

'Stay,' she told her dragon, resting one hand on her ruff of feathers. 'I'll be right back. And if anyone threatening appears you fly away, okay?'

Torsgen had promised her two days before he set the Vorjagen on Inelle, but Elka still felt uneasy about leaving her by herself. Inelle lowered her head and took Elka's wrist in her teeth, not biting down, just holding her. Elka looked up into her dragon's eyes.

'I know, we're family and I'll come back, I promise.'

She hurried to the end of the bridge then turned and looked back. Inelle was watching her, yellow eyes the same colour as the lanterns all along the bridge. Her long talons wrapped around the metal railing and behind her tall houses reached into the sky. She looked so out of place, but also beautiful.

Claujar was waiting outside Ottomak's house and Elka ran along the street to meet him. She started up the steps to the front door but Claujar grabbed her arm.

'Not that way.' He shook his head then his eyes drifted to the scimitars on her back. 'It's good you brought those.'

Elka had half forgotten she was wearing them. She'd strapped them across her back more from habit than need.

'Why? I thought we were here for Ottomak to sign a

contract.' She patted the wallet of papers in her pocket.

'We are, but we may need to apply some force, just to ensure Ottomak signs. Are you up for that?'

'Of course,' Elka bristled. 'But I thought Torsgen had this deal all sorted.'

'We're not the only people who want the land Ottomak is selling. Come.'

Claujar pulled her down the little alley between Ottomak's house and his neighbour. Elka shook him off but followed. At the back Claujar knocked three times on the servants' entrance. It was a plain old-fashioned door, not one of the new mechanised ones, and after the click and slide of a bolt it opened. An older woman in a maid's uniform ushered them inside.

'Thank you, Marla. How's your son?'

'Still got two years inside to go.' She looked at the stump on Claujar's left hand and he patted her gently on the shoulder. 'The master is upstairs?'

'In his study, third floor, second door on your left.'

Claujar nodded his thanks and motioned for Elka to follow. Claujar strode through the narrow servants' corridors and into the house proper.

'Why did we have to come this way?' Elka asked.

Claujar shushed her and started up the stairs. She seemed to have lost the upper hand with Claujar and wanted to get it back. On the third floor landing she barged past him then raised a hand to knock on the study door. But Claujar causally pushed her aside and kicked open the door.

Elka got almost as much of a fright as Ottomak did.

He jumped up from behind his desk, knocking over a glass of red wine that spilled all over the papers on his desk.

'Sparks!' he swore, hastily gathering up his now soggy papers.

'Evening Mr Klein,' Claujar said, walking calmly into the room and sitting down, not in the chair in front of the desk but in the big leather armchair by a bookcase. He crossed his legs, resting his hands on his knee. Elka followed him in and stood awkwardly, not sure where to put herself. This wasn't how she'd expected business meetings to be conducted.

'What are you doing in my house?' Ottomak demanded. 'I'll call the Zachen Guards.'

Claujar raised an eyebrow. 'You pay one of the guards extra to patrol your street specifically, don't you?'

Ottomak glared at him and Claujar continued.

'I didn't notice him tonight. Perhaps he got a better offer from someone else.'

Elka could easily picture Claujar slipping a purse of galders to one of the Zachen Guards but wondered why that had been necessary.

'What do you want?' Ottomak demanded.

'Torsgen has sent us with the contract of sale for you to sign.' Claujar waved in Elka's direction and she hurried forward, pulling the leather wallet of documents from her coat.

'Apologies for disturbing you.' Elka opened the wallet and removed two sheets of paper. She *would* take back control of this meeting. It was her Torsgen had given this job to after all. 'We just need your signature in two places, then we'll leave you to enjoy your evening.'

'What is this?' Ottomak directed the question at Claujar while waving a hand at Elka as if she was a servant who'd overstepped.

'It's the contract of sale for the land which you, as Head of the Landowners Guild, have agreed to sell to the Hagguar family,' Elka said, trying to get his attention back. 'Land where we'll build our new mill and bring more wealth to the city,' she added because it sounded like something Torsgen would say.

'I made no such agreement!' Ottomak objected, still speaking to Claujar and ignoring Elka. He slapped his hands down on his desk, then swore when he splashed wine on his trousers. 'That land has been earmarked for a hospice and homeless shelter. The sale is already lined up, the buyer has paid the deposit and the balance will be transferred tomorrow.'

Elka was lost. Torsgen hadn't mentioned a rival purchaser. He'd made it sound like the deal was already done. Claujar smiled like they were all friends here just sharing a drink.

'I've noticed that there are fewer homeless people around these days. Haven't you seen that too?' He directed the question at Elka but then continued without waiting for an answer. 'So maybe a shelter isn't really what the city needs.'

'I—' Ottomak spluttered, his nose quivering.

'And, as I think my employer has already mentioned, we will be paying half again what the Healers Guild have offered you. So, shall we?'

He gestured to Elka and, desperate to play a part in securing this deal, she placed the paper down on a dry corner of Ottomak's desk. Taking his own pen she held it out to him.

'I... the sale has already been agreed.' Ottomak held up his hands as if there was nothing he could do.

'Indeed it has,' Claujar said calmly, 'with us. Now please, your signature.'

Elka waggled the pen at him. Claujar slowly uncrossed his legs, leaned forward and his eyes slid from Elka to the hilts sticking up above her shoulders. She took his meaning but she hesitated, feeling uneasy about using her Rider's blades to threaten an innocent man. But it would only be a threat, she'd never actually hurt him, and she needed to prove her loyalty to Torsgen. So she reached back and placed a hand on the hilt of one scimitar. She didn't draw the blade, not yet.

'I think you may have forgotten who we represent. The Hagguars are not a family you wish to cross,' Claujar told Ottomak.

Elka saw it then, the flash of fear in Ottomak's eyes. He snatched the pen from Elka and scribbled his signature on both documents. With the job done Claujar was on his feet and already opening the study door. Elka hurried to follow him. Marla let them back out the servants' door and they'd reached the main street again before Claujar spoke.

'You did well.'

Elka stood, hands on hips and tried to soak up the praise. She'd known this was a test and that Claujar would be reporting back to Torsgen. It seemed she'd passed.

'I'll see you back at home then,' Elka said.

'Not yet, we have one more errand to run,' Claujar replied, already heading off down the street.

'What?' Elka ran after him then matched her pace to his. 'Torsgen didn't mention another job.'

'It's a quick one. This way.' Claujar turned onto Klimstraab.

'But…' Elka's voice trailed off as she looked back towards where Inelle waited. She could feel prickles of anxiety in her mind and wasn't sure if they came from her or Inelle, but either way she'd left her dragon alone long enough. 'I'll just get Inelle,' she said, turning away from Claujar.

He grabbed her arm and squeezed. 'Where we're going, you don't want to bring a dragon.'

Elka wanted to object, to stamp her feet and demand that Claujar listen to her because she was the Hagguar here, and that meant she was in charge. But doing that would make her seem childish.

'Fine,' she snapped, shaking him off.

She sent Inelle a pulse of love and reaffirmed the command to wait. They walked down Klimstraab, the canal to their right and a row of shops and cafes, all closed up for the night, to their left. They reached the end of Klimstraab and turned into Lockstraab where a small spur of the canal created a docking area for barges.

A soft drizzle had begun to fall, dappling the water. Barges, tied up at the docks, creaked as they bobbed. The brick wall to Elka's left was plastered with overlapping bills and posters. The top layer caught her eye. Posters of more missing teenagers. Something Claujar had said back in Ottomak's office made her look around, eyes seeking out doorways. They were all empty. There were no beggars, no one sleeping rough.

'Was that true, what you said about there being fewer homeless people in Taumerg?' Elka asked.

Claujar had stopped beside the dock master's office and turned, giving her a shrug. 'Seems to be.'

'But why? Where have they all gone?'

Claujar shrugged again and the movement made Elka want to clamp her hands down on his shoulders to stop him doing it. Further discussion was curtailed as a figure emerged from the shadows. Instinct kicked in and Elka pulled a scimitar free, sweeping into first stance, blade extended and ready.

'She's a jumpy one,' a woman's voice laughed.

Claujar waved for her to stand down. Elka relaxed her stance but kept her blade bare. Large metal arms, known as grabbers, lined the side of the dock, their pulleys and gears all still for the night. Grabbers were for hoisting goods on and off barges. A tall woman stepped out from between two of them and leaned causally against one. The drizzle pattered on her shaved, tattooed head. She was one of the Vorjagen. Elka felt a jolt of surprise—she'd presumed the hunters were all men.

'I assume you have my payment, Tori?' Claujar

asked, hand outstretched.

'Well, I'm not out in the rain because I needed to wash my hair,' Tori shook her head and laughed.

Elka didn't trust her smile and squeezed the hilt of her scimitar. Tori tossed Claujar a jingling purse which he caught and slipped into his pocket. Elka watched the exchange with narrowed eyes. This must be payment for the deal Torsgen had mentioned yesterday. But why did Claujar need her here for this collection?

'Did you complete that crossbow you were building?' Claujar asked.

Tori's face split into an even wider grin. 'Oh yes, and she's a beaut.'

She patted her own shoulder and Elka saw it then. In the dark she'd mistaken the lines of shadow behind Tori for part of a grabber, but she saw now that the woman had a huge crossbow strapped to her back.

'Here, I'll let you admire her.' Tori swung the weapon from her back and held it reverently. 'No touching, though. She doesn't like the hands of a stranger on her.'

The crossbow was easily three times the size of a normal one. There were two huge springs fixed along its length, connected to two large cogs fitted beside the limbs and a trigger on the stock. Rain droplets beaded on the metal. It was an ugly, brutal-looking weapon.

'You modified the mechanism from a clockwork pistol,' Claujar said, sounding impressed.

'That I did,' Tori patted her crossbow. 'And with this, I could easily shoot a dragon from the sky.'

Elka's heart went cold.

'I've noticed a dragon flying across our city lately.' Tori's eyes shifted to Elka. 'And I know a man in Soramerg who'd pay me a lot of galders to have its head on his wall.'

Elka didn't think, she just acted. Darting forward she smashed Tori in the jaw with her elbow and as the Vorjagen's head snapped back Elka pressed her blade to her throat.

'If you go near my dragon, I'll slit your throat,' she hissed.

From three streets away she heard Inelle roar. Tori's eyes flicked in that direction but it wasn't fear that filled them, it was lust. Lust for a kill. Elka had grown so used to seeing women bonded with dragons that seeing a woman eager to kill one felt unnatural.

'The dragon is off limits until Torsgen says otherwise.' Claujar's calm voice sounded behind Elka.

'She's off limits forever,' Elka spat, pressing her blade till a trickle of blood ran down Tori's narrow throat.

The claws of a beast tattooed on Tori's head curved down around her eyes, almost like elaborate makeup. She stared at Elka for a moment, then grinned. This was why Torsgen had ordered Claujar to bring her here. It wasn't about collecting payment, he wanted her to see his threat was real. Either she got rid of Inelle or this harpy would shoot her from the sky and cut her head off to sell as a trophy.

'Elka.'

Claujar's voice was firm behind her. But Elka couldn't turn around and be calm, couldn't just head home like tonight had been a job well done. The unease she'd felt in Ottomak's office returned, and she felt scared, and out of her depth. The only thing that was making sense was to protect Inelle.

Elka pulled her blade from Tori's throat, spun the grip in her hand, then punched the hilt into her temple. She hit Tori right in the sweet spot Aimee had shown her, knowing it would knock her out cold. Tori's legs crumpled and she landed on the cobbles in a heap. Sheathing her scimitar Elka knelt and rolled her over. Then, with a throwing knife she cut the straps holding her horrid crossbow to her back. It was even heavier than it looked and Elka struggled to lift it as she stood.

She took a staggering step to the edge of the canal and dropped the crossbow. It disappeared under the dark water. A moment later the surface was calm, nothing disturbing it but the rain. She looked over her shoulder to see Claujar watching her, a single grey eyebrow raised. He hadn't tried to stop her.

'There will be retaliation for this,' he said, coming to stand beside her at the canal's edge.

Elka looked down at the unconscious Vorjagen.

'No there won't,' she said with a confidence she didn't feel. 'I'm a Haggaur. They can't touch me.'

She could feel the pull of Inelle in her mind, restless and wanting to be reunited with her Rider. Elka turned and walked away. Claujar called something to her but she ignored him, focused on walking down the street with her back straight, even though her legs felt wobbly. She rounded the corner onto Klimstraab and sank to her knees as the adrenaline abandoned her. Her hand was shaking so badly it took three goes to slide her throwing knife back into its garter.

Watching Tori collapse had stirred up the memories she was trying so hard to bury. She saw Halfen's face again as he fell, saw her hands covered in his blood, saw Aimee's eyes roll up in her head as the redbane sucked her under.

Elka's stomach cramped and she bent over, retching. She gasped and wiped the drool from her lips.

She'd attacked a Vorjagen.

But she'd done it to protect Inelle. And besides, she knew Torsgen had no problem using violence to get what he wanted. He wasn't squeamish about doing what needed to be done, so she wouldn't be either. Standing quickly before Claujar found her there she forced her unsteady legs into a run. Inelle was flapping her wings, ruff of feathers all stuck out, as Elka ran onto the bridge and sprang into her saddle. Inelle took off and Elka closed her eyes, letting the rain beat against her face.

CHAPTER 19

TRACKED AND FOUND

Elka and Inelle had flown all night, back and forth across the city, then up along the River Ireden until Taumerg was nothing but a blur of orange light on the horizon. By the time they got home, she was soaked and Inelle was tired, but she'd thought of a compelling argument that might allow her to keep her dragon.

Back home she ran herself a bath, then dressed quickly, and made it down to breakfast before Torsgen and Frannack left for the day. She sat at the large dining table opposite Frannack and beside Torsgen, and smiled at Ida as she placed a cup of steaming black coffee in front of her.

'Claujar told me what happened last night,' Torsgen began without saying good morning.

'Yeah, Ottomak signed, so the deal is done and the land is ours,' Elka replied breezily, helping herself to some toast and slathering it with butter.

'I was referring to the member of the Vorjagen that you knocked unconscious.'

Frannack looked up from his notebook. 'You attacked a Vorjagen?'

'She was low-life scum.' Elka shrugged, feigning nonchalance.

Tori collapsing, Halfen falling, blood on her hands. She shook off the images and took a bite of her toast but instantly felt sick and struggled to swallow it. Frannack gaped at her but Torsgen's gaze was cool and assessing.

'I've shown the Vorjagen what happens if they threaten my dragon, and you can take back your ultimatum.'

'I can?' Torsgen asked, still watching her intently.

'Yes, because last night I closed an important deal for us, and I defended our family name. Thugs don't get to threaten any one of us and get away with it.' Elka took a sip of her coffee, warming to her argument now that she had her brother's attention. 'I've proven that I am a Hagguar, not a Rider, therefore I will be keeping my dragon.'

'I will not take—'

'No, Torsgen listen!' Elka shouted over him. Frannack was watching the two of them, his eyes flicking between them. 'Think what an advantage Inelle gives us. I can be anywhere in the city in minutes. Even your network of runners can't get messages across Taumerg as quickly as I could. And who's going to mess with a family with the only dragon in Taumerg.'

Elka sat back, argument laid out. Frannack pointed his pencil at her and looked to their older brother.

'She's got a point.'

'Frannack stick to solving your spark-damned problem and keep out of this.'

'What problem?' Elka looked at Frannack. 'Is this the same one that you mentioned yesterday?' But he turned away and didn't answer.

Elka brushed her long fringe out of her eyes and watched Torsgen, waiting for his answer about Inelle. Moving annoyingly slowly he poured himself another coffee and settled back in his chair, cup held in both hands. He looked at Frannack then Elka.

'No.'

'What! Torsgen, but—'

He slammed his cup back down on the table. Hot coffee sloshed onto the tablecloth. 'Disobey me one more time, Elka, and the bounty will be on your head as well.'

She opened her mouth to argue but his glare dried up all her words. 'You were a baby so you don't remember what it was like to be destitute, living in the basement of that orphanage, damp crawling up the walls and rats scuttling on the floor. But I do. I remember it every day. Do you think we got from there to here by magic?' He waved at their luxurious dining room. 'We're here because I took every job I could, legal or not, and pulled us out of that hole. Frannack has more than paid me back, he's the cleverest engineer in the city and thanks to him our factories are far more advanced than anyone else's. But you, Elka, I'm not convinced you've proved yourself yet.'

'I have!' she objected.

'You can't take orders. You shirk your duties. I don't—'

'When did I ever shirk my duties?' she yelled.

'When you spent two years messing around down in Kierell.'

'Messing around? You, with your soft-city lifestyle, can't even imagine how hard it was training to become a Rider! My whole body hurt so much! And I spent hours every night searching for Pagrin's bracelet!'

'Stop it! Both of you!' Frannack jumped to his feet, startling them both. Elka had never heard him raise his voice like that. 'Elka has a valid point regarding her dragon. It could be an asset. No, let me finish,' he directed his words at Torsgen as he was about to interrupt. 'Give Elka the Britte job if you feel she needs one last task to prove her allegiance. And call off the Vorjagen for now. If Elka fails, then you can put out the bounty on her dragon's head.'

'What's the Britte job?' Elka demanded, seizing on the chance Frannack was offering.

Torsgen downed the remains of his coffee in one gulp. Then he pulled a folded sheet of paper from his waistcoat pocket. 'The details are on here. Hertham was going to go and do it. He's outside waiting so take him with you.'

Elka reached for the paper but Torsgen held it back. 'You will do this job without taking your dragon. You will prove to me that creature isn't a crutch you're leaning on.'

Elka snatched the paper and held her brother's cold

stare. 'Fine.'

She mouthed a 'thank you' at Frannack as she left the table but he already had his nose stuck back in his notebook. Out in the hallway, Hertham was sitting on a bench by the door. He was another of the men Elka had grown up seeing around but had never really known what his job was. But he'd always been kind to her, sneaking her sweeties when Torsgen wasn't looking. She hadn't seen him since she'd returned to Taumerg.

'Hert, how's things?'

'Well, look who it is, little Elka.'

He'd called her that even after she put on a growth spurt at thirteen and grew taller than him. Just like no time had passed he took a paper bag of boiled sweets from his pocket and held it out. Smiling, Elka took a mint one.

'I've had no one to share these with for two years. Had to eat them all myself and I swear my teeth are going to fall out now. That's your fault.' He gave her a wink and she laughed. 'You accompanying me to see Britte?'

Elka waved the folded piece of paper. 'I'm the one with the instructions, so you're accompanying me.'

Hertham smiled. 'Lead on.'

Outside the rain had cleared up, leaving the air fresh and chilly. Inelle was perched on the roof of their townhouse and Elka had to crane her neck back to see her. Her dragon clung awkwardly to the roof's peak, one wing and her long neck wrapped around the chimney. She'd taken to doing that, pressing herself against the warm bricks of the chimney. Back home she'd have slept in the Heart, the cavern warmed by the heat of other dragons.

'He's pretty impressive,' Hertham said, nodding up at Inelle.

'She,' Elka corrected.

'Torsgen letting you keep her then?'

Elka frowned. Did everyone in Taumerg know she'd been ordered to get rid of her dragon?

'Come on, there's work to be done.' Elka waved Torsgen's note at him and turned away from Inelle. It felt like leaving a part of herself behind and she imagined their connection unspooling between them like ribbon from a bobbin. Hertham offered her another sweet but Elka was still sucking her mint. They reached the end of their street and stopped.

'You know the way to Britte's place, yeah?' Hertham asked.

Elka didn't want to admit that actually she had no idea who Britte was. 'Remind me,' she replied. 'I've been away from the city for a while.'

Hertham gave a chuckle and waved for her to follow him northwards. Elka tried to think of a subtle way to ask what they were doing but eventually gave up.

'So who's Britte and why are we going to see her?' she asked.

'Britte's a puffer, and a good one from what I hear.' Hertham's words had to squeeze their way out around another boiled sweet. 'She lives in one of the tenements up near the Ultrich pottery factory.'

'Okay, great. So why are we visiting her?'

Hertham nodded to the paper in her hand. 'That's what your note will tell us.'

Elka unfolded it as they walked. There were three things written on it in Torsgen's slanted handwriting. Britte's name, her address and the words 'right hand'. Confused, Elka showed the note to Hertham.

'Ah, makes sense.'

'Does it?'

'Yeah, I heard Frannack and Mila talking about this. Apparently Britte broke her contract, took a job working for someone else when your brothers had employed her exclusively.'

'So?'

'This is her punishment. Torsgen obviously thinks she could be useful in the future or he'd have us break her legs too.'

Elka stopped walking. 'What *are* you going to break?'

Hertham realised she wasn't beside him and turned back, pointing at the note she still held. 'Just her right hand.'

'Just her…'

Elka couldn't finish the sentence, it was too horrible. They were going to go break some steam engineer's hand because she'd taken a contract working for someone else. She felt the imagined ribbon, tying her to Inelle, pulling at her. She wanted to go back. To climb into her saddle and do nothing today but swoop over the city. Maybe fly out to the hills around Vorthens.

'Hert, what if Britte reports us to the Zachen Guards?'

Hertham's sweetie rattled against his teeth as he chuckled. 'No one would be stupid enough to rat a Hagguar out to the guards. Come on.'

A year of training to become a Rider and at the completion of it she'd sworn to protect people. And here she was off to help break someone's hand.

But she wasn't a Rider anymore and could never go back to being one. She'd well and truly burnt that bridge till it was nothing but ashes. This is who she was now, a Hagguar. It was what she'd chosen and it was her last chance to prove herself to Torsgen. If she did this, Inelle would be safe. And people recovered from broken hands, right?

Elka forced herself to keep walking, even though it felt like she had heavy stones in her boots. Hertham clapped her on the shoulder and said something that didn't register. The streets around them grew narrower, the buildings shabbier as they entered the area of the city where most workers lived.

Elka's steps began to slow, her conscience dragging her to a halt. She was desperately trying to think of some lie she could tell Hertham that would sound convincing when she heard a commotion from an alleyway. Someone was shouting, their words slurred. She slipped a hand to her thigh, fingering her throwing knives. Three men stumbled from the alley, two of them propping up the one in the middle. It was the middle one who was shouting, words and gestures slack with drink. He was young, Elka's age, but his clothes were dirty, his hair all sticking up. Out of work and down on his luck maybe. The man on the left sank a punch into the boy's belly and he doubled over, coughing watery sick down his front.

'Alright Hert?' the man on the right said as he spotted them.

'You got another one for us?' Hertham asked, nodding to the drunk boy.

'Yeah, so best get him away before he drowns his spark in gin. We need them full, don't we? Nice to see you, Hert.'

Elka watched, very confused, as the two men dragged the drunk boy away. 'They've got another what?' she asked Hertham.

'Hmm, I thought Torsgen would have told you.' He looked at her thoughtfully then shrugged. 'Ah well, in that case it's nothing for you to worry about.'

'Told me what?' Elka demanded but Hertham had started walking again. 'Hert! What's going on?'

'Come on, we've got an appointment with a puffer and a hammer.'

Hertham kept walking, waving for her to follow. Elka ran to catch up with him and grabbed his arm, pulling him to a stop.

'I'm a member of the Ragel now so that means you take orders from me as well as my brother. And I order you to tell me where they were taking him.'

'Listen, girl, there—'

'Don't call me girl. I have a name, and it's Elka

Hagguar, emphasis on the Hagguar.'

Hertham sighed. 'Pardon me then. But your brother's plans are not mine to share. You'll need to ask him if you want the particulars.'

'I will,' Elka vowed. It was going to be the first thing she did when she got back home. A thought suddenly occurred to her. 'Does this have something to do with all the missing people posters?'

'Posters?' Hertham had started walking again and Elka found herself following him.

'Yeah, I keep seeing posters for missing teenagers and well… I dunno.' Her words petered out because she wasn't sure where her thoughts were taking her. She remembered Daan insisting that Jennta had disappeared too. Was any of this connected?

'Sweetie?' Hertham offered as they turned onto a cobbled lane between rows of high tenements.

Elka shook her head, still distracted by her fragmented thoughts. But they scattered the moment Inelle sent her a warning. She felt it as a rapid pulse along their connection. Every instinct in Inelle had just gone on high alert. Elka dropped to a crouch, one hand on her knives, the other on the hilt of her scimitar, eyes wide as she looked for the danger.

'What is it, Inelle?' she whispered. 'What have you seen?'

She could sense Inelle was still perched on the roof of her house. The impulse to run back to her dragon was so strong that her whole body quivered.

Then she heard the worst possible sound she could

hear.

Wingbeats. Dragon's wingbeats.

They echoed down into the narrow street and Elka tilted her head back in time to see the shadows of three dragons pass overhead.

'No, please no.'

In her heart she knew who it would be but she had to check. Ignoring Hertham's shouts she sprang at the wall of the nearest tenement. A jumble of pipes snaked up the brick and Elka climbed them easily. Maintenance valves made ideal handholds and though some of the pipes were scalding hot she hardly noticed. In a few minutes she was level with the top floor. A pulley jutted out from the building's eaves, used normally to hoist work crews up the building if pipes needed fixing. Elka used it to climb up onto the roof.

She flattened herself to the tiles and peered over the peak. Looking south, back the way she'd walked, she saw Inelle still perched on her rooftop. Clouds hung over the city, mingling with the smoke from chimneys. Elka scanned the skyline, hoping against reason that she'd imagined the dragons. But then she saw them.

Three dragons emerged from the clouds to the west above where the Amms Canal cut through the city.

'*Mi sparken!*' Elka swore.

She watched as the Riders flew across the city, their dragons' wings swirling the clouds. For a moment her chest felt so tight that she couldn't breathe, like her spark was draining away. Aimee and the others had obviously spotted Inelle but they had no idea where she was. Elka heard her dragon call out to Jess as she flew a wide circle around Elka's house. Elka felt like her heart might break because her dragon had called out a greeting. She could feel in their connection that Inelle was delighted to be reunited with the others in her clutch. Inelle didn't know, she couldn't understand.

Elka had to get rid of the Riders before Torsgen learned they were here. She lowered herself off the roof and climbed back down the pipes quicker than she'd gone up, adrenaline flushing through her veins. She jumped the last few feet, landing in a crouch on the street. As she straightened Hertham grabbed her arm.

'Elka, who are they?' He pointed at the sky.

'I don't know,' she lied. 'They must be here on some diplomatic mission. Maybe just stopping off on their way to Soramerg.'

She knew it sounded flimsy and Hertham's raised eyebrow told her he didn't believe a word of it.

'Look, please can you go and deal with Britte and I'll sort the Riders.'

'What's to sort if they're nothing to do with you?'

Elka ground her teeth in exasperation. 'I just need to gather some info, so please, handle the job and I'll meet you back at home.'

Hertham scrutinised her for a moment longer before nodding. As he turned away Elka called to him.

'And don't mention any of this to Torsgen.'

'You know I can't do that.'

'Please, for me. Just for now. And when I get my share of the profits from our new mill I'll buy you a sweet shop and you can retire and work there till all your teeth fall out.' She forced herself to smile at him.

And it worked. He gave her a wink like he'd done when she was a little girl and headed off down the street. Elka ran. It felt like her mind was on fire, thoughts tearing through as she desperately tried to work out how to get out of this mess. She splashed through puddles, rainwater spraying up her legs, and reached Ornstraab, a wide open street which followed the Rorg Canal all the way back to her house.

She realised her mistake a few seconds later.

Taumerg was a noisy city. The machines in the factories whirred and clunked all day and night. Workers shouted to each other on the dozens of barges on every canal. Steam hissed from the network of pipes that covered every building. Steam-powered carriages rattled on the cobblestones. But above it all Elka heard the roar of an angry dragon and knew she'd been spotted.

CHAPTER 20

CAN'T RUN FOREVER

The sky above the canal filled with blazing orange wings as Malgerus swept down towards them. All along the street people screamed and ran for cover. Elka caught a flash of Nathine's face and saw nothing but pure hatred. Malgerus's huge wings almost touched the buildings on each side as he dived at her, teeth and talons ripping the air.

'Shit!'

Elka dropped to the cobbles but that wouldn't be enough. He'd snatch her up like a hare. Wind blasted her face as Malgerus closed in on her. Wincing at how badly this was going to ruin her clothes, Elka rolled to the side and dropped off the edge of the street. She hit the cold water of the canal and sank. Pressing herself against the slimy stones lining the wall, she counted to thirty before she risked sticking her head up. Malgerus was back in the high sky. But Jess and Skydance were skimming the street's rooftops.

'Hey, miss!'

The shout came from a barge behind her but Elka ignored it. Taking a deep breath, she dived back under and swam through the murky water. A shadow loomed towards her. Panicking, she kicked, diving deeper as a barge touched against the canal's side. She only just avoided being crushed by it. Breaking the surface she gasped for air. Another barge was chugging towards her, its occupants all shouting at her. She couldn't stay in here. She'd either be pulped by a barge or the shouting would draw Nathine's attention.

She hooked her elbows up onto the street and heaved herself out of the water. Her clothes reeked of stagnant water and engine oil. The street that had emptied as Malgerus swept down it was now filled with people, jostling and pointing upwards. Elka forced her way through them, catching an elbow to the side of her head as one man jabbed excitedly at the sky. The buzz rose around her like a kettle coming to the boil and Elka knew the dragons were flying back for another pass.

'Move, move!' she yelled, shoving her way through.

She felt the air swirl and heard the flap of wings. Riders were under oath never to harm a civilian but Nathine had looked so pissed that Elka half expected she'd let Malgerus tear the crowd apart to get to her. She sprinted down a side street, too narrow for wings. The townhouses crowded her and she couldn't see Inelle but she could hear her roaring.

'Stay, I'm coming!' she yelled the command to her dragon.

She ran down the street, careened off the wall at the

bottom and turned into a narrow alley. It ran along the back of her street. Ahead she could see her house and Inelle on the roof. It felt like the ribbon between them was being wound back in by an out-of-control spooler. She told herself everything would somehow be alright if she could just get back to Inelle.

Elka kicked open the gate to her back garden and sprinted across it. She'd drank two cups of strong snathforg brew this morning but she hadn't expected to be climbing buildings. The ache in her ribs pulsed down her whole side and Elka wished she'd had three cups. She leapt at the wall of her house. Ida was on the back steps, washer bucket in her hand and she gaped as Elka began to climb. Hand over hand, up she went, using the pipes and valves. The scrape of talons filled her ears as Inelle scrabbled at the roof, desperate to take off.

'Wait,' Elka ordered her, bracing a foot on a windowsill and pushing herself up to the third floor.

She felt so exposed that her back tingled, expecting at any moment to feel Malgerus's talons sinking into her.

'Ah!' she hissed as hot steam rushed through the pipe she was holding, scalding her hand.

Another couple of minutes of climbing and she was pulling herself up onto the steep slope of the roof. Inelle was on the roof's peak, wings open fully, ruff of feathers all standing on end, roaring into the sky. But she wasn't roaring to scare off the other dragons, she was roaring to greet them. Elka could feel Inelle's excitement at being reunited. She longed to fly with her clutchmates again.

'They're not our clutch anymore,' Elka tried telling her dragon.

Balanced precariously on the rooftop, she followed Inelle's intent gaze. Jess, Skydance and Malgerus were flying in a wide circle around Inelle, waiting. Orange wings cut across the sky and Elka heard Nathine yell. She'd been spotted. A second later Malgerus was diving at her, talons outstretched. Elka dropped to a couch, gripping the peak of the roof with one hand and Inelle's back leg with the other. Inelle rumbled a confused growl as Malgerus cut through the air just above them.

Before Nathine had time to turn her dragon for another pass Elka sprang up, grabbed her saddle and threw a leg over.

'Go!' she yelled.

Inelle launched from the roof and into the sky, her long powerful wings quickly carrying them high. Elka pushed her fringe from her eyes and wished she still had her flying goggles. The rain had started again. She looked down through it and saw the three dragons converge then climb up into the sky after her. Elka didn't wait for them to catch her. She squeezed Inelle's ribs with both knees and pushed on her spiralled horns. Her dragon shot through the sky, wingbeats sending raindrops flying in all directions.

Elka glanced behind and saw the others give chase. She had to find a way to lose them. Malgerus and Skydance were both larger than Inelle and they'd catch her in the open sky. But Elka and Inelle knew the city, its twists and turns, the routes through the rooftops.

They could lose them there.

Elka guided Inelle into a dive. Her dragon tucked in her wings, stretched out her neck and shot towards the city. Rain battered Elka's face as they dived at a diagonal back down towards the Rorg Canal. Adrenaline tingled in Elka's body. As Inelle opened her wings with an audible snap, stopping their dive and gliding over the rooftops, Elka was thankful for all the times she'd practised flying really fast. A quick glance over her shoulder showed that she'd taken the Riders by surprise and they were only now dipping into their own dives to come after her.

She and Inelle followed the rooftops heading west, skimming over tiled peaks and swerving around chimneys. They moved as one, Elka shifting her weight exactly as she needed to, and Inelle obeying her commands as soon as Elka thought them. It felt incredible to be so in tune. She tried not to think about the fact that it had been Aimee who'd first described this feeling to her, back when she was a recruit.

Inelle's confusion at running from other dragons was gone now, replaced by Elka's desperate desire to get away. And in return Elka knew that Inelle would fly until she dropped if it meant keeping her Rider safe.

Where the Rorg Canal intersected with the Njmega Canal Elka and Inelle turned sharply left, wings almost vertical and with one tip trailing in the water. Elka heard the panicked cries of workers on the barges as she and Inelle skimmed their boats. She glanced behind in time to see Malgerus and Skydance shoot past, missing the turn. But emerald-green wings shimmered through the rain as Aimee and Jess cut round above the canal.

'Sparks!' Elka swore and pushed Inelle for more speed.

There was a small courtyard ahead and Elka sent an image of it through her connection to Inelle. At the last moment Inelle tucked her wings and bent her long body. Their momentum carried them into the courtyard. They were flying low and as Inelle flapped again, the wind swirled by her wings buffeted a cafe's empty tables and chairs, scattering them across the cobbles. Inelle grabbed the pipes running up the courtyard's far wall and pressed herself against the building. Elka hung on tight to her horns so she didn't slip backwards out her saddle.

'Shh,' she told her dragon then held her breath.

Had she lost them? Jess hadn't followed them into the courtyard. Voices sounded below and Elka flinched.

'Blazing sparks! What are you doing?'

A couple had emerged from the closed cafe and stared in disbelief at their scattered tables and the dragon clinging to their wall. Elka ignored them.

'Got her! There!'

The cry came from above. Blinking in the rain Elka looked up to the square of grey sky and saw three winged shadows.

'Damn it!' she yelled and Inelle pushed away from the wall. 'Blast through them!' she ordered her dragon.

Inelle's rapid wingbeats took them shooting up out of the courtyard like the bullet from a clockwork pistol.

Elka pulled a throwing knife from the garter on her thigh. The Riders swore in various languages as Inelle burst into the sky, forcing them to scatter. As she shot past them Elka threw her knife at Nathine. It went wide, slicing the air above Nathine's left shoulder.

Elka and Inelle were engulfed in a low raincloud, the world becoming soft and grey around them. Pulling her horns and guiding with her knees, Elka steered Inelle out of her upwards dive and they levelled off, high above the city. Elka shoved her wet fringe from her eyes with the back of her arm. Rain droplets ran in sparkling rivulets down Inelle's indigo scales. She pulled another knife free. They couldn't hide in a cloud forever. Ideas for escape spun through her mind like the hundreds of threads in one of Frannack's looms. But none of them were any good and they all tangled together.

The cloud around them became wispy and a moment later she and Inelle emerged back into the open sky.

'There!'

The shout came from her left and Elka yelled in frustration. The Riders raced towards her in an arrow-tip formation.

'Up!' Elka ordered.

Inelle flapped desperately, sharing her Rider's panic. They climbed higher in the sky until Elka tugged on Inelle's left horn and they swooped that way, gliding above the Riders passing underneath. Elka threw her second dagger, aiming again for Nathine. It bounced off one of Malgerus's horns and pinged away into the sky.

'Elka, stop!'

She recognised Aimee's voice as the Riders turned their dragons, coming after her.

'We only want to talk to you,' Aimee continued.

'Speak for yourself, I'm still going to kill her!' Nathine yelled across the sky.

'Nathine, shut up!' Aimee ordered, but it was no use because out of the two of them, Elka believed Nathine the most.

Despite what Aimee might promise there would be no 'just talking', not after what had happened to Halfen and not after the way she'd left them on the tundra. Nathine would kill her and then Aimee and Pelathina would be forced to slaughter Inelle. Because without a Rider she'd revert to being wild.

But Elka wouldn't let that happen, not to Inelle, the one being in the whole world who loved her without Elka needing to prove anything in return. Even now, Torsgen was still treating her like a nobody, but to Inelle, Elka was everything. There was no way she'd let anyone take that away from her.

She just needed a plan.

'Elka, we only want the bracelet back. Please!'

This time it was Pelathina shouting. Elka glanced over her shoulder and saw they were gaining on her.

'You're lying!' Elka yelled back, switching back to Kierellian without even realising. Because even if she gave them back the bracelet, which she couldn't do, she'd never be a Rider ever again. Not when she'd betrayed them all.

'Traitor! Murderer!'

Nathine was only a few dragon's lengths behind her now, Malgerus's huge wings carrying her ahead of the others. Her accusations cut Elka like claws tearing at her heart. She'd said those things to herself but hearing them out loud from someone else's mouth made it feel so much more real. The haunting image of Halfen's shocked face flashed through her mind again. She wanted to say sorry, to explain again that she hadn't meant it, but there was no way Nathine would give her that chance.

'Nathine, wait!'

Aimee's yell gave Elka the warning she needed. She pushed on Inelle's horns, her dragon tucking into a dive just as Malgerus launched at her. Inelle roared in pain as Malgerus's talons scored the flesh of her tail. Blood splattered Elka's back. But Malgerus's talons had sliced clean though Inelle's scales and hadn't hooked on. They shot back down towards the city as Malgerus and Nathine flew straight ahead. Nathine's curses followed her.

Pain washed through Elka's brain in a red wave as she felt her dragon's injury. 'I'm sorry, Inelle.'

Upturned faces and cries of alarm rushed towards them and Elka pulled on Inelle's horns. Her dragon levelled off above the canal. Elka heard the flap of wings behind and gritted her teeth. She needed to lose them, but how? She wasn't wearing any gloves and her fingers were wet and freezing cold as she gripped Inelle's horns, but she couldn't stop, not for a second.

The streets gave way to the treetops of Rokspaark. Inelle's belly skimmed the autumnal leaves, making them shudder. Her dragon growled, long and low, and Elka knew she'd caught scent of the deer that lived at the back of the park.

'No, Inelle, we're not hunting now,' she told her dragon.

And then the idea sprang into her mind, fully formed. It was awful and brilliant at the same time. Elka didn't take the time to consider it—she didn't want to—she just acted. Steering Inelle across the park, they headed for the line where the cultivated trees turned into the deep tangle of forest at the city's edge.

Inelle wanted to hunt deer in Rokspaark but beyond the park, in that forest, lived others who wanted to hunt. No one went there because everyone knew that's where the Vorjagen had their headquarters. And if Elka couldn't shake the dragons following her, she'd get someone to hunt them for her.

She spotted a long low roof, half concealed by branches, a little way into the forest. The trees crowded right up to the hunting lodge, their branches brushing against the wooden shingled roof. It reminded Elka more of the buildings she'd seen down in Kierell. Dozens of prowler skulls had been nailed to the lodge under its eaves, leering out with their empty eye sockets and teeth-filled jaws.

The reality of what she was about to do pressed up against her. But after Halfen, after the meeting on the tundra, there'd never been a way back to the Riders. All her bridges were burned and their ashes trampled into the mud. And she'd failed Torsgen's test today by leaving Hertham to deal with Britte. She was in danger of losing her seat on the Ragel, of being kicked out of her family. And enemies were lining up to kill Inelle—Torsgen, the Vorjagen, Nathine.

She had no choice. She had to do this or she'd lose everything.

Pushing Inelle's horns she guided her high above the treetops. Looking back across the park, she saw the three dragons closing the distance towards her.

'I'm here!' she yelled, and sharing her desperation, Inelle roared.

Nathine screamed across the sky at her and Elka saw her push Malgerus for more speed. His orange scales blazed in the sunlight.

'No! Nathine, wait!' Aimee shouted from behind.

'Blazing sparks, Aimee! She's right there!' Nathine slid free a scimitar and pointed it at Elka.

'Yes, and she's led us here!'

'I don't care if it's a trap!'

Nathine's voice sent a shiver of fear up Elka's spine. Her words were thick with her rage and grief and right then Elka had no doubt she'd risk death to get revenge for Halfen. If the Vorjagen didn't kill Nathine for her, Elka was going to be hunted for the rest of her life.

'And if I die, then you do too,' she whispered to Inelle. Her dragon twisted around and gave her wrist a gentle bite. Elka stroked her feathers. 'Yes, family. Come on.'

Elka hunched her shoulders and pushed Inelle into a dive. She was taking a huge risk and hoping it would pay off. Wind whipped into her face, making her eyes stream as Inelle shot towards the treetops. At the last second, Inelle opened her wings with a snap and they glided above the trees and out over the roof of the Vorjagen's hunting lodge.

Flinching, Elka waited to hear the shouts. They came moments later—voices scrambling up from the trees and the lodge. Then came the grinding of gears and the clicking of crossbows being wound.

'Dragon!' an excited voice yelled.

'Fly!' Elka screamed at Inelle.

Her dragon pumped her wings, fast as she ever had, and they cleared the lodge in a wide arc, heading back towards the park. Elka shot past the Riders coming the other way to catch her, hearing them swear at her sudden change of direction. Then Aimee, Nathine and Pelathina were above the Vorjagen's lodge and Elka heard the weapons fire.

'Sparks!'

'Aimee! No!'

The Riders screamed behind her. She didn't want to look. But she had to know. Twisting in her saddle Elka watched as dozens of bolts shot from the trees towards the Riders. They scattered, dragons swooping in every direction. Blood was already spurting into the sky from a deep gash along Jess's back leg. Elka heard the grinding of gears and something shot from the roof of the hunting lodge. A net. It ensnared Skydance. He roared, biting at the thick rope even as it crushed his wings.

'Pellie!'

The desperation and fear in Aimee's voice tore right through Elka's heart. She turned away. Her last glimpse of the Riders was of Skydance being dragged from the sky while Aimee screamed and Nathine unsheathed her second scimitar. Elka was responsible but she couldn't face watching their sparks go out. Inelle roared, her neck twisted around to look behind. Elka could feel her desire to fly back and help the dragons she still thought of as part of her clutch.

'We can't. I'm sorry.'

Elka tightened her hold over Inelle and pushed her for more speed. She looked at her hands, gripping Inelle's horns so tight that her knuckles where white knobs. They were wrinkled from the rain but her skin was clean. Only it wasn't. Her hands were covered in blood—first Halfen and now Aimee, Pelathina and Nathine.

CHAPTER 21

TRAITOR

THE WORLD SPAN and Elka retched. Leaning from her saddle she threw up, vomit splattering the trees below. She felt so dizzy she was in danger of slipping from her saddle.

'Inelle, we need to land.'

Her dragon obeyed, swooping down between the trees and into Rokspaark. The moment Inelle's talons sank into the wet grass Elka let herself fall from her saddle. Inelle caught her with her long neck, stopping her from hitting the ground. Elka smelled grass and mud, and tasted sick in the back of her throat.

'Be stronger,' she whispered to herself, voice croaky. 'Be like Torsgen.'

But she was shaking so much she could hardly stand, never mind straighten her spine and put on the cold mask Torsgen wore. It felt like the sky was tugging at her, trying to pull her back into it, urging her to get in her saddle and go rescue Aimee and the others before there was no one left to save.

But she couldn't. This was the path she'd chosen to walk and she had to stick to it, no matter how painful it was.

Instead she looked across the park. The rain had stopped but drips still fell from the trees and ran in rivulets down the windows of the cafe. Daan. This was one of his family's cafes. Was he here today? Elka desperately needed to see a friendly face. With Inelle following she hurried across to the building. The doors and windows were closed against the rain, the metal tables outside all empty. She pressed her face up to the glass and peered inside. Immediately her eyes found him. She banged on the glass, not caring that half the room turned to look, and beckoned to Daan.

With Inelle she headed back under a hoolegode tree, its heart-shaped leaves turned red and gold by autumn. Daan appeared a few minutes later, running across to her. Seeing the warmth of his smile, Elka couldn't hold herself together any longer. She fell to the ground so quickly that this time Inelle didn't catch her. But her dragon dropped beside her and wrapped a wing around her shoulders.

Daan skidded to a halt on the muddy grass and stared down at her.

'I…Elka? Are you…?'

He stuttered then gave up, staring at her with a mix of confusion and fear rumpling his pretty face. Daan's usual repertoire was bad jokes fuelled by too much caffeine and he obviously realised that was going to fail him here.

'I had to,' Elka mumbled before giving in to tears.

'Em...okay.'

Daan stared down at her for a moment longer before rallying himself. He pointed at Inelle. 'Can I hug you without getting my head bitten off? Because I'm quite attached to it.'

Elka nodded, tears dripping from her chin, and told Inelle that Daan was a friend. She snorted a puff of smoke in understanding. Elka saw that Daan's hands were shaking with nerves but he crouched down, then sat in the mud beside her. He took her hand in both of his, wrapping it in his long fingers. His skin was hot against hers.

'Your fingers are freezing. Why are you soaked through?'

Elka shook her head, wondering how to explain to him why she'd dived into a canal.

'What happened?' His voice was soft and he was slowly running a finger across her knuckles, not quite a caress, but almost.

Elka couldn't tell him, shouldn't tell him, but she blurted out everything anyway. Except that her words came out garbled as she sobbed, choked on snot, and wailed. She felt like she was falling apart, a little piece at a time.

'What have I done? Oh sparks, what have I done?' she asked, squeezing Daan's hand.

'Okay, so I didn't get any of that. Elka.' He put a finger under her chin and gently lifted her head. She peered at him through the wet tangles of her long fringe.

'Is it Torsgen? Has he done something?'

Elka's face screwed up. 'No, it was me. I did it all.'

Because I wanted to be like Torsgen, she finished the thought inside her head. And that was still what she wanted, wasn't it? Everything used to be so clear, back before she went to Kierell, before she made the climb. Now she didn't know what she wanted, except to keep Inelle safe.

'Elka, why don't you come and stay with us for a few days,' Daan was saying. 'You can bring her.' He nodded towards Inelle. 'She can perch on our roof.'

His hand had dropped from her chin and rested now on the side of her hip. She liked it there. The subtle pressure of his fingers was comforting.

'I was gone for two years,' she said.

'Yeah, I noticed.'

'Why did you wait? You could easily have found some pretty girl to tell your terrible jokes to.'

His hand tightened gently on her hip. 'Prettier than you?' He leaned in and brushed her long fringe from her eyes. 'Not possible. Elka, I've loved you since we were twelve and I tried to kiss you but you shoved me in the canal.'

Elka had forgotten that but the memory surfaced now, making the corners of her mouth twitch.

When she didn't say anything, Daan kept speaking. 'Whatever it is that Torsgen is making you do it isn't worth it. Your spark is brighter than his, way brighter. And I know he's your big brother but he's... well, you know.'

'Know what?' she demanded.

'Come on, Elka. It's the worst kept secret in Taumerg that your brother rules the criminal underworld.'

'He doesn't.' Elka pulled her hand free of Daan's. 'When he was younger he did some jobs for a few unsavoury people but that was only because he had to. We had nothing and he saved Frannack and me. And yes, now a few people do him favours but he's not some master criminal.'

The look Daan gave her was so full of pity that it sparked anger in her chest. What did he know about her family? The little voice at the back of her mind told her that he was right, and that she knew he was. But if she couldn't be a Rider then she had to be a Hagguar.

'No,' Elka shook her head. 'I have to impress Torsgen. I need to be strong and prove myself to him.'

'Why?'

'It's the only way to keep Inelle safe.'

'Elka, I don't understand.'

'Then you can't help me.'

She uncurled his fingers from her hip and stood, Inelle rising behind her.

'Elka—'

'No. Family is all that matters.'

She turned away but Daan's fingers slipped into hers. The feel of his skin sent tingles up her arm. He pulled her towards him, resting his other hand against the small of her back so gently that Elka wondered if she was imagining his touch. His face was inches away. She let her eyes flutter closed, breathing in the black pepper and oak moss scent he wore. It felt like she could breathe that smell forever and never get enough of it.

'Elka.'

The way he whispered her name made her open her eyes. He was watching her, his gaze gentle but intense. His dark eyes held hers and wouldn't let go.

'Don't let him turn you into one of them,' Daan said, his voice hushed.

Then his lips were on hers, soft, warm and unexpected. His hand on the small of her back gently pulled her closer. She let him, surrendering to the kiss, then throwing herself into it. She wrapped an arm around his waist, her other hand reaching up, running fingers through his tight curls. He moaned and she kissed him deeper. She remembered another kiss two years ago, shared and enjoyed on a barge in the summer sunshine.

But she'd been a different Elka back then. A girl without blood on her hands. And kissing Daan had her longing to be that girl again. She broke the kiss and pushed him away.

'I can't do this.'

She hadn't meant to hurt him but she saw the pain of rejection in his eyes.

'I'm sorry,' she told him. 'Just not right now, okay?'

Daan took her hand again and squeezed. 'Whatever's going on, you don't have to do it. Pick another outfit to wear. You don't have to be a Hagguar.'

'But that's who I am. It's who I've always been.'

She took back her hand and boosted herself in

Inelle's saddle, gritting her teeth against a grinding in her sore ribs. Daan scrambled backwards, barely avoiding being slapped by Inelle's wings.

'I'll be at the Fischer bakery this afternoon if you need me,' he yelled after her.

'I don't,' Elka said softly as Inelle carried her up into the sky. She shouldn't have gone to see Daan. She was being weak and that was the last thing she could afford to be right now.

In the sky above the city she shivered. Her clothes were wet from the canal, right through to her underwear, and the cold wind was pressing them against her body. As she guided her dragon across the Amms Canal and towards the industrial northern sector of the city, she didn't look west towards the Vorjagen's lodge. Her skull tingled, making her want to look around but she resisted. She couldn't hear the flapping of wings other than Inelle's and no shouts had erupted when they lifted into the sky. That meant the Vorjagen had killed the Riders, and their sparks that had been shining bright this morning were now extinguished.

Elka swallowed the lump in her throat and angrily brushed tears from her lashes.

It was done and there was no going back.

They flew high above the city, tearing apart the last of the rain clouds. She needed to think. Torsgen would be angry that she'd lied about dealing with the Riders when she left them on the tundra, and he'd be disappointed that she left Hertham to complete the Britte job. Leading the Riders to the Vorjagen would have bought her a little more grace and proved her dedication to their family. However, Elka thought it would still be best to keep Inelle out of Torsgen's sight for now.

Her mind sifted through ideas for places to hide her dragon. She wanted her close by, because the thought of taking her out of the city and leaving her somewhere was like taking away the vital part that made a machine work.

They reached the River Ireden at the city's northern edge. Below them, flat-bellied barges carried stacks of timber down from Fir du Merg. They shared the river with passenger boats carrying people back and forth between Taumerg and Soramerg. All of the boats were steam-powered and their chimneys pulled lines of smoke along behind them. The docks bustled, the gears of the grabbers hissing and clicking as they unloaded crates from the boats. Elka needed somewhere quiet to hide Inelle but Taumerg was so busy everywhere.

As they flew over the long roofs of the dock's warehouses she checked through her mental notes of every property her family owned. There was an old warehouse, over near the last lock on the Laren Canal, right where it met the river. It had been empty when she left for Kierell. If it still was then it would be the perfect place to hide Inelle. And a spacious warehouse with sunlight streaming in from skylights in the roof would be almost like the Heart.

Elka pushed for speed and Inelle's wingbeats increased. They were past the docks in minutes and the narrow Laren Canal came into view. The street behind the warehouse was empty and they landed there.

'Wait on the roof while I check this out,' Elka ordered and after snorting a puff of smoke in her face Inelle flew up to the roof. Elka felt wary about leaving her in so obvious a place but they were right at the other side of the city from the Vorjagen and she'd only be in the warehouse for a few minutes.

The building's big double doors were scuffed and battered, the green paint peeling away all around the edges. Weeds had grown tall in the cracks by the doors showing they hadn't been opened in a long time. That was good. Less good was the large new-looking padlock securing the main cog that would release the lock. Elka didn't have a key. She tried opening the little door, further along the wall from the main doors, but it was locked too. There was a long, narrow window above the main doors. That would do.

Elka found hand and footholds between the bricks and climbed up to the window. Bracing one foot on the lintel above the doors, she broke the window with her elbow. Glass tinkled on the floor inside. She waited ten breaths to see if anyone appeared and when they didn't she wriggled through. A line of metal shelves made climbing down the other side easier.

As she'd hoped, the warehouse was empty. It housed nothing but rows of bare shelves and a jagged heap of broken crates in the far corner. But there was a line of footprints and drag marks through the dust on the floor. Elka frowned at them. She couldn't leave Inelle here if someone was using it. So she followed the drag marks, her own boots leaving wet footprints. At the far end of the warehouse, where there were no skylights and shadows gathered, a metal staircase led down under the floor.

She remembered now that the warehouse had a basement. They used to keep vats of fabric dye down there. Some colours were sensitive to heat and light, and the basement was always cold and dark. Black paint flaked off the metal steps as Elka crept down, the darkness swallowing her.

At the bottom a short corridor led to a heavy steel door. A row of old-fashioned candles, standing on a shelf, lit the corridor with a flickering yellow light. There was another door to her left and as Elka approached she heard the scape of a chair pushed back. A moment later the door opened and Torsgen stepped out. Elka was surprised to see him here, but when he spotted her, he nodded.

'Good, you got my note. How did it go with Britte?'

Elka was too confused to reply. What note? What was Torsgen doing in an empty warehouse? And what lie could she spin to make her failure to break a puffer's hand sound acceptable? Torsgen didn't wait for an answer, though. Instead he nodded towards the steel door.

'It's time we tested what you brought us.'

Elka watched as he pulled a hexagonal key from the pocket of his silk waistcoat and slotted it into the steel door's mechanism. After a few seconds of grinding gears and a puff of steam, the door swung open. Torsgen's tall body filled the doorway and Elka couldn't see inside to the room beyond, but she could hear the sounds from within. Crying, whimpers of pain and someone begging for water.

'What...?' the question died on her lips as Torsgen stepped into the room, gesturing for her to follow.

She did, and gasped.

'Sparks!' she swore.

There had to be almost one hundred people squeezed into the room. Elka corrected her thoughts—one hundred prisoners. They sat huddled on the dirty floor while men with clockwork pistols stood around the room's edges. The stench hit Elka as she stood beside Torsgen. It was stale sweat and piss, the rusty tang of blood, mouldy clothes and the smell of fear. She saw hollow cheeks and glassy eyes, collarbones showing at necklines. These people looked like they'd been kept in here for weeks and hardly fed.

'Torsgen, what is this? Who are these people?' Elka asked, turning from the fearful faces to look at her brother.

'They are the solution to our problem with the bracelet,' Torsgen replied, watching her out of the corner of his eye. 'They have the bright sparks we need.'

'Bright sparks?'

Then Elka realised that most of the people huddled on the floor were her age, or a handful of years older. There were a few men and women with grey in their hair, but the vast majority were teenagers. People young enough to still have lots of energy in their sparks.

Torsgen took a book with a green cover from his

pocket and Elka recognised Callant's *Saviour of Kierell.*

'Is that mine?' she demanded.

'Ida found it in a search of your room.'

Torsgen opened the book, skimming past the line drawing of Aimee and Jess, and flipped towards the back. Then he pulled something from his pocket—a wide gold cuff. Pagrin's bracelet. Torsgen pushed back the sleeve of his silk shirt and held the bracelet around his wrist.

'Wait, Torsgen, what are you doing?' Elka grabbed his arm. 'You can't put that on. If you've read Callant's book then you know it'll drain your spark and kill you.'

'Only if I don't have any other sparks.'

'But you don't. You're not a Quorelle. Frannack was supposed to be working out a way to use the bracelet without you needing hundreds of sparks.' Elka shook his arm. 'Torsgen, if he hasn't done that yet then you need to wait.'

'Frannack has been working on something else,' Torsgen replied without looking at her. His eyes were still on the bracelet balanced around his wrist.

'But…'

Elka's voice trailed off as she looked back towards the prisoners huddled on the floor. Torsgen's words slotted into place like gears in her mind. He was going to steal their sparks, all of them. And with hundreds of sparks in his blood he could use them to create the Endless Workers Elka had proposed. They wouldn't be Empty Warriors—their purpose wouldn't be to kill people—but every single one of them would be created from the murder of an innocent person.

CHAPTER 22

SPARKS AND PISTOLS

'NO, NO, NO. Torsgen, this is all wrong! This isn't what was supposed to happen.' Elka gasped, tugging on her brother's arm.

But Torsgen ignored her. A plea from the prisoners drew her attention back to them and her eyes caught on a face. She stared hard. It couldn't be, could it? Then the young woman turned to speak to the man beside her and Elka pressed her hands to her lips in shock. It was her old friend, Jennta. Daan had been right; she hadn't moved to Soramerg with her family, she was being held captive by Torsgen. Elka baulked to think how long her friend had been down here, scared and starving.

It was as if Jennta's face had unlocked the crowd for her because now Elka saw them as individuals. They were teenagers just like her, but they wore tattered clothes and had the wary eyes of people living in fear. She remembered Claujar's evasive comments about there being fewer homeless people in the city. That's because they were all here! Rounded up and held captive. A face turned in the crowd and Elka recognised the drunk boy from this morning. This is where he'd been dragged to. And his bright, young spark would be used to create a worker tied forever to Torsgen's will.

Her brother and his criminal network of thugs had been snatching up young people they thought the city wouldn't miss and hiding them here.

'To our new future.'

Torsgen sounded so pleased with himself that it made Elka's skin crawl. Before she could stop him, he snapped the bracelet closed around his wrist. His cry of pain filled the room, echoing off the bare brick walls. He dropped to one knee, clutching his arm. Elka knew from reading Aimee's story that the spike on the bracelet had just pierced his vein, linking the bracelet to her brother's spark. She held her breath as she waited for Torsgen to rise. He did, slowly, his cold stare travelling around the room.

'Sparks,' he breathed. 'Elka, you were right, it works.'

For the first time in her life she wanted to shove his praise away. She tried to imagine what it would be like, suddenly being able to see the sparks of everyone in the room. She reached for her brother but he took one step away from her, turned over the bracelet on his wrist and she saw him flick the dial to *ura*.

'If your book is correct, Elka, then I wouldn't try touching me,' Torsgen warned.

Elka's hands clenched into impotent fists. With the bracelet in *ura* if her skin was touching Torsgen's then he could steal her spark. He could kill her with a touch.

'Let's test this.' Torsgen nodded to one of his men, then towards a skinny boy huddled on the floor gripping his own knees. 'Bring me him.'

'No!' Elka yelled but her cry was lost amongst all the others as the prisoners realised something was happening and it wasn't good.

The thug grabbed the boy, hauling him to his feet, a pistol pressed to his temple. The boy wore the faded boiler suit of a factory worker. Elka stared into his terrified eyes. He was her age. Had his head been full of dreams for his future before he was snatched and dragged here? The thug forced the boy to his knees in front of Torsgen and shoved back one of his sleeves.

'Torsgen!' Elka cried.

'Hold her,' Torsgen ordered without even looking at her.

Before Elka could get a knife out or a scimitar unsheathed, she heard the telltale click of a clockwork pistol and felt the muzzle press against the back of her skull.

'I can pull the trigger quicker than you can draw one of those knives, girl.' A man's voice, right in her ear.

All Elka could do was watch as Torsgen wrapped his fingers around the bare skin of the boy's arm. The boy gasped like a fish out of water and tried to yank away. But Torsgen held on, draining the spark from him. Murdering him.

It seemed to take forever. The other prisoners had no idea what was happening, why the boy looked like he was in so much pain from a simple touch. They watched in horrified silence. Finally, the boy dropped, dead. Torsgen stared down at his own chest. The thugs around the room were all watching him and the looks of respect on their faces turned Elka's stomach.

'Bring me another one,' Torsgen ordered.

Panic swept through the prisoners. They scrambled and shuffled backwards, yelling protests and begging for their lives. The men stepped up, pistols aimed. Torsgen was staring at his wrist, flexing his fingers.

Elka thought of her brother's cold determination and knew he wouldn't stop until he'd drained the spark of every person in the room.

One thug grabbed a girl wearing a tatty coat with dozens of pockets. She was younger than Elka and he threw her at Torsgen. She screamed as he wrapped his hand around her throat, sucking the spark from her.

'Stop it!' Elka yelled.

She was powerless. Worse—she was to blame. The girl dropped to the floor like a broken doll. Dead. And it was Elka's fault. She was dead because of what Elka had done. The boy too. When Torsgen had killed everyone in this room, she'd be just as responsible for their deaths as he was.

And where would it end? What would she do if Torsgen offered her a turn of the bracelet? If he asked her to prove her dedication to the family by stealing sparks.

Suddenly Elka couldn't remember why she had ever wanted to be like Torsgen. Right then she wanted to be like Aimee, who'd held this power to kill and given it up, saving thousands of lives. A memory barged into Elka's mind of standing in the high gallery of Kierell's Council Chamber and swearing an oath to protect people.

She had to stop this.

The thug's pistol was still pressed to her skull, so, very slowly, Elka raised one leg—then stamped the heel of her boot down on the man's foot. She felt the crunch of his toes. He howled in pain and Elka dropped her weight, crouching down. A moment later he fired but the bullet whizzed over her head, biting into the far wall. She spun around as she straightened, filling the gaps between her fingers with her throwing knives.

Her first knife sank into the man's shoulder. He yelped and staggered backwards. Her second knife pierced the meat of his thigh. She was aiming to injure not kill. She'd done enough killing. Another of the thugs fired at her and she ducked, the bullet shooting out the door behind her. Still crouched, she flicked her wrist, sending another knife flying. This one sliced the man's ribs and her second one stuck in his bicep. Blood spurted and he dropped his gun.

She had two knives left.

Torsgen hadn't noticed her fight. He'd grabbed another young man and was lost in the power of the bracelet. Elka didn't stop to think, just flicked her wrist and threw. The blade cut the air between her and Torsgen's back. But at the last moment another of the men shoved his boss aside. Instead of piercing Torsgen the blade sank into the thug's upper arm. Elka swore. Finally Torsgen spun around, the young man hanging limp from his hands.

It was the first time she'd ever seen real surprise on Torsgen's face. She threw her last knife, right at Torsgen's throat. But he dragged up the half-dead boy and it sank into him instead. Elka caught the sound of clicking and spun aside as another bullet whistled past her head. It lodged in the wall, spraying chips of stone. Elka continued her spin, unsheathing her scimitars as she did and came back around to face Torsgen with a blade in each hand.

'Stop!' she ordered her brother.

Torsgen dropped the dead boy and shook his head at Elka. It wasn't anger that clouded his face, it was disappointment. 'I should've known not to waste my time with you. It's clear that you don't have the metal in your spine to take what you want from the world.'

He waved at her clothes, ruined now but they had been expensive, made with the most luxurious fabrics from Hagguar mills. 'You've always just taken what I've provided for you with no idea of its real cost.'

Elka wanted to tear off her coat but it would mean dropping her blades. 'I would rather wear a plain black coat, and own nothing except my dragon, than wear anything else that you've bought with money made from murder!'

Anger flared in Torsgen's eyes, as cold and deadly as ice sheering off a cliff. 'You ungrateful child! You've never understood that building something, being someone, it requires sacrifice.'

Elka squeezed the leather of her hilts and thought of the year she'd spent training to be a Rider. 'You're right, being someone does require sacrifices. Such as keeping running when your legs feel like they're burning, lifting a training blade when your arms feel like they're going to drop off, working hard day after day out in the cold and the rain instead of curling up inside with a coffee. Sacrifices should not be other people's lives!'

Elka sprang at her brother. Three guns fired at once but no bullets bit her flesh. The thugs rushed her before she reached Torsgen. She spun and slashed, keeping them back, using every skill Aimee had taught her. Dancing on the balls of her feet she attacked them one after the other, forcing them to jump back or dodge, stopping them from bringing up their pistols to fire again. She felt her right scimitar slide through the thigh of one and heard his grunt of pain. She swung a high kick at him, knocking his pistol away and hearing it clatter along the floor.

'Dull-sparked turncoat!' someone spat and Elka ducked and rolled on instinct. The bullet tore through her coat hem and into the floor. She heard the clicking of cogs as he wound his pistol to fire again. She leapt and slashed. Her scimitar sliced through his thumb and cut into the wooden grip of his pistol. The thug burbled curses as he dropped his pistol, and his thumb, to the floor.

One man left, and he'd moved back to protect her brother. Torsgen had taken a pistol from the first thug she'd downed and had it aimed right at Elka's heart.

'You won't kill me, I'm family,' Elka said.

Torsgen sneered at her. 'You don't deserve to be a Hagguar.'

'Elka, run!'

The cry came from the crowd of prisoners. Everyone turned to look, everyone except Torsgen. A girl elbowed two other prisoners out of the way. She was all too-thin limbs and boney joints, and her blond hair hung lank around her face, but Elka recognised Jennta.

The pistol in Torsgen's hand clicked as he fired. Right at the same moment as Jennta barrelled into him. Elka flinched, expecting to feel her heart explode as the bullet tore through it. But Jennta had knocked off Torsgen's aim. The bullet still found Elka, though, slicing a line of fire along her left hip. The pain of her torn flesh washed down her leg and she collapsed to one knee. She felt blood soaking into her already damp trousers.

But she couldn't succumb to the pain, she had to get up and save the prisoners. It was what Aimee would have done.

A shadow loomed over her and she heard the grinding gears of a pistol winding up to fire. The edges of her vision had gone black with the pain so she struck out blind, slashing her scimitars in a wide arc. She felt her right blade connect with something and was rewarded by a gasp of pain. A pistol clicked and Elka dived forwards. Pain lashed her injured side like a whip.

As she landed on the floor her left scimitar went

skittering from her hand, spinning away across the stone. Elka rolled over. The thug she'd just wounded was lying right beside her, cursing and clutching his lower leg. Blood gushed from between his fingers. Elka swung up her legs, kicking him in the stomach. He jackknifed and she smashed her heel into his face, feeling his nose crunch. It wasn't very dignified—lying on the floor, kicking someone—but right then Elka didn't care. Aimee would have fought with more style and grace but she wasn't here. She was gone.

'Elka, move!'

Jennta's warning cut through the pain throbbing in Elka's whole left side. She shoved up to her knees and threw herself over the groaning man, hiding herself behind his bulk. Bullets peppered the floor where she'd been. One hit the man and he yelled obscenities. Elka glanced over the hump of his shoulder. Torsgen and two of his thugs stood with pistols smoking in their hands. For a moment, Elka regretted only injuring them.

She had only seconds as they clicked their clockwork pistols, reloading. With one scimitar still in her hand she leapt to her feet and sprinted for the door, her breath coming in ragged gasps. Pistols fired and bullets pinged off the steel door. Elka ducked behind it, safe for the moment. But the prisoners weren't safe. She hadn't saved them.

She peered around the door. Two men were down, groaning on the floor. The one with the broken nose was coughing blood. Of the other two, one stood with Torsgen and the other had turned his pistol on the prisoners. Elka saw Jennta crouched beside her parents and her chest tightened like overwound cogs. Her friend hadn't seen her for two years, but had still saved her life. Twice. Elka had to rescue her.

The pain from the bullet wound on her hip was making it hard to think. Another click and burst of smoke. Elka yelped and ducked back behind the door as Torsgen's bullet ricocheted off the metal.

'You two, stay here and watch them,' Torsgen ordered. 'I'll deal with Elka then return to harvest their sparks.'

She heard the sound of steel on stone and peered around the door to see Torsgen picking up her scimitar. Seeing him hold it felt like a violation. She sucked in enough breath to yell.

'Put it down! You haven't earned the right to touch that blade.'

He raised his pistol and fired. Elka swore and ducked behind the door. Her rescue mission had gone all wrong. She wondered if Aimee had ever felt this useless. But Aimee didn't save the world alone, she had friends to help her. That's what Elka needed.

'Jennta! Hold on, I'll come back for you!'

She hoped her friend heard her. Then she sprinted along the short corridor. Her wounded hip screamed at her and shadows crowded the edge of her eyes.

'Elka!' Torsgen roared behind her and she heard his boots on the stone, chasing her.

Every step of the metal staircase was an agony. She pulled herself up using the handrail, dragging her wounded leg. Another bullet pinged off the metal just as she turned at the top, back into the warehouse. The distance from where she stood to the door looked like a million miles.

The staircase rattled and Torsgen appeared. She didn't give him a chance to fire, attacking with a series of short slashes. He clumsily blocked her blade with the one he'd taken, the ring of steel echoing in the empty warehouse. Elka caught his blade on hers and twisted her wrist. It was a move Pelathina had taught her. The scimitar spun from his fingers and clattered down the staircase. The pang of loss in Elka's chest almost stole her breath. She'd lost her Rider's clothes, her flying goggles and now one of her scimitars.

All she had left of the Rider she'd been was her dragon.

'Inelle!' she yelled. But she was trapped in here and Inelle was alone on the roof.

Facing her brother, she held up her free hand. She could feel blood running down her leg, pooling in her boot and her breaths were ragged in her throat.

'Torsgen wait, I'm sorry I should...' her words fizzled out. She was stalling for time and had been about to feed her brother lies about being overwhelmed by what she'd seen and that she'd been wrong to attack. But she was sick of lying.

Torsgen pointed his gun at her head. He wasn't even out of breath from the fight, the sparks he'd stolen giving him extra strength.

'If I could spin a cog and turn back time I'd go back

to the day you asked to go to Kierell, and this time I'd refuse you permission. And maybe you'd thank me for that too.' Elka could see his knuckle was white on the trigger. 'You've lost yourself, Elka. If I hadn't let you go to that city you would never have forgotten that you are a Hagguar. Because above all else, family is what matters.'

'Yes,' Elka agreed and felt tears in her eyes. 'But family doesn't have to mean the people you're stuck with from birth. I found a different family and they loved and respected me, more than you ever did.'

'What? Those luddites with their dragons?' Torsgen's mouth twisted in a sneer. He stepped forward, pressing the pistol's muzzle to her forehead. 'You're fighting against a pistol with a sword. This,' he pushed the cold metal against her skin, 'represents progress, efficiency, the future. You'd swap that for a backward city that has only just discovered the printing press?'

A memory popped into Elka's head of sitting in Anteill's dining cavern, dragon's breath orbs glowing above her head, eating porridge she'd helped cook and listening to Aimee and Nathine have some ridiculous argument that seemed to mainly involve giggling.

Yes, she'd trade every luxury in her townhouse, every convenience of Taumerg's city life, even her place on the Ragel to be back there with those women.

She threw that sense of longing into her connection with Inelle. The crash of breaking glass drew Torsgen's eyes to the roof and in that moment Elka smacked her knee into his groin, aiming upwards at just the right angle to cause maximum pain. Nathine had taught her that. All the breath went out of Torsgen as he doubled over. Another crash sounded above and Elka wrapped her arms over her head as broken glass rained into the warehouse.

'Inelle!' Elka yelled in delight as her dragon swooped through the skylight she'd smashed open with her tail.

CHAPTER 23

SOMEBODY

INELLE'S ROAR BOUNCED off the warehouse walls. She flew towards Elka then twisted aside at the last moment. One of Torsgen's men had appeared at the top of the stairs and he fired at Inelle. She dodged and roared. Fear for her dragon flushed ice cold through Elka's veins. The thug fired again and this time the bullet tore a hole in the membrane of Inelle's wing. Elka screamed as she shared her dragon's pain.

'Go!' she yelled to Inelle, ordering her dragon to leave.

But her dragon wouldn't leave without her Rider. In that moment Elka truly understood what it meant for someone to have her back. A warm flush of gratitude swept through her.

Torsgen's man fired a third time. Elka felt her dragon's intent and realised she was about to let loose a blast of dragon's breath. Elka wouldn't care if the thug got incinerated but she couldn't risk a fire tearing through the warehouse. Not when the prisoners were still trapped below.

'No!' she ordered Inelle and felt her dragon's confusion. She was only trying to protect her Rider. Elka had to get her out of here.

Torsgen staggered upright. Elka had dismissed him since she'd disarmed him, but he still had a weapon. He lunged for her, arm outstretched. Elka only just managed to jump aside, avoiding his grip. If he grabbed her he'd suck the spark right out of her. Something jangled on the floor and Elka saw the hexagonal key had fallen from Torsgen's pocket. Thinking it might thwart Torsgen in some way she snatched it up. Then Elka held Torsgen back with her blade, the tip pressing lightly against his chest.

'Go on then,' Torsgen dared her.

His face was still an impassive mask, cold as always, but there was a hunger in his eyes that hadn't been there before. All Elka had to do was push and her scimitar would pierce his heart. But he was her brother. He'd raised her, given her a life after their parents died. He'd pulled them all up out of poverty. And Elka didn't want more blood on her hands.

Over Torsgen's shoulder she saw Inelle dive at the thug. He dropped back down the stairs and Inelle's talons screeched on the metal handrail as she skimmed overhead.

'Stupid creature!' the man yelled and fired again.

'No!' Elka cried as his bullet scored the muscle of Inelle's back leg. She roared and Elka swore the beams of the warehouse shuddered. Inelle flew towards the broken skylight, blood dripping from her leg, but she turned at the last moment, swooping down towards Elka. Even injured she wouldn't leave her Rider.

Despite her pain Elka smiled. That was family.

She landed behind Elka, wings outstretched to their fullest and roared at the two men. Biting her lip against the oncoming pain, Elka turned and ran towards her dragon. She felt fresh blood trickle down her leg as she boosted herself into her saddle. Torsgen had tried to follow her but Inelle lowered her head and breathed a small burst of flames. The fire swirled in the air, forcing her brother back.

Inelle took off, her wings swirling up a storm of dust in the warehouse. She shot back through the hole she'd smashed in the roof. The disappointment in Torsgen's eyes followed Elka into the sky. Above the city she could feel Inelle's relief at being free of the men with pistols but also her hurt. Guilt at leaving the prisoners behind needled her gut but Elka couldn't save them alone.

She remembered Daan saying he'd be at the bakery this afternoon if she needed him. She spotted its roof a few minutes later, a graceful curve of glass and metal with cast iron chimneys like a spiky spine along its length. Inelle landed in the large cobbled courtyard where wagons delivered supplies. A warm orange glow came from a set of wide-open double doors and Elka's nose filled with the smell of fresh bread and cinnamon.

Inelle growled in pain. Feeling her dragon's hurt intensified her own and suddenly Elka's mind was awash with it. She bent over in her saddle, resting her head against Inelle's spiralled horns. Her hands were dangling down either side of Inelle's shoulders. Her dragon twisted her long neck and gently clasped her teeth around Elka's left wrist. Elka felt the heat from Inelle's fire and her nose filled with her dragon's familiar smokey smell.

Inelle tugged carefully but instantly on her wrist. It was her way of reminding Elka that they were family. And she was right, they were. Elka had gone to Kierell to steal a bracelet. She hadn't gone looking for friends, or a real family who would love her whether she proved herself to them or not. But that's what she'd found. And then she'd torn it all up. Tears ran from her eyes, dripping off her chin and splashing on Inelle's indigo scales.

She'd only ever been a pawn to Torsgen. As a child she'd been kept in the background till he could see if she was of any use to him and the criminal empire he was building. In her early teens he'd decided her role—to be a hostess, smile sweetly and keep her head out of their business. After returning from Kierell with Pagrin's bracelet she thought she'd finally won Torsgen's approval. She'd been given a place on the Ragel after all. But it wasn't enough. To truly earn her place she'd have to become as cruel and heartless as he was.

The blood of Halfen already coated her hands and it would never come off. She'd extinguished his spark and she'd need to live with that. Now Torsgen was going to steal the sparks from dozens of people. Teenagers that he'd decided should be sacrificed so he could become more powerful. And she'd given him the means to do it.

Inelle pressed down on her wrist, more insistent, not quite breaking the skin.

'I know,' Elka sobbed. 'You've been telling me for a year and I haven't been listening. We're family and *we* are what matters. And we had a clutch that we belonged to, one that loved us, and I ripped us away from them.'

Elka tugged her wrist free and stroked the smooth scales of her dragon's head. Footsteps battered the cobbles as Daan came running towards them. He skidded to a halt out of range of Inelle's teeth.

'I know, I can't stand to be away from my glowing company for long either,' he joked. Then he squinted, suddenly catching sight of the state they were in.

Elka lowered herself from her saddle and tried to walk towards him but her hip was on fire and her leg buckled. She fell to the ground, and a moment later Daan's arms were around her. He smelled of pastry and vanilla.

'Hey,' he said softly.

'I wanted so badly to be someone,' Elka told him, words pouring out like a burst dam. 'I wanted to be noticed, and valued, and listened to. I wanted to be crucial and to take up space, not fade into the background while other people did all the important stuff.'

'You can be all those things without being a criminal,' Daan told her. 'And if it makes you feel better, I always noticed you.'

Elka shook her head. 'Is this the part where you belittle me up by telling me that you'd like me even if I was always Elka the nobody.'

'Sparks no!'

Daan genuinely sounded insulted and Elka turned to look at him in surprise.

'I always liked you *because* you wanted those things. I admire you *because* you're ambitious.'

Elka felt tears prickle her eyes. 'Back in Kierell people would nod and smile at me. Little gestures that meant they were thanking me for being a Rider and for protecting them. And the council, Daan, they'd ask my opinion on important things that were shaping the city's future. And Aimee, she...' Elka's words caught on the lump in her throat.

'Elka, what's—'

'No, shut up,' she ordered. 'Aimee would pull me into every conversation because I was part of their group. I was their friend, their family.'

Daan pulled her into a tighter hug and the movement jarred the wound on her hip. Pain flickered black at the edge of her vision but it was nothing compared to the agony in her heart.

She felt Daan go completely rigid as Inelle lowered herself to the cobbles.

'It's okay, she won't hurt you,' Elka promised.

'I don't care. I'd always risk getting my head bitten off to give you a hug.'

Inelle pressed her snout against Elka's thigh and she stroked the smooth scales of her dragon's head.

'Oh Inelle, what did I do?' Her words came out as a wail. 'I...they...I can't...'

'Oh, hey.' Daan's words were soft as a blanket.

'I've screwed everything up.'

Then her words were lost in a torrent of tears and snot. Inelle nuzzled against her, the ruff of feathers around her neck quivering with her anxiety.

'Elka!' The panic in Daan's voice pulled her out of her sobs. He was holding up his hand and it was wet with her blood. 'Oh that's not good. Let me see. What can I do?'

As if mention of it had reactivated it, the bullet wound in her hip began to throb. Elka ground her teeth against the pain but Inelle felt it along with her and her dragon rumbled a low growl. Daan flinched, scooting back from her as Inelle nudged aside Elka's coat and licked her wound. Her dragon's rough tongue sanded her skin but her saliva was cooling and the pain began to ease.

'What the blazing sparks is she doing?' Daan gasped.

Elka winced before answering. 'Dragon's saliva has healing properties. But ah, sparks! Bullet wounds really hurt.'

'Yeah, I could have told you that and I've never been shot. Who shot you?' Daan's eyebrows had risen so high they almost disappeared into his curly hair.

'Torsgen.' Elka shoved the name out between clenched teeth.

Daan's eyes narrowed but he didn't say anything. Instead he jumped to his feet and ran back into the bakery. Elka felt a pang, thinking he'd abandoned her until he came running back out with a leather case in his hands. He turned the clockwork lock and it popped open. Bandages and bottles.

'The bakery has this in case of accidents and burns. Will you let me patch you up properly?'

Elka nodded, grateful that she wasn't going to have to dress her own wound.

'Okay, enough.' She gently pushed Inelle's head away. Wincing at every movement, she peeled off her coat. It lay in a soggy heap on the ground, stained with canal water and blood.

'It used to be my favourite.' Elka mourned it.

'That's what you're worrying about right now?'

'Yes, everything else is too scary to think about.'

She leaned back on her elbows and let Daan pull aside her shirt and the top of her trousers. Back before she'd left Taumerg she used to dream of Daan undressing her, but her fantasies were way more romantic than this. And they didn't involve her being wounded. She glanced down, saw a deep gash in the flesh above her hipbone and tasted sick in the back of her throat. Pelathina had taught her about field dressings for wounds but she'd honestly hoped to never use those skills.

She felt Daan's fingertips pressing at her torn and bloody flesh, bits that should have been on the inside now open to the air.

'Daan, I—' was all she managed before she twisted her head to the side and threw up. Vomit splattered the cobbles. Inelle looked up from licking her own wound and Elka felt her rueful reproach in her mind.

'Yeah well, we can't all be as stoic as you,' she told her dragon and received a wave of love in return.

'Huh?' Daan didn't look up from applying the bandage.

'I was talking to my dragon, not you.'

'Oh sure. That might take some getting used to.'

'What were you doing at the bakery?' Elka asked to take her mind off the pain and the sour taste of sick in her mouth. 'Checking up on your family's orders?'

Daan shook his head, curls bouncing. 'Nah, we trust the Fischers to get our orders right. I just like baking.'

'Baking?'

'Yeah, you know where you take flour, yeast, sugar, maybe eggs and turn it into something delicious.'

'You like doing it?'

Daan tied off the bandage and looked up. The smile on his face warmed Elka's heart. 'I love it. There was one day when I shaped the pastries into something rude and managed to bake half the batch before Fischer caught me.'

'What shape did you make them?'

Daan looked down at his groin then grinned.

'No!' Elka laughed.

'I think I'd like to have my own bakery one day,' Daan admitted.

Elka realised then that, since forever, she'd been so obsessed with carving out her own future that she'd never stopped to ask any of her friends what they wanted for theirs. The image of Daan in his own bakery, flour dusting his hands, slotted together perfectly in her mind. Then when her mind panned out from that image she saw that his bakery wasn't squeezed into one of Taumerg's narrow streets, it was facing a wide thoroughfare in Kierell. And when she imagined walking in, she had Aimee and the others with her, with Nathine buying three of everything and Daan smiling at them all.

Her tears came back with a vengeance. It felt like her sorrow was pushing her through a mangle, squeezing everything out. Her chest hurt and her throat was raw. Daan sat cross-legged on the cobbles beside her and held one of her hands in both of his, like he'd done earlier.

'Tell me what you did that's making you so upset.'

Elka gasped for breath then choked on snot. 'Everything.'

She told him, about becoming a Rider to steal Pagrin's bracelet, about how she betrayed the Riders by bringing the bracelet back to Taumerg, how she gave the bracelet to Torsgen and what he was using it for. She told him about the prisoners locked under the old warehouse, about Jennta, and how they were all going to die. She admitted that she'd caused Halfen's death and now he'd never get to read the book Aimee had loaned him. And finally she told him about what she'd done to the Riders, how she'd led Aimee, Nathine and Pelathina to their deaths.

As she spoke she could feel Daan's rising horror in the way he became more and more tense. When she'd finished, she fully expected him to stand up and walk away. But he didn't.

'You have to stop him,' Daan said. The horror was there in his voice but it wasn't directed at her.

'Torsgen?'

'Yes, he...sparks!' Daan squeezed her hand. 'He can't get away with murdering people, stealing their sparks and using them to make slaves. And he won't stop at making workers for one mill. How many hundreds of people will he kill to keep building the Hagguar empire?'

'I know! I tried to stop him but Inelle and I both got shot. We're going to need help, Daan, we can't do this alone. Torsgen has dozens of thugs who have no doubt been ordered to shoot me on sight, and he's now a weapon himself. All he'd need to do is touch one of us and he'd steal our spark.'

'Can you report him to the Zachen Guards?'

Elka snorted. 'Torsgen's paid off most of the guards. They look the other way in return for Hagguar galders.'

'What can I do?' Daan asked.

Elka shook her head. 'I don't know. I don't even know what I can do but this is all my fault so I have to find a way to fix it.'

She thought back to reading the *Saviour of Kierell*. Aimee always had a plan. Elka realised then that she'd lived her life being a follower, not a leader. She'd let Torsgen steer her life wherever he wanted. It was time she found her own path.

Tears threatened again as she thought of Aimee and she tilted her head back to stop them from falling. And saw smoke in the sky. Not the usual smog from the city's factories, but a wide plume from somewhere south-west.

'It can't be.' Elka stood, winced, wavered as her vision went black then cleared.

'What?'

'That fire.' She pointed at the sky then clambered painfully into her saddle.

'Should you be flying? I only just patched you up.'

'I need to see,' she called down as Inelle took off. Daan held a hand over his face against the wind from her wings.

They rose above the walls of the bakery.

'Yes!' Elka yelled.

The smoke was coming from beyond Rokspaark, and there was nothing out there except the Vorjagen lodge. And if it was burning, then the Riders had fought back. And maybe they'd won. Maybe they were still alive.

CHAPTER 24

BURNT BRIDGES

'Elka!'

She looked down into Daan's upturned face and hoped it wasn't the last time she'd see it. Because if the Riders were still alive then they'd want to capture or kill her, so going to find them was a huge risk. She regretted now not kissing him before she'd mounted up but there was no time to fly back down.

'I'll kiss you later,' she yelled the promise at him.

Inelle shot across the sky, long wings eating up the distance to Rokspaark. The grey smoke rising from the Vorjagen hunting lodge was thick and billowy. As they skimmed the treetops of the park the acrid stench of it caught in Elka's throat. She and Inelle circled the plume three times but couldn't see anyone moving below. The peaked roof of the lodge was gone, and there was nothing left of the walls but blackened timbers spearing the sky. Inside the empty shell of the lodge, flames still crackled. The shimmering heat in the air was intense. Only dragon's breath could burn a building down that quickly.

Still no one moved below.

Even though they might kill her on sight, Elka hoped with all her spark that Aimee and the others were still alive. She pushed Inelle into a dive. Her dragon tucked her wings and slipped between the trees. They'd been burnt back beside the lodge, leaving space for Inelle to land. Ashes swirled in the air and sweat beaded Elka's forehead. She lowered herself painfully from her saddle.

From the smoke at the side of the ruined lodge three dark shapes materialised. Elka held her breath. The figures wore long black coats and carried bloodied scimitars. Riders. Elka let out her breath in a whoosh of relief. Then she stepped towards them, holding up her empty hands. Spotting her the three Riders raised their blades.

'Don't kill me,' Elka said quickly, switching to Kierellian. Speaking the Rider's language again made her feel, for the briefest of moments, like one of them.

Nathine spat a stream of curses at her, calling her names far more vile than traitor. Elka didn't move when Nathine pressed the tip of her blade to her chest. The Rider's face was smeared with soot and the ends of her ponytail were singed. Elka looked beyond Nathine's anger to the two others standing behind her, their bloodied blades held ready. Their faces were just as hard. Aimee's wide eyes were swimming with pain and Pelathina's were full of accusations. A streak of blood marred the colourless half of Aimee's face.

Elka took a deep breath. 'I need your help.'

The pressure on Nathine's scimitar increased and Elka felt a trickle of blood run down between her breasts. Still she didn't move. The time for running had passed. It felt good, to have finally chosen a path of her own, and she was going to stick to it.

'Nathine—' Aimee began but her friend cut her off.

'No, Aimee. If this sparkless double-crosser spouts one more lie I'm going to slice her tongue out.'

'Pellie.' Aimee spoke again, her voice wobbling. 'I'm dizzy. I can't…'

Her words trailed off as she collapsed. Pelathina and Nathine ran to her immediately, Elka forgotten for the moment. She pressed her fingers to her chest and they came away bloody.

With the others distracted it gave her a chance to take in the scene. To her right Malgerus had slunk around to the edge of the trees and was snarling at Inelle. Crispy black leaves drifted down, settling on their scales.

Aimee had curled into a ball on the ground, Pelathina and Nathine crouched above her. There was a deep cut on her temple, blood streaking down to her ear and Elka saw now that her eye was swelling shut.

Behind them the blackened ribs of the hunting lodge smouldered. And crouched at the corner of the building, scales sooty, were Jess and Skydance. Jess was lying down, wings folded, tail curled around her body. Skydance had draped himself across her as if protecting her. Elka's heart twinged when she spotted the large, ragged hole in Jess's wing. She'd been shot by one of the dragon-killing crossbows. It hurt to see Jess, the beautiful dragon from Callant's book, wounded and weak.

Elka blinked away tears. Everything she saw here, all the pain and injuries, it was her fault. She'd done this. But she was going to make up for it.

Pelathina had helped Aimee to sit up and she leaned against her girlfriend. Elka longed so badly to help as well. To go back to when she was part of their world.

'I'm alright,' Aimee insisted, trying to smile but it looked more like a grimace.

'Feeling dizzy because of a head wound, then collapsing, is not alright,' Pelathina disagreed.

Nathine had stood and now faced Elka again, blade twitching in her hand. In three steps she was back in Elka's space, scimitar pressed to her throat. Elka held up her hands but didn't fight back. That wasn't the way to win the Riders' trust.

Over Nathine's shoulder she saw Pelathina help Aimee to her feet and they both came to stand beside their friend.

'Where's Pagrin's bracelet?' Aimee asked. Her voice was sad, tinged with fear, but not angry.

'That's what I need your help with,' Elka replied, still holding her hands up and hoping with every breath that Nathine's blade wouldn't cut deeper.

'No. You tell us where it is, then I slit your traitorous throat, Mal guts Inelle, and we fly off to retrieve the bracelet.'

'Nathine,' Aimee said gently, 'that's not our plan.'
'It's my plan!' Nathine yelled. 'She killed Halfen!'

Nathine blinked and tears spilled down her cheeks, catching beads of sweat on their way. Elka's heart twisted in her chest like it was caught between two cogs. When Nathine was angry she was scary but somehow seeing this strong young woman breaking was even worse.

'She'll face judgement from Jara for what she did to Halfen, I promise, Nathine. But killing her isn't justice,' Aimee said, still leaning heavily on Pelathina.

'I don't give a damn for justice, I want revenge!'

'I'll go!' Elka cut in, directing her words at Aimee. 'After this is over I'll fly back with you to Kierell and face whatever justice Jara and the Riders want.'

Elka was surprised to say the words and realise that they weren't a lie. As long as she could stop Torsgen, after that she'd go back to Kierell. At least then she and Inelle would get one last chance to be with their clutch, to stand in the Heart together, before Jara meted out punishment.

Nathine turned to Aimee, mouth open to argue, but a look passed between the two. In that moment they shared something that only years of mutual support and friendship could allow. Elka felt a pang of longing.

Slowly the blade retracted from Elka's neck, though Malgerus continued to threaten Inelle. Nathine stepped back but Elka noticed she didn't sheath her scimitar. Aimee pushed free of Pelathina's arms and took Nathine's place standing right in front of Elka. She had to tilt her head back to look up into Elka's face.

'You lied to us for years,' Aimee began and there was a determined set to her small face. 'You stole a dangerous artefact, and led us into a trap where we were shot from the sky. I'm injured. Jess is injured. I trained you, Elka. We gave you a home.' Aimee looked into her eyes. 'You betrayed us and our friend is dead because of you.'

Elka knew what she'd done, but hearing Aimee, the Saviour of Kierell, list out her crimes made her feel so much more ashamed. She'd always wanted to be someone, but not if that someone was an infamous traitor. She felt tears run down her cheeks and didn't wipe them away.

'Yes, I did all that. It was my plan to betray you from the day I arrived in Kierell,' Elka admitted. She'd always thought saying those words to Aimee would be impossible but they'd slipped out easily. For the first time she wanted Aimee to really know her. She'd been hiding all the bad stuff she'd done, and why she'd done it, but now she wanted Aimee to see it.

'I only ever became a Sky Rider so I could steal the bracelet.'

'Traitor!' Nathine hissed.

'Let her speak.' Aimee held up a hand to quieten Nathine.

Elka made sure to look all three of them in the eye as she spoke, even Nathine. She wanted them to understand. 'I know now that I chose wrong. I should have made the climb and never looked back at Taumerg. And if I could go back in time I would. I'd be a Rider forever.'

'You'll never—' Nathine hissed but Aimee shut her up with a look.

Elka was trying to swallow her sobs and it was making her chest shudder, pain gnawing at her ribs.

'I screwed everything up, and I'm really sorry. I know I can't go back to being a Rider, but I need you to know that I wish I hadn't done what I did.'

'Why did you betray us, Elka?' Aimee asked.

Taking a shuddering breath she told them, for the first time, the truth about her life before she made the climb. She admitted that she'd almost forgotten about her mission to steal the bracelet and would happily never have done it if Torsgen hadn't sent Nail to kill her dragon. She saw an understanding in Aimee and Pelathina's eyes as she described being forced to complete her mission to save Inelle. And surprisingly she saw the tiniest melting of the glacier that was Nathine's face as she described how her family had lied to and controlled her.

'And I know that you hate me for what I've done, and that's fine but—'

'I loathe you. I hope your spark withers,' Nathine cut in.

'Okay, you loathe me,' Elka continued, 'but I still need your help.'

'Why?' Aimee asked.

The more she admitted the easier it became to tell them all the bad she was to blame for. She explained what she'd done with the bracelet and how Torsgen was using it. Fear stole onto the Riders' faces.

'Right now, I'm not your enemy, but my brother is. You have to help me stop him.'

No one spoke. She could see their distrust of her swirling in their eyes.

'I'm not lying anymore, I promise! And when you became Riders you swore to protect innocent people, didn't you? Does that only apply to people in Kierell? Some of the kids trapped in that basement are younger than me. Are they not good enough to be protected because they aren't Kierellian?'

'Of course they need to be saved.'

It was Pelathina who answered. She wrapped an arm around Aimee's waist again.

'Fine, so we'll rescue the kids then come back and cut her throat,' Nathine spat. 'Where are they?'

Elka could do that, she could tell the Riders where to find Torsgen and let them handle it. But she'd made a choice, and even if they didn't want her, she'd chosen the Riders. That meant she'd fight alongside them.

She directed her words at Aimee. 'I know the city, and four dragons are better than three, especially if Jess is injured.'

'She's injured because of you.' Nathine stabbed towards her with her blade.

'I know!' Elka yelled back.

Aimee stepped between them, glaring at both Elka and Nathine. She was about to speak but Elka got there first.

'Torsgen's going to take those people's sparks, and

along with them their dreams, their skills, their passions and use them to make blank-faced slaves. He's going to make those people nothing! Just like he…' Elka's words softened to a whisper. 'Just like he tried to do with me.'

Aimee pushed Nathine back then stood in front of Elka, her arms folded and her face set with determination.

'I've learned a lot from working with our recruits,' Aimee began. 'I've learned that when you train someone day after day, forcing them to push themselves beyond where they think their limits are, you get to see the person they keep deep inside. I've seen the girls that doubt what they can do, the ones that fear they'll never be good enough, and the ones that get angry with themselves for being rubbish. And then I've seen them reach out, taking strength and inspiration from the girls around them, and succeeding where they never thought they could.' Patchwork fingers slipped between hers as Aimee took her hand. 'I've seen who's inside you, Elka, and she's not a bad person.'

'I didn't mean to kill Halfen.' Elka's voice wobbled. 'He tried to stop me taking the bracelet, we fought and then…he fell. And the whole time I told myself I was only doing what Torsgen would have done.'

'And what would Elka have done instead?' Aimee asked gently.

Elka fumbled for an answer. She thought back to that night in Vunskap Tower. If she hadn't been forced to complete her mission would she have been there? She'd been trying to win Torsgen's approval for so many years that she didn't know what else to strive for. She'd tried so hard to be like him, so that he'd value her, that she'd lost track of what it was to make her own decisions.

'I'd have never gone to the university,' Elka admitted as she realised the truth. 'I'd have been curled up in bed, in my little cave, dreaming of flying.'

'No, Aimee you can't trust a word this twisted snake is saying.' Nathine shoved Aimee in the shoulder as if trying to press her words into her friend. 'Don't you dare go believing her and fly off into another trap.' Nathine shoved her again. 'No, stop it with your stupid determined face. Pelathina?'

She appealed to the other Rider but Pelathina pushed Nathine back and wrapped an arm around Aimee, letting her girlfriend lean on her.

'Sparkly sparks, Nathine, if you knock Aimee over I'm going to make you do every one of my night shifts from now until I'm thirty.'

Elka watched as Aimee kissed the side of Pelathina's face. 'I'm alright,' she insisted.

'Fine, no more shoving.' Nathine held up her hands but kept glaring.

The three of them had slipped into familiar banter and Elka stood on the edge of it, longing to join in but knowing she wasn't welcome. She didn't even look like one of them anymore. The three Riders' black boots were dirty, Aimee's coat was smeared with mud down one side and one lens in Pelathina's flying goggles was cracked, but they looked like Riders. Their dark coats with upturned collars and slits to their hips were stylish in a kick-ass sort of way. The flashes of their Rider's jewellery added a feminine flare and the beautiful scimitars, in their hands or strapped to their backs, made them look awesome and deadly.

Elka looked down at her own red trousers and patterned pink waistcoat, pretty and fashionable this morning, now damp, dirty and ruined. Her garter of throwing knives was empty and she'd shoved her solitary scimitar through her belt because she'd left her sheath with her coat back at the bakery. She looked like a girl playing at being a Rider.

'But come on, she's a liar, and a thief, and a murderer.' Nathine stabbed a finger at Elka.

'But if there are people trapped in that warehouse then it's our duty to save them,' Pelathina eased out her words.

'And if Elka's brother has put on Pagrin's bracelet then we have to stop him. Nathine, the bracelet's power will corrupt him and he'll create monsters,' Aimee added.

'It didn't corrupt you,' Nathine pointed out.

'It nearly did.' There was a waver in Aimee's voice. 'And I was only able to resist because I had Jess's help and the support of the Riders.'

Nathine was shaking her head and she folded her arms like the matter was final. 'I don't trust her and if you fly into an unknown fight with her at your back then you're an idiot, Aimee Wood.'

'But I'll be at *your* back, so you won't need to worry,' Aimee countered.

Nathine was still shaking her head, burnt ends of her ponytail swishing.

'What if it was your brother kidnapped and held in that basement? What if it was Lukas's spark that Torsgen was going to steal,' Aimee said.

Nathine threw up her hands in surrender. 'Ugh, fine. But to steal Pelathina's idea, in return you have to do all *my* night shifts until I'm thirty.'

Aimee smiled at her. 'Deal.'

'I wouldn't actually have made you do it,' Pelathina said.

'Yeah well, I'm definitely going to hold Aimee to this.' Nathine gave her a pointed look but Aimee still only gave her a smile and squeezed her arm.

Elka heard a low growl and felt a cautious wave of relief from Inelle. Malgerus had backed off, though he kept his teeth bared and his wings unfurled. With her eyes locked on him, Inelle slowly edged towards Elka until she could press herself against her Rider. Elka reached up and stroked her feathers.

'Thank you,' she said to Nathine.

'I've not forgiven you, and as long as my spark burns I never will.' Nathine tossed the burnt ends of her ponytail over her shoulder. Malgerus had appeared beside her and he rested his head on her shoulder. Her eyes still shimmered with tears and anger as she looked at Elka. 'But let's say for now that I understand that the family you grow up in might not be the safe place you thought it would be.'

The three Riders all looked to Elka. Their dragons were arrayed behind them and their reptilian eyes were fixed on her too. Elka straightened her spine and tried to keep down the smile twitching her lips. They hadn't accepted her back, and probably never would, but the Saviour of Kierell and her friends were looking to her to lead them and that was more than she could have hoped for.

'So, what's your plan?' Aimee asked.

CHAPTER 25

NOT A TRAP

Elka led them back across the city, Inelle in front, the other dragons following. She imagined the awe on faces down below as they saw four dragons glide across the sky. Inelle's saliva had cooled the worst of the hot pain in her hip, and Daan's bandage actually seemed to have stopped the bleeding. It still ached but it wasn't as bad as having your spark sucked from your chest. Aimee had needed Pelathina's help to mount up and the air whistled through the tear in Jess's wing, making her slower than the others.

Still, Elka was flying to a fight alongside the heroes of the Battle for Kierell, and that felt unreal.

Her plan was simple. They needed to break into the warehouse fast and en masse, and their dragons would let them do that. They'd swoop in through the hole Inelle had made in the skylights and deal with any thugs inside. And she fully expected there to be more of Torsgen's men now. He'd know that she'd be coming back, and he'd be prepared. Hopefully the sound of fighting would bring up any others from the basement into the warehouse. Then from the back of their dragons they'd have the advantage and could take them out. Elka was insistent that they try where possible to maim the men, not kill them.

As they followed the Amms Canal towards the river, Elka wished for a moment that she could show the Riders around her city. Take them to Daan's coffee shop where Pelathina could enjoy proper Marlidesh coffee. Visit Makje's Bakery on Tinstraab and listen to Aimee and Nathine argue over which pastries to buy.

The River Ireden was shimmering with the colours of sunset, the orange and pink waters cut apart by dozens of barges coming and going. The streets they flew over were busy, as factories closed for the night and people headed home to food and families.

Elka pointed out the warehouse and its shattered skylight to the others. They nodded, faces grim, weapons drawn.

'Have you fought against pistols before?' Elka called over to the others. In two years she'd never seen a pistol in Kierell.

'Not until those mad brutes at the lodge started firing at us,' Nathine replied, just reminding Elka of what she'd done to them. As if she'd forgotten.

'Any advice?' Aimee called.

'The clockwork pistols don't reload as quick as crossbows, so let them fire a shot, then attack.'

'Easy,' Pelathina called over.

Inelle took point, then Malgerus and Skydance. Jess

would bring up the rear. Aimee had argued with Pelathina about that but her girlfriend was determined to keep her as safe as she could from further injuries.

They flew once over the warehouse roof so Elka could check inside. Torsgen's men had fortified it, building a barricade from boxes and knocked-over shelves. Elka counted at least half a dozen of them kneeling behind it. But a barricade was only of use when an enemy attacked head on. These men weren't used to factoring in dragons who attacked from above.

Elka yelled a battle cry and pushed Inelle into a dive. Malgerus was right on her tail. They swooped in through the smashed skylight and were on top of the men before they'd a chance to take proper aim. Most just jabbed their pistols skywards and fired. Bullets shot between wings and swishing tails, pinging off the metal rafters above. Inelle grabbed one thug in her talons and flung him across the warehouse. He crashed into a stack of crates and slumped. He didn't get up again. Malergus tossed away another and he slid along the floor, stirring up clouds of dust.

Then Elka was turning in the air, Inelle's long wings brushing the walls of the warehouse. Malgerus roared as he too swept around. Skydance had swooped down after them but the remaining men had got their aim by then and all four fired directly at him. Pelathina cried out as Skydance tilted in the air, wings going vertical, bullets whizzing up past where he'd just been. Skydance's manoeuvre saved them from being shot but took him away from the fight.

They'd agreed not to use dragon's breath for fear of starting a fire that would burn down a whole neighbourhood. As Elka and Inelle flew along the ceiling, just under the network of metal rafters, Aimee and Jess attacked. And with absolutely no finesse. Aimee pushed Jess's horns till they were in a low dive and they smashed straight into the barricade. Boxes and broken shelves exploded into the air. Jess thrashed her tail smacking a whole rack of shelves into one of the thugs. He fell, shelves pinning him to the floor.

Elka watched, gaping in amazement, thinking of the line drawing in Callant's book of a poised young woman and her dragon. She actually liked this gung-ho version of Aimee better.

Two thugs had escaped the barricade carnage and Elka heard the tell-tale clicks as they reloaded.

'Pistols!'

She yelled the warning as Inelle swept underneath Malgerus, their wings almost clashing in the tight space. Inelle dived towards the men from the warehouse's end, Malgerus from the roof and Skydance from the corner behind them. The thugs hesitated, swivelling their pistols wildly at the converging dragons. One fired at Skydance who swerved high, spiralled horns almost scraping the roof. The other fired at Malgerus who continued his dive but skewed to the side. His talons raked the air above the broken barricade, missing his target, but his tail whipped out and smacked into the other thug who screamed as one of the barbs on Malgerus's tail pierced his thigh.

The second man was aiming at Elka now, spinning the gears on the side of his pistol, desperately trying to reload before Inelle reached him. As they flew along, only a few feet above the warehouse floor, Inelle stretched out her long neck. The man was still fumbling with his pistol when she head-butted him. He yelped, pistol flying in one direction as he was thrown in the other. Elka told Inelle to land and she furled her wings, dropping down beside the fallen thug. She placed one clawed foot on his chest.

'Only my control over her is stopping a dragon from cracking all your ribs like kindling for the stove,' Elka told him.

He splayed his fingers in surrender, wide eyes flicking between Elka and Inelle. She looked around. The others had landed too, guarding their own downed thugs though none of them looked like they had any fight left in them. Intimidating buttery-soft councillors and low-level engineers was one thing, but none of them had joined Torsgen to fight dragons.

'All of you, get out!' Elka ordered, and Inelle stepped back, releasing the thug.

She watched as around the warehouse the men looked at each other as if not wanting to be the first to move, the first to abandon their job.

'Go!' Inelle punctuated Elka's shout with a roar.

The men scrambled to their feet, one or two clutching bloody wounds.

'Leave the pistols,' Nathine ordered as one thug bent to scoop his up.

As they filed out Elka turned to the others, a sad smile slipping onto her face. She'd just flown into battle with Riders and their dragons beside her, and done it to save people. The adrenaline of it fizzed in her fingertips and her heart felt like someone had turned up the speed, increasing its beats.

But the victory was bittersweet because she knew it wouldn't last. And even more poignant was the knowledge that this could have been her life, if only she'd chosen it earlier.

Still on their dragons, the Riders met at the staircase.

'Everyone alright?' Aimee asked.

'Are you?' A frown crinkled Pelathina's brow. Aimee nodded and blew her a kiss.

'Did that seem too easy to you? Nathine asked. She'd picked up one of the clockwork pistols and was poking at its cogs.

'Easy?' Elka gaped at her and pointed around at the destruction they'd caused in the warehouse.

'Even if they were expecting Elka to return, I guess no one was expecting four dragons to show up to the little party they clearly had planned,' Pelathina replied.

'I'd still say that taking out six of Torsgen's thugs without any of us getting injured wasn't "easy",' Elka argued.

'Compared to fighting sparkless monsters this was flying on a sunny day with no wind.' Nathine pointed the pistol at Elka. 'Think you could fire one of these from dragonback?'

'Nathine, leave the pistol before you accidentally

shoot someone. And let's hope Elka never experiences a fight with Empty Warriors,' Aimee said, dismounting. 'Alright, this is where we leave our dragons.'

Elka could feel that Inelle was less wary about being left behind this time because the other dragons were with her. She leaned her face into Inelle's feathers.

'It's good, isn't it. Feels like being home,' she whispered. Inelle twisted her neck around and gently bit her wrist.

The Riders crept to the metal railing around the top of the staircase and listened. It was silent below which Elka found strange. She'd assumed Torsgen would still be here, and even if the fighting hadn't brought him upstairs more of his men should have come running.

'What's the layout down there?' Aimee whispered.

'This staircase, then a short corridor with a door on the left. But the one we want is straight ahead, that's where the prisoners are being kept,' Elka replied.

'If your brother hasn't stolen all their sparks already,' Nathine added.

'If he is down there, you can't let him touch you,' Aimee warned.

'Yeah, Aimee, we know.' Nathine rolled her eyes.

'But Elka doesn't.' Aimee looked at her. 'There's a dial on the bracelet and if Torsgen turns it to—'

'To *ura* and then touches someone he can suck out their spark and kill them.' Three faces were watching her. 'I know how the bracelet works, I've…' She'd never told Aimee this before. 'I've read *The Saviour of Kierell* four times.'

She felt an uncharacteristic blush in her cheeks and was surprised to see a matching one on Aimee's face. Pelathina smiled at Elka and nudged Aimee gently with her shoulder.

Nathine snorted. 'I still think Callant could have made me sound more heroic.'

They all hovered there for a moment, balanced on the edge of friendship, until Nathine dragged them back.

'Who's taking point?' she asked, her voice reverting to its brusque tone.

'I will,' Elka volunteered before anyone else could.

Nathine shrugged. 'Just so you know, it's fine by me if you get killed.'

'Nathine!' Aimee warned.

Without realising she'd done it, Elka gave Nathine one of Torsgen's cold stares. 'Likewise.'

'Enough.' Aimee glared at them both.

Elka started down the stairs, her footsteps soft, hardly making a sound on the metal treads. She looked back, just before she disappeared into the darkness, and saw Inelle crouched, wings furled, with Jess and Skydance on either side. Dragons mirrored their Rider's emotions so she wondered if maybe, just maybe, Aimee and Pelathina might think of her as one of them again.

The candles that had lit the short corridor were all snuffed out and Elka couldn't see a thing. She stopped at the bottom of the stairs, feeling the others press in behind her. The metal door to the room must have been closed. This was starting to feel like a trap. Were there dozens of men crouched in the darkness waiting to blast them with bullets? Elka blew her long fringe out of her eyes, as if that would help her see in the darkness.

Well if it was a trap, she may as well spring it. She didn't like sneaking. The part of her that would always be a Hagguar wanted to march down the corridor.

'Hello?' she called.

'Oh yeah, just tell them all we're here,' Nathine hissed behind her.

But there was no answer. Aimee took a dragon's breath orb from her pocket and held it low. The soft yellowy glow spilled along the floor, coating Elka's boots. She saw the stone corridor and the metal door with its cog lock at the end. There were no waiting thugs. But standing before the door with his back to them was Torsgen. Even half in shadow she recognised his straight spine and the hairstyle that made his head look narrower.

'Torsgen!' Elka called, the name bouncing off the walls.

He didn't turn. That was odd. The last thing Torsgen would ever do was stand quietly and not dominate a space. Elka made to move forward but Aimee grabbed her arm, tight and fierce.

'Wait,' she cautioned.

Then Torsgen turned. As Aimee lifted her orb the yellow light travelled up his immaculate suit before settling on his face.

'*Mi sparken!*' Elka swore in Glavic.

It was Torsgen but not Torsgen. The thing standing

before her had her brother's face but his eyes were dull grey steel. No pupils, no irises, no whites, just metal. And there was not a scrap of humanity in them.

'Oh great, he's made an Empty Warrior!' Nathine filled the corridor with curses.

Elka couldn't stop staring at the thing that wore her brother's face. She knew this was what happened when a bracelet wearer combined a spark with an element. The thing they made looked like them but wasn't human. But knowing that, and then seeing an actual monster wearing her brother's face, were two very different things.

'He's learned quickly how to master the bracelet's powers,' Pelathina said.

Elka wasn't surprised. 'He'll have been studying for months, reading Callant's book over and over. He was ready to embrace the power and use it the moment he snapped the damn thing on his wrist.'

And of course he'd used metal. Machines were what their family's empire was built on. But the other thing he'd needed was a spark. Elka thought of the teenagers she'd seen Torsgen murder—the boy in the faded boiler suit and the girl wearing the coat with dozens of pockets. The life, dreams and future of one of them was now powering this monster.

'Why isn't it moving?' Pelathina managed to ask when Nathine took a breath between swears.

'I'm guessing its purpose is to guard that door,' Aimee replied.

Elka felt anger clawing its way up her chest and into

her throat. For years she'd begged and cajoled Torsgen to let her into his inner circle and he'd rejected her, his own little sister. But he'd given this sparkless monster a job. This was what Torsgen really wanted their family to be—replicas of himself that he could control.

'Ideas, anyone?' Nathine stopped swearing long enough to ask.

Elka tightened her grip on her single hilt and charged.

'Looks like we're attacking,' she heard Pelathina say as she slashed at the monster.

The Torsgen-thing didn't even move as her blade sliced across his chest and up into his shoulder. Elka's arm juddered as her scimitar clanged off steel. She stumbled, thrown off her attack because she'd expected her blade to slice into flesh, not be repelled by metal. The monster reached out to grab her and Elka yelped, but another hand tugged on her waistband, pulling her back.

'Thank you,' she said but Aimee was already pushing past her, launching her own attack, Pelathina right on her shoulder.

The corridor was too narrow for Nathine and Elka to fight as well. The edges of the Riders' blades gleamed in the light as they slashed. Elka watched in horrified amazement as the Torsgen-thing used his arms to block them. Aimee's scimitar slashed right across his wrist. Had he been human, his severed hand would have dropped to the floor. Pelathina aimed for his groin but he blocked her with his other arm, her blade slicing through his coat and screeching up the metal underneath.

'Watch out!' Nathine yelled but too late.

The monster swung the arm Pelathina had cut, easily knocking aside her scimitar and backhanding her across the face. The force of his blow threw her backwards into Elka. She grabbed the Rider but they both fell to the floor.

'Pellie!' Aimee yelled but she didn't take her eyes from the monster.

His arm shot out and he grabbed her blade. It sliced his skin but not the metal underneath. With a twist of his wrist he snapped the sharp curve of metal in two and tossed the broken-off half to the floor. Aimee scampered back. The monster didn't follow, simply crossed his cut-up arms and stared at them with his blank metal eyes. Aimee had placed her dragon's breath orb on a shelf and from its light Elka could see the metal gleaming dully where they'd sliced him open. There was no blood.

'He's made of steel inside,' Elka said.

'Yeah thanks, we'd worked that out,' Nathine replied sarcastically.

'How do we kill him then, smart-ass?' Elka threw back at her.

Nathine narrowed her eyes but she didn't have an answer.

CHAPTER 26

STEEL AND NETS

Elka glared at the monster wearing her brother's face. He wasn't going to let them pass and if they cut him enough would all his skin just slide off? Would he still stand there with his metal arms folded?

'It's horrible.' Elka shivered as if cold metal fingers stroked her spine.

'I know,' Aimee's voice was sad, 'and if there's more of them…'

She let her words hang but Elka didn't need her to elaborate. She was already picturing Torsgen's thugs replaced with metal monsters. They wouldn't take bribes and no amount of begging would make them break some fingers instead of a leg. Torsgen would control the city. And where would he stop? He'd take other businesses by force. She imagined metal monsters storming into Fischer's bakery and dragging off the bakers, kicking and screaming, to have their sparks sucked out. Instead of Daan baking rude-shaped pastries, loving what he was doing, the bakery would be filled with sparkless slaves working all day and night. Daan's jokes would be replaced with nothingness.

'Hey, this isn't the same as last time.' Pelathina's voice was soft as shadows.

Elka turned to see her take Aimee's hand and kiss her patchy knuckles.

'It is the same,' Aimee insisted.

'There's only one,' Nathine pointed out, stabbing towards the Torsgen-thing.

'He'll make more,' Aimee's voice was hard.

'You don't know that.'

'I do because the longer Torsgen wears the bracelet and the more sparks he steals, the more it will corrupt him.'

'What if he was already corrupt?' Elka asked.

'Then by now he's probably lost his humanity.' Aimee looked straight at Elka.

Elka's anger bubbled up again and without thinking she grabbed the dragon's breath orb and flung it at the monster—the thing her brother had chosen over her. It smashed against his solid skull with a crack and a whoosh of flames. Freed, the dragon's breath inside set him alight. His mouth opened into a dark hole but no scream came out as the flames ate his face. The heat from the dragon's breath pressed the Riders back along the corridor. The flames blazed down the monster's body, turning his clothes to ashes in moments and melting the metal underneath.

Elka shoved the others back further as he dropped to his knees. His head was already half-melted, her brother's face gone, liquid metal pouring down his chest.

'Yes! Dragon's breath works on these guys!' Nathine narrowed her eyes with grim determination. 'See, Pellie's right, it's not the same this time. If there are any more of these freaks out there we'll just blast them with dragon's breath, and job done.'

The corridor darkened as the flames began to dissipate. The monster toppled forwards, hitting the stone floor with a clang. The last of the dragon's breath danced along his back but he was nothing but a misshapen lump of steel now. Elka spared him no more thoughts and jumped over him to get to the door. She pulled out the hexagonal key, thanking her earlier self for grabbing it, and slotted it into the door's mechanism. Before she turned it, she looked back at the others.

'Do you think there's more of those monsters inside?'

It was Aimee who shook her head first. 'Why guard the door if there's an army waiting for us behind it.'

'And I don't think your brother will have had the time to make dozens of warriors, not yet,' Pelathina added.

Aimee collected the broken pieces of her scimitar from the floor and sighed. 'Dyrenna's going to kill me. I'm already on my second set of these.'

Their reassurances were good enough for Elka. After a few seconds of grinding gears and a puff of steam the door swung open. Elka braced herself, the leather grip of her scimitar a comfort in her hand.

She stepped around the door and into the room.

'Elka!' a voice yelled before someone barrelled into her, pinning her arms to her side and wrapping her in a hug.

Elka panicked for the briefest of moments until she realised it was Jennta.

'You stayed alive.' Elka squeezed her friend tight.

'Huh?' Jennta asked, pulling out of the hug because Elka was still speaking Kierellian.

Instead of answering she looked around the room. The huddle of prisoners was smaller than it had been and Elka swallowed the nausea in the back of her throat.

'Where are the others?' she asked Jennta, switching to Glavic this time. 'Did Torsgen…'

She couldn't finish as she noticed the horror lurking in the whites of her friend's wide eyes. Jennta pointed, her finger shaking. Elka looked, saw, then ran to the corner of the room, dizzy and sick. She tried to throw up but she'd nothing left in her stomach. The other Riders had seen the pile of bodies too and moved towards it, weapons lowered because there was no one in here except victims. Pelathina crouched beside the still form of a dark-skinned boy and placed a hand on his chest.

They'd all had their sparks taken, nearly thirty of them, and then they'd been discarded like old machine parts no longer of any use. All of them had been young, and all dead because Elka's brother had stolen their lives. She heard a rumbling from above and knew Inelle and the others had all roared, sensing the horror their Riders were witnessing.

Thankfully, Aimee took charge because right then Elka felt lost. With Pelathina's help she got the remaining prisoners to start filing out of the room. Many had been locked down here for months and were very weak. Elka hung back with Jennta by her side. She didn't know what to say to the friend she'd left two years ago without even a goodbye. Jennta's face was white as fresh snow except for the deep purply hollows under her eyes. Her clothes were filthy, crescents of dirt under all her fingernails and the haunted look in her eyes said that she'd have night terrors of this place for years.

'Elka, what did Torsgen do to them?' Her eyes darted to and away from the tangled pile of bodies.

'He sucked out their sparks and took them for himself,' Elka answered, her every word edged in anger.

'What! How is that even possible?'

'You remember the book I used to have, the one about the Battle for Kierell?'

'Of course, you spent a whole afternoon talking about it once. I had to ply you with sparkling wine to get you to shut up. But…' Jennta shook her head. 'It was fiction, wasn't it? A fairytale about monsters.'

This time it was Elka who looked to the pile of bodies. 'No, they were real monsters. And now Torsgen is one of them and he's going to make more, hundreds more. He's going to steal people's sparks and replace us all with slaves made from metal.'

'Sparks,' Jennta swore.

'I'm sorry I left you,' Elka said, meaning earlier today but also two years ago.

'You came back, but Elka you shouldn't have.'

'What? As if I was going to leave you here to die.'

'But it's a trap.'

'I thought that too but it's not.' Elka waved around at the now almost empty room. The weakest of the prisoners were being carried out. Nathine had a young girl in her arms, her head resting against Nathine's broad shoulder. 'Torsgen left this place protected but he didn't set a trap. I don't suppose you know where he's gone?'

The thinness of Jennta's face made her eyes bulge as she stared at Elka. 'I've heard the men talking in the last few days about a workshop outside of the city.'

'What sort of workshop?'

'I don't know. But I'm sure one of them said Frannack was running it.'

Elka checked through her mental map of all the Hagguar property in and around Taumerg. They didn't own any workshops outside of the city. 'Did anyone say where it was?'

Jennta shook her head. 'Somewhere north of the river. That's all I got.'

'The river stretches the length of the city!'

Jennta gave her an apologetic shrug and Elka took her friend's hand. It was so skinny that she felt all the bones in Jennta's fingers like twigs.

'Look at you,' Jennta said, somehow managing to

smile. 'Elka, you're a Sky Rider! How did that happen?'

Elka wished that her friend could have seen her a few weeks ago instead of now. She wished that Jennta had seen her wearing her proper Rider's clothes, standing atop one of the peaks in the Ring Mountains with the wind blowing back her hair and Inelle by her side, sunlight shining on her beautiful indigo scales.

Jennta nodded towards Aimee and Pelathina, helping the last of the teenagers from their prison. 'They let someone from Taumerg join them?'

Elka's smile was bittersweet. 'They accept anyone who can survive the climb.'

Jennta looked thoughtful, her eyes far away. 'Is it hard?'

'It's awful.'

'You managed.'

Elka looked down at her old friend and remembered the way Jennta had risked her own life just hours earlier to save hers. Starved, weak and scared, she'd still attacked Torsgen and done so without a weapon. There was a strength in her friend that she'd never bothered to notice before.

'You would make a good Rider,' Elka told her. 'I'm sorry this happened to you.'

'Elka, it isn't your fault.' Jennta gave her a sad smile.

'It is. I'm to blame for all of this.'

'Elka, shut up. You have to get out of here before the trap springs.' Jennta pulled her hand from Elka's and gave her a shove. She was so weak that she couldn't push Elka even one step.

'You said that before but you're wrong. This isn't a trap.'

'It is!' Jennta insisted. 'Torsgen knew you'd come back and he ordered Nail—'

Elka didn't hear the rest of her words because the tug in her mind almost jerked her off her feet. She was running before she even knew it.

Inelle. Something was wrong with Inelle. Waves of fear pulsed into her brain from her dragon. She elbowed through the prisoners in the corridor.

'Hey, what's—'

But the rest of Aimee's shout was drowned in the thumping as she sprinted up the metal staircase. The bullet wound on her hip was a line of burning fire, her cracked rib a dull ache behind it. It didn't matter. Nothing did except protecting Inelle. Protecting her family.

'Inelle!' she cried as she burst up into the warehouse.

Her brain was flooded with her dragon's fear and panic and she couldn't think straight, couldn't make sense of what she was seeing. Inelle was ensnared in a net. The large doors to the warehouse were opened wide and her dragon was being pulled through them.

Elka ran towards her but the click of multiple pistols pulled her up short. Inelle snapped and bit at the huge net that had trapped her. She roared as barbed wire woven through the rope cut into her mouth.

'Let her go!' Elka yelled.

Men crowded around her dragon, pistols aimed at her. More stepped towards Elka but they were only dark shadows at the edge of her vision. All she could see was Inelle, the blood on her scales and the horrible way the barbed net crushed her wings. She forgot the pistols and took a step forward. Cold metal pressed to her temple.

'Our orders aren't to kill you, miss.' Elka recognised Nail's voice. 'But I am at liberty to take out your kneecaps if you stop us. I think you'll find it hard to fly with legs that don't work.'

'Why are you doing this?'

Elka couldn't tear her eyes from Inelle. More of Torsgen's thugs had dragged her out into the courtyard now. She tried to fly, seeing sky and freedom but unable to get to it. The barbed rope shredded the edges of her wings and she roared in pain and fury. Elka felt every desperate emotion, and thought her brain might explode.

'Torsgen's orders,' Nail answered her question. 'I am sorry, miss.'

'No you're not! If you were you wouldn't be doing this!'

Elka raised her hand to fight him off but it was empty. When had she dropped her scimitar? She couldn't think straight with Inelle's fear pulsing through her. She raised her fists anyway but Nail deliberately moved the pistol to point at her knees. Fury boiled in her. She'd do it, attack him and take the risk that she could bring him down before he fired a shot. Her muscles coiled, ready to spring. But she heard the click of six other pistols and looked out from the corner of her eye. She was surrounded by men with pistols, all aimed low. If she moved they'd shoot her legs full of bullets and if she was broken like that then she'd never be able to rescue Inelle.

But she wasn't alone. Hope flared in her chest. She looked around for the others, and her hope died.

Thugs, more than she ever knew her brothers employed, had pistols aimed at Aimee, Nathine and Pelathina. Three Vorjagen, who must have survived the fire at their lodge, had their evil-looking crossbows trained on the Riders' dragons. The anger twisting their faces said they'd fire them if the dragons even twitched a feather. As Elka stared one of the Vorjagen turned and threw her a wicked grin. She recognised Tori and fear squirmed in her gut.

Elka's heart felt like it was being torn in two as men dragged on the net, pulling Inelle up onto the open back of a wagon. She snapped and snarled at them but couldn't get her teeth past the barbed rope. Blood was streaming from a hundred cuts in her mouth, painting her teeth a frothy pink.

'Stop, Inelle!' Elka yelled at her, terrified her dragon would kill herself trying to get free. 'I'll come and get you out, I promise.' She glared at Nail. 'Where are you taking her?'

'I'm not at liberty to tell you that, miss.'

'Coward,' she spat. 'Does my brother tell you when you can piss too? Do any of the three thoughts swimming around in the sludge of your brain even belong to you?'

Nail didn't rise to the bait, he simply walked backwards from the warehouse, keeping his pistol aimed at her. Elka glared at him and longed for her throwing knives. Outside, Inelle cowered in the wagon, indigo scales criss-crossed with lines of blood.

'We're family and I won't let Torsgen hurt you,' Elka promised, pushing the words along their connection with a wave of love. Inelle growled and snorted a puff of smoke.

She watched the Vorjagen jump up and perch on the sides of the wagon. Tori aimed her crossbow at Inelle, the other two aimed theirs at the sky. If Aimee and the others tried to attack they'd be shot down. It felt like all Elka's strength was being dragged away with Inelle as the steam-powered engine pulling the wagon puffed alive and made its way out of the courtyard.

Elka stood tall, like her spine was riveted together with iron bolts. She'd dared to defy Torsgen and this was her punishment, but she wouldn't give him the satisfaction of hearing that he'd broken her.

CHAPTER 27

HIDDEN

She stared at the gate through which Inelle had been taken until she felt a smaller hand slip into hers. She looked into Aimee's mismatched face.

'We'll get her back,' Aimee promised.

'You'll help me?' Elka asked.

'Of course. A gang of thugs can't take a Rider's dragon from her and not have to deal with me.' Aimee gave her hand a squeeze.

'But I'm not a Rider anymore.' Elka looked over Aimee's shoulder towards Nathine. 'And I'd have thought you'd all see having my dragon stolen away as a fitting punishment for how I betrayed you.'

Aimee followed her gaze to where Nathine was helping Pelathina bandage a young girl's arm. 'Nathine doesn't do emotions by half measures, and she will hate you forever. And I have this big lump of disappointment that's sitting right here.' She tapped her chest. 'But I trained you, and I've seen how strong you can be. I know what evil looks like and it's not you.'

'I—'

'Ah, I'm not finished.' Aimee gifted her a small smile before her brow crinkled in a frown. 'When I was seventeen I chose myself a new family. I chose to belong to the Riders. But,' she waved a hand over the colourless half of her face, 'not all of them wanted me as one of them. Nathine was the worst. But I fought to belong and I'd have done anything to earn my place among those women. You chose a family too, and you've been fighting to prove yourself to them. That's what made you betray us and that's something I can understand. But, you chose the wrong family.'

'I know that now,' Elka admitted.

'Riders stick together, and when one of us is hurt, we'll all fight to help.'

'What about Halfen?'

Sorrow turned down the corners of Aimee's mouth. 'You'll still need to answer for his death.'

'I really didn't mean for him to die.'

'I believe you.'

And those three words almost made Elka weep. It wasn't absolution, but maybe, just maybe, she and Aimee could be friends again one day.

'Are they taking her to your brother?' Nathine asked brusquely, coming to join them. Elka nodded. 'So if we track Inelle we can find Torsgen. It's handy that they took her then,' she added flippantly.

Elka threw Nathine a glare but decided against starting another fight. It took effort to uncurl her fists, though.

Aimee looked to Elka. 'Can you track Inelle?'

Elka flicked her long fringe out of her eyes. 'How?'

'Through your bond with her,' Aimee replied. 'Close your eyes and concentrate.'

Elka looked suspiciously at Nathine.

'I won't let her punch you while you're not looking, promise.'

So Elka closed her eyes and touched the connection she shared with her dragon. She'd never used it to look for her before because she'd always known right where she was. It felt weaker than it ever had, stretching out like thread unravelling. She could feel Inelle's pain but it was getting fainter, like she was losing her.

'No,' Elka whispered.

When they'd first been bonded Elka had resisted letting Inelle fully into her mind, not committing properly to their bond, but now her dragon felt like a piece of herself housed in another body. Elka blocked out the sounds in the warehouse—weeping from some of the freed prisoners, swearing from others, and the impatient rustling of dragon wings—and let her mind float. She felt Inelle tugging, pulling her towards the river. She held on to that sensation and opened her eyes.

'I can follow her,' she told Aimee. 'Someone will need to let me ride with them.' She jerked her head towards Nathine. 'But not her.'

She didn't trust Nathine not to push her off once they were up in the sky.

'You can ride with me and Jess,' Aimee offered.

'What about these people?' Pelathina asked, coming

to stand with them by the warehouse doors. 'What do we do with them? Half of them are just kids and they say they don't have anywhere to go.'

'They don't.' Elka shook her head. 'My brother's been rounding up homeless people and taking workers from the poorest tenements. The ones he thought no one would miss. The people he figured he could take sparks from and no one would care.'

She looked at the sad gaggle. Most looked relieved to be free of the basement but confused about why they'd been kidnapped and unsure what to do now. She felt a stab of pity for them and a bigger stab, one of anger, at her brother.

'Elka!'

A voice yelled from the courtyard and dozens of footsteps echoed into the warehouse. Elka spun to see Daan rushing towards her. He grabbed her in a bear hug and swung her around.

'Ouch!' She slapped him on the shoulder till he put her down.

'Ah, in my delight at seeing your face, I forgot your heroic injury,' he joked but also cast a guilty glance at her hip.

'You were the one who patched me up.'

He shrugged, bouncing on the balls of his feet.

'Daan, how much coffee have you had today?'

'Wow! More dragons! I am loving the orange one. He looks so mean!'

Daan was looking beyond her now, his eyes bright with excitement. Elka in turn was looking beyond him and stared amazed as half a dozen of Taumerg's guards stepped cautiously into the warehouse. They wore long daggers on one hip, a pistol on the other, and stern expressions on their faces. Each one had the badge of the city on their chests.

'Daan, did you bring the Zachen Guards?'

'What?' He was still staring at the dragons who watched everything with their yellow eyes, wingtips fluttering. 'Oh yeah, but you've no idea how hard it was to persuade them to come. They didn't believe a single word I said about bracelets and Empty Warriors and stealing sparks. So I told them Riders from Kierell were robbing a Hagguar warehouse.' He shrugged.

'You what?' Elka exclaimed.

She saw now the way the guards were ignoring her and Daan, and watching the Riders intently, fingers hovering over hilts.

'Is there a reason these fellows are looking at us like we might have stolen their purses and had our dragons swallow the evidence?' Pelathina asked in Kierellian.

'Because my friend here is an idiot,' Elka replied in the same language. 'But he was just trying to help,' she added, before Nathine decided to punch him or something.

'Daan,' she switched to Glavic and grabbed his arm to get his attention. 'We have to go, Torsgen wasn't here and he's taken Inelle. Don't interrupt, we haven't got time. I need you to get the Zachen to help these people, and talk to them. They'll back up your story about my brother and Pagrin's bracelet. They've seen him use it to kill.'

'Where are you going?' His dark eyes were full of concern.

'To rescue my dragon and stop my evil brother.'

'Sure, why not. Sounds like an ordinary day for a Sky Rider.'

Elka turned to go but Daan took her hand. 'Wait, here.' He had a bag slung over his shoulder and from it he pulled out a coat. It was long, sunshine yellow, and embroidered all over with little stars. He held it out towards Elka.

'You bought me a new coat?'

Daan nodded and shrugged, acting overly casual, like it was no big deal. 'I thought the colour would match your dragon and well, you left yours in a soggy heap at the bakery. It's totally ruined. And you'll get cold, flying around in just your shirt.'

Elka took the coat and slipped it on. It wasn't a Rider's coat, didn't have the slits from hem to hip, but if she wore it open she'd still be able to climb onto a dragon.

'It complements your hair too,' Daan said, admiring her.

Elka grabbed him and kissed him. 'Thank you,' she whispered as they pulled apart.

Then he cupped her face. 'Be careful.'

She felt all the Riders' eyes on her when she turned, but only Pelathina gave her a cheeky wink. As she walked towards Jess she felt something in the pocket of her new coat. Reaching in she pulled out a pair of puffer's goggles. They weren't flying goggles but with their round lenses and leather strap they looked near enough the same. She waved them in the air and called back to Daan.

'Thank you!'

Slipping them over her eyes she looked down at herself—dirty red trousers, a torn pink waistcoat and a new yellow coat on top. She was the most mismatched Rider ever. She didn't even have a weapon. Scanning around she spotted a clockwork pistol on the floor. She scooped it up, tucking it into her belt.

Then Aimee was swinging up into her saddle. Reaching a hand down, she helped Elka up too. Daan watched them take off and Elka smiled to see his wide eyes and the huge grin on his face. They rose above the roofs of the warehouses and into the evening sky. Lights twinkled as Taumerg spread out below them.

'That way.' Elka pointed north over Aimee's shoulder, towards the docks.

Elka wished for a moment that Tariga could see her riding Jess. Though it was probably a good thing that she wasn't here. If she was, she'd be so envious that she'd likely explode.

The air whistled through Jess's torn wing as Aimee steered her northwards. The sunset was an orange smudge on the horizon. Elka closed her eyes and reached out to Inelle. Their connection was stretching thin, and heading north. Jess flew over the docks, still busy with the hiss and clank of grabbers unloading barges as workers got on with their jobs by lantern light.

Beyond the docks, the River Ireden glittered with the last vanishing rays of the sun.

'Wow. That's the best bridge I've ever seen.'

Elka looked around Aimee's shoulder and saw what she was seeing. The bridge crossed the river in three graceful arcs, the middle one larger than the two either side. Through a complex series of cogs and gears, it opened up to let fully-laden barges pass underneath. It was mechanical genius but also, the bridge was beautiful. The intricate network of metal girders supporting it made it look like a spider's web—delicate but super strong—and at the southern end there was a tower, round and bulbous as a dragon's egg, with porthole windows looking in every direction.

'It's called Carneela's Bridge, named for the puffer who designed it,' Elka explained as the dragons soared above it. 'She was one of the first female engineers and apparently no one would give her a job, so she designed and built this bridge to prove she was just as good, if not better, than the male puffers.'

'I like her.'

Elka could hear the smile in Aimee's voice. 'I wish I could show you more of Taumerg,' she found herself saying.

'Maybe you can,' Aimee replied. 'After this.'

Elka didn't reply. She didn't want to risk putting that hope into words. Instead she closed her eyes again, reaching for Inelle. She felt closer now. Inelle's panic and fear was coming through stronger and it twisted Elka's heart. She snapped her eyes open and scanned the road below them. From Carneela's Bridge a road wound its way into the rolling foothills of the Schonlight Mountains. Beyond the craggy peaks of the mountains lay Marlidesh.

'There!'

It was Pelathina who spotted the wagon. A thin trail of smoke puffed skywards from the steam-powered engine as it disappeared into the foothills.

'Inelle!' Elka yelled. 'Fly down, get closer,' she ordered Aimee.

'I'm sorry, we can't,' Aimee said over her shoulder. 'We can't risk the hunters shooting the rest of us so we need to stay high.'

'If we attack quickly we can take them.'

Aimee shook her head, her soft curls brushing Elka's nose. 'If your brother and his men had wanted to kill Inelle then I think she'd be dead already. She's safe till they reach wherever they're going.'

A lantern bobbed on the tail of the wagon and by its yellow light Elka could see Inelle cowered beneath the net that bit into her scales and stopped her from flying free. She sensed her Rider was near and was about to start struggling again. Elka could feel her intentions.

'No, just wait,' Elka whispered in Glavic. She held her breath but thankfully Inelle didn't move. She'd tear herself to pieces if she did.

'We need to follow them to find your brother,' Aimee was saying. 'I'm sorry. I know it's hard to see her in pain and not be able to help.'

'Like watching someone break your fingers and not

being able to stop them.'

'We'll get her back,' Aimee promised again. And if anyone else had said that to her Elka might have been distrustful of such an assertion, but Aimee was a hero, so Elka believed her.

It was too dark now for Elka to see the Vorjagen riding on the wagon but she knew their crossbows would be tracking the dragons across the sky. They had to stay out of range. After another twenty minutes the wagon turned off the road to Marlidesh and onto a track heading into a valley between a curve of hills.

'Do you know where they're going?' Aimee asked as she pushed on Jess's left horn, turning them to follow the wagon.

Elka shook her head then remembered Aimee couldn't see her. 'No. As far as I knew my family doesn't own anything way out here.'

Jess was the tip of the arrow that followed the wagon, Malgerus and Skydance flying to either side of her. Elka stared at the little bobbing light of the wagon's lantern and kept sending thoughts of comfort to Inelle. She could sense her dragon had calmed now that her Rider was close but under that Elka could feel her pain and her fear. She vowed that Torsgen was going to pay for hurting Inelle.

'Elka, I need to be able to breathe to fly.' Aimee's voice sounded strained and Elka realised she was gripping her too tightly.

'Sorry.' She quickly released her arms, resting her hands on Aimee's hips instead.

The star-sprinkled sky had darkened, making the hills into soft round shadows, the track a faint line between them. Elka shook her head. This didn't seem right. Torsgen never left Taumerg. It was his city and he loved it. He hated grass and mud and roads that weren't paved. Why had he come out here?

Then a soft orange glow lit the sky around the next hill. The wagon headed towards it, the dragons following on quiet wings. Rounding the final curve into the valley proper Elka saw something she'd never have expected out here. Nestled at the head of the valley, hugged on three sides by hills, was a large building.

'Sparks, what is this place?'

Elka shook her head because she didn't have an answer for Aimee.

'It looks like a clutch of dragon's eggs,' Aimee said and she was right, it did.

The building was made up of one large dome in the centre but attached to it all around were dozens of smaller silo-like additions. The front of the nearest silo was made up of hundreds of square windows and orange light spilled from inside, lighting up the track and the wagon puffing towards it. A network of pipes snaked up and around the building. Columns of chimneys stood tall on more than half of the curved roofs.

The wagon with Inelle had reached the building's large double-doors and stopped. The doors were opening. Inelle was going to be taken inside and Elka had no idea what was in there. The need to get her back before that happened was pushing at her like a storm wind. She stood strong against it, though. Because as Aimee took Jess as low as they dared to go she could see the Vorjagen, now standing guard by the doors, crossbows aimed up at them. Elka could feel the wrongness in her bones as she watched a member of her family being taken away from her and she could do nothing to stop it.

Aimee must have sensed her anguish because she reached around and took Elka's hand, squeezing tight.

'Aimee, there!'

It was Nathine, calling across the sky. Aimee and Elka both turned to see her pointing at a rocky outcrop on one of the hills overlooking the valley and the building nestled at its heart. Elka watched Aimee judge the distance between the outcrop and the Vorjagen's weapons before nodding.

The dragons landed together, talons clacking on the rock. Elka jumped off, ignoring the throbbing pain that seemed to be everywhere in her body now, and crouched at the edge of the outcrop. She was too far away to see faces but a handful of figures had appeared from the building, the orange glow from inside casting their shadows long up the track. The wagon began moving again and Inelle roared.

The sound felt like claws tearing at Elka's heart. She grabbed her own wrist, just as Inelle would have done if she'd been beside her.

'Family,' she whispered. 'I'm coming, Inelle.'

The wagon and the men disappeared inside the building and the big double doors shut with a resounding clang.

CHAPTER 28

LOYALTY AND BRAVERY

INELLE'S PANIC AT being trapped washed through Elka's mind like a tidal wave. It was too much and she fell backwards, landing on her bum. Hugging her knees to her chest, she squeezed her eyes shut and pushed through her dragon's fear to take hold of their connection. It was like trying to catch a hummingbird. Inelle was everywhere in her mind, pushing herself into all the corners, desperate to feel closer to her Rider. Elka took a deep breath and pushed back, grabbing their connection.

'I'm still here, I promise.'

But Inelle wouldn't settle.

'Elka?'

She opened her eyes to see Pelathina beside her, hand on her arm.

'Whatever's in that building, it's making her terrified,' Elka explained.

She heard a rustle of wings and looked around to see Jess, Malgerus and Skydance all perched on the rocky lip of the outcrop. Their wings were only half furled, tips quivering, their ruffs of feathers all standing on end and each had stretched out their long necks, yellow eyes staring intently down at the building. Their colourful scales shimmered in the rising moonlight. They looked beautiful, and deadly.

'They know one of their clutch is in there,' Aimee said, pointing down into the valley, 'and they want her back too.'

'So how do we get in, rescue Inelle and stop Torsgen, without all getting killed?' Pelathina asked.

Elka brushed off Pelathina's hand and stood. Her legs felt shaky, but that could have been from either the pain of her own injuries or the fear Inelle was still pumping into her mind. Taking a deep breath she imagined turning a valve and half closing her connection to Inelle, not enough that her dragon would panic that she was no longer there, but enough that she could think straight. She stepped to the edge of the rock beside Jess and studied the building. The yellow glow from the lights inside lit the ground around it, and above the sky was clear, the rising moon casting soft silver light across the roofs.

'I think it used to be an observatory,' she said.

'And? So?' Nathine asked.

Elka shook her head. This looked like something else Torsgen had desired and so had taken. But it had been modified too because an observatory didn't need pipes and chimneys. Jennta had said Torsgen's men talked about a workshop. Is that what this was? But a workshop for what?

'In an observatory the roof is designed to open so you can see the stars.' Elka pointed to the large dome in the middle. 'If I can get that roof open you can fly in and attack.'

Aimee came to stand beside her. Elka didn't look at the small Rider, keeping her eyes on the workshop and thinking through her plan.

'I'm assuming the roof can only be opened from the inside?' Aimee asked.

Elka nodded. 'I'll go in. It's me Torsgen's wants. That's why he has taken Inelle.'

There was silence for a long moment until Aimee spoke. 'Are you sure this is what you want to do?'

Elka did turn and look at her then. 'Are you still worried I'm some sort of spy and I'm going to sell you out to my brothers?'

'Yes,' Nathine called from the other side of Malgerus.

Aimee shook her head, curls bouncing in the darkness. 'No, I'm worried you might be about to watch your family die. Because the only way to stop Torsgen now is to kill him. If he's using the bracelet to make Empty Warriors then the power of it has already corrupted him. He's not going to give it up willingly.'

'I know that. And I know the bracelet began draining his own spark the moment he put it on, just like Kyelli's bracelet did with you. I had two choices—stand down there with Torsgen or stand up here with you. This is the path I've chosen and I know where it leads.'

Elka turned up the collar of her yellow coat and took the clockwork pistol from her belt. 'Inelle is my family, and even if you never let me back into Anteill, the Sky Riders are my family. Torsgen isn't, not any more.'

'Shut up, Nathine,' Aimee said quickly before she could throw any insults. Then she looked around at the others. 'It's a good plan, and I trust Elka to do her part.'

'Thank you.' Elka checked the pistol for bullets. Four. It would have to do.

'You'll need to watch carefully for the Vorjagen,' Elka added. 'I can't see where they've gone and Torsgen will have paid them to protect his workshop from your dragons.'

Aimee nodded in understanding.

'Elka, what if Torsgen simply kills you the moment you step through those doors,' Pelathina asked. The concern in her voice hurt in a good way.

Elka thought of her cold, calculating brother. 'He won't. He wants me here for a reason.'

'What reason?' Aimee asked.

'I don't know.'

Torsgen could easily have left enough men with pistols at the warehouse so that when Elka went back she wouldn't have stood a chance. But he didn't. Instead he sent Nail and the remaining Vorjagen to capture Inelle. He knew Elka would follow her dragon. That meant he knew she was coming here. Torsgen did nothing without a reason and everything he did benefitted himself, and their family. So where did a secret workshop and a captured dragon fit into that?

Elka felt like she was fifteen again, left out of her brothers' plans, kept in the dark. Just like then she really wanted to unpick Torsgen's secrets, but now she wanted to do it not to be like him, but to thwart him.

She turned back to look at the Riders. With their proper Rider outfits they blended into the shadows. Clouds had scudded across the moon and they were all in darkness now. Elka couldn't read their expressions.

'If my other brother, Frannack, is in there, don't kill him,' Elka asked. 'He's not evil, he just does what his big brother tells him to because he thinks he owes Torsgen.'

'Torsgen is the only one who needs to die,' replied the smallest shadow. Aimee.

'And any other Empty Warriors he's got tucked away in there,' Nathine added.

'Here.' Aimee's face appeared from the darkness as she pulled a dragon's breath orb from her pocket and passed it to Elka.

She cupped a hand around the textured glass and held it out from her body to light her way. The dragons and Riders watched her, still as statues as she began to make her way off the rocky outcrop and down the grassy hill. She reached the valley floor and turned to look back up at where she'd left the others. The moon had poked out from behind the clouds and it bathed the Riders and their dragons in soft silver light. They looked like something from one of Callant's stories.

Stones crunched under Elka's boots as she stepped down onto the track. Holding the dragon's breath orb high she marched towards the workshop. With every step she could feel Inelle growing more insistent in her mind. She reached the workshop. The doors had been closed behind the wagon and they stood firm against her now. The light from her orb spilled across the ground and up the legs of two men standing guard. They didn't move as she approached and Elka saw that their eyes were solid metal.

Empty Warriors or Endless Workers. Was there a difference? She'd thought that there would be, but she'd been wrong. These sparkless monsters wearing her brother's face had no humanity. If Torsgen ordered them to kill everyone in Taumerg they'd do it, without pause, without hesitation. And they wouldn't stop until everyone was dead.

Elka stepped up to the doors. The Empty Warriors watched but didn't stop her. They wore identical suits made of the finest Hagguar fabrics and each carried two clockwork pistols. She'd always thought Torsgen's pale eyes were cold but they seemed full of emotion when compared to the eerie blank metal that stared at her from these replicas of his face. Hoping she wasn't about to get stabbed in the back, Elka passed the monsters, pushed open both doors and stepped into the workshop.

The heat hit her first and then she couldn't see as her puffer's goggles steamed up. She pushed them up onto her forehead and had to untuck her fringe which caught in the strap. She imagined her spine was riveted together with the strongest steel as she strode into the workshop, tall and straight. She walked through one of the silo-like structures. A tangle of pipes, valves and cogs snaked from floor to ceiling. Steam puffed from small release valves and a glass dial was showing a needle working steadily from blue to green.

An archway opened into the main space of the workshop, below the big dome, and Elka stepped through. The walls curved upwards, brick at the bottom, turning to panels of metal in the top half. And everything was lit by the orange glow of a furnace. It was like being inside the belly of a giant dragon.

She heard the roar of her own dragon and Inelle's relief at seeing her washed through her mind. Elka's eyes skimmed over everything in the room until they found her.

'Inelle!' she yelled and managed two steps towards her before she felt the muzzle of a pistol against her temple.

Inelle roared again, the sound echoing back from the huge curved ceiling. Hearing her nearly tore Elka in two. Inelle was still tangled in the net which had caught her, but now she was trapped in a cage as well. Thin bars of metal curved around her, as if she was being held in a giant bird cage.

Elka twisted her head as far as she could against the pistol and saw its owner, Claujar. He was neat and perfect as always, not a single grey hair out of place.

'You can let her go now, she's served her purpose. I'm here,' Elka told him.

Instead of answering Claujar pushed with the pistol making Elka walk further into the workshop. Their boots clopped on the wooden floor but the sound was lost amongst the hissing of steam and grinding of gears. Elka saw that all the equipment for watching the stars had been removed and replaced with machines she didn't understand. To her right a large copper tank stood on its end, a porthole window in the front and a series of pipes emerging from the top. Elka followed them with her eyes over to a workbench that took up the whole back wall of the room.

She felt Inelle watching her and told her dragon to stay calm. As she walked she scanned the room, searching for the levers that would open up the roof. Claujar shoved her and she stumbled. Steam puffed across her vision and Elka stepped through it. As it cleared, she recognised the man at the workbench.

'Frannack!' Elka called.

Her brother turned and looked surprised to see her. He wore puffer's goggles over his glasses and had his sleeves rolled up. In his hands he held an empty bottle, about the size of a gin bottle, made of pale green glass. The workbench was littered with tools, lengths of pipe, wires and cogs. Frannack cleared a space and reverently placed the empty bottle in it.

'Elka, why are you here?' Frannack asked. He didn't seem to have noticed that Claujar had a pistol to her head.

'I came to get her, of course.' Elka pointed at Inelle.

Frannack blinked—the glasses and goggles combination made his eyes look huge. He seemed surprised to see the dragon in his workshop as if he hadn't noticed her being dragged in. Elka knew that when Frannack's mind delved into an engineering problem it forgot the rest of the world until he'd solved it.

'What are you working on? And why are you out here?' Elka swept out a hand, taking in the retrofitted workshop.

'Our future, Elka.'

The reply came from Torsgen as he emerged from one of the other silos. Men followed him—thugs and Vorjagen—and took up positions around the room. Footsteps sounded from Elka's left and she turned to see five Empty Warriors wearing Torsgen's face appear from another silo. Five more innocent lives that Torsgen had stolen and used to make these sparkless monsters.

Torsgen strode across the workshop floor, lantern light shimmering on the gold thread at his cuffs, on his highly polished boots, on the silver links of his pocket watch, and on Pagrin's bracelet clasped around his wrist.

Frannack had turned back to his workbench and was fussing with something there. Elka noticed Mila appear, tool belt around her waist, goggles pushed up onto her forehead. She paid no attention to Torsgen or anyone else; all her focus was on whatever Frannack had in his hands.

'Claujar,' Torsgen spoke the word and nodded. Elka felt the pistol disappear from her temple. Freed, she longed to run to Inelle but she needed to find the roof's levers first. Then when the others flew in and attacked, she could rescue her dragon.

She watched Torsgen walk calmly towards her and

held herself steady. Out of habit she pulled on the same cold expression that he wore but then realised that mask didn't fit her anymore. Instead she set her face into the determined frown she'd seen Aimee wear. Torsgen scowled as he looked her up and down, taking in her mismatched outfit, the dirty clothes under a new coat.

'You seem to have let your standards slip, sister.'

Elka glared at him. 'Take off the bracelet, Torsgen.'

She could shoot him now, but how many sparks did he have inside himself? Enough to heal from a bullet to the heart?

'You don't remember it, the basement we lived in after our parents died, but I can still see it every time I close my eyes.' He walked around her as he spoke. 'There were four families crammed in down there and one of the women looked after you. I don't remember her name but I remember her saying that you cried a lot.' He stopped in front of her, looking her in the eye. 'It was my job to get us out of there, to make a life for us where we'd be safe and my baby sister didn't cry all day because she was cold and the air she breathed was rank with damp.'

'And you did that, Torsgen.' Elka grabbed on to the hope that maybe there was a chance she could talk him out of this. He'd killed, but so had she. There could be a way back for them both. 'We're already one of the richest families in Taumerg, we don't need any more.'

'Ah, Elka.' Torsgen began circling her again. 'That's what you never realised. It's not about the galders, it's about power. In that basement we were nobodies, but by this time next year, we'll rule Taumerg.'

'It's wrong.' Elka looked to the Empty Warriors standing patiently at the edges of the workshop.

Torsgen was behind her and the back of Elka's neck prickled. All he had to do was grab her and he could steal her spark. She felt sick at the thought of all she was—her skills, her loves, the dreams she had for her future—being turned into an Empty Warrior.

She flinched when Torsgen leaned in, his words loud in her ear. 'It was all your idea.'

Torsgen's voice had always been edged with frost but a force thrummed behind it now too. It was the power of the bracelet, the power Aimee had resisted but that Torsgen had embraced. And now it was corrupting him.

'I made a mistake,' Elka said. 'I shouldn't have taken the bracelet. It should have been destroyed after Pagrin was defeated.'

'All of this is thanks to you, Elka,' Torsgen continued as if she hadn't spoken. 'You took too long to retrieve this bracelet, and you've become unnaturally attached to that dragon, but I'm willing to forgive you those mistakes.' He came to stand beside her and Elka forced herself not to show weakness by edging away. 'Because actually the two years you were away gave us more time.'

'Time to do what?'

'This.'

Torsgen waved a hand to take in the workshop. Elka still didn't understand. Torsgen walked away from her, over to the workbench where Frannack, Mila and Claujar were already crowded around something. Elka spotted the gears high up on the wall that would open the roof. Her eyes followed the rods down from them but they disappeared behind the tall copper tank. The levers must be behind there. Elka took a slow step in that direction. Around the room the eyes of the thugs, and Vorjagen, were on Torsgen. The shiny metal eyes of the Empty Warriors were unreadable. Elka took another three steps, slowly, carefully.

Torsgen aimed a pistol at her without even turning from the workbench. 'Come,' he ordered.

Elka hesitated until Torsgen stepped aside and she saw what everyone was looking at.

'No, no, no.' The word escaped her in a panicked gasp. Elka ran to the workbench and grabbed her middle brother. 'Frannack what have you done?'

Torsgen's smile was cold, calculating and proud. He clapped a hand on Frannack's shoulder. 'I always knew you had the best brain in Taumerg.' He looked back to Elka. 'And I told you that we'd put the two years you delayed us to good use.'

Elka barely heard him. She was staring down at the wooden box on the workbench. Its heavy lid was open, the inside lined with purple velvet, and sitting in a row were three identical metal cuffs. They were made of steel, not gold, and the dial on each one was clockwork, but Elka still recognised them for what they were.

Frannack had copied Pagrin's bracelet and made more.

CHAPTER 29

AT WHAT COST

Elka remembered Torsgen telling Frannack at breakfast to keep working on his spark-damned problem. This is what he'd been talking about. In the days after she returned from Kierell, Torsgen had taken the bracelet and Elka hadn't seen it again until he put it on today. That's because he'd given it to Frannack. Not so Frannack could engineer a way for it to work without stealing sparks but so Frannack could manufacture more.

'Do they work?' Elka asked, dreading the answer.

Frannack picked one up and turned it over in his hands. It looked so clunky and industrial compared to the beautifully engraved gold cuff on Torsgen's wrist.

'This has been the most challenging engineering problem I've ever come across,' Frannack said, staring at his homemade bracelet, admiration shining in his eyes. 'Thank you for bringing me the solution, Elka.'

'I would have got Inelle to melt Pagrin's bracelet to slag if I thought for even one second that you could do this, Frannack.' Elka wanted to reach out and touch her brother's arm, to pull his gaze away from the horrific thing that he'd created.

'I still don't know what powers Torsgen's one,' Frannack continued as if Elka hadn't spoken. He gestured at their brother's wrist then began flipping through a notebook on the workbench with one hand. Elka saw it was filled with scribbled drawings of the bracelet and copied-out passages of the Quorentin engraved upon it.

'We've tried everything we can think of to work it out but it's powered by some ancient Quorelle magic,' Mila added, shrugging her shoulders.

'It doesn't matter what powered this one in the past, what matters is powering these ones now.' Torsgen took the bracelet from Frannack's hands and tossed it in the air, catching it and smiling.

'You've all gone insane!' Elka yelled and across the room Inelle roared. 'The Quorelle bracelets kill anyone who puts one on unless you start murdering people by stealing their sparks! But you thought that sounded like such a great idea that you've made more of them! Frannack?' Elka had to repeat his name three times before he pulled his attention from his notebook and looked at her. 'Do they work?'

'They didn't, not at first.' It was Torsgen who answered. 'But once you brought us Pagrin's bracelet, Frannack studied it and found a way.'

'You see, whatever powers the Quorelle bracelet doesn't require a spark to work,' Frannack took up the explanation, his voice exactly the same as it had been when Elka was little and he was trying to teach her about the machines he built. 'Torsgen's bracelet draws on the wearer's spark to power it, which is why it'll kill someone with only one spark in their chest, but it doesn't need a spark inside it before it starts working.' He took another of his bracelets from the box and held it up. 'When we first put these ones on, nothing happened.'

'You put one on?' Elka gasped, horrified.

'Of course,' Frannack frowned at her. 'How else was I going to test it? But nothing happened. That's when Mila came up with the theory that these ones need something to power them *before* they start working.'

'They require a spark to be already in them before the wearer puts one on. Though that spark seems to get used up when the bracelet is activated. So the bracelet still draws on the wearer's spark, draining it and killing them,' Mila added.

The horror grew wings in Elka's mind as the full meaning of Mila's words settled on her. This time she did grab Frannack's arm and pulled him around to face her.

'Where did you get the sparks from to test this theory?' When he didn't answer Elka shook him. 'Frannack! Where? And how do you know your bracelets will drain a wearer's spark?'

'Torsgen got me sparks,' Frannack answered as if that was the least important part of all this.

'He took them from people!' Elka yelled.

Frannack tugged himself free of her arm. 'Science requires sacrifices.'

'Not people's lives, Frannack!'

'Your vision always was too short, Elka, your dreams too small,' Torsgen handed the steel bracelet back to Frannack.

As her brother reached out to take it his sleeve slipped up his arm and Elka saw it—dull metal and little copper cogs.

'You're wearing one! A working one.'

Elka stepped back in shock and bumped right into Claujar. The older man clamped a hand on her arm and pressed the muzzle of his pistol to the back of her neck.

'Shhh, enough shouting.'

Elka ignored his command and screamed at her brother. 'Frannack, take it off! You don't have to do this just because Torsgen is. You don't owe him anything!'

Frannack looked around at her, magnified eyes wide behind his goggles, brow creased in confusion. 'I thought you understood, Elka. About the machines and their beauty, with the complex interplay of cogs and pistons and steam, of theories and minds.'

Elka shook her head, struggling to make Frannack see beyond the engineering he loved to the people it would hurt and kill. 'Those bracelets aren't just machines, Frannack, they're tools for murder.'

'Science requires sacrifice,' he repeated and Elka knew then that Frannack was beyond saving too. She felt tears heavy on her lashes and blinked them away.

She had to stop this. Had to get free of Claujar and

open the roof. She scanned the workshop, noting where all Torsgen's thugs were standing, where the Empty Warriors waited. She thought of the pistol pressed to her neck and how close to her Torsgen stood. She tried to use everything Aimee had taught her about fighting when outnumbered. But in those practised scenarios she'd always had her dragon and Inelle was still trapped under the net inside the cage.

Before she could make a move, or even think of one, Elka heard the clang of a door behind her and then footsteps on the floorboards. Torsgen looked over her shoulder and nodded.

'Bring him here,' he called, then turned to Claujar. 'And hold her,' he ordered.

Elka felt Claujar's grip tighten on her arm till it felt like he'd crack her bones, and the cold metal of the pistol pressed harder into the back of her neck. The footsteps came closer then Nail walked into view, marching a young man at pistol tip before him. The gas lanterns were in the centre of the workshop and above the workbench rather than out at the edges, meaning Nail and his prisoner walked through shadow until they finally emerged into the orange glow.

The prisoner was Daan.

'Get off him! Let him go!'

Elka's yells drew Daan's attention and his eyes locked on hers. Elka sucked in a breath as she saw his busted lip, the blood on his nose and chin, and the purpling around his left eye that was already swelling shut. Another man appeared behind Nail wearing the outfit and badge of the Zachen Guards. Events clicked into place in Elka's mind. The guard was one that Torsgen had paid off. She knew she was right when after a nod from Torsgen one of his men tossed the Zachen guard a purse. He snatched it from the air and left without a word.

'Where do you want this one?' Nail asked, giving Daan a push. He stumbled to his knees but Nail grabbed his elbow, pulling him up again.

'In the tank,' Torsgen replied, nodding towards the copper tank with the small porthole window and the pipes coming out of the top.

Nail raised an eyebrow at this but did as he was ordered, dragging Daan towards the tank.

'What are you doing? Torsgen, let him go!' Elka yelled. 'Daan, run! Get out of here!'

She began swearing at her brother but her words were swallowed by Inelle's roars. Claujar's pistol still pressed against her neck, and she watched helpless as Torsgen flicked the dial on Pagrin's bracelet to *ura*. Daan was kicking and shouting but he was eighteen and a baker, not a fighter. Nail was twice his weight and easily held him pinned while Frannack opened the door of the tank. Nail threw him inside.

'Daan!'

'Elka! You were always—'

The clang of the door slamming shut stole whatever Daan wanted to tell her.

Elka couldn't stand it. She wouldn't sit by while something terrible happened to Daan. Claujar had one of her arms pinned to her side but Elka raised the other, elbow up, about to smash it backwards into Claujar's face. But a hand grabbed her arm and pulled it out straight. Yelling in frustration Elka turned to see Mila. The puffer was strong from a lifetime of working with machines and she held Elka fast.

Torsgen strode towards her, pulled on a leather glove and backhanded her across the face. Pain exploded across Elka's cheekbone and the workshop filled with Inelle's roars. Torsgen pulled off the glove, finger by finger, and held his deadly hand inches from her face.

'You think you can just walk away from this family? Chose a different life? This is who you are, Elka.' Torsgen strode back over to the copper tank. 'You almost made a mess of things with your stunts, bringing Riders to our city, releasing the sparks we'd gathered in that warehouse, burning out the Vorjagen.' Torsgen smoothed his hair back, hands rasping on the shaved sides of his head. 'And now you're running around shouting murder. This isn't murder, Elka, this is progress. This is what you wanted to be part of and I won't let you turn your back on us now. Because above all else, what matters?'

'Family matters,' Elka gave the answer, but when she said it, she wasn't thinking of her brothers. Inelle knew and growled. The sound drew Torsgen's attention to her and Elka saw the cold fury seep into his face as he looked at her dragon.

'Open it!' Torsgen called the order.

Elka twisted around enough to see one of the Empty

Warriors pull a lever in the wall. Beside him a metal door clanged open, and an intense wave of heat blasted out. Elka saw the huge iron grill and the flames behind it. Then her eyes spotted the track Inelle's cage was affixed to. One pull of a lever and she'd be dragged into the furnace.

'If you hurt her, I'll kill you!' Elka screamed at Torsgen.

'Seems to me that you should only have one family.' Torsgen turned from her and called over to where their brother was adjusting dials on the side of the copper tank. 'Frannack, are we ready?'

The pipes that stuck out of the top of the tank ran down the side, through a series of valves and into a small distillation chamber welded to the tank's side. Frannack took the pale green glass bottle he'd been holding earlier and fitted it to the tap at the bottom of the distillation chamber.

He nodded and stepped back. 'Good to go, Torsgen.'

Elka watched, held and helpless, as Torsgen opened a small panel on the tank's front and slipped his hand and wrist inside.

'I always knew Frannack was a genius, but this is exceptional.'

Frannack smiled at Torsgen's praise and began explaining to Elka. His eyes and face lit up like a gas lanterned turned up full. He saw the excitement of solving a problem, of making a machine work the way he wanted it to. He didn't see the life if affected. Daan's life.

'Copper was the key. It seems to conduct a person's life energy so much better. But even then we couldn't get it working until we tried using Pagrin's bracelet as well.'

'Working to do what?' Elka demanded, though she dreaded the answer.

'To take out a spark, of course, but collect it so we can then put it in a bracelet.' Frannack spoke as if she was stupid and hadn't been listening.

Daan. They were going to remove his spark and put it into one of Frannack's steel bracelets. They were going to kill him.

'No! Torsgen stop!' Elka screamed and thrashed but Claujar and Mila held her firm. 'Don't do this!'

But Frannack stepped to his workbench and threw a lever. The tank began to hum. Daan was shouting inside, his cries muffled by the thick metal. Torsgen closed his eyes and activated Pagrin's bracelet. Elka saw Daan's face through the porthole window, head thrown back, screaming. Then the inside of the tank began to glow as the power of Pagrin's bracelet combined with Frannack's machine sucked out his spark. But Torsgen wasn't touching Daan, so instead of being pulled into his chest, Daan's spark was sucked into the pipes and out through the distillation chamber.

Elka watched in sickening horror as Daan's life energy condensed into a stream of greenish-white light and poured into the glass bottle. Then she heard the muffled thump as Daan collapsed inside the tank. Dead.

'Put it back!' Elka yelled, still thrashing, still held firm. 'Frannack, put Daan's spark back!'

Elka couldn't tear her eyes from the glowing bottle in Frannack's hands. Everything Daan ever was or could be was in there. The glow of it was beautiful, but it was so, so wrong. Moving with care, Frannack took the bottle to his workbench and screwed it into the end of a curving copper pipe. Then he attached one of his steel bracelets to the other end. There were three valves on the pipe, and he opened all three and stepped back.

'Daan.' Elka's throat was hoarse from screaming and the word was nothing but a croak.

Daan's spark emptied from the bottle and into the bracelet. Tears streamed down Elka's face. There had to be a way to reverse it. If Frannack built this machine then surely he could make it work the other way around.

When the glass bottle was empty Frannack disconnected the bracelet and held it up.

'All good?' Torsgen asked.

Frannack nodded and passed him the bracelet. Torsgen's pale eyes turned to her and Elka saw in them what was coming. She screamed, her voice cracking. She thrashed, her wounded ribs and hip a throbbing agony. But Claujar pressed the pistol harder against her skull and Mila tightened the vice-like grip on her arm.

The steel bracelets required a spark to be already in them before a wearer put one on, that's what Frannack had said. And he'd also told her that the spark in the bracelet got used up when the bracelet was activated.

Elka could hear Inelle thrashing and roaring in her cage, tearing her wings and her scales, desperate to escape and help her Rider. Elka's mind was too flooded with her own horror to calm her dragon.

Torsgen pushed up the sleeve of Elka's new coat. The yellow coat Daan had bought her because it would look good against Inelle's indigo scales. He opened the catch on the steel bracelet and placed it around Elka's wrist. Torsgen knew the pain this was going to cause her. He was punishing her for her disloyalty by ensuring she could never leave the family.

'Please,' she begged. 'Please don't.'

'You are one of us, Elka,' Torsgen said.

Then he snapped the bracelet closed.

Icy pain shot up Elka's arm and she screamed. The spike on the bracelet pierced her vein, connecting it to her spark. Her vision faded to black as a wave of energy washed up through her arm and pulsed across her heart. Daan. This was his energy. The bracelet had just used up all that he was to connect itself to her. Daan was gone. Mila and Claujar released her and Elka slumped over, hands on knees, gasping.

As Elka straightened her vision cleared. All around the workshop she saw balls of greenish-white light in people's chests. Sparks. She could see everyone's sparks. The bracelet was working. She felt fresh tears spill down her cheeks. Her own spark glowed in her chest, bright as a small sun.

She looked up and was pleased to see that Claujar's spark barely flickered in his chest. But as Elka watched, still feeling nauseous, Claujar began rolling up one sleeve. There were still two more steel bracelets on Frannack's workbench. Enough for Claujar and Mila to get one each. Torsgen was calling to Nail, telling him to bring them another spark. Nail nodded and disappeared into one of the back silos. They must have prisoners locked in there too. Elka's vision swam and she had to put her hands on her knees again. Torsgen was about to murder two more people, steal their sparks, and use them up to give Claujar and Mila bracelets.

And then what? Would they keep stealing sparks from teenagers Torsgen had decided didn't deserve their lives? Would they use them to create Empty Warriors or Endless Workers? Elka looked down at the cuff of steel fixed to her wrist. A line of blood ran from under the bracelet and across her palm. Did Torsgen expect her to use the bracelet too?

Elka shook her head.

'No more bloody hands.'

She'd promised herself.

Torsgen thought he had her subdued and for now she was ignored. She looked across the workshop at Inelle. Her dragon was curled up under the barbed net, bloody tail wrapped around her body. The edges of her wings were shredded and her snout was criss-crossed with cuts. She looked like she'd given up.

Elka closed her eyes and touched their connection, relieved to find it still there and that the bracelet hadn't affected it. Her whole body ached, and her heart felt wrung out, but Elka scraped together what strength she could find and sent it along her bond to Inelle.

'I need you to wait and then be ready. Can you do that for me?'

The sorrow Elka felt from her dragon was almost too much. She was scared, hurting, lonely without her clutch and desperate to be reunited with her Rider. As Elka watched, Inelle slowly opened her mouth and bit down gently. Fresh tears welled in Elka's eyes as she looked at her wrist, the one she'd hurt, the one Inelle always gently bit, and saw the cold metal of the bracelet stuck on it.

Anger shot through her like a fresh burst of steam. 'I am not one of you,' she told the bracelet then looked to Inelle. 'You're my family.'

She heard the clang of a door and echoed shouts from beyond the workshop. Nail was bringing another victim for the tank. She had to stop this and fill the workshop with her real family.

CHAPTER 30

FIRE AND METAL

WHILE EVERYONE'S ATTENTION was on Frannack and his bracelets, Elka slipped into the shadows at the workshop's edge. She climbed through a tangle of pipes and over a cog bigger than she was. It was attached to the ceiling with chains and beyond it were two levers, each as tall as her waist. Elka grabbed them both and pulled. With a grinding of gears and a clanking of chains the curved roof of the workshop began slowly opening, revealing a sliver of night sky.

'Come on,' Elka urged it to move quicker.

Shafts of moonlight streamed into the workshop, followed a moment later by three dragons. The snap of their wings echoed around the workshop and for a moment surprise froze everyone except Elka. Malgerus landed on top of the copper tank that still contained Daan's corpse and roared. His orange scales blazed in the lantern light. Skydance swooped around the workshop, his talons scoring bloody gouges into three men before they'd a chance to aim their pistols. And Jess landed in the middle of the floor, talons scraping the floorboards, scales shimmering like emeralds, and lashed out with her tail. It smashed into the workbench, tearing off the legs. Frannack's equipment scattered across the floor in a mess of broken pipes and shards of glass.

'Take down the dragons!' Torsgen roared at the Vorjagen.

Elka used the distraction to run from the shadows and across the workshop floor. She'd dropped her pistol when Torsgen had snapped the bracelet around her wrist but she scooped it up now and ran for Inelle. Bullets shot through the air around her as Torsgen's men recovered from their shock and fired at the dragons. Elka skidded to her knees, tearing a hole in her trousers. Aiming at a thug, she squeezed the pistol's trigger. He screamed as her bullet shattered his kneecap.

Jumping up, Elka sprinted on. She heard the rustle of wings and saw sapphire scales flash past. Men were shouting, pistols were firing, gears were grinding as the roof continued to open fully and the three dragons were roaring. But above it all Elka heard Inelle call to her.

'I'm coming!'

Something moved at the edge of her vision, lightning quick, faster than a man. Elka was knocked sideways and fell, jarring everything, pain firing everywhere. Dizzy, she scrambled back, heels kicking. Above her loomed a monster with metal eyes wearing her brother's face. Her hands were empty. Her pistol lay on the floorboards five steps behind the Empty Warrior.

She wished that before she'd entered the workshop she'd thought to tie the damn thing to her wrist.

'Elka!'

The cry came from above and she looked up in time to see Skydance sweep overhead. Pelathina leaned from her saddle and dropped a dragon's breath orb. Elka snatched it from the air and threw it at the Empty Warrior. It smashed open on his chest, freed flames instantly burning through his fancy suit and the metal shell underneath. He took a step forward but the dragon's breath had melted his whole chest and it caved in. He toppled forward and Elka leapt over him as he hit the floor.

She ran. Inelle roared, twisting inside the net, cutting herself, trying to get free. Behind her through the open door of the furnace the flames crackled, throwing out their terrible heat.

One of the Vorjagen lunged at her and Elka dropped and rolled. Agony flared in her hip as she sprang back to her feet and she stumbled. The Vorjagen was Tori, and she grabbed Elka around the throat and lifted her up till her toes were scraping the floorboards. Tattooed beasts snarled on her shaved head and fury brimmed in her eyes.

'You and me have unfinished business. Torsgen's orders are to keep you alive but you need to pay for stealing my crossbow and for what your friends did to our lodge,' she spat. Elka felt the cold tip of a dagger slide up her cheek and press against her lower eyelid. 'Taking your eyes ain't enough for what you did, but it'll do for a start.'

Shadows crowed the edge of her vision as Tori squeezed her throat, but her hands were free. All she had to do was turn the cogs on her bracelet, switch the dial to *ura*, and touch Tori. Her fingers found the edges of the bracelet, pawed at it, groping for the dial. She found it, but didn't turn it. If she did, she'd be giving in to Torsgen, becoming like him. Tori glared at her and lifted her wrist up, ready to press her dagger into Elka's eye.

Then she was gone. Snatched into the air as Jess flew past. Tori yelled curses as Jess carried her high then, with a flick of her strong body, threw her out the roof and into the night sky.

'Thank you!'

Elka yelled to Aimee, already running towards Inelle. She ran so hard that she couldn't stop and smacked right into the cage. Her dragon pressed herself against the bars, barbs on the net cutting into her scales. The rumbling sound she made was almost like a purr.

'I'm here,' Elka told her.

There was a lock on the cage. Elka stepped back and kicked it. Pain jarred up through her heel but the lock held. Holding onto the cage's bars she kicked it again. A bullet whizzed past her and pinged off the iron. Elka yelped.

'Can't let you free her, miss.'

She turned to glare at Nail. Behind him, thugs and Empty Warriors were fighting dragons and Riders. Flames crackled in patches all over the workshop. But

Elka's full attention was on Nail. His spark glowed bright in his chest, almost as bright as her own. Back in Kierell when he'd dragged her into the alley and threatened her, Elka had been too shocked at seeing him to fight back. Not now. She had no scimitars, no pistol and her dragon was caged behind her. But she was still a Rider.

Her first high kick knocked the pistol from Nail's hand and it skittered along the floor. She followed with a punch which cracked satisfyingly into his nose. Blood splattered her knuckles. He swore and lashed out but Elka ducked under his swing and jabbed another punch into his ribs. Nail grunted and jabbed downwards with his elbow. It caught the edge of Elka's shoulder as she danced back. It knocked her off balance and she stumbled. Nail's next punch glanced off the side of her skull and black spots flickered in her vision.

But she would not be beaten by this thug. She *would* defend her dragon.

Elka skipped back, drawing him towards her, then punched. He knocked aside her right fist but her left connected with the top of his breastbone, right above his spark. He gasped as the air whooshed out of his lungs. Springing off her left foot, Elka kicked him straight in the centre of his thigh. Nail howled as his leg buckled. He fell to one knee and Elka sank a kick into his belly. She put all her anger into it, and the force of it threw Nail backwards. She heard the crack as his skull hit the floor.

She waited, fists held high, bouncing on the balls of

her feet, but Nail didn't get up again. His spark flickered but it didn't go out. He was unconscious, not dead. That would do. Grabbing his pistol Elka ran back to Inelle's cage.

'Move!' she yelled to her dragon. Inelle understood and shuffled as far back in the cage as she could.

Elka aimed the pistol at the lock and fired, blowing the mechanism apart. The cage door sprang open and she clambered inside. Inelle's joy flooded Elka's mind. She tried to wrap herself around her Rider, but she was still caught in the net. Its barbed rope pressed painfully against Elka's skin as Inelle nuzzled her.

'Hang on, stop, Inelle. Let me get you out of here.'

She needed a blade. She spun, about to leap out of the cage and find one when suddenly a scimitar fell from the sky and stabbed into the floorboards by the open door. There was a white domed dragon's tooth on the pommel. Aimee's scimitar.

'Don't lose it! It's the only one I've got left!'

Aimee and Jess swept past the cage and Elka thought she saw a smile on the Rider's face. Reaching out she grabbed the blade and quickly began cutting through the net. Inelle was so desperate to get out that as soon as the hole in the net was large enough she sprang free, knocking Elka over on the way. Elka lay on her back in the cage and laughed as her mind flooded with her dragon's joy. Inelle jumped down to the floor and stretched out her wings to their full extent. Through their connection Elka shared the relief Inelle felt at being able to spread her wings after hours spent cramped inside that net.

Elka scrambled out of the cage and wrapped her arms around her dragon's neck, pressing her face against her cool scales. Inelle rumbled a dragon's purr. Elka could see how tattered her wings were from where the net had torn them, and blood streaked her scales from a hundred small cuts. Elka nearly laughed again when she saw a streak of viscous dragon's blood on the arm of her new coat, thinking Daan would be disappointed that she'd ruined it already. Then she remembered that Daan was dead.

Anger pushed aside Inelle's joy and Elka grabbed her saddle.

'Can you fly?' she asked her dragon. Inelle's head swivelled round on her long neck and she licked Elka's face. 'Ugh, horrible beast.' But she sent Inelle a wave of love as she mounted up. She pulled down the sleeve of her coat to hide the bracelet. She didn't want to look at it.

From her saddle, Elka got a better view of the battle raging around them. Torsgen's thugs had rallied to him and they were crouched behind the overturned workbench, firing at the dragons. Frannack and Mila were there too. Mila had grabbed a Vorjagen's crossbow, the weapon looking almost as big as she was, and was tracking Malgerus across the ceiling. Frannack, though, was scrabbling around behind the workbench trying to gather up the pieces of his broken equipment, ignoring the battle around him. Mila fired and the bolt shot towards Malgerus but he dodged at the last moment and it lodged in the curved wall. Malgerus roared and blew a small jet of dragon's breath. None of them would risk a full blast in such an enclosed space.

Elka saw Jess launch herself from a rafter, aiming for the workbench, but the moment she moved Claujar stepped out from behind a cluster of pipes, pistols in both hands. Elka felt a cold spike of fear as he aimed at Jess and Aimee. Pelathina must have seen the danger too because her shout rang out above the noise of the fight.

'Aimee, swing!'

Without even looking round Aimee did exactly that. Jess went from diving straight to swinging round in a wide arc, wingtips fluttering, in half a second. She tucked in her feet and lifted her tail so she didn't hit the walls, and Aimee must have known exactly what Jess would do because she shifted her weight perfectly, staying in her saddle, staying in control. It was beautiful to watch. As they swung around the far wall Jess tilted her wings back to horizontal and flapped twice, heading straight for Claujar. The older man had tried tracking the dragon with his pistols but he was too slow. Jess and Aimee were on him before he could fire.

Jess grabbed his arms with her forelegs and tore. She ripped both his arms off. Claujar dropped screaming to the floor and Jess tossed his arms away in different directions. Elka thought of the kids locked in a dank basement waiting for their sparks to be harvested; of the councillors and puffers Claujar had threatened and hurt over the years; of the hands and legs he'd broken. The lives he'd ruined. She felt not a single drop of sympathy for him.

Inelle called out to the other dragons and Elka felt her delight at being reunited with her clutch.

'Alright, let's go and help them.' She pushed on Inelle's spiralled horns and her dragon took off.

The click and blast of pistols sounded instantly as she and Inelle joined the fray. Elka held on tight as Inelle tipped her wings and they soared around the outer edge of the workshop. Below her a bullet tore through Skydance's wing as he swept low, grabbing two men in his talons. Pelathina guided him high and when he reached the roof Skydance dropped them. One smacked off the cage that had held Inelle, his scream cut short as his spine cracked.

The air smelled of smoke and blood and hot metal. Malgerus dived for the workbench. The men behind it ducked and fired up at him. His talons scraped wood and pipes but missed hooking into anyone's flesh. Nathine, though, leaned out of her saddle and Elka saw the glint of metal and polished wood in her hand.

'Sparks! Who let her have a pistol?' Elka asked Inelle. The thought of Nathine with a pistol made her shoulder blades itch.

Nathine fired and even from the back of a swooping dragon her aim was true. A Vorjagen dropped, the tattoos on his skull exploding apart in a mess of brain and shards of bone. Elka had to admit that the move was pretty spectacular and Nathine looked awesome. Malgerus roared their triumph as he swept back around, tail flicking aside to avoid another hail of bullets.

'Elka!' Aimee called as Jess flew towards them.

'Where's Torsgen?' Elka called back as Jess grabbed a metal rafter just above them, perching for a moment.

Aimee pointed to the tank that had stolen Daan's life. 'He's behind there with three Empty Warriors. I think he's trying to close the roof and trap us.'

Just as she said this Elka heard the grinding of gears and above them the curved ceiling began to move, shutting out the night sky.

'Can you take care of the workbench thugs if I go after Torsgen?' Elka asked and Aimee nodded. 'But watch out for Frannack, he's wearing a bracelet.'

'Torsgen took it off?' confusion scrunched Aimee's face.

Elka shook her head. 'No, Frannack's been making more. Torsgen's still wearing Pagrin's bracelet and Frannack's wearing one he made.'

'Kyelli's sparks! How is that possible?'

'Fight now, explanations later?' Elka suggested.

'Alright,' Aimee looked down towards the tipped over workbench. 'Frannack is…'

'Dark hair, long on top, shaved at the sides.'

'Elka, if he's wearing a bracelet, we either kill him or he takes it off and he dies.' Aimee's eyes were soft with sympathy.

Elka blinked and felt tears on her lashes. 'I know. And if he made more bracelets once then he could do it again. That's not knowledge that anyone should have.' She looked down to the workshop floor. 'I'm sorry, Frannack,' she whispered.

Pagrin's bracelet might have corrupted Torsgen, but he'd corrupted her and Frannack years before. Elka had been an idiot and only saw it now.

'Make it quick,' she said, turning back to Aimee.

'I promise.'

'Do you want this back?' Elka held up Aimee's scimitar but the Rider shook her head.

'I'll probably just lose it. I've got a habit of that.' She threw Elka a swift smile before Jess pushed off the rafter and back down into the battle.

Inelle had been hovering, her wings' backbeats swirling the air, but now Elka pushed her into a dive. A pipe in the workshop's wall had burst, steam spewing out and Inelle swerved around it. Under the hiss of the steam Elka didn't hear the pistol firing but she felt Inelle jolt as the bullet hit her. She saw a man below them, crouched behind a wooden crate. A moment later he was gone as Malgerus grabbed him, tossing him across the room.

'Inelle, please tell me you're alright?'

Panic made Elka's voice tight. She couldn't stop to see where her dragon had been hit. She'd felt a burst of pain through their connection when the bullet bit but it was gone now.

'Inelle?' All she got back from her dragon was a strong sense of determination. 'Okay, just a flesh wound then.'

Inelle's wingtips brushed the wall as they swept down behind the copper tank. Elka tried not to think about Daan's sparkless body slumped inside. Three Empty Warriors aimed pistols at them.

'Hold!' Torsgen ordered and the warriors lowered their weapons.

Inelle landed, talons clacking on the floorboards, growl rumbling in her throat. The warriors watched them with their creepy solid metal eyes. Behind them, Torsgen stepped away from the roof levers. And above them Elka heard the thunk as the roof closed, shutting off the dragons' escape.

'I gave you the future, Elka!' Torsgen's normally calm voice was rough with anger. It was the first time Elka had ever heard him like that. He spread his arms wide. 'I offered you the place in our family that your childish little mind always dreamed of. And you toss it away for what? Some freaks and their dumb beasts?'

Elka needed to be eye to eye with her brother, so she slipped from her saddle, Aimee's scimitar in her right hand. Watching the warriors warily she stepped around her dragon. She stood with Inelle at her back, her wings spread as wide as they'd go in the narrow space, and her head over Elka's shoulder, both of them staring down Torsgen.

Torsgen glared at her appearance as if she was fifteen again and had just returned home with her nose freshly pierced. 'You look ridiculous,' he spat.

Elka smiled. 'Wrong, I look awesome.'

All her life she'd listened to Torsgen, eavesdropping on him when he wouldn't let her into the room. She'd absorbed his words and used them to shape the person she wanted to be. But now, she didn't need him to be somebody. She was a Rider, and that was a million times better than ever being a Hagguar. She squeezed the hilt of Aimee's scimitar. No more words. It was time for action.

CHAPTER 31

NO CHOICE

TORSGEN MUST HAVE seen the intent in her eyes because he took a step back. His Empty Warriors closed ranks in front of him. It was eerie, staring down four identical brothers but knowing only one was real.

'I've imbued these three with the purpose of protecting me,' Torsgen called over the warriors' shoulders. 'You'll never get through them, Elka.'

Three lives, ripped from their owners so Torsgen could have bodyguards. In that moment Elka truly hated him. Inelle growled and the warriors raised their pistols. Armed with only a scimitar, their bullets would find her before she could attack.

Torsgen looked so sure of himself and Elka realised that even now he underestimated her. That gave her an advantage. All her life she'd followed Torsgen, but now it was his turn to follow her. She sent her plan as a series of images to Inelle. Her dragon growled and snorted a puff of smoke that drifted above Elka's head.

'Now!' she yelled.

Inelle took off, and while the Empty Warriors raised their pistols to track her, Elka sprinted between them and grabbed Torsgen. She hoped the fact that they were both wearing bracelets would cancel their power out. She head-butted him and felt his nose crunch. Blood splattered across both their faces. While he was dazed, she hooked an arm around his throat and dragged him backwards. She couldn't feel her spark draining from her chest, so her theory about the bracelets must have been correct.

They'd been standing right by the open door to one of the building's silos and Elka dragged Torsgen inside. In the workshop the warriors fired at Inelle but she blasted them with dragon's breath. One was completely engulfed, the fire peeling back his skin and melting the steel underneath. But the other two dived aside and into the silo behind Elka.

Torsgen spluttered blood but Elka still had him around the throat, and now she pressed Aimee's scimitar to the side of his ribs. One twist of her wrist, a push of her arm, and she'd skewer his heart. Torsgen grabbed her hand, skin against skin, but nothing happened.

'You made me one of you so your hateful bracelet can't hurt me,' Elka spat the words in his ear.

'Elka, this,' he clanged his gold bracelet against her metal one, 'is the future.'

Elka shook her head. 'No. People are the future. Taumerg needs all their different ideas, dreams and ambitions, not just yours.'

The two surviving Empty Warriors aimed their

pistols at Torsgen and at Elka hidden behind him.

'Wait!' Torsgen called to them. 'That shot's too risky.'

But the warriors couldn't listen to reason, they could only act on their purpose to protect Torsgen. They took the shot, aiming at Elka just over Torsgen's shoulder. But Elka ducked and spun her brother with her. Both bullets slammed into his shoulder, spraying blood. He screamed and fell, landing on top of Elka.

'Inelle, head height!' She had to force the words out because Torsgen was crushing her chest and her cracked rib felt like it had been lit on fire.

Inelle stuck her head through the door of the silo and blasted flames. Her dragon's breath exploded outward, setting alight the two Empty Warriors' heads. They beat silently at the flames as the fire melted the skin from their faces. Torsgen groaned, bleeding from his broken nose and the bullets in his shoulder. His immaculate suit was splattered with blood and caked in dust from the floor, and his hair was a straggly mess.

Elka kicked out from under him and wriggled away. One of the warriors had fallen to his knees, still not making a sound as the metal of his head softened and caved inwards. The other one ran at the wall, smacking into it. He knocked over a shelf of lanterns and gas canisters. They clattered to the floor, lanterns smashing, canisters rolling.

'Sparks!'

Elka swore, and though everything in her body hurt she got to her feet and ran for the door. Inelle filled it, her indigo scales streaked with blood and soot. Elka ducked under her wing and span on her heel. Back inside the silo, Torsgen had staggered to his feet. Flames crackled in the silo, Elka's face was sticky and wet with sweat, but her brother's eyes were as cold as ever.

'Elka!' he yelled.

'Do it!' She sent the command to her dragon and crouched down, wrapping her arms around her head, squeezing her eyes shut.

Above her Inelle roared and gave a full blast of dragon's breath, emptying herself out. The flames, hotter than the hottest forge, shot into the room and in the second before they reached the gas canisters Elka sprang to her feet and slammed the door shut. Gritting her teeth against the pain in her side she heaved on the cog mechanism, locking the thick iron door in place. As she slumped back against it she heard the boom of the explosion.

She'd had no choice, but still Elka rested her head against the door and cried for her brother. Inelle hunkered down beside her and rested her head in Elka's lap. She stroked her dragon's feathers and watched her own tears fall and bead on them. The door to the silo grew uncomfortably hot against her back as Inelle's breath burned everything inside to ashes.

When Elka shuffled away from the door she realised the sounds of battle were absent. She gently pushed Inelle off her lap and got painfully to her feet. She noticed as she stood that the hem of her yellow coat was singed black. Fresh tears spilled from her eyes, these ones for Daan. She hobbled around the copper tank, everything seeming to hurt a hundred times more now that the adrenaline was ebbing away. She gripped Aimee's scimitar and placed one hand on Inelle's cool scales, ready to climb back into her saddle and fight if she needed to.

Relief washed through her as she saw that the battle was over. Jess, Malgerus and Skydance had coordinated an attack, landing together on the upturned workbench, their weight pushing it over. The men behind it had been crushed. Elka hobbled over, Inelle following. The three Riders turned at her approach, weapons up, but they lowered them when they saw it was her. Though Nathine was a little slow to lower the pistol she'd aimed at her.

Elka wrinkled her nose as she stepped over one of Claujar's severed arms. She stopped beside Aimee, her boots inches from the pool of blood seeping from beneath the workbench. Shattered glass and bits of broken pipes decorated the floor. Elka's heart twisted as she spotted the bottle Frannack had captured Daan's spark in. It was whole. How was it still whole? Angry, Elka stooped to pick it up, glared at it in her hand for a moment, then hurled it at the wall. Satisfyingly it shattered into a hundred pieces.

Aimee and Pelathina both cocked their heads at her like dragons and Nathine raised an eyebrow. But none of them questioned her.

'Is it over?' she asked.

'Almost,' Aimee replied. 'We need to destroy

Pagrin's bracelet and any others that your brother made.'

'Pagrin's is already gone,' Elka told her.

'Prove it,' Nathine demanded and Aimee threw her friend a frown.

Elka pointed to the silo door behind her. Through the porthole window they could all see the swirl of dragon's breath, like it had been trapped in a giant orb. 'Unless gold can survive dragon's breath I think we can safely say Pagrin's bracelet is destroyed.'

'Your brother?' Pelathina asked softly.

Again, Elka pointed to the silo door. Aimee's face softened with sympathy and she took Elka's hand, giving it a squeeze. Elka squeezed back then quickly pulled away. Not because she didn't want the comfort—she really, really did—but because she didn't want to start crying again. She was trying to be strong, like a Rider, because this wasn't quite over yet.

'How many bracelets did Frannack make?' Aimee asked. If she was upset at Elka pulling away her hand then she didn't show it.

'Three,' Elka replied, telling one last lie because there had been four. 'He was wearing one and there were two others in a box.'

She looked around at the destruction of the workbench and half the workshop too.

'How can you be sure he didn't have more stashed here somewhere?' Nathine demanded.

It was Aimee who answered. 'We can't, so we'll destroy the ones we know about and then burn the whole place down just to be sure. Agreed?'

Elka was surprised when Aimee looked to her but she nodded quickly. 'Agreed.' All around the workshop small fires crackled and it wouldn't take much to set the whole place alight.

'I think there are prisoners here somewhere,' Elka suddenly remembered. 'Same as back in the warehouse.'

'It's okay.' Pelathina sheathed her blades. 'I'll find them and get them out. You three destroy the bracelets.'

She brushed Aimee's sweaty cheek with her lips then ran towards the doors at the back of the workshop. Skydance glided along behind her, sapphire-blue scales shimmering and rainbow-coloured ribbons streaming from his saddle.

'Last one to find the box of bracelets is buying breakfast,' Nathine said as she began digging through the wreckage.

Elka's stomach growled at the mention of food but then soured a moment later when she saw an arm she recognised. The cuff of the silken shirt was embroidered with gold thread but it had been turned back to make room for a metal bracelet. Frannack. She knelt, blood soaking into her now irredeemably ruined trousers, and tugged planks from the workbench off his body. Underneath, Frannack lay stiller than she'd ever seen him. Elka's eyes scanned his body, searching for a spark. There was nothing. He was dead.

Mila was curled up beside him, the shattered remains of the Vorjagen's crossbow scattered across her body. No spark shone in her chest either.

Elka closed her eyes for a moment, remembering a younger Frannack, one overflowing with curiosity and talking endlessly about all the machines he was going to build. She used that memory to push aside the one of the man her brother had become.

Then she heard a thud and opened her eyes. With no spark powering it anymore the bracelet on Frannack's wrist had snapped open and fallen off. She reached over her brother and picked it up.

'Aha! I win,' Nathine called as she tugged the splintered remains of a box from under a jumble of broken pipes. She plucked the two bracelets from inside. One was spattered with blood.

'I've got Frannack's,' Elka said, holding it up.

'Great. What's the best way to destroy them? Dragon's breath?' Nathine asked.

Aimee picked her way over the wreckage as Elka stood up and shook her head. 'How about the furnace?' She pointed to the open maw where Torsgen had threatened to send Inelle.

Aimee smiled a grim smile. 'Perfect.'

Elka took a step towards the furnace but then collapsed.

It wasn't her legs that had given out, though, it was Inelle's. Sudden pain and weakness had made Inelle collapse to the floor and she'd shared it all with Elka full on. For a moment Elka couldn't move, she was so crippled by her dragon's pain.

'Elka! What's wrong?' Aimee was shaking her and Elka opened her eyes only to be blinded by Aimee's spark as she tried to pull her up.

'Move!' Elka shoved Aimee out of the way and crawled across the floor to her dragon. Shards of glass crunched under her palms but Elka didn't feel them. Inelle was lying down, her wings draped across the floor, her beautiful head twisted to the side. Her brain was full of her dragon's pain and Elka struggled to fight past it, to work out what was going on. She reached Inelle and wrapped her arms around her. Instantly her arms felt wet. Pulling back, Elka saw that she was covered in blood. Inelle's blood. Lifting up her wing, she crawled underneath and saw the ragged hole a bullet had torn in her belly, the bullet that Elka had thought was just a flesh wound because Inelle had carried on. Her dragon had hidden her hurt from her.

'Why didn't you tell me, Inelle?' Elka demanded, crawling out from under her wing and lifting Inelle's head into her lap. Her world filled with the comforting smell of woodsmoke. But blood bubbled on Inelle's lips and frothed between her sharp teeth.

'You didn't need to be brave for me,' Elka told her even though it was futile. From the day they'd bonded Inelle had always tried to impress her Rider, to be the absolute best for her. Elka stroked her feathers and they quivered with pleasure at her touch. 'You are the best,' Elka told her.

Inelle nudged her wrist with her snout, too weak to do anything else. 'Yes, we're family.'

Elka sensed their connection fading, felt Inelle drifting away inside her mind. She tried desperately to hold on to it but it was like trying to grab steam. Slowly she slipped away and then was gone. Inelle's head lay motionless in her lap. Elka shook it and howled. But Inelle didn't come back. She was all alone in her head and her mind felt too big and empty now without Inelle sharing it.

Someone crouched and put a warm hand on her shoulder. Inelle's head had become an indigo blur and Elka blinked furiously, trying to shift her tears and see her dragon clearly again. Gently she shook Inelle, willing her to still be alive.

'Elka.'

Someone was shaking her and saying her name. Elka got the impression they'd been talking to her for a while. Her neck felt like it was on gears clogged with rust and turning to look at Aimee was a huge effort. With the cuff of her yellow coat she wiped away her tears but, even though the coat was ruined, couldn't bring herself to wipe her nose on it too.

'I screwed up,' Elka said then kept going as Aimee shook her head. 'I did. I screwed up everything.'

Elka let Aimee lift her hand from Inelle's scales. She slipped her patchy fingers between Elka's, her colourless spots of skin looking even paler against Elka's tanned hands.

'You protected innocent people and you've stopped an ancient power from being used to create monsters,' Aimee said.

Elka looked down at her mismatched outfit, torn and bloody, and her dead dragon's head in her lap. 'I look like a failure.'

'You look unconventionally fantastic,' Aimee told her.

'I would have been a good Rider.'

Aimee grabbed her chin and forced Elka to look her in the eye. 'You *are* a great Rider.'

'Yeah?'

'Sparks, yeah.'

Surprising herself, Elka snorted a small laugh at the ferocity in Aimee's tone.

'Now come on, you've got a mission to finish.' Aimee tugged her upwards.

Elka gently set Inelle's head aside and stood. 'I'll be right back,' she told her dragon, and she meant it because Aimee's words had ignited an idea.

Hobbling beside Aimee, Elka made it over to the furnace. She threw a glare at the cage that had held Inelle. Heat from the furnace pressed against her face, sticking her fringe to her forehead with sweat. As Aimee joined her, she gave Elka a hug. She squeezed too hard and Elka's ribs hurt but right then Elka would have chosen a hundred painful hugs over standing there alone.

Nathine was standing by the door to the furnace, two metal bracelets held awkwardly in her hands. As Elka stepped up with Frannack's bracelet, Nathine threw her a look. There was still anger in the set of her lips, but her eyes had softened ever so slightly with pity.

'She was beautiful, and brave,' Nathine said, nodding back towards Inelle.

'Thank you,' Elka replied. Then she nodded to the furnace. 'After you.'

One after the other Nathine lobbed the bracelets into the roaring flames. The relief at watching them disappear was like heavy chains being cut from Elka's body. As Nathine stepped back, Elka stepped forward and hurled Frannack's bracelet into the furnace. She didn't even feel bad for destroying something her brother had worked hard to create. The bracelets were too evil to exist.

'Oh sparks.'

Elka turned at Aimee's words. She was leaning against her friend, Nathine's arm around her shoulders and their dragons crouched behind them.

'It's actually over this time, isn't it?' Aimee asked, looking around at the destruction in the workshop.

Elka ran her fingers over the bracelet still stuck on her own wrist. She'd been too ashamed to tell Aimee about it before. Now she turned up the sleeve of her coat and stuck out her arm.

'It's not quite over,' Elka said, voice loud above the roaring flames behind them.

'Oh, Kyelli's sparks, Elka!' Aimee exclaimed.

Elka didn't miss the way Nathine's tightened her grip on her scimitar and how Malgerus rose from his crouch, wings unfurling.

'It's in neutral, and I won't touch any of you, just in case,' Elka reassured them.

But Aimee was looking at her and a single tear slipped down her cheek. She stepped away from

Nathine and over to Elka. Aimee trusted her enough to stand within arm's reach. That meant a lot to Elka.

'You didn't use it to steal anyone's spark, did you?'

Elka knew from Aimee's tone that she wasn't asking because she thought Elka had, she was asking because she already knew Elka hadn't, and she didn't want to say aloud what that meant.

Elka placed a hand on her own chest, right above where her spark glowed. 'It's only me in here.'

'Then the bracelet will drain your spark,' Aimee said. 'I don't know how long you've got left. Is your spark bright? It might last months, maybe longer. I don't know. I managed to get Kyelli's bracelet off before I found out how quickly it would kill me.'

Aimee was babbling, her words tumbling out and over each other. Elka looked down at her spark, its greenish-white light shining out between her fingers.

'My spark's bright, really bright.'

'And if you try to take off the bracelet it'll pull out your spark, killing you. Oh Elka, it's not fair.'

Aimee's words continued to rush out. Elka looked down into the face of the one girl in all the world who knew exactly what it felt like to hold in her hands power over other people's sparks.

Torsgen took that power and used it for his own greed. Frannack took it for its mechanical wonder but didn't see the lives it destroyed. Aimee had held it, resisted its evil pull and used it to save a whole city.

'What will I do with it?' Elka whispered, looking down at the metal cuff on her wrist.

CHAPTER 32

HERO

'Elka?'

She looked over into Aimee's face and smiled. 'It's okay,' Elka told her, and it was.

Her idea had turned into a decision, and what was most important was that it was hers. She was doing what she wanted to do, not what she felt she had to do to please her brothers.

'When I was growing up I always wanted to be somebody.' Elka found herself smiling. 'The problem was, I didn't know who that somebody was. I let my brothers push me down one path. And when I found another with the Riders I didn't see it for what it was. I was an idiot and I stubbornly kept my feet pointing the wrong way.'

Aimee had a small, pleased smile on her lips but a confused frown on her forehead. 'Okay, so who are you?'

'I'm a hero.'

And for what felt like the first time in a long while

Elka smiled a genuine smile. Then she pushed past Aimee and began running across the workshop.

'Elka, what about the bracelet?' Aimee called after her.

'Blazing sparks, what is she doing?' Nathine added.

Elka passed Inelle's body. 'Soon,' she promised her dragon.

The fires were spreading around the workshop and smoke was billowing against the roof. The Riders would need to get out soon before the whole place exploded. She spotted Pelathina. The Rider was ushering half a dozen young teenagers out of the workshop and through the silo to the front door. Skydance hovered above them, protective but keeping back in case he scared the rescued kids. Elka saw their bright sparks—all that life, glowing in their chests—and was thankful that it was still there. Her brothers would have sucked it out and killed them.

With the prisoners freed it was time for the Riders to escape as well. Elka sprinted for the roof's levers, barely feeling the pain in her body now. She grabbed the levers, pulled them and heard the grinding of gears as the roof began to open again. Smoke was sucked out into the night sky.

'That's your way out!' Elka called to the others as she rounded the copper tank.

Aimee and Nathine had followed her and their dragons watched with yellow eyes and fluttering wingtips.

'Ours?' Aimee asked. 'What about you? You can ride

back to Taumerg with Jess and me.'

Elka shook her head, though the offer made her smile.

'I'm not going back to the city,' she told her. 'I'm being a hero.' She put a hand on the copper tank, the one that contained Daan's body.

'Elka, we'll find a way to get the bracelet off you,' Aimee said but Elka shook her head again.

Looking around the room she could see a few sparks scattered amongst the debris. Some were faint, one was really bright. That meant some of Torsgen's men were still alive, though probably injured. Elka could suck the spark from one of them and use its energy to then take off the bracelet. That's what Torsgen would have done. But not what Elka was going to do.

Turning the dial, she opened the copper tank. Everything was hurting again and she didn't have the strength to lift out Daan's body so she had to pull him. Aimee moved close to help her but Elka waved her away. She winced as Daan's head bounced over the lip of the door.

Then she slumped to the floor and gathered him in her arms.

His eyes were closed, long lashes resting against his cheeks, and that was all wrong. They should be open and bright, darting around, looking for the next thing he could crack a joke about. His mouth was slack and that was wrong too. It should be smiling that beautiful smile, the one that had promised if she stuck with him, she'd spend her days smiling too.

Elka turned the cogs on her bracelet, watching them click around until the little needle of the dial pointed to *zurl*. Her family had stolen lives but Elka had the power to give one back. Aimee crouched beside her and Elka held up a warning hand.

'You can't come near me,' she warned, holding up her wrist. Though it was an empty threat. As if she'd ever steal the spark from Aimee, Saviour of Kierell.

Aimee held up both hands as if calming a wary dragon. 'I won't, but I can see what you're thinking of doing. Are you sure?'

'For the first time ever, yeah, I'm really sure.' Elka looked across at Inelle's body. 'I want to be with my family.'

'What's she going to do?' Nathine demanded. She was standing behind Aimee, scimitar in one hand, clockwork pistol in the other.

'She's going to give Daan her spark,' Aimee answered.

Elka looked up and thought she saw a flicker of respect in Nathine's eyes. 'I would have given it to Halfen if I could but it's too late for him. I'm sorry.'

Aimee sat down, cross-legged beside her as if they were little girls sitting down to play a game. Except Elka held the body of her first love in her arms and the workshop around them was burning and littered with bodies.

'I'll be right here,' Aimee told her.

Elka nodded and a tear dripped from her eyelashes. 'When I'm gone you'll take the bracelet and throw it in the furnace, won't you?'

She didn't ask because she was worried Aimee wouldn't do it. She just needed to say the words out loud.

'Can I ask more favours of you?'

Aimee nodded. 'As many as you like.'

'Will you tell Daan to make the trip to Kierell and once he's there, will you make sure he opens his own bakery. And will you go there all the time and buy what he makes.'

'Nathine can eat three pastries for every one I can, so Daan better be able to bake fast.'

Elka could see that future, and was sad she wouldn't share it but was happy that she'd be able to give it to Daan. He'd love to be the Riders' favourite baker. Maybe he'd learn to make pastries in the shape of dragons instead of rude things.

'And if, one day, Jennta comes to Kierell and makes the climb, will you let her become a Rider?' Elka asked. 'I know I was the first Rider from Taumerg and I betrayed you, but not everyone from my city is a screw up like me.'

'I've learned that girls from Taumerg are braver and stronger than they think they are.' Aimee smiled at her. 'Jennta would be very welcome.'

Elka looked down at Daan then back at Aimee. 'Okay, last favour. Tell Tariga that I'm glad she was the recruit I trained with. She was a kinder friend than I deserved. Tell her I think she's awesome.'

'I will,' Aimee promised.

Elka looked across the broken workshop to Inelle's body. Even in death she was beautiful, reflected firelight dancing across her indigo scales. Elka had known when Halfen fell from Vunskap Tower that she'd never be allowed to be a Rider again. But still, she'd chosen the Riders over the family she was born into. That decision had cost her life, but she'd make the same choice a hundred times over.

Reaching under her shirt collar, she pulled out a chain she'd been wearing around her neck. Unclasping it she held it up and let a small gold ring fall from it and into her hand. She slipped it onto the index finger of her right hand and smiled down at the little ship with its mother of pearl sails. She really had been planning to leave it behind on the tundra but in the end it had meant too much to her. So she'd brought it, and hidden it, and hadn't dared wear it.

But she did now. Because Aimee had given her this ring for being brave and protecting people.

She smiled at Aimee. 'Do you think Callant would write a book about me?'

'A story of impossible choices, betrayal and redemption?' Aimee smiled back. 'Callant will love that.'

Elka imagined a young girl, bursting with ambition, reading that story, and learning from the mistakes she'd made. Being that role model would be a good somebody to be.

'Tell Daan I love him,' Elka said.

And then it was time. She took Daan's hand, pushing her fingers in-between his. Instantly she felt the bracelet begin to work, pouring her life into him. A tiny spark appeared in his chest. Then it grew, growing brighter as the one in her chest faded.

Daan's eyes flickered, then opened. And Elka got to see them one last time before the world slipped away.

CHAPTER 33

SMOKE AND TEARS

Aimee stood on the grassy hillside beyond the hidden workshop, Jess beside her. She heard Malgerus land near them but her eyes were fixed on the building. It was properly ablaze now, flames crackling and roaring, shooting bright embers up into the night sky. The wind picked up the smoke and dragged it across the stars. The world smelled like burning wood and sadness. In the flickering orange glow of the flames, Aimee watched Pelathina help the freed prisoners into the back of a wagon she'd found. It hurt Aimee's heart to see them. Most must only have been thirteen or fourteen and they were scared and alone. Pelathina left Skydance to watch over the wagon and ran up the grassy slope.

'Where's Elka?' Pelathina asked.

The fire's light caressed the side of Pelathina's face with a soft orange glow and Aimee marvelled, as she always did, that this beautiful girl was hers. Needing to feel Pelathina's skin against her own she took her girlfriend's hand and pulled her close.

'Aimee?' Pelathina's voice was the softest of whispers.

Instead of telling her what Elka had done, Aimee pulled Pelathina around to the other side of Jess. A little way off, hunkered down in the grass, Daan hugged his knees and cried.

'She gave her spark to him,' Pelathina said, understanding. 'Brave girl.'

'She was,' Aimee agreed.

Pelathina turned her around and gently cupped Aimee's face in her hands. Her palms were warm. 'Are *you* okay? Because this must have dredged up memories of Pagrin.'

Aimee took one of Pelathina's hands and gently kissed her knuckles. 'I'm fine.'

'Aimee, don't just shove all this into a box at the back of your mind,' Pelathina said, her voice unusually stern. 'I will always hold you after any nightmare but it would also be nice not to go through all that again. I like sleeping.'

'Honestly, I'm genuinely alright.'

Pelathina looked at her for a long moment before turning to regard Jess. Because if Aimee was lying her dragon would give her away. Aimee smiled, pleased, as her dragon stood perfectly calm, wings tucked in, eyes watching the horizon.

'Good girl,' Aimee whispered to Jess then gave Pelathina's nose a kiss. 'See?'

Aimee really was okay because this time she hadn't

needed to pick up the burden and be a hero. Though, of course, she would have done if it had meant saving Elka. No one else would ever really understand the power Elka had wielded, wearing that bracelet. The fact that she'd resisted it, and instead used it to sacrifice herself for Daan, more than redeemed her in Aimee's eyes. It proved she was a proper Rider.

After Elka died, Aimee had taken the metal cuff from her wrist and chucked it into the furnace as promised. Daan had been confused and then distraught when Aimee told him what Elka had done. But there hadn't been time then for anger or tears because the workshop was rapidly burning around them. Daan had wanted to take Elka's body but Aimee wouldn't let him. He'd yelled at her in Glavic and though Elka had never taught her any swear words, Aimee could recognise them easily enough. She'd motioned to Nathine and the other Rider had mounted up, then Malgerus had picked up Daan in his talons. The boy had continued to yell as Malgerus carried him up and out of the roof.

If Aimee had been bigger and stronger she'd have carried Elka over to Inelle. That would have been more dignified, but Elka had been a lot taller than she was and so Aimee had to drag her body across the floor. She felt bad as she saw streaks of dirt and soot appear on Elka's yellow coat. To Aimee she'd looked strange in her mismatched, colourful outfit. Elka had liked it, though, and so it was fitting that it was the last one she'd ever wear. Aimee felt bad that she also looked so dishevelled. Elka had always seemed so careful with her appearance.

'I'm sure Inelle won't mind,' she told her as she placed Elka against the body of her dragon so they were lying curled up together.

Then she and Jess had followed Malgerus out of the roof. Now she stood and watched the smoke from the burning workshop drift into the sky. It wasn't quite a Rider's funeral but it wasn't far off. She smiled to think of Elka and Inelle flying forever together across the sky.

'You'll need to let me treat this properly,' Pelathina was saying, pressing her warm fingers close to the cut on Aimee's temple. It stung and her eye was so swollen now that she could hardly see out of it. Still, she pushed Pelathina's fingers away.

'Not right now.' She wanted to watch until the workshop was completely destroyed. Partly out of respect for Elka and partly for her own peace of mind. She needed to know that the bracelets were well and truly destroyed.

'You're going to have an epic black eye,' Pelathina told her, moving her fingers from Aimee's head to stroke the back of her neck.

Movement caught Aimee's good eye as Nathine dismounted. It felt like claws were squeezing her chest as she looked at her best friend in all the world. Aimee might be okay but Nathine wasn't. For all that she teased him, and pretended she didn't care, Nathine had loved Halfen deeply. It was going to take a long time for that grief to heal and Aimee wanted to help.

Nathine walked towards her and Pelathina but then kept going, striding past them.

'Nathine?' Aimee called after her.

'Yeah, I know, we'll do the hugging thing later,' Nathine called over her shoulder.

'Do you think she's planning to keep that pistol?' Pelathina whispered in Aimee's ear.

'I think we might need to fight to get it off her.'

'Is Nathine with a pistol a good thing?'

Aimee shrugged. 'I dunno, but she does look pretty impressive with it.'

They watched as Nathine sat on the grass beside Daan and shoved him with her shoulder.

'Budge up,' she told him, 'you're hogging the comfiest tussock.'

Aimee saw the shine of tears in his eyes as he turned to look at her, surprise and confusion fighting for a place on his face.

'What do you want?' Aimee heard him ask.

'Oh good, you speak Kierellian. My Glavic makes me sound like I've only got half a brain,' Nathine told him.

'I learned while Elka was away because I didn't know if she was coming back and I thought maybe I'd have to go to Kierell and find her.' Daan rested a hand on his own chest, right where his spark would be if Aimee could see it. 'I never told her that.'

Aimee hesitated, wondering if she should intervene. Nathine was still hurting over Halfen and she carried around anger like it was her favourite blanket. And Daan had Elka's spark inside him. The spark of the girl responsible for Halfen's death.

'Just wait, give her a minute,' Pelathina said, taking Aimee's hand and pulling her back a step.

Aimee watched, still nervous as Daan went back to staring down at the burning workshop. Nathine stared too. They both jumped a little as the roof collapsed inwards, shooting up thousands of embers like little fireworks.

'There was this boy with a stupid face and idiotic notions about being a hero. But I loved him, and he gave his life to protect Kierell. I'm guessing all that snot and those tears mean that you loved Elka?'

Daan nodded.

'She's not gone, you know. She gave you her spark. All the years that she was going to live, she smooshed them into you instead.'

'Smooshed?'

'Yeah, smooshed.'

'Well I would smoosh them back into her if I could.'

'You can't. But she was super ambitious, yeah? So take her ambition, because you've got it now, and use it to do something that would make her proud.'

'Like what?'

'Maybe make the journey to Kierell and open your own bakery.'

Aimee took Pelathina's hand as she watched Daan pull his eyes away from Elka's dramatic funeral pyre and look at Nathine.

'You'd help me?'

'Yeah. I mean not with the actual baking because I'm worse at that than I am at speaking Glavic. But if you come to Kierell you'd have one friend to start with.'

'She told me, you know. Elka told me what happened to a guard in Kierell the night she stole the bracelet. That guard was your boy, wasn't he?' Nathine nodded. 'So why help me if I'm sort of her now.' He looked down at his chest then back to Nathine.

'Because life has just dealt you the same hand of grief it has given me,' Nathine told him, and Aimee longed to run over and give her a hug but instead she squeezed Pelathina's hand. 'So maybe we can prop each other up when we fall.'

Daan watched her for a moment that seemed to stretch out forever. Then he nodded. 'Alright.'

'In exchange for a lifetime of free cake, of course,' Nathine added, and to Aimee's amazement Daan smiled.

Then they both returned to watching the fire, their grief a little lighter for being shared. Aimee turned her gaze to the sky. The stars above were the same ones she knew from home but they were all in slightly the wrong place. She had a sudden pang of homesickness that was so strong that Jess growled and flapped her wings.

'What's the plan, Aimee?' Pelathina asked.

Aimee smiled. 'Time to go home.'

Acknowledgements

Book 4, guys! Woohoo! The idea for this fourth Sky Riders book popped into my head back when I was writing the first draft of book 1. I had to put it aside, but it has been waiting there patiently, waving at me every now and then. It was such good fun to finally get to write it.

As always, a huge thanks to my beta readers—Colin Sandie and Penny van Millingen. Thank you for the time you've given to the Sky Riders over the years. Penny—I'm sorry my books have made you cry. Colin—I'm sorry I let your feedback make me cry! Once again, this book is better because of you both.

Thank you to my editor, Rheanna-Marie Hall, who once again did an amazing job on this book. I'm extremely grateful for the time you've dedicated to the world of the Sky Riders. And I love that I learn something every time you work on one of my books.

The cover of this book was created by the wonderful team at Damonza. And I really love this one. Isn't it perfect?

Thank you to my mum and dad who have always supported me, in this project and everything I've ever done in life.

One of the most lovely things I've discovered on my

writing journey has been you lot—my readers. I've been absolutely blown away by the way you've embraced the world of the Sky Riders and I've enjoyed having you on this journey along with me. Thank you for letting the incredibly brave young women of the Sky Riders into your hearts.

Finally, thank you for all the brilliant reviews (keep them coming!) and for the shares and likes on social media. I think the world of the Sky Riders is yours now as much as mine. I'd give you all dragons if I could. What colour would you like?

About the Author

Kerry Law grew up reading Tolkien and David Eddings, and has never looked back. A love of the past took her to the University of St Andrews where she did an MA in Medieval History. During her degree she learnt all about castles, but her imagination had to fill in the dragons.

The Rogue Rider is her fourth novel and is book 4 in the *Sparks* series.

Kerry enjoys exploring uniqueness in her books and takes inspiration from her own interesting skin condition—vitiligo. She's also inspired by the incredible magical-looking landscapes of her home in Scotland.

Kerry lives with her husband and cat in a small town in the Scottish Borders where there are more trees than people.

Contact Kerry:
kerrylawbooks.com
facebook.com/kerrylawbooks
instagram.com/kerrylawbooks

Also by Kerry Law

Sparks Series
The Sky Riders
The Rider's Quest
The Immortal Rider
The Rogue Rider

Printed in Great Britain
by Amazon